When I'm W...

New Hope Falls: Book #5

By

KIMBERLY RAE
JORDAN

THREE**STRAND**
P R E S S

A CORD OF THREE STRANDS IS NOT EASILY BROKEN.

A man, a woman & their God.
Three Strand Press publishes Christian Romance stories
that intertwine love, faith and family. Always clean.
Always heartwarming. Always uplifting.

When I'm With You/ Kimberly Rae Jordan. -- 1st ed.
ISBN-13: 978-1-988409-45-0

A man's heart plans his way,
But the LORD directs his steps.
Proverbs 16:9 (NKJV)

CHAPTER ONE

Michael Reed's text alert chirped, disturbing the light sleep he'd been drifting in and out of since his alarm had gone off earlier. He'd forgotten to shut it off the night before, so the alarm had gone off at seven o'clock, which was usual for him for a Saturday.

It wasn't often that Michael had a whole day off work other than Sundays, but he'd made sure to completely clear his schedule for that day. The day he was to stand up with another friend as he married the love of his life.

Stretching, he reached over to pick up his phone from the nightstand to see who was texting him so early. He figured it would be Kieran Sutherland, the groom, or someone else involved with the wedding.

Instead, he recognized his sister's name, so he tapped the screen to have the phone read the message to him.

Tay: *I'm not going to make it to set up the flowers, but they're all done and in the cooler in the shop. The directions for what goes where is with them.*

Frustration warred with unease as Michael lifted the phone to dictate a message back to her. *Why aren't you going to make it? This is important.*

As he waited for her to reply, he debated calling her since he found it easier to talk than text. Unfortunately, with the way things had been going recently, chances were she wouldn't answer even though she clearly had her phone in hand. In the end, it took several minutes before her response showed up.

Tay: *I'm not feeling well. Everything is there. You'll do fine.*

Except this wasn't his part of their business, so it was entirely possible that he—and the flowers—*wouldn't* be fine. This was Taylor's responsibility.

What about the shop?

Tay: *I called Emma and she said she could open it for a few hours.*

While he was glad she had someone to open the flower shop, Michael was still disappointed—and frustrated—that Taylor wasn't available to help with the wedding flowers.

With a sigh, he dictated a response. *Can't you just come to give me directions? I doubt there will be anyone at the church this early. I'll do everything. You just need to tell me what to do.*

When there was still no reply to his text after fifteen minutes, Michael figured he had his answer. Flipping back the covers, he swung his legs over the side of the bed and leaned forward, scrubbing at his face, suddenly feeling tired even though he'd just woken up.

So much for his hope for some quiet, relaxed moments before the day got busy. Not that he wouldn't have been there to help Taylor with the flowers. He would have been at the church with her, but the responsibility for setting it all up and making sure everything met the bride's wishes would have fallen on Taylor, not on him.

Plus, this all just highlighted, with a glaring spotlight, what had been going wrong between them lately. It wasn't that he really thought Taylor was lying, but he had to say that he was no longer one hundred percent certain she was telling the truth all the time either. He really hated that since it meant their relationship was changing...devolving...from what it had always been.

Resigned to doing what had to be done, Michael threw on a pair of jeans and a long-sleeve T-shirt then headed for the shop to pick up the flowers and the instructions. Once there, he found everything just as Taylor had said. A bit of his worry eased when he saw that she'd left him drawings clearly indicating the flower placements instead of a bunch of written instructions.

When he got to the church, the pastor was there, but otherwise, the building was empty.

"No Taylor?" Pastor Evans asked after coming to let him in.

"She isn't feeling well." Saying that kind of felt like a lie, but it wasn't his since he was just passing on what Taylor had told him. "So I'll be doing the flower set-up."

"Do you need a hand?"

"I think I'll be okay."

"Good," the pastor said. "I'm going to head back to my place. Just let me know when you're done, and I'll come back and lock up."

"Thanks for coming to open the church for me."

The pastor clapped him on the shoulder. "Anytime, son."

The first time the older man had called him that, Michael had fought the urge to wince. Being a son had only ever brought him pain and suffering. But in the years since Pastor Evans had first called him that, he'd never once felt either of those things with the man.

Left alone, Michael got to work carrying in the floral arrangements, bouquets, boutonnieres, and flowers to finish the wedding arch at the front of the sanctuary. Taylor had done a lot of work on the arch the night of the rehearsal, but the fresh flowers had to be added last.

He referred to the illustrations Taylor had left for him often, and by the time he was done, he felt relatively—okay, maybe *sort of*—confident that things were as they were supposed to be. The last thing he did was to put the ladies' bouquets in the room where they would be gathering once they arrived at the church.

Taking one more tour of the church and hall, Michael hoped that the bridal couple would be happy with everything. With a sigh, he left the hall and headed for the exit of the church, dictating a text message to let the pastor know he was leaving.

He still had to get home and change into his suit since he was a groomsman for Kieran. Though he was honored to have been asked to stand up with the man, after the way things had unfolded with Taylor, he wished he could have just focused on one thing that day.

It took him fifteen minutes to get back to the mobile home he shared with Taylor. Or rather, that he used to share with her. Just before Christmas, she'd told him that she'd found a roommate and was going to be moving to an apartment in Everett. It wasn't that he begrudged her moving out on her own, but the way she was going about everything was a bit distressing.

They were supposed to be a team. Everything he'd done over the past ten years had been for her, and now she was distancing herself from him. He didn't know how to process that because if she didn't stick around, his life was going to become much more of a struggle.

Those had to be thoughts for another day, however.

At home, he took a shower then changed into his suit. Given that he really had no reason to ever wear a suit, he was glad that they were wearing the suits from Eli and Anna McNamara's wedding, so he hadn't had to lay out money for another one.

As he left his room, he glanced around at the mobile home that was now bereft of Taylor's presence as well as the furniture she'd taken earlier that week. She was drifting away from him, and the life he'd carefully built for them was in danger of collapsing completely.

With a frustrated sigh, Michael once again tried to drag his thoughts away from his sister. For now, he needed to focus on the wedding. Taylor and the potential disaster he suspected was heading his way could wait for another day.

Anna McNamara gave him a concerned look when he walked into the church a short time later. "You okay, Michael?"

Apparently, he hadn't done a very good job of putting the stress aside. "I'm alright. Did you check the flowers? Taylor wasn't able to make it to set them up, but she gave me directions for what I needed to do."

"It all looks great," Anna assured him. "Is everything okay with Taylor?"

"Yes." As far as he knew. "She just wasn't feeling well this morning."

Again, it felt like a lie.

"Well, you did a great job. I know Cara and Kieran will love it all."

Some of the worry in Michael's gut eased. At least he wasn't letting down the couple who'd thought enough of him to ask him to be part of their wedding. He counted Kieran among his closest friends, along with Carter Ward and Eli McNamara. They were men he looked up to, even though they were all around the same age.

"The ladies will be arriving shortly," Anna said. "But the guys are already in the pastor's office, if you want to join them."

Michael nodded then headed down the hallway to where the offices for the church staff were located. The door to the pastor's study stood open, so he stepped into the room. Eli was also there, though he wasn't one of the wedding party.

"Hey there, Michael," Kieran said with a broad smile. Clearly, the man was looking forward to the day, and Michael couldn't blame him.

"How're you doing?" Michael asked after giving the man a quick hug. "Ready to end your single days?"

"I most definitely am," Kieran said with a nod. "And hopefully, Cara feels the same way."

Carter scoffed from where he sat relaxed back on the couch, his legs stretched out in from of him. "As if she wouldn't."

This wedding was much simpler than Eli and Anna's, so Taylor had only had to arrange half the number of flowers. Which was a good thing, considering she hadn't shown up at the church.

Aaaand he was thinking about the situation again. With a huff of frustration, Michael dropped down on the couch beside Carter.

Anna appeared a little while later to escort the guys to the foyer. The ladies had all arrived and were waiting in another room for the ceremony to start.

Michael and Eli were to usher people to their seats, which, with fewer guests, would hopefully be an easier job than it had been at Eli and Anna's wedding. Kieran was going to escort his mom to her seat at the front of the sanctuary, and Cara's brother would be the one to walk her down the aisle to meet Kieran.

The next little while went by quickly as people began to arrive, then the ceremony began, and he was walking down the aisle with Jillian Hall, Carter's girlfriend. Carter walked behind them with Cara's maid of honor, Sarah McNamara, who was Eli's sister.

Soon, they were all at the front of the sanctuary, and Michael was finally able to keep his focus on what was happening around him. The love that Cara and Kieran had for each other was evident as they exchanged the vows they'd written for each other.

Getting married wasn't something he'd spent a lot of time pondering. It wasn't until he had gotten involved with Eli's group at the church that he'd seen loving relationships. Prior to that, the only marriage he'd had an up-close and personal look at had been his parents', and based on what he had seen, he had come to the conclusion that marriage wasn't something he wanted for himself. Ever.

Still, watching as one by one his friends took the plunge, helped him see that not all relationships or marriages were as awful as his parents' had been. Did that make him reconsider marriage for himself? Not so much. He knew nothing at all about being a good husband, and would no doubt fail if he ever decided to try.

Lately, the one role he'd thought he was doing a decent job at had taken a turn for the worse. If he couldn't even manage to be a good brother to Taylor, he definitely wasn't going to attempt the role of husband.

Michael sighed, frustrated that it was such a struggle to keep his thoughts off the deteriorating relationship with his sister.

When the pastor finally presented the new couple to the friends and family gathered in the church, Michael clapped and cheered with everyone, then offered his arm to Jillian so they could follow the bride and groom up the aisle. As soon as they were gathered in the foyer, Jillian headed to Carter's side.

They were yet another couple that Michael was sure would be tying the knot in the near future. If nothing else, the weddings were good for business, since so far, they'd all come to Taylor for their bouquets and floral arrangements. He had no idea what would happen with the shop if Taylor suddenly decided she didn't want to be involved with that anymore.

"You doing okay, man?" Eli asked as he thumped Michael lightly on his shoulder. "You seem a little distracted today."

Michael didn't want to be a downer at the wedding, so he tried to give his friend a reassuring smile. "I'm fine. How're you doing?"

Eli regarded him for a moment as if trying to judge the honesty of his response. "I'm doing good. Glad that the Christmas rush is over. I'm ready for a bit of a breather."

"Is the lodge quiet now?"

"It is, thankfully. Just a few guests on the weekends."

They continued to chat until Anna herded the wedding party off to where Cara and Kieran had decided to have their pictures taken. Thanks to Anna's organizational skills, that all went smoothly, and they were back to the church for the reception right on schedule.

Michael was glad he knew the guys around him at the head table, so he didn't need to force conversation. He was sure the food was good, but the taste just didn't register over the unease in his stomach.

When it was time to catch the garter, he went up with the rest of the single guys, but he made no effort to grab it. Beau Allerton, Sarah's boyfriend, however, made it two for two when he got hold of the garter at this wedding, just like he had at Eli and Anna's. Sarah also managed to snatch the bouquet out of the air, which didn't appear to be too difficult of a feat since none of the other women were trying very hard to catch it.

All in all, the reception appeared to go off without a hitch, and there were several comments on how beautiful the flowers were, so that made Michael feel a bit better about the whole situation. Taylor may have bailed on the set-up, but she'd made sure all the arrangements and bouquets were done to the bride's specifications.

Maybe things would work out okay after all.

Leilani Alexander stared at the screen on her laptop, wincing at the bottom line of the report from the bookkeeping program she used. She rested her elbows on the desk and covered her eyes with her hands. After counting to ten, she looked at the screen again, but nothing had changed.

With a sigh, she shifted her gaze out the living room window of her second-story apartment. Warm light spilled out of the windows of the houses across the street. A few still had Christmas lights up that they turned on in the evening, and a couple even had their trees still up.

Her mom would have smiled at that since Christmas was her favorite holiday. Just like it had once been Lani's. It wasn't anymore, however, as the holiday just magnified her loss. She'd decorated the shop since it was expected, but she hadn't done any decorating in her apartment. Unlike the homes across the street, she'd already taken all the decorations and lights down in the shop.

She knew a few of the people who lived in those homes, but not very well. As she gazed at the houses, she wondered what kind of worries those people had in their lives. Lani wasn't naïve enough to think that they lived worry-free lives, but there were days when she wondered if she was the only one struggling with such a heavy weight.

You're not alone, Leilani Kalea, my darling.

The words came to her in her mom's voice. It was something she'd told Lani so many times over the years, even more so during the years they'd been apart. But Lani hadn't realized how truly alone she could be until her mom died.

Something needed to change, but she wasn't sure what. Part of her wanted to go back to Hawaii. To finish the degree she'd had to abandon just one semester shy of graduating and to the job that had been more fun and less stressful.

But she wasn't going to abandon her mother's dream. Instead, she was going to have to find a way to keep it alive.

She picked up her phone and tapped the number she'd called so often over the past few months. It only took one ring for the call to be answered.

"You better be calling to tell me you're coming back," Nina Webster said. "Or you can just hang up right now."

Lani laughed, her mood lifting just a bit. It seemed these days, she only smiled genuinely when speaking to her family or to her former boss.

"Well, guess I'm hanging up then."

"Don't you dare," Nina snapped out. "Don't you dare."

"Okay. If you insist." Lani lowered the lid of the laptop then leaned back in her chair.

"What's up, darling?" Nina asked. "How're you doing?"

"I'm doing okay." Lani didn't have to say more than that to Nina. They talked enough that she knew how Lani was really doing without her having to say the words.

"You sound tired."

"Yeah. I just finished cooking the week's meals for Dad and me."

"How's he doing?" There was a hard edge to Nina's voice, betraying her true feelings about Lani's dad.

"Same as usual." Which meant he was bitter and angry, and taking his frustrations out on everyone around him. Especially her.

"One of these days..." Nina never finished that sentence, but she didn't really need to.

After they'd talked for a few minutes, Lani got to the point of her call. "I need a favor."

"Anything, darling," Nina said without hesitation.

"I need you as a reference."

"A reference? Like for a job?"

"Yes. I'm applying for a part-time job."

Nina scoffed. "Have you suddenly discovered you have more hours in your day than the rest of us?"

"Nope. I'm just swapping some of them."

"Explain."

"A flower shop in town is looking for someone to help with flower arrangements for a few hours in the morning. If I get the job, I'd start opening my shop at eleven. It will help to bring in some extra money, and I'll actually get to do more of what I enjoy."

"And what you're really good at," Nina added.

"Well, if I am, it's because of what you've taught me."

"You were already well trained, thanks to your mom. I just helped you to hone that skill a bit more."

"So, will you give a reference?"

"Is this for the shop that your dad blames for killing the business at your mom's store?"

Lani sighed. "Yeah. Which is kind of why I need a big favor from you. I don't want them to know who I am. So I was wondering if you could maybe not be too specific about exactly *when* I worked for you. Maybe make it seem like it's been a bit more recently than it's actually been."

"Are you sure this is a wise move, darling?" Nina asked, concern lacing her voice. "You're already so tired."

Lani knew that it might stretch her even more, but if it relieved some of the financial stress, it would be worth it. "I want to at least try."

"Well, you know I'll do it for you, but I want you to promise me that if it gets to be too much, you'll quit. You're already on close to burning out. I don't want this to be the thing that pushes you over the edge."

The reality was that it wasn't the shop that was burning her out. It wasn't so much a physical burn-out as it was an emotional one, and that was because of the toll of dealing with her father.

"Promise me, Leilani."

"I promise."

"Then I will sing your praises when they call for a reference."

"*If* they call you for a reference."

"*If* they're smart, they'll call."

Lani really hoped that was the case. She really, really needed for this to work out the way she hoped it would.

They talked for a few more minutes, then ended the call. Lani felt a sense of relief and a little bit of anticipation.

Reaching out, she lifted the lid to the laptop and clicked to minimize the bookkeeping program. The ad she'd been reading over earlier remained on the screen. The one looking to hire someone to make flower arrangements for three hours each morning. Those hours would be perfect because it would still leave her time to have her own shop open for a few hours each day. Even the salary was more than she might have expected for New Hope.

As Nina had said, her dad blamed that shop for the decline in sales for her mom's business. Having looked at the books, Lani wasn't so sure about that. Certainly, it hadn't helped, but from what she could see, there had been financial issues even before that, starting back before she'd left New Hope to go to college.

Lani already knew what her father would say about what she was considering. But since she didn't plan to tell him, she wouldn't have to listen to his disapproval. The only thing that might cause a problem was if the job required her to interact with customers. All she wanted was to make the flower arrangements because if she had to deal with customers, word would likely get back to her dad about where she was working.

She shuddered, thinking of the explosion that news would cause, fueling the anger he already directed at her.

However, she had no choice but to consider it. He had left her with no other alternative. Though she'd tried to convince him that it was time to close the business and cut their losses, he'd refused. Repeatedly and loudly. He refused to listen to reason.

Lani hadn't had a chance to grieve her mother the way she wanted to because she'd been too focused on dealing with her father during his stay in the hospital and also after he was home, all while trying to keep a struggling business afloat.

And now, over a year since the accident, things weren't any better. If anything, they were probably worse, but she tried not to dwell too much on that. She had to just take things one day at a time. Anything more, and she became overwhelmed by it all.

Resolved to see if this might be the one thing that could ease the financial burden a bit, even if it made her already long days even longer, Lani decided to apply for the job. If it was meant to be, she'd get it. If not, she'd try something else.

Once the application was completed and submitted, Lani shut the lid of her laptop without going back to the bookwork. It would still be there the next day, and sadly, the numbers wouldn't have changed at all.

Sunday might have been the one day the shop was closed, but it wasn't a day of rest, that was for sure. Her kitchen looked like a bomb had gone off, so she still had to clean all that up before she got ready for bed.

A new week lay ahead. Maybe it would be the same as every other week had been in recent memory, or maybe, just maybe, it might hold something a bit different. She could only hope.

CHAPTER TWO

Michael swung the van into a spot behind the shop and slammed on the brakes. Frustration swirled inside him as he climbed from the vehicle, shutting the door with a little more force than necessary.

Things hadn't improved with Taylor in the two weeks since the wedding. She was coming to work later and later when she used to come in early to get a jump on the flower arrangements for the day. And when he was around her these days, she was sullen and withdrawn, barely speaking to him.

Today, however, he'd reached his limit. His one job for the shop was picking up the floral orders from a wholesaler about forty-five minutes away from New Hope. That meant a super early morning for him, but he'd been willing to do it for Taylor since he was more of a morning person than she was.

The only thing he'd asked was that she provide him with a clear list of what he was picking up, something that he could listen to and confirm before accepting the order. That day, however, she hadn't sent him anything, so he'd had to trust that the company had given them exactly what she'd ordered. The way her change of attitude was starting to impact the business was troubling and frustrating.

Michael strode toward the shop, planning to give Taylor a piece of his mind. His steps faltered when he spotted a figure standing by the back door. With the sun not rising until close to eight, he couldn't see who it was. Since it was only a little after seven, he wasn't sure who it could be. Prior to everything that had transpired lately, Taylor would have been there to take care of whoever was waiting.

"Can I help you?" Michael asked, his movements turning on the motion sensor light above the door.

A young woman with dark hair stood there in a thick jacket, likely in deference of the chilly morning air. She crossed her arms, hugging herself. "I'm here to work?"

He frowned at the uncertainty in her voice. She didn't *know* what she was doing there? "At the flower shop?"

"Yes." She sounded more sure of herself with that answer. "Taylor hired me to work for three hours each morning. Seven until ten."

Frowning, Michael punched in the code on the door lock then into the alarm pad. He flipped on the lights then held the door open for the woman, noticing that she hesitated for a moment before stepping into the back hallway.

Once they were inside the building, he turned and held out his hand. "I'm Michael Reed. Taylor's brother."

She took his hand, and Michael couldn't help but notice how small her hand felt in his. Now that they were in the light, he could see that she had eyes of a color he'd never seen before—blue-ish-green with light brown around the pupil—and skin that hinted that perhaps she was of mixed race.

"I'm Lani Alexander."

"Nice to meet you, Lani," Michael said as he released her hand. "I'm sorry that Taylor's not here to meet you. Hopefully, she'll be in soon. In the meantime, maybe you can help me bring in the flowers I just picked up at the wholesaler."

"Sure," she agreed readily. "I can do that."

He propped the back door open then led her to the van where they began to unload the flowers. It didn't take them too long to get the flowers into the larger walk-in cooler where they kept all the flowers both before and after they were arranged.

Once they were done, he showed her where to hang up her coat in the small office. By that point, he was usually leaving to start his day, but with Taylor not there yet, he wasn't sure about just leaving Lani.

"Did Taylor speak to you at all about the orders you'd be working on?" Michael asked, taking in the simple outfit of jeans and a long-sleeve, dark blue T-shirt she wore.

She shook her head. "She said she'd tell me when I got here."

Michael let out a sigh. "Okay. Let me give her a call and see where she is. In the meantime, feel free to look around and familiarize yourself with the shop."

She nodded and walked into the back area of the shop where there was a large worktable set up with ribbons and the other things Taylor used in her arrangements.

Once she was out of earshot, Michael walked back into the office and placed a call to Taylor.

"Please tell me you're on your way here," he said when she answered.

"I am."

Michael dragged a hand down his face. "She was standing outside in the cold, Taylor. You need to be more considerate."

"Chill out, Michael," Taylor said with a sigh. "I'll be there in a couple of minutes."

She hung up before he had a chance to say anything further. It felt like maybe this was going to be the thing that pushed them to the confrontation he really had been trying to avoid.

Hiring a new employee and not telling him about it? And then not being there when said employee shows up, so they're left standing out in the cold?

None of that was acceptable.

They'd always discussed things like hiring new employees. They were supposed to be a team.

The worst part was that he *needed* her. If Taylor decided she was going to bail on the business they'd built together, they were going to lose it all. Everything he'd worked so hard for would be gone.

But that was a discussion for another day. Certainly, they weren't going to be talking about it while she had a new employee to orientate.

Michael left the office and found the woman standing at the worktable, flipping through the binder Taylor had filled with pictures of arrangements she'd done in the past. As he neared her, she looked up, her gaze watchful.

"Taylor will be here in a few minutes," he said. "She's just running a little late."

"Is it okay that I'm here?" she asked, clasping her hands on top of the binder.

"It's fine." For some reason, Michael felt the need to reassure her. "This is Taylor's side of the business, so if she's decided she needs help, then this is exactly where you're supposed to be."

"Okay. I just thought maybe I got the day wrong."

"Nope. It's all good." He hesitated then said, "Are you from New Hope?"

"Yes. I lived here until I moved away for college a few years ago."

"What brought you back?" Michael asked, leaning a hip against the worktable as he crossed his arms.

She hesitated a moment then said, "My family needed me."

He knew there was a story there—wasn't there always when it came to families? For some, it was a good story. For others, like him, it wasn't.

There was a flurry of activity as Taylor rushed in, looking more disheveled than usual, and tossed her coat over a chair. "I'm sorry I'm late, Lani."

"That's okay," Lani said with a smile.

"The flowers are all in the cooler," Michael said as he zipped up his jacket. "Hopefully, the order is all correct."

He knew Taylor caught the edge to his voice when she scowled at him. "I'm sure it's fine. They've never gotten our order wrong before."

Knowing it wasn't the time or place to address what was going on, Michael turned to Lani. "Nice to meet you, Lani. Thanks for helping me with the flowers. I'll see you around."

She gave him a nod and a small smile as her gaze darted between him and Taylor, clearly having picked up on the tension between them.

With a final look at Taylor, Michael left the shop. He climbed into his truck, leaving the van there for any deliveries Taylor might need to make later.

As he drove away, he blew out a long breath, feeling exhausted even though he hadn't done anything really physical yet. But he knew from previous experiences that emotional stress could be exhausting. So very exhausting.

However, he'd survived back then, and he'd survive this. But in order to do that, he needed to just take the bull by the horns and talk to Taylor about what was going on. Just hoping whatever it was would go away clearly wasn't going to work since it hadn't so far.

Michael had never imagined he'd get to this point with Taylor, but here they were...

~*~

"Sorry I'm late," Taylor said again as she slumped down on one of the stools at the worktable. The woman's hair was pulled up in a messy bun on the top of her head, and she looked tired. She wore a baggy cardigan over a loose T-shirt and jeans. "Hit snooze one too many times. Were you waiting long?"

"No. Not long." Which was true. She'd only been at the door for a couple of minutes, but the chilly morning air had made it feel longer. Thankfully, she'd been dressed for the weather...for the most part. She should have just stayed in her car, but she'd honestly thought that Taylor would be there before seven to let her in. Next time, she'd just wait in her car.

Taylor gestured to her. "I see you've been looking through the binder."

Lani moved her hands off the binder. "Yes. The arrangements are beautiful."

"I look forward to seeing what you can do. The pictures you showed me were lovely, and your previous boss gave you a great reference. She said you quit in order to come back to New Hope."

"Yeah. I had family issues that required me to come return home."

"It seems like perhaps your boss's loss will be my gain."

Lani hoped she continued to feel that way. She had to admit that things were off to a shaky start. Not just because Taylor hadn't been there when Lani had arrived, but because the tension between the brother and sister had been so thick, Lani wasn't sure she would have even been able to cut it with a knife. She probably would have needed a chainsaw.

"Well, let's see what's on the schedule for today?" Taylor said as she got up from her stool. She stood for a moment, gripping the edge of the worktable, before heading for the cooler.

Lani looked over her new boss's appearance, taking in the pallor of her skin and the dark smudges beneath her eyes. Taylor had said that she didn't have anyone else to help her out with floral arrangements. However, she did have a woman who handled the front of the shop on an as-needed basis and also someone who helped with deliveries.

Though Lani also worked alone, her shop wasn't as busy as this one. It was no wonder that Taylor looked so run-down. Lani might have come to work in the shop in order to make extra money, but if she was able to also help Taylor out with the stress she was clearly under, that might be a good thing.

"First up, we need to put together a few floral arrangements for the seniors' home. It's a standing order, and they leave the decision on the specific flowers and such to us."

Lani listened closely as Taylor explained what sort of bouquets she usually put together. Once she was done, Taylor waited long enough to answer any questions Lani might have, then she went to her office.

Hoping it would be okay, Lani loaded up her favorite playlist on her phone, keeping the volume low as she began to assemble the arrangements. It didn't take long for her to get into the zone, enjoying the chance to arrange flowers once again without the stress of the shop hanging over her head. It was surprisingly therapeutic and took her back to her days working with Nina.

"Those are all lovely."

Lani looked up from the arrangement she was finishing to see Taylor standing on the other side of the worktable. Reaching out, she shut off her playlist.

"I'm almost done," Lani said as she put in the last bits of greenery on the arrangement she had in front of her. "Do they look okay?"

"They're perfect." Taylor gave her a smile, looking a bit better than she had earlier. "I know the home will be so happy with these. Unless Emma can come, I usually close the shop from noon until one to make deliveries, so we can just put these in the cooler for now."

Lani helped Taylor carry them to the cooler then said, "Is there anything else you need me to do?"

"Not today. It's almost ten, so you can feel free to go." Taylor touched her arm. "I'll try and make it on time, but maybe you'll want to wait in your car, just to be safe. Did you park on the street?"

"Yes. Shouldn't I have?"

"That's fine, but tomorrow you can park around the back. That way, you can stay in your car if I'm running late."

"Does your brother make a daily flower run?"

"Not unless we need a large number of flowers for a special order. Otherwise, he usually makes a trip two or three times a week."

Well, if Michael wasn't going to be there to let her in the next day, she was definitely parking in the back. Two days standing out in the cold wasn't her idea of a good time.

"I'll see you tomorrow then," Lani said as they walked to the office so she could get her jacket.

She headed out the back door even though Taylor had said she could go through the front. The last thing she wanted was for someone to see her coming out of the rival florist shop and report back to her father. There were still a handful of people who he tolerated and who tolerated him.

As Lani drove from the florist shop on Main Street to her own shop several blocks away, off the main drag, she thought back over the events of the morning. She'd forced herself to have no expectations of any sort for the shop or the owners. Her decision to go this route had nothing to do with any of that, and everything to do with trying to save her business.

Still, it seemed that perhaps the Reed siblings were dealing with some issues of their own. Their shop was beautiful though, everything that Lani knew her mom would have wanted for her own shop. A whole cooler room instead of just a large cabinet style cooler. A Main Street location.

Sadly, between her mother's lack of business sense and her father treating her shop more like a hobby than an investment, it didn't seem like there had been much hope for *Luana's Blossoms.* Even now, with her degree—her *almost* degree—Lani wasn't sure she could get the business to where her mom had wanted it. And her father couldn't seem to let go of his anger and guilt in order to see that there was no sense in keeping the business going when it was floundering so badly.

After parking in the back of her shop, Lani headed inside. She unlocked the front door and flipped the sign to *Open* then got the cash tray from the safe in the back. It didn't take long to get the shop ready for the day, then she settled down at the worktable in the back with her music to put together a small bouquet for Mr. Adams.

For as long as she could remember, he had come to the shop once a week to buy flowers for his wife. Even after they'd been closed for a while following her mom's death, he'd shown up as soon as she reopened the shop and had been coming weekly ever since. He could be counted on to appear at three o'clock each Tuesday to pick up his bouquet.

This bouquet was simpler than the ones she'd been working on that morning, but she liked knowing that this one was being given with a heart full of love.

She hadn't been working on it long when the bell above the front door jingled. It was a rare enough sound that it took her a bit by surprise. Setting aside the flower stems she'd been trimming, Lani got to her feet and went to the front of the shop.

"Oh. Hello, Mrs. Lange." Lani moved to stand behind the counter, gripping the edge of it as she waited for the woman to get to the reason for her visit.

The woman made her way around the room, trailing her fingers across the front of the smaller glass-front cooler that Lani used for an assortment of cut flowers. She paused for a moment to look out the front window—the one that looked across the street to her own home—then turned around to pin Lani with a look.

"You opened later than usual this morning," she remarked sharply. "Aren't you supposed to open at ten?"

Lani sighed inwardly but managed to give the other woman a smile—a small one, to be sure, but a smile nonetheless. "I've made a change to the hours and will be opening at eleven from now on."

"Does your father know about this?" she asked with the lift of a single brow. "Does he approve?"

A frown almost managed to overtake the smile on her face, but Lani fought to hold it back. "My father has other things to worry about, and I need a couple of hours in the morning to do a few other things."

"I would think this would be something he'd like to know about," Mrs. Lange said with a huff.

Lani wondered if her mom had had this much trouble with the woman. She didn't know much about Mrs. Lange beyond the fact that she had grown up in New Hope and was divorced. Oh, and that she apparently had nothing better to do than keep track of everything going on in her neighborhood.

"If I need to justify it to him, I certainly can," Lani said, doing her best to keep from giving in to the urge to justify it to Mrs. Lange.

The woman looked at her for a moment before giving a sniff and lifting her chin. "Well, maybe your mother should have been open fewer hours and spent more time with your father."

Say... *what?*

But nope! She was *not* going to respond to that. It was definitely a smack at her mom, and part of Lani wanted to defend her, but she could almost hear her mom's voice.

You never need to defend me, Leilani, my love. Only someone hurting tries to hurt others—especially those who aren't around to defend themselves.

Rather than respond, Lani just amped her smile up a bit and hoped that Mrs. Lange had somewhere she needed to be. Soon...

"I do think you should let your father know about this change," she said instead of leaving the shop like Lani wanted. "Before he finds out from someone else."

The *like me* was as silent as the *t* in *castle.* Which is where Lani kind of wished the woman would go. Preferably to one in England. She had an idea the Queen would be able to tell Mrs. Lange to butt out in a way that would leave the woman feeling complimented instead of insulted.

Lani lifted her arms and crossed them, glad that she'd inherited her mother's patience rather than her father's lack of it. They were in a waiting game. Mrs. Lange was waiting for a response while Lani was waiting for her to leave. She was confident that she'd be able to win this particular battle.

When several minutes had passed without the woman leaving, Lani changed up her tactic.

"What would you like to buy today, Mrs. Lange?"

The woman's eyebrows rose at the question. "Uh, what?"

"People usually come into the shop to buy something, so what can I get for you?"

That appeared to fluster the woman who then said, "Oh. I've changed my mind." She headed for the door. "I'll just be going."

As the door swung shut behind Mrs. Lange, Lani let out a huff of laughter then returned to the worktable to finish the bouquet. She couldn't help but wonder how long it would be until her father called demanding to know why she hadn't opened at ten that morning.

She could hardly wait...

CHAPTER THREE

When he arrived at the shop on Thursday morning, Michael spotted a car he didn't recognize, but there was no sign of Taylor's. And, just like on Tuesday, she hadn't verbally confirmed the flower order with him. Thankfully, he had taken the time the night before to record it for himself. It had taken him ages, and he'd had to type certain words into his phone in order to figure everything out.

He'd been exhausted by the time he'd finished, and a headache had been threatening to take him down for the night. Still, he was glad he'd done it since he'd proved that he *could* do it if he had to.

After he got out of the van, Michael walked to the back door, glancing over at the car in time to see someone climb out. It appeared that Taylor's employee was once again there before her. He certainly hoped that Taylor was paying Lani from the time she was supposed to work, not when Taylor actually showed up to let her in.

"Good morning, Lani," Michael said as the woman approached him.

"Morning." She glanced over at the van. "Do you need help bringing in the flowers?"

"Sure. Just let me get the door unlocked."

After he'd punched in the code on the door and the alarm, he propped it open. It didn't take them long to get the flowers out of the van and into the cooler. He had a job to get to, but he didn't feel comfortable leaving Lani on her own in the shop just yet.

It wasn't that he didn't trust her... Well, okay, maybe that was definitely a big part of it. He didn't know her at all, and though she seemed perfectly nice, he had no way of knowing she wouldn't mess with the shop if left there on her own.

Michael headed to the Keurig machine to make himself some coffee. "How have you been finding working here?"

"It's been great," Lani said as she sat on a stool at the worktable once again.

"Good to hear." Michael added some cream to his coffee then screwed the lid on his travel mug. He turned to lean back against the counter, taking a sip of coffee. "Did you have to wait long for Taylor yesterday?"

Lani's brow furrowed for a moment, but her gaze never left his. "Not too long."

Michael appreciated that she wasn't throwing Taylor under the bus, but he wasn't sure she was being entirely honest in her response. Though he wanted to phone Taylor to find out where she was, he resisted.

"Taylor said that you do landscaping work?" Lani said, turning her statement into a question. As if seeking clarification.

Michael nodded. "I have a few guys that work for me, and we do a little bit of everything. Tree pruning and removal. Chopping wood. Mowing grass. Planting flowers. We pretty much do any outdoor stuff that people need doing."

"That sounds amazing," she said, her eyes shining with interest. "Do you get people demanding you plant a certain type of plant or flower, even if it's not suitable for this area?"

He was a bit surprised at her question, as well as her interest. "We do a lot of planting for older people who still want flowers but can't do the work themselves anymore. They're usually pretty knowledgeable about what grows well around here. It's often the people who are new to the area that make requests that aren't the best for our growing environment."

"Did you study horticulture?" Lani asked as she leaned forward, bracing her elbows on the worktable. A hunk of dark hair fell against her cheek, and with a quick movement, she tucked it back behind her ear.

"Uh, no. I kind of fell into doing this kind of stuff in high school, and then learned on the job once we moved here." Michael didn't want to have to explain how college had never been an option for him.

"And you enjoy the work?" she asked with a tilt of her head.

Michael wasn't used to being the subject of such a focus and shifted a bit under her gaze. He took another sip of coffee before saying, "I do enjoy it. Being outside is preferable to being inside. At least for me."

Lani nodded. "I kind of like a bit of both. I enjoy working with flowers like I do here, but I also enjoy spending time out in nature. Haven't done much of that lately, though."

Michael wondered what she did to fill the hours she wasn't there at the shop. Since she was asking questions of him, it seemed only fair that he be able to ask some of her as well, satisfying the desire to know more about the woman who was now part of the shop family.

But before he could form his first question, the alarm chirped, alerting him that the back door had opened. Lani turned to look as Taylor walked in. Without even glancing in their direction, she shrugged out of her jacket and went into the office.

Lani swung back around, her gaze meeting his long enough for Michael to see the curiosity there. It made him wonder how the two of them had worked together over the past few days.

Michael didn't move, just continued to sip on his coffee as he waited for Taylor to join them. He didn't plan to confront her about anything, but he hadn't seen her since Monday, and he wanted to check on her. It had been weird going from seeing her every day to now just a couple of days a week.

They'd had a schedule of sorts, a pattern to their days. They'd gone back and forth on who cooked and who cleaned. She would tease him about cooking the same three dishes—the only ones he really knew how to make—while she added spice and variety to their meals.

Now he made meals for one and ate alone.

But more than that, he missed talking with her. Hearing what she thought about things going on in the business or even in the world. Where he struggled with reading and learning, she was super smart. He wasn't dumb. It was just that it was so much harder for him to learn in a way it wasn't for her. When she talked about things, he learned stuff.

All that was gone now, because not only had she moved out of their home, she'd shut him out of her life almost completely.

"Morning, Lani," Taylor said as she came out of the office and walked toward them. "Michael."

"Morning," Lani chirped, while Michael kept his greeting a bit more subdued.

He took the time to run another small cup of coffee into his travel mug then, even though in the past he would have spent a few minutes chatting with Taylor, he just said goodbye to the two of them and left to start his day.

"Hey there, Michael."

Michael turned from where he'd been adding mulch to the latest bit of landscaping he'd been doing for Beau. The man had brought him a lot of business over the past several months since buying his home. He'd given Michael a vague idea of what he wanted but then had basically left the yard design up to him. At Beau's request, Sarah had given a bit of input when she was around, but even then, it hadn't been too specific.

"How's life?" Michael asked as he used the rake to continue to spread the mulch around the base of the tree for his last job of the day.

"Can't complain," Beau said. "How about with you? How's Taylor doing?"

"She's...okay, I guess." He'd shared a bit with the guys in his Bible study group about what was going on with Taylor. Not everything, but enough that they knew he was struggling with the changes. "Still showing up late for work in the mornings. Still not talking to me much."

"I'm sorry to hear that." Beau paused then said. "This might not be the time to mention this, but I still haven't gotten an invoice for the work you did last month. I just want to make sure I pay you, and maybe if I haven't received an invoice..."

Beau didn't have to finish his sentence. Michael felt nauseous as proof that things with Taylor were now affecting his side of the business came into glaring focus. He wished that he could just go into the office, sit down at the computer and bang out the invoices himself, but he couldn't. He relied on her to do that for him.

"I'll talk to Taylor about it." He didn't want to have what was probably going to turn into a confrontational conversation with her, but it seemed inevitable.

After he finished his job at Beau's, he packed up his truck and headed into town. Hopefully, Taylor would still be at the shop even though it was closed. Previously, she would have been, but who knew anymore.

He only had to turn down the lane that ran behind the buildings on that block of Main Street to see that Taylor's car was gone. If he knew where she'd moved to, he might have driven there to talk to her, but since he didn't, he had to just head for home.

All the way there, Michael rehearsed what he was going to say when he called her because he couldn't let this go on too long. Other customers might not be as forthcoming as Beau had been about following up if they didn't receive an invoice. Now was not the time to have their income drop because invoices weren't being sent out.

He was battling worry and a bit of anger by the time he got home, which wasn't a good combination, but it propelled him to make the call without putting it off like he had been previously.

The worry and anger spiked when Taylor didn't answer his call. Her voicemail was full, so he settled for sending her a voice note.

"Beau said he didn't receive an invoice for the work I did for him last month. Can you please make sure we are up to date on all the invoicing we need to do for the landscape side? We can't afford to lose out on the money that's owed us. Also, I hope everything was okay for payroll this week."

Michael never would have found it necessary to remind her about something like that before, but he just didn't know anymore. He wished that he had some sort of manual for how to deal with this situation. They'd always communicated really well, and now they weren't. He just didn't know what to do about it.

~*~

Lani was sitting in her car, sipping the last of a rare cup of coffee, when Michael's truck swung into one of the parking spots. She frowned as she watched him climb from the vehicle and head for the back door. Since the van had been there when she'd arrived, she'd assumed Michael wouldn't be there that morning.

When he reached the door, he punched in the code then turned toward her car, giving a jerky wave of his hand. Lani took a final sip, set the mug in the cup holder, and got out of the car. It was a chilly morning, so she hurried to where Michael stood holding the door open.

"Good morning, Michael," she said as she walked past him into the building.

"Is it?"

She glanced over her shoulder at his mumbled response. If she hadn't dealt with him early in the morning without him being grumpy, she might have assumed that he wasn't a morning person. The fact that he looked like he hadn't slept at all gave her pause.

Without taking off his jacket, Michael made a beeline for the Keurig, looked around, then opened the cupboard above it and grabbed a mug. Lani took off her jacket and went into the office to hang it up.

When she came back out, Michael was doctoring his coffee. Content with the amount of caffeine she'd ingested so far, Lani settled at the worktable yet again. She was beginning to think she should just not bother to show up until seven-thirty since Taylor hadn't made it in by seven yet.

Michael came to sit across from her at the worktable. With his gaze lowered, the man took sips of his coffee, leaving Lani free to observe him.

He wasn't a conventionally handsome man, with sharp features that gave him an intense look. His dark hair was cut close to his head, and his body spoke to the physical job he worked. His forearms were muscled, and his shoulders were broad. But it was the dark circles under his eyes and his troubled expression that left Lani curious about what was going on with him. Taylor hadn't looked very happy over the few days Lani had been working with her either.

When she'd made the decision to work for the enemy—so to speak—she hadn't thought much about what the brother-sister team would be like. All she'd cared about was making some extra money. And if it came from the enemy's coffers, all the better.

Now that she was there, however, her curiosity was getting the better of her.

Maybe it was just nice to focus on someone else's problems rather than her own. Hers still hadn't gone away, and really, the longer days were starting to wear on her, especially the ones that started with a super early morning flower run like that day had. But for a few hours each day, she was able to check out of those problems and just do what she loved.

"Is everything okay, Michael?"

He glanced up at her for a moment, then ran his hand over the back of his neck. "Just dealing with some business stuff. Sometimes being the boss isn't all it's cracked up to be."

Lani could definitely agree with him, but instead of making it seem like she knew exactly what he meant, she said, "I'm sure that's true."

Michael didn't say anything further, and the silence that fell between them was weighty. Rather than just sit at the table with him, Lani got up and went to get the binder that Taylor used to track orders. She brought it back to the worktable and sat back down.

"Do you have a lot of orders to work on today?" Michael asked.

His hands were cupped around the mug where it sat in front of him, and his gaze was on the binder. She found it interesting that he didn't pull out his phone to kill time while he waited for Taylor.

Flipping it open to the top page, Lani checked the date then ran her gaze down what Taylor had written there. "Looks like there are a few arrangements for a funeral as well as a wedding consultation."

Michael gave a grunt in response, and Lani wondered if he was concerned that there wasn't more work for the shop. Honestly, from what she'd seen, they did a profitable business for being in a small town. They had several weekly orders from corporate customers—a couple of care homes, a funeral home, a B&B, as well as a bulk order of cut flowers from a high-end restaurant in a nearby town, among others. It also appeared that they got customers from Everett, though, so that probably helped as well.

Lani opened the flower binder and matched the pictures to the orders, making a note of the changes to each that Taylor had written down. She appreciated how organized the woman was because it made it easy to understand what she needed to do without constantly going to Taylor with questions.

When the chirping of the alarm announced Taylor's arrival, Lani glanced at Michael. He got to his feet and went to put his mug in the sink.

"Michael," Taylor said. "What are you doing here?"

The sharp edge to Taylor's words had Lani looking over at her. She stood with her hands on her hips as she glared at her brother. She once again wore a baggy sweater over a loose shirt and pants. The woman had a curvy figure, but the clothes she wore did nothing to flatter it.

"We need to talk."

Well, that didn't sound ominous *at all.* Weren't those the most dreaded four words in the English language? In contrast to Taylor's defensive tone, Michael just sounded weary.

"I don't think—"

"In the office, Taylor," Michael said with a sigh as he walked by her.

Taylor hesitated for a moment before following him, but the slamming of the door let Lani know that she wasn't happy about it.

Lani's heart pounded, reminding her of the times her parents had argued. And like back then, she found she couldn't just sit there, especially since it was all too easy to hear the conversation going on through the thin walls of the space.

At first, it was muffled enough that she would have had to strain to hear what was being said, but that didn't last too long.

"What you're doing is starting to affect the business, Taylor," Michael said. "That's not acceptable."

Lani got up and started to pace, thinking that maybe she should just leave since this really wasn't any of her business.

"Did you ever stop to think that this isn't what I wanted for my life?" Taylor demanded loudly. "This is what *you* said I should do."

"We discussed this before we ever made the decision to open the shop. You said you wanted to do it."

"I lied, okay?"

"Why would you do that?" Michael asked, his own words half-way to a yell.

"Because you needed my help with the business, so it seemed that the best thing would be to just go along with it since I did have some experience with it." There was silence for a moment, then Taylor said, "I'm just *so* tired of doing what you think I should do with my life."

"Are you kidding me?" Michael shouted. "Do you think I wanted to drop out of high school? Do you think I wanted to stick around after that? Absolutely not, but I did it because I love you, and I had to do what I could to protect you."

"Don't blame me for that, Michael. I didn't ask you to do any of that."

"Where do you think you'd be right now if I hadn't? If Gran hadn't helped us move here? Are you telling me that you'd really rather be back in Spokane, living with Mom and Dad?"

There was silence for several beats, and Lani glanced at the door, expecting to see it burst open, but it stayed closed, their conversation lowering to a murmur once again.

Unable to do nothing and wishing fervently that she'd brought her headphones with her that morning, Lani went to the front of the shop and opened the cooler. She lifted out one of the cylindrical vases that held the cut flowers and returned to the sink, wanting to stay as far from the office as possible.

After emptying out the water, she trimmed up the ends, then returned the blossoms to the vase and added fresh water. She hummed as she worked, trying to block out the words that were still being said in the office. Once done with the first vase, she went and swapped it out for another.

As she stood at the sink, she could hear the words again, even over the running water.

"Why won't you just talk to me?" Michael demanded. "You can't just drive the business into the ground and then run away."

"Would it really have made a difference? Or would you do what you're doing now? Trying to convince me that I can't move on with my life? Why I need to stay here and devote my time to a business I don't want to be part of?"

Lani stood with her hands braced on the counter. She understood all too well how it was to feel like you had no control of your own life.

"How am I supposed to run this without you? You know I can't do it all on my own."

"Hire people," Taylor said. "That's what people do when they have parts of a job they can't do themselves."

"Just give me some time, okay?"

The conversation dropped back down to a muffled level after that, so Lani continued to work on refreshing the flowers from the front. She was standing at the sink, rinsing out a vase when she heard the office door open, and then the alarm chirp as the back door opened then thudded shut.

She finished the flowers then returned the vase to the cooler at the front. When she returned, Taylor was standing at the worktable, staring down at the binders.

"What would you like me to start working on?" Lani asked as she approached her.

The conversation she'd overheard bits and pieces of wasn't any of her business, so she didn't bother to broach it with Taylor. The other woman let out a long sigh, and for a moment, Lani thought she was going to volunteer some information on what had gone on with Michael.

"Go ahead and make the arrangements for the funeral." She gave a few more details about them, and then the two of them went to look at the flowers in the walk-in cooler.

Lani could see the woman's focus wasn't on the flowers, so she wasn't too surprised when Taylor retreated to the office once Lani assured her that she knew what she was doing.

As she worked, she struggled with her feelings. On the one hand, having this shop close might mean that she could finally get her mom's business back on track. However, the strain it was putting on the brother and sister wasn't easy to witness.

Lani didn't want to care about these two. She really didn't want to waste time thinking about their problems when she had enough of her own.

But it seemed that she couldn't help but do a little of both.

CHAPTER FOUR

Michael felt sick to his stomach as he drove back to the mobile home, and he was half-tempted to call Ryker, his right-hand man, and have him take care of that day's job.

Usually, he enjoyed the drive, leaving the town behind and meandering along the more rural road to his property. For the past several years, he'd thought it was nothing short of a miracle that he and Taylor had ended up there.

The twists and turns that had led him to New Hope Falls and eventually to the man who had taken him under his wing, teaching him all about his business and then leaving it to him on his death, had felt like God's leading.

However, the gut-wrenching conversation he'd just had with Taylor was making him question it all. How had he missed seeing how unhappy she was?

He wasn't the smartest guy around when it came to stuff like reading and math, but he'd always thought he did a pretty good job of listening to his sister. He really didn't think he'd misunderstood how Taylor had felt about things when he'd suggested that she might like to go into the florist business. Clearly, he had though.

So now he was left with a mess and no idea of how to clean it up. Maybe it would be best to just let the flower shop go entirely, and then hire a bookkeeper to help with the paperwork that he couldn't do for his landscape business. And any plans they'd had to expand to greenhouses and growing some of their own flowers would have to go by the wayside.

If that was what would keep Taylor happy, then he'd do it. They just needed to have a conversation when they'd both settled down.

It was rare that they raised their voices with each other, but emotions had definitely been running high that morning.

He could only imagine what Lani must think of them. No doubt, she'd been able to hear a good portion of their conversation. Or rather, their argument. That hadn't been any sort of conversation. He had a feeling that neither of them had walked away with a clear understanding of where the other stood.

Michael wasn't altogether sure what he thought of Lani. She had a very calm air around her, which he appreciated, and he was also glad that she hadn't pried too much into why he'd been there that morning.

It was possible—likely, even—that she'd ask more questions of Taylor now that he had left, but that was fine. Taylor would shut her down if she didn't want to share any details about what seemed to be bothering her.

He was tired, though. Tired of trying to figure out where Taylor's head was. Tired of thinking of what he'd need to do to keep things afloat. All he wanted was to do his part of the business. The part he knew how to do.

Once he met up with the guys who were working with him that day, Michael did his best to put everything else out of his mind. With a tree removal scheduled, he needed to make sure he was focused, so no one got hurt, and no property was damaged. The problems with Taylor would still be there when the job was done. And honestly, he needed something else to focus on for a bit.

The next morning, Michael wasn't surprised to find Lani sitting in her car once again when he arrived with the flowers he'd picked up. She got out as he headed for the back door.

"Morning," he said with as much of a smile as he could muster.

"Good morning," Lani replied.

He propped the back door open, and then they began to bring in the flowers. They worked in silence, Michael uncertain of what to say to the woman whose calm presence was an odd reassurance in the midst of the storm of chaos his life seemed to be in at the moment.

"Thanks for your help," he said once the flowers were all unloaded.

"You're welcome." Lani smiled at him in a way that helped settle some of the worry and unease that seemed to be constantly churning in his gut.

She seemed like one of those people who cared about those around her even without knowing them. In the short time he'd known her, she'd shown herself to be sensitive and approachable. It made him want to spill his guts and share everything with her...but he wouldn't. No one but Pastor Evans knew about everything he'd already dealt with in his life as well as what was currently going on with Taylor.

And for now, he was going to keep it that way.

"I'm going to head off. Hopefully Taylor will be here soon."

"You're just going to leave me here on my own?" Lani asked, her brow furrowed.

Honestly, Michael wasn't sure he should trust her, but he did, so he just shrugged. "You're an employee. Taylor hired you to work here, so if she doesn't want you to be in the shop on your own, she needs to get herself here on time."

Lani was silent for a moment before she said, "You trust me?"

He frowned at her. "Shouldn't we?"

"Well, yes. Sorry. It just feels a bit weird."

"I'm sure it will be fine. You seem to have picked up on how Taylor does things around here. I assume you must have the experience she needs."

"I do have lots of experience working with flowers."

Michael gave a quick nod. "So I'll leave you to it. Give me a call if something comes up and Taylor's not here yet."

"I don't have your number," Lani stated.

"Oh. Right." Michael waited as she pulled out her phone, then recited his number. After she'd input it, his phone beeped.

"There you go. That's my number, so you have it too." She paused. "Uh, if you need it."

"Thanks." Michael didn't check his messages since he'd need to have his phone read it to him in order to understand it. "I'm off. See you later."

"Yep. Have a good day."

Michael headed for the back door, hoping he wasn't making a mistake by leaving a virtual stranger alone in the shop. Unfortunately, he just didn't think that he was ready to deal with Taylor. The sting of the fight they'd had the day before still hadn't abated, and he didn't want to relive it.

Sooner or later, they'd have to talk it over because Taylor seemed determined to move forward, away from him and their business. They had to figure out what to do.

From the shop, he headed over to the church to do the weekly lawn care. That was where things had started for him. Where he'd made his first connection in the town that had become his home. Now he did the work for free as part of his commitment to the church.

As he weeded the flower beds he'd created around the building, Michael prayed. He'd prayed a lot during his life, starting at the urging of his gran when he was just a teen, struggling to deal with a father who could only be described as abusive. Though at that time, he hadn't been sure that God even existed.

When his gran had helped him and Taylor get away from that situation, Michael had begun to consider that maybe God really did exist. He'd then prayed that God would lead them to where they should be, and they'd ended up in New Hope Falls. Meeting Pastor Evans and witnessing his faith and devotion to God had been what had helped Michael truly accept God into his heart and life.

Now he once again pleaded for God to give him wisdom and understanding. For certain, he was lost in how to deal with Taylor and needed God's help. He just hoped that that help would come sooner rather than later.

~*~

Lani turned on her music and began to look through the binder for what sort of work they had on the schedule for the day. It was weird to be in the shop alone, and she wondered why Michael had left her today when he hadn't the other days. Had something changed in how he viewed her? Or was the situation with Taylor forcing him to do things he might not usually do?

It was almost eight o'clock before Taylor showed up. She didn't look so great, and she'd no sooner arrived when she headed into the bathroom. It sounded like she was sick, which made Lani a little nervous. She didn't want to catch anything because frankly, she didn't have time to deal with any sort of illness.

When Taylor came out of the bathroom, she murmured a greeting as she went to the kitchen area and got herself some hot water from the Keurig machine. She brought it along with a teabag to the worktable.

"Sorry I'm late," she said with a sigh. "I guess Michael let you in?"

"Yes. He dropped off the flowers then left."

Taylor just nodded, dunking the teabag in her mug of hot water. "So what are you starting on?"

Lani watched her for a moment then dropped her gaze to the binder, reading out what was written on the page for that day. Though she knew she shouldn't be interested in these people—that she should just concentrate on earning money from them—it was kind of hard not to be curious about what was going on between the siblings.

"Are you doing okay?" she asked when Taylor made no move to start on any of the orders.

The other woman continued to dunk her teabag before lifting the mug to take a small sip. "I'm fine. Just tired." She glanced up and gave her a small smile. "You know how it can be."

Lani didn't know why Taylor assumed she'd know that. It wasn't like they knew that much about each other. However, be that as it may, she did, in fact, know. "Yeah. There certainly are days."

Taylor sighed, but didn't say anything further, just drank more of her tea while Lani began to gather the flowers for the first order. She would have thought she'd feel uncomfortable working under Taylor's scrutiny, but she'd worked like that plenty of times.

Her mom had been the one who had started to teach her when she'd been just eight or nine, then later, she'd worked under Nina's watchful eye. It didn't make her nervous because while there were plenty of things that Lani wasn't confident about, arranging flowers wasn't one of them.

"Are you sure you can't stay a little longer?" Taylor asked when ten o'clock rolled around.

"Sorry. I have other commitments for the rest of the day."

"Do you have another job?" Taylor asked.

Lani hesitated, not wanting to lie, but there was no way she was revealing who she really was. It was entirely possible they'd fire her, and she couldn't let that happen. Sure, she wasn't earning a lot of money working there, but she made more in that time than she did in her own shop for those three hours.

"I have family stuff that needs my attention. My dad isn't well, and I help to take care of him."

"I'm sorry to hear that."

"I appreciate being able to work for these hours each day. It gives me a break, and it allows me to do something I really enjoy."

"Well, you're very good at it, so we're fortunate to have you."

Lani told herself not to be pleased with Taylor's words, but it was hard not to be. Clearing her throat, she said, "I'd better go."

"You're okay to work tomorrow?" Taylor asked.

"Yes." She was there to work any day they were open. But unlike Lani's shop, which was open six days a week, Taylor's was closed on Sundays and Mondays. Lani wished that she could have an extra day off, but she really couldn't afford it. Being open on a day that Taylor's shop was closed had gotten her a bit of business.

"Thanks for your help today," Taylor said as Lani gathered up her things to leave. "See you tomorrow."

As she drove to her shop, Lani once again found herself wondering what was going on with the siblings. From the way her father had talked about them, she'd expected a much more cold and ruthless attitude from the pair. He made it sound like they'd arrived in town determined to take over her mom's business.

The thing was, New Hope was a small town, but it wasn't *that* small. The two businesses should have been able to co-exist without one going under. There had been times when her mom's business had gotten almost too much for her to handle on her own.

There had been more going on with their shop than just a competing shop coming into town. Unfortunately, her mom wasn't there to cast any light on the situation, and her dad only had one response whenever she brought up the subject. From what she could see, her mom had taken more money out of the business than she should have, meaning she didn't have enough to buy the stock she needed to keep filling orders.

What she'd done with the money, Lani hadn't discovered yet, and it was possible she never would if she had to rely on her dad for an explanation. Sure, the arrival of another florist shop hadn't helped. But she was beginning to think that her dad's painting of the Reeds as cutthroat competitors wasn't entirely accurate.

Not that she'd ever tell him that.

When she showed up at the shop the next morning, Lani was surprised to see Michael's truck there. She didn't think Taylor had placed another flower order unless some orders had come in later in the day.

His truck was empty, so she assumed he was already in the shop. The unlocked door when she pulled on the handle confirmed that, and as soon as she walked in, she could smell coffee.

"Good morning, Michael," she said as she took off her jacket.

The man was seated at the worktable, a mug of coffee cupped between his hands. He looked up and gave her a smile. Though it was brief, it took his expression from stern to something softer. "Morning."

He looked as weary as she felt that morning. After working at the shop the day before, then trying to finish a few projects that she'd been working on in hopes of selling them online to help supplement the shop's income, she'd gone to her dad's, only to have to deal with his raging temper. That had left her agitated and unable to sleep well the night before.

There were times she'd wondered what her mom had ever seen in him. He'd never been a gentle man. His military career had hardened him, and even after he'd left the service, he'd never softened in his attitude.

While she'd seen him offer her mom sporadic affection over the years, it wasn't something he'd given to Lani. She'd asked her mom about it, but her mom's response had been that it was just how he was.

Now, there was no affection of any kind left in the man. He was bitter, overflowing with anger and resentment. The night before, she'd been ready to just pack up the shop and fly back to the life she'd abandoned in Hawaii. But even though Hawaii had been her mom's home before meeting and marrying her dad, the shop in New Hope had become her mom's dream. The thing she'd wanted the two of them to share.

Abandoning the shop would feel like she was abandoning her mom and the dream she'd had for them. Maybe someday she'd be able to walk away, but not yet. The shop was the one place where she felt her mom's presence most keenly, and she needed that still.

"Did you bring a load of flowers?" Lani asked as she glanced toward the temperature-controlled room.

"No. Taylor called me a bit ago and said she wasn't feeling well and wouldn't be in until later. I figured I'd come in and do a few things and make sure you were okay on your own here."

Lani wondered what was wrong with Taylor, and once again, she hoped it wasn't anything contagious. "I'm sorry to hear she's not feeling well."

Michael just sighed and said, "Yeah. I'm sure she'll be fine once she gets in."

"Well, I'll get started on the bouquets she needs for today." Lani pulled the binder toward her. "What time does she think she'll be in?"

"She said by ten, but I'll stay until she gets here if you have to leave."

Lani appreciated that since she couldn't stay late. Michael continued to nurse his coffee as she checked on the orders for the day. There were only a couple, so Lani felt like she could just take her time doing them.

"Have you always wanted to do flower arranging?" Michael asked as she began to assemble the things she needed for the first bouquet.

Lani glanced at Michael, meeting his gaze for a moment. "I don't suppose that I thought of it as a career until I was in my teens. But ever since I was a kid, I loved planting flowers and picking bouquets for my mom. How about you? Did you always want to do your job?"

"Not really. As a teen, I didn't realize that what I did could be made into a career." He took another sip of coffee. "I did a lot of yard work stuff. Cutting grass in the summer. Weeding. Shoveling snow in the winter. Just stuff to earn money, you know. It wasn't until we moved to Seattle for Taylor to go to school that I realized that maybe it could be more than just a casual job."

"It's always great when you can have a career doing what you enjoy," Lani said as she trimmed the stems of the flowers for the first arrangement. "What's your favorite part of what you do?"

"I don't know that I have one favorite thing. I like the variety. No two days are ever the same, you know."

From hearing his argument with Taylor, Lani had some idea of how they'd ended up with a florist shop, but she was curious about the whole story. However, she wasn't sure about asking him for details. Was she ready to hear about what had drawn them to New Hope Falls to set up a business that was a competitor to her mom's? Maybe not just yet.

Before she could think of something more to say to Michael, he lifted his mug and drained it, then got to his feet. "I'd better get to work. If you need anything, just let me know."

Lani nodded and watched as he went to the sink and washed his mug before heading to the small door that led to a utility closet. He pulled out a vacuum and headed for the front of the shop.

She stood for a moment holding a Delphinium stalk, listening as the vacuum roared to life. The man was a really interesting mix of...stuff. Basically the opposite of what she'd expected when she'd imagined the owner of the florist shop who'd taken away the business from her mom.

With the sound of the vacuum in the background, Lani quickly got back to work. Out of the corner of her eye, she saw him bring the vacuum back and then pull out a yellow mop bucket. She continued to assemble the arrangement while Michael worked at the front. Washing the floor took longer than vacuuming as there was more tile than carpet there, but soon he was back to get something else before returning to the front.

Lani tried to focus on what she was doing, but as she carried the finished arrangement to the cooler, she glanced through the doorway. Michael was squirting glass cleaner on the front of a cooler door then wiping it off.

It seemed the man was willing to do pretty much anything, though he probably should have done the window cleaning before he mopped the floor.

When his phone rang, he had to come back into the workroom to get it from where it lay on the table. It had stopped ringing by the time he picked it up, and he stared at it for a moment before muttering something. He gave her a small smile as he made his way to the office and shut the door.

It was then that Lani wondered if he had a girlfriend. Or maybe a wife. Maybe he even had some kids. She was pretty sure that Taylor was single from some remarks the woman had made, but she hadn't mentioned anything about her brother.

Not that it mattered.

Nope, it didn't matter at all.

With that in mind, she focused on working her way through the remainder of the arrangements. That was what she was there to do, after all.

To arrange some flowers and to earn some money.

Not to wonder about her bosses' personal lives.

Never that.

CHAPTER FIVE

By the following Friday, Michael had a feeling that nothing had changed in Taylor's schedule, but he didn't ask Lani for confirmation of that. They hadn't had any more personal conversations. It wasn't that he didn't want to get to know Lani better. It was just that he'd had so much else going on. He was grateful, though, for their unexpected rescuer—because he was sure she was definitely that.

He wasn't sure Lani knew that, and maybe even Taylor wasn't aware of it. But that was definitely how Michael had come to view her. He was beginning to think that if it weren't for Lani, there wouldn't be many floral arrangements getting done on time.

"Good morning, Michael," Lani said as she joined him at the van to carry in the flowers.

"Morning." He gave her a smile, the movement tugging at muscles in his face he hadn't been using much recently. When he opened the door, the interior light inside the van came on, chasing away the darkness, and Michael was able to see unusual circles beneath Lani's eyes, the dark smudges highlighting her uniquely colored irises.

Peering into the back of the van, she said, "Guess this was a larger than usual order, huh."

"It sure seemed like it was," Michael agreed.

Since he hadn't had time to work through the order the night before, it had caught him off-guard. Before accepting the order, he'd texted then called Taylor to confirm, but—surprise, surprise—she hadn't answered. He'd been forced to just take what they said she'd ordered.

"Yep. Apparently, there's a wedding on Saturday that we're getting ready for, and we're prepping for Valentine's Day as well."

The idea that he was going to have to rely on Taylor to be on her game for both a wedding and their busiest day of the year made Michael feel a little sick. Lani had already made it clear that she wasn't available to help beyond ten o'clock on Saturday, so he wasn't sure what he'd do if Taylor bailed on him yet again.

The wedding wasn't for anyone he knew, so it wasn't like he could prevail upon the bride and groom to cut him a little slack if things weren't exactly to order, like he would have been able to do with Cara and Kieran. He hated the idea of letting someone down on their special day.

After all the flowers were in the cooler, Michael grabbed a mug and filled it with coffee. He sat down on a stool, taking in Lani as she bent over the binder, her elbows braced on the table, her hands tucked under her chin.

"So you're not able to help with the wedding on Saturday?" Michael asked.

Lani looked up at him, then straightened with an apologetic look. "I can't, I'm sorry. But I did tell Taylor that I could come in on Sunday until one or so since she wanted to open for Valentine's Day."

That was a bit of a relief. He'd told Taylor that he'd do deliveries that afternoon, so at least he didn't have to worry about the bouquets not being ready to go.

How sad was it that he felt he could rely on someone he'd only known for a few weeks more than the sister he'd known since the day she was born?

Very sad.

"I would imagine it's going to be a bit of a crazy weekend," Lani said. "I'm sorry I can't be around to help more."

"It's fine," Michael said. "Any help you can give is greatly appreciated."

She gave him a smile. "I enjoy working with flowers, so this is no hardship."

Michael wished he could talk frankly with Taylor about how Lani was doing. While he'd been around flowers a lot because of the shop, he wasn't a great judge of what made a bouquet look good and what didn't. Taylor, however, did, so she'd be able to tell him if Lani really was doing a good job, in addition to taking pressure off Taylor.

The alarm chirped, and Lani turned to look toward the door while Michael looked over her shoulder. Michael was more than a little surprised to see Taylor come through the door. Not that anyone else would have been coming in, especially at that time of day.

Michael considered making a comment about her showing up for a change, but he bit his tongue. They still hadn't hashed out what Taylor was doing with her life, and it wasn't the time right then to do it.

"Morning, Taylor," Lani said.

"That it is," Taylor murmured as she shrugged off her jacket and laid it on the table. "Guess we've got our work cut out for us today."

Lani nodded. "You can say that again. Who has ten brides-maids?"

"A young bride who is trying to please everyone," Taylor responded. "And a father who is willing to pay whatever makes her happy."

Michael watched a look of sadness cross Lani's face and wondered about it.

"Well, that's good for your business," Lani said. "If only every wedding party was that big."

"Are you okay to do the bouquets while I work on the large floral displays?" Taylor asked as she picked up her jacket.

"Yep. I can take care of those."

"Did you need my help?" Michael asked. "I've cleared my schedule for the weekend."

It wasn't that he could do any arranging, but Taylor had always managed to put him to work when she needed an extra set of hands. If nothing else, he could trim stems on flowers and cut ribbons as needed. He knew how to do that much.

Lani glanced between him and Taylor, obviously understanding that there was still tension between them. She probably didn't want to get stuck in the middle, but he had no intention of adding to the stress of the weekend by trying to have a serious conversation with Taylor in the midst of it all.

"I'm sure we can find something for you to do," Taylor said. She disappeared into the office with her jacket then reappeared a minute later. "Let's get this organized."

Michael continued to sip his coffee as Taylor and Lani discussed things.

"So we'll do the bouquets today, and then the boutonnieres for the men tomorrow morning." Taylor bent over the binder, running a finger down the page with the details. She looked up at Michael. "The order was complete?"

He raised his brows at her question. "I assume so."

She pushed away from the table and headed for the cooler. Michael didn't bother following her. Either the order was complete, or it wasn't, and there wasn't much he could do about it. He'd tried his best to check it, but she knew that it was a struggle for him, especially when he didn't have a lot of time.

Lani had been watching Taylor, but when she disappeared into the cooler, she shifted her gaze to him. Michael was sure she was curious about what that all meant, but that was definitely the last thing he was going to reveal to her. Let her think that Taylor just didn't trust him to check the order.

"It looks like everything's there," Taylor announced when she came back into the room. "So let's get this order going."

Having worked with Taylor before, Michael knew what to expect, and that was to just wait for her to tell him what to do and then do it. Soon enough, she had both him and Lani working on bouquets.

"Let Michael know how much you want trimmed from the stems and the length of ribbons you need. He's helped me plenty with that in the past, so he knows what he's doing."

Lani wasted no time in telling him what she needed, and they fell into a rhythm. With ten identical bouquets needed, there was plenty of repetition.

"Does it get boring making the same thing over and over?" Michael asked as they began to work on the third bouquet.

She smiled at him, some of the tiredness easing from her face. "I try not to think of them all together. Rather, I approach each one like it's the very first one I'm making like that. It helps to alleviate the boredom of making the same thing a bunch of times."

"Well, I hope the bride likes them even if they aren't the most original," Michael said as he looked at the pink and white roses that Lani was assembling. "But I guess they work for a wedding this close to Valentine's Day."

"I guess that's one way to make sure the groom never forgets their anniversary since it will always be the day before Valentine's Day."

Michael grinned at that. "So maybe there is some method to their madness."

"With a wedding party of twenty-two, it's definitely going to be madness," Lani said with a shake of her head. "Especially when it's time for the pictures. Getting that many people to smile at the right time must be an impossible task."

"Hopefully their photographer is a pro at photoshopping. Then, if someone smiles in one picture but not another, they can just swap heads."

Lani looked at him for a moment before she giggled. "What would happen if they accidentally picked the wrong head and ended up with two of the same person?"

"They'd have to make up a story about twins or something," Michael said, thinking of Eli McNamara's twin sisters. "But that could lead to a convoluted story if they had to explain why someone was a twin who'd never had a twin before."

"Separated at birth." Lani paused for a moment, holding a length of ribbon between her hands. "That would be quite the story."

As they continued to chat about the wedding and all the issues they might encounter, Michael found himself in a weird situation. He had long ago resigned himself to remaining single—for so very many reasons—and while that wasn't going to change, he did find himself enjoying Lani's company. It made him wonder what it would be like to be open to a relationship, to flirt and fall in love.

He'd seen three of his friends do just that, and he was happy for them. It was kind of nice to see loving relationships. Goodness knows he hadn't seen that from his parents. His mom's parents might have had a good relationship, but by the time he was old enough to see past the horror of his homelife, his grandfather had passed away.

"Let me take that to the cooler for you," Michael said, needing a minute to himself.

"Thanks." Lani gave him a smile. "Three down. Seven to go."

Taylor glanced at him as he walked by her on his way to the cooler. She had earbuds in, so he wasn't sure if she was paying much attention to what he and Lani were saying. Without commenting, she turned her attention back to the elaborate display she was working on. There were two white wicker stands that needed to be filled. But she'd done plenty of them over the years, so Michael was sure they'd be beautiful once she was done with them.

He carefully put the bouquet stems into the vase of water next to the others Lani had already completed. Though he wasn't thrilled about Taylor's reasons for hiring Lani, Michael was glad that she was there to help them out. It might only be for a few hours each day, but she did take some of the pressure off Taylor, and that could only be a good thing.

After a moment, he returned to the workroom. Lani was focused on another bouquet, her movements quick and sure. With so many to do, he had thought that Taylor might still have to do some of the bouquets, but from the way Lani worked, she might get them all done before she had to leave.

"I'm starting to think you've done bouquets like these before," Michael said as he settled on his stool and began to cut more lengths of the pink and white ribbons the bride had chosen to go with the flowers.

"You'd be right," Lani said as she bent over the flowers she was assembling. "The shop I worked for in Hawaii did lots of wedding flowers."

"Did you mostly use conventional flowers?" Michael asked. "Or did brides tend to want something native to the area?"

Lani leaned over to take one of the ribbons he'd cut. "We got both, but if a bride could afford it, they tended to go for orchids."

"Orchids? Really?"

"Yeah. Those bouquets were always gorgeous cascades of blossoms." Even though he could only see her profile, her smile was visible. "Those weren't bouquets that were quickly done, I have to say."

"Did the bridesmaids carry those types of bouquets too or just the brides?" Michael wasn't sure why he was asking so many questions about the flowers. He never asked Taylor those types of questions.

"It usually depended on how rich the bride's father was. But mostly, those bigger, more elaborate bouquets were just for the brides."

At Lani's instruction, Michael switched from cutting the ribbon to trimming stems. Though the work was physically easier than what he usually did, he felt a bit like he was all thumbs. Taylor and Lani worked so deftly with the flowers and ribbons, while he struggled to cut the stems at the right angle.

"I'm going to have to head out, Taylor," Lani said when ten o'clock rolled around. "I got all but two of the bridesmaids' bouquets done."

"That's great," Taylor said as she slumped down on one of the stools. "Thank you so much. I'm not sure I could have done this without your help."

"You're welcome. I've really enjoyed working on them."

"You'll be in tomorrow?" Taylor asked, her brow furrowed as she looked at Lani.

"Definitely. Although I'll still have to leave by ten," she said. "Sunday, however, I can stay until one."

"That would be very much appreciated." Taylor blew out a breath. "I'm not sure what I was thinking when I agreed to do a wedding of this size the same weekend as Valentine's Day."

"Do you have someone to do deliveries on Sunday?"

"That would be me," Michael said. "I'll be here to do them once I'm done at church."

"It's so much easier when Valentine's doesn't fall on a Sunday," Taylor muttered. "And when we don't have a wedding the day before."

"Well, I'll do my best to help as much as I can," Lani assured her. "We'll get through it, and then you can crash on Monday."

"I can't wait," Taylor said as she pushed to her feet.

After Lani got her jacket from the office, she said goodbye and left the shop. The silence that lingered in her absence was deafening, and Michael wasn't sure how to break it. Instead, he went to the front of the shop and turned on the lights before flipping the sign and unlocking the door. Knowing that Taylor liked her jazzy music, he turned on the shop's sound system, which was already set to her favorite playlist.

He'd barely stepped into the back when the bell over the door jangled. Though he wouldn't be able to take any detailed orders, if all they wanted was a dozen roses, he could help them with that.

"Hi, Michael," Beau greeted him as Michael returned to the front of the shop.

"Hey, Beau. Here to get some flowers for Sarah?"

"You know it." Beau wore a suit, so he was either on his way to the office or on a break from work. "My inclination is to ask for several dozen roses, but something tells me Sarah wouldn't appreciate that. Too un-original for her."

"Well, we do have plenty of roses, if that's what you want."

"How about a random assortment?" Beau asked.

"Once you get past roses, I'm afraid I'm out of my depth," Michael said with a laugh. "Let me get Taylor for you."

"Thanks."

Michael walked back into the workroom to find Taylor. "We have someone who needs your expertise, Tay."

"Okay." She set the flowers she was holding onto the worktable then went to the front of the shop.

Michael trailed after her. Normally, he wouldn't have, but this was a friend.

"So you just want an assortment of flowers?" Taylor asked.

"Yep. The more colorful, the better," Beau said, a beaming smile on his face. "Sarah loves colors. She's a painter, you know."

"That's sweet of you to get her something she'd like rather than going for the most expensive option," Taylor observed. "Most guys just go for roses."

"I do get her roses, but they're more of a spur of the moment thing. If I'm planning this in advance, I'd rather get her something I know she'd really like."

"Did you want to pick them up or have them delivered?" Taylor had a sheet of paper out, making notes on it.

It was a reminder of why he couldn't do this part of the job. Why he couldn't do this without her.

Once Beau and Taylor had finished, and Beau had paid for the order, he spoke with Michael for a few more minutes then left the shop. Taylor had disappeared as soon as the order was completed, and when Michael went back to the work area, she was once again focused on the floral display.

"Do you have anything you need me to do?" Michael asked, not wanting to leave Taylor floundering, but if she didn't need him, he wasn't keen to just hang around in tense silence.

"I think I'll be alright," Taylor said with a glance in his direction.

Michael nodded. "Okay. Call if you need me to come back. I'm just going to be at the house."

Grabbing his jacket, he left, the weight of their fractured relationship once again pressing down on him. It felt even heavier than usual because of the moments of lightness he'd experienced with Lani.

He wished that Lani could come work for them full-time. Maybe it would take some of the pressure off Taylor and help them mend whatever had broken between them. Although it was probably wrong to rely on someone else to try and fix the issues between him and Taylor, no matter how tempting it was.

CHAPTER SIX

The next morning, Lani wasn't surprised to find Michael in the shop but not Taylor. Thankfully she didn't need Taylor there to get started on the boutonnieres for the groom and the guys standing up with him. Since she only had a few hours to help out, she wanted to make sure she didn't waste any time.

At least she had a little more energy and hadn't needed coffee that morning. The previous day, she'd had to make a super early morning run to the wholesaler for flowers since she actually had some orders for Valentine's Day that weekend. By the time she'd gotten to Taylor's shop, she'd already been up for a couple of hours and felt like she was running on fumes.

As she walked in the back door of the shop, she was greeted by the aroma of coffee. She kind of wished that she liked coffee more. She could drink it if she was desperate—like on days she had to get up well before the sun—but it had to be so filled with sugar and flavored creamer that the coffee taste was pretty much gone.

As she stepped into the workroom, she spotted Michael at the counter with the coffee machine. "Good morning."

He turned with a mug in hand and smiled. "Good morning."

It had been strange working with him the day before. Her dad would never have stepped in to help the way Michael had. He would have just given her a lecture on time management. Though he had left the military not long after she was born, he'd continued to operate as if she and her mom were his personal military squad.

"I guess we've got some work to do," Lani said after she'd hung up her jacket.

"Yeah." Michael came over and sat down at the table. "Not sure what, though."

Lani pulled the open binder toward her and scanned it, looking for any notes that Taylor may have left for her. "Looks like she finished up all the bridesmaids' bouquets as well as the bride's. I just need to work on the boutonnieres."

"Well, tell me what to do to help you out," Michael said, setting his mug on the table. "I would imagine that you don't need me cutting long lengths of ribbon for those, huh?"

Lani glanced up and laughed. "No. I think the bride would be asking for a refund if we did that."

A small smile tipped up the corners of Michael's mouth. "Well, we don't want that."

"Okay. Let me get organized and see where we are." For all that she didn't always appreciate her father's approach to life, one thing she'd inherited from him and always needed was organization.

After referring to the notes for the boutonnieres, she went to the cooler and took out the flowers and greenery that she'd need. After a bit of discussion, they decided that Michael would look for the best leaf to go behind the flower and a bit of baby's breath. Lani would then assemble them and wrap the stems.

"What's your favorite flower?" Michael asked after they'd been working for a few minutes.

"Oh. That's a tough one. I like all kinds of flowers for different reasons." Lani finished the boutonniere she was working on and set it aside. "Although, for me, there's nothing like the scent of lilacs on a warm spring day. Orchids and roses are beautiful, but I also like daisies."

"I guess that was a bit of a difficult question," Michael conceded.

"Kind of like asking a librarian what their favorite book is," Lani said with a laugh. "Although I might have a hard time picking a favorite book too."

"You like to read?"

"I do. Next to flowers, books are my favorite thing." She took a leaf from him and laid it on the table. "Do you enjoy reading?"

"I'm more of an audiobook guy," Michael said after a brief hesitation.

"You're definitely not alone in that. I prefer to read, but sometimes, I'll listen to an audiobook while I'm working." She glanced up at him and smiled. "The best of both worlds. What sort of books do you listen to?"

Michael's brow furrowed as he continued to sort through the leaves. "I guess I like action-adventure the most. Suspense, too. I'm not really into sci-fi or non-fiction."

The alarm chirped as the back door opened, and Taylor walked in. She headed straight for the office, and when she reappeared, she went to the bathroom. When Taylor finally came out, she didn't look so great, and Lani wondered if she still wasn't feeling well.

"You okay, sis?" Michael asked, concern in his voice.

"Yeah."

Lani kept her gaze on Michael as he watched Taylor walk over to the coffee machine. She got a mug from the cupboard and pulled out a box of teabags. After putting one in her mug, she got hot water from the Keurig.

The tension had spiked when Taylor appeared, and Lani braced herself for some sort of confrontation between the brother and sister. She kind of hoped it didn't come to that since they had lots to do, but it seemed like whatever they'd had their big fight over hadn't been resolved yet.

Thankfully, rather than press Taylor about her blatant lie, Michael let it go, choosing instead to shift his attention back to the leaves he was sorting through.

"Are you free to go with me to the church with the flowers this afternoon, Michael?" Taylor asked as she joined them at the table, both hands cupped around the mug she held.

"Is Emma available to watch the shop?" he asked, glancing up at her briefly before returning his attention to what he was doing.

Taylor hesitated before she said, "No. She said she couldn't."

"So who's going to?"

"My roommate said she'd come and take care of the shop."

That got Michael's attention. His head jerked up, and he stared at Taylor. "Your roommate? Does she even know anything about running things here? Do you trust her?"

Lani didn't want to be in the middle of this discussion, but she couldn't very well walk out. There was work to be done, and she had a job to do.

Keeping her head bent, she focused on wrapping the floral tape around the ends of the flowers. It seemed odd that Michael wouldn't know more about Taylor's roommate, but maybe it was a recent thing.

"Of course, I trust her. I wouldn't have asked her to keep an eye on things if I didn't."

The indignant tone of Taylor's voice made Lani hunch further over her work. She wished she could shrink down in size and just slip away.

"I haven't met her, so how would I know if she's trustworthy or not?"

"You hadn't met Lani, but you seem to trust her just fine."

"We didn't leave her unattended in the shop until after I'd met her, and I'm usually a fairly good judge of character."

"Whatever," Taylor muttered. "I didn't have a choice since Emma had something going on with her sheep and couldn't come in to cover for me."

"So why don't you just go, and I'll watch the shop?" Michael asked. "You don't need me there, do you?"

Lani wished that she could offer to stay at the shop, but she couldn't do it for two reasons. First, she couldn't risk someone who knew her dad finding her there in the shop. Second, she was hoping she'd get some extra orders since it was the day before Valentine's. She couldn't do a bunch of deliveries, but she hoped that people would walk in to buy a bouquet or some roses.

"How much good are you going to do here?" Taylor asked. "You can't even—"

"Taylor."

At Michael's sharp tone, Lani glanced up to see him glaring at his sister. She looked at Taylor to see her reaction. Taylor had lifted her mug but kept her gaze lowered as she took a sip.

"We don't have a choice," she finally said. "It's Britt, or we close the shop."

"Fine." Michael got to his feet. "What time do we need to leave?"

"The wedding starts at three, so we need to leave by noon. They want the flowers for pictures beforehand."

"I'll be here." With that, Michael left the shop, the back door thudding closed behind him.

Lani felt a bit sick, and her fingers trembled a bit as she held the stems together to wrap them. She hated the tension that seemed to be present whenever the siblings were together. Maybe it would help if she understood it, but she didn't feel it was her place to delve into whatever was causing such tension between the two of them. And frankly, she wasn't really sure she wanted to know.

"I'm halfway done with the boutonnieres," Lani said. "Was there something else you needed me to work on?"

"No. You can keep going on those. I need to finish one of the displays, but everything else is done for the wedding. Once you're done those, you can tackle some of the orders for tomorrow."

"Sounds good." Lani turned her focus back to the flowers she needed to finish. She almost wished it was a more complicated task because then it might capture her thoughts, thus keeping them from wandering to things that were absolutely none of her business.

Instead, the simplicity of the boutonnieres and the fact she'd already made several meant her mind was free to wander.

Lani made quick work of the remaining boutonnieres then turned her attention to the orders in the binder. Taylor finished the remaining floral display then also began to work on the Valentine's orders. The other woman worked in silence, though she'd turned on some music, so it wasn't dead quiet.

By the time ten o'clock rolled around, Lani was more than happy to be leaving. Taylor had barely said a handful of words to her, and while she didn't think Taylor's silence had anything to do with her in particular, it still hadn't been a very comfortable work environment.

Though she might be curious about what was going on with the siblings, Lani knew she had enough of her own issues to not be taking on someone else's. Not that she would have brushed Taylor aside if she'd wanted to talk, but clearly she hadn't wanted to, so it was all good.

Once she got to her shop, Lani quickly opened it up, hoping against hope that she'd get some business that day. Even though Sunday was usually her day for doing her cooking for the week, she was considering opening once she was done at the Reeds', just to take advantage of the holiday. It would mean doing the cooking daily instead of for the week, but if she could get some extra sales, it would be well worth it.

~*~

Michael didn't hang around at church once the service was over since he'd promised Taylor he'd be there to make deliveries throughout the afternoon. In past years, Valentine's Day could be fairly busy with deliveries. With it falling on a Sunday, though, it seemed there weren't as many deliveries.

He spotted Lani's car in the parking lot, but he knew that she wasn't hanging around too long. Given that Taylor had taken a chunk of the previous afternoon off to take care of the flowers for the wedding, he was glad that Lani was there to help.

The shop was quiet except for the jazz music Taylor liked, but there was no sign of her when Michael walked into the workroom.

"Good afternoon," Michael said when Lani glanced up and gave him a quick smile before turning her attention back to the arrangement she was working on. "How's it going here?"

"Pretty good. I think we've got most of the orders done for today."

Michael stood across the table from her and watched as she added some flowers to the container in front of her. She wore a light pink T-shirt that accented her tanned skin, and her dark hair was pulled up in a bun, leaving just a few tendrils free to frame her face.

"That's an interesting arrangement," he said, dropping his gaze from her face to the flowers. "It looks like something you'd gather from the side of a road."

She laughed softly. "Well, then I guess the customer will be happy. That's almost exactly what they asked for."

"Really?" Michael leaned down to rest his arms on the worktable. "Why? I mean, why didn't they just go pick some flowers?"

"Who knows," Lani said as she sat back a bit, tilting her head as she checked out the arrangement. "But it's all the better for the shop that they didn't."

"True."

"We need to get started on the deliveries."

Taylor's words had Michael straightening and turning toward her. Her brows were pulled together as she glared at him. With a sigh, he gave a nod then followed her to the cooler. They'd worked out a system that allowed him to be able to make deliveries with minimal chance of him messing up.

"I'll send you voice memos of the address info for each of the arrangements along with pictures of them."

For the first time in his life, Michael heard impatience in Taylor's voice as she spoke about the things she had to do to accommodate his inability to read very well. She was one of the very few people who knew his secret. Technology had allowed him to adapt, but there was no way he could do this without her help.

Maybe she had finally tired of helping him.

The thought caused his stomach to knot, and shame swept in. She'd never made him feel dumb, but maybe she'd just been hiding how she truly felt about him. Maybe she felt the same way about him that their father had...she'd just been better at not letting it show.

"Are you listening to me?" Taylor asked sharply.

"Yes."

"If you're not paying attention, you're going to screw everything up."

The knot tightened, and Michael swallowed hard as he fought to keep his focus on everything Taylor was saying. He was glad when it was finally time to load up the deliveries. Having finished the arrangement she'd been working on, Lani helped carry the flowers out to the van before she left for the day.

Michael sat out in the van waiting for the first voice memo and picture to come through so that he could plug the address into the GPS. As he left the shop for his first delivery, Michael wondered if perhaps it would be best to just close it down so that Taylor could go do whatever it was that she wanted to do with her life.

He had never wanted to hold her back, but recently he felt like that was all he was doing. Whether it was with the shop or his own failings.

Once the deliveries were all done without any mistakes, Michael took the van back to the shop and swapped it out for his truck. Taylor's car was already gone, which was yet another change. In years past, she would wait around for him to get back, then they'd go out for dinner to celebrate another successful Valentine's Day at the shop.

They'd never gone to any of the restaurants that were frequented by couples since the wait to get in would have been horrendous. Instead, they usually chose a fast food place where they could indulge in fries and burgers.

Sunday nights usually meant a gathering at Anna and Eli McNamara's place, but because Valentine's Day fell on a Sunday, they'd decided not to have anything that evening so that the couples could celebrate together. That meant that Michael had nowhere else to go but home.

He hated the silence that greeted him as he walked into the mobile home. Maybe he should look into getting a dog. They'd never gotten a pet before because Taylor hadn't wanted to have to deal with one, especially a dog. Now, though, if she wasn't going to be living with him anymore, maybe it was time to do something he wanted.

But since he wouldn't be getting a dog that night, he'd just have to accept the silence.

On Tuesday morning, Michael found himself looking for Lani's car as he pulled the van into the shop's parking lot. As soon as he realized what he was doing, he frowned.

There was no way he could allow himself to become interested in a woman, no matter how nice she was. And Lani had proven herself to be very nice, always friendly and willing to talk to him even when Taylor ignored him.

Was that the main reason he was drawn to her? Was he trying to fill the void Taylor had left in his life?

Still frowning, Michael pushed open the driver's door and climbed out of the van. Lani's car wasn't there, but he was early, so that wasn't unexpected.

After propping the back door open, he began to carry the flower order from the van to the cooler. He was just closing the rear doors of the van when Lani's car appeared.

"Am I late?" she asked as she got out of her car.

"Nope," he assured her. "I just got here a bit earlier than usual."

At the back door, Michael waited until she walked inside before kicking the brick he'd used to prop open the door to the side. Following her into the workroom, he went right to the Keurig and opened the cupboard to take out one of the travel mugs he kept there.

"Do you not drink coffee?" he asked Lani as he waited for his mug to fill. It occurred to him then that he'd never seen her drinking any at the shop.

"Sometimes, but it's not my favorite drink." She wrinkled her nose. "By the time I've added enough cream and sugar to make it palatable, I might as well just skip the coffee part and eat a bowl of coffee ice cream."

Michael laughed. "What do you like to drink then? Tea?"

She gave a shrug. "I usually drink a cup of green tea each day, but that's more for its health properties than because I like it."

"So just water?"

"Well, I know a lot of people would cringe at this, but if I really feel the need for a drink in the morning, it's usually pop."

"Really?"

"What can I say? If I'm going to drink a sweetened drink in the mornings, I'd rather it be one I enjoy."

"Can't say I've ever tried it myself. Coffee is my go-to."

"I don't do it every day because I know it's not very healthy, but a couple of days a week, I'll indulge."

"Should we start stocking pop for you?" Michael asked, gesturing to the small fridge at the end of the counter.

"Please don't," she said with a shake of her head. "If the temptation is there, I'll drink more of it than I should."

Having realized what he had just a short time ago, Michael knew he should leave the shop, but he didn't want to. He liked Lani's company. These light moments with her were like bright spots in his day.

Taylor still wasn't in when he finally had to leave a short time later. Lani assured him she'd be okay, and while he'd had reservations about Taylor's roommate being alone in the shop, he no longer had any about Lani.

Michael was sure that Taylor would have something more to say about that if he voiced it, but he wasn't going to do that. He might not be the smartest guy around, but he wasn't that dumb.

CHAPTER SEVEN

Lani let herself into her dad's house, tension already gathering in her shoulders. With quiet movements, she closed the door and began to walk toward the kitchen.

"You're late."

The harshly spoken words were like a punch to the stomach, and Lani had to pause for a moment to gather her wits about her. Knowing that ignoring him wouldn't lead to anything good, she turned to the arched doorway leading to the living room where her dad spent the bulk of his days.

He sat in the wheelchair that had become his mode of mobility after the accident, his legs covered by a plaid blanket. The television was tuned to some sort of historical documentary, which seemed to be all he wanted to watch anymore. He glared at her, his thick brows drawn low over his faded blue eyes.

"Why are you late?" he demanded.

"I needed to finish getting your supper together," she said, wishing she didn't have to explain why she was five minutes later than usual. "It took me a few minutes longer than I thought it would."

"What did you make?"

"Meatloaf, mashed potatoes, and green beans." It was one of his favorite meals, so she hoped that he'd focus on that rather than on the fact she was late.

He harrumphed and shifted his gaze back to the television, effectively dismissing her. Lani didn't mind that at all and quickly left the living room. In the kitchen, she set the bag she carried on the counter. Though she could have finished cooking the meal at her dad's, the less time she had to spend there, the better, so she did as much preparation as she could in her own kitchen.

She'd cooked the meatloaf and potatoes the night before but hadn't had a chance to do the green beans, which was why she ended up being late. After unpacking the bag, she went about dividing the food between two plates, giving him the usual amount that would hopefully guarantee that he wouldn't complain about her starving him.

As it was, he would probably complain about the potatoes since they were instant and not real. When she cooked for the week, she usually did a batch of real mashed potatoes. But this week, since she had to cook daily, he was getting instant.

Once she had the food on the plates, she put one in the microwave, and as it warmed up, she put plastic wrap over the other one. He would heat it up for his lunch the next day. Thankfully, he was okay with having the same meal two days in a row.

She put the second plate in the fridge, making sure it was on a shelf he could easily reach. While she was in the fridge, she checked over its contents to see if he needed anything. Since he ate pretty much the same things each week, keeping his fridge stocked with what he wanted was fairly easy, but she never wanted him to get upset because he ran out of something.

When the microwave dinged, Lani took the plate out then grabbed a beer from the fridge. She knew she shouldn't be giving it to him, but the vitriol he directed at her when she tried to tell him that, was more than she could stand. She didn't buy it for him, but whenever he ran out, he just called up one of the few buddies he still talked to and had them bring him some.

Though he hadn't been much of a drinker when she'd lived at home, on the night of the accident, his blood alcohol had been double the legal limit.

Lani had tried to talk to her dad about the details of the accident, but he'd shut her down. So much about it didn't make sense to her. Why had they been driving so late at night? Or rather...early in the morning? Her mom had been driving, even though her dad was usually always the one to drive. Of course, given how drunk he was, that was probably the wisest choice. But why had he been drinking so much?

Though she'd tried to ask him those questions, he'd refused to answer them and continued to drink more than he should, especially considering that he still took medication for chronic pain. It was possible that he carried some guilt for what had happened, but if he did, Lani knew it would never be something he'd admit to.

"Is that food almost ready?" her dad shouted.

Lani closed her eyes briefly and blew out a breath. After almost a year and a half of doing this, it should have been easier to hear his angry demands. But it wasn't.

Bracing herself, Lani took the plate and beer into the living room. He already had his rolling table in front of him, so she put the plate and beer down on it. When he'd first come home from the hospital, she'd tried to get him to eat at the table with her, but it had quickly become apparent that neither of them enjoyed the experience.

After a few attempts at family dinners, Lani had given up, finding that dealing with his anger had robbed her of her appetite. Now, she brought him his dinner, then ate hers alone back at her place. It didn't seem to matter to him that she wasn't there for dinner.

Even now, his attention was divided between his food and the television. Before she left, Lani took a tour of the house, checking to make sure that the person who came each day to help her dad for a few hours was taking care of the things she was supposed to.

Thankfully, the laundry was all done up, and the sheets on her dad's bed appeared to be fresh. Though her dad never voiced any appreciation for what was done for him, Lani still did her best to make sure that he was comfortable in his own home.

"I'm going to head home, Dad," she told him once she had checked everything.

With his gaze still on the television, he said, "I hear you're opening the store later than you should."

Lani's shoulders slumped at his words. She was kind of surprised it had taken this long for him to hear that news.

"It's just an hour later,"

"You getting lazy? I can't see that closing for an extra hour a day will help the sales, especially since you say sales are low."

"I need that hour to do other things for the shop that will help bring in some money."

She wasn't about to try and make him understand how working for three hours a day was beneficial for her and the shop. The money helped to cover the mortgage on the building—the mortgage her mom had taken out after the small building had already been paid off.

"I think you need to go back to opening at ten. It's what your mother would have done."

Lani hated when he threw that in her face, but she wasn't going to budge on this decision. Still, to keep the peace, she said, "I'll think about it."

"You do that."

With that, she was dismissed. Lani picked up her bag and empty containers from the kitchen and slipped out the front door. Twilight had settled over the town while she'd been at her dad's, bringing with it a chill.

Lani wrapped her arms around herself, walking as quickly as she could along the sidewalk. It was broken up in spots, so she had to keep her gaze on her path. The large trees along the sidewalk cast dappled shadows from the streetlights that had come on with the darkness.

It was a walk she'd been on almost her entire life, but she didn't enjoy it much. Especially when it was cold and wet. It was both those things that night, and she wished she'd brought the car, but it would have been a waste of gas.

That night as she hurried along the deserted sidewalk, she tried not to dwell on her latest encounter with her dad.

Instead, Michael's face came to mind. The way he looked at her, his face serious until she said something that made him smile. Then his eyes would crinkle at the corners, and small dimples would appear beside his mouth.

She knew she shouldn't be feeling any sort of way about Michael. But with so much having gone wrong in the past couple of years, who could fault her for taking a little joy where she could find it. Given who she was and who he was, nothing could come of it...not if she didn't want her life to implode.

Her last date had been before her rapid exit from Hawaii back to New Hope Falls after getting the news about her mom's passing. But even though she and the guy had been dating for almost a year, he'd been quick to end things when it became clear that she wouldn't be going back to Hawaii. He hadn't been interested in a long-distance relationship.

So while she'd been grieving the loss of her mom, she'd also been grieving the loss of a relationship she'd had high hopes for. Now, almost a year and a half later, the grief over her mom still had a tight hold on her heart, but the hurt over her failed relationship had faded.

She rarely thought about the man anymore. But there were moments she was lonely, and she wondered if she'd ever have the chance to share her life with a man and build the family she'd always hoped to have.

When she reached the building that housed both the shop and her apartment, she went around to the rear door. She keyed in the code to unlock the door, then stepped into the back hallway. She ignored the door that led into the shop and climbed the stairs to her apartment.

She let out a sigh of relief as she walked in, glad to be out of the cold and away from her father's attitude. After putting the dirty containers in the dishwasher, she pulled her phone out and went to sit in her favorite chair.

Flipping it over and over in her hand, she fought the intense urge to call her cousin. If she could get in and out of her dad's house without any sort of confrontation, her homesickness for Hawaii stayed low. But after an interaction like she'd just endured, followed by a cold walk home, all she wanted to do was go back to the place that had become her home—a place filled with warmth and love.

Aware that reaching out to her cousin wouldn't help her current mindset, Lani set her phone aside and went to the computer to enter the numbers from the day. She couldn't wait to get up the next morning and go to work where she could just focus on what she loved doing without the worry of paying bills for a few hours.

The next few weeks fell into a rhythm that Lani treasured. The side of her that she'd inherited from her father enjoyed the schedule, especially since it kept her busy. The days might have been long, but that was fine with her.

When she didn't have any customers or orders, she filled her hours creating floral watercolors to sell in the shop and online. She wasn't the artist that Sarah McNamara was with her portraits and landscapes, but one thing Lani could draw was flowers. Starting from a young age, she'd taken to drawing the flowers she saw in the shop. In time, she'd started applying watercolors to the sketches she'd done and giving them as gifts.

Now she saw it as a way to add to the income of the shop. She didn't sell a ton of them directly to customers. Most of her sales came through her online store. It wasn't what she'd ever planned to do, but after discovering the actual state of the store's finances, she'd been forced to become creative.

She still enjoyed—for the most part—the hours she spent at the Reeds' shop. The only thing she didn't like was the ongoing tension between the siblings. Anytime the two were in the same room, Lani wished she could be anywhere but there.

Taylor still kept a distance from her—much like she did from Michael. The woman was all business, never revealing anything personal about herself. Michael, on the other hand, was much more approachable and friendly.

"How are you doing this morning?" Michael asked as he opened the back door to the shop. Once again, Taylor was nowhere to be seen.

"I'm fine," she replied as they walked inside. "How about you?"

"Can't complain."

Lani grinned as he made a beeline for the Keurig to make his coffee, convinced that he was addicted to the beverage. Meanwhile, she sat down at the table and pulled the binder toward her.

"I have to head out," Michael said once his coffee was made. "I have a tree removal about an hour from here, and I'm meeting my guys there. You okay to stay here on your own?"

"I'm fine," Lani assured him.

It looked like there were a few orders for a funeral, and that would keep her busy for the duration of her shift.

Michael took a sip of his coffee, and rather than rushing out, he regarded her intently for a moment. Lani wasn't sure what was going through his mind, but he clued her in soon enough.

"I just want to thank you for all your help," he finally said. "I'm sure you've noticed that Taylor isn't quite as focused on the shop as she should be."

Lani gave a small nod but didn't say anything.

"I'm not sure what's going on with her, but I do know that without your help, the shop would truly be suffering. I just want you to know how much I appreciate what you've done here."

"I'm glad I could help." It certainly hadn't been on her mind that they might really need her help when she'd accepted the job. She'd figured it would just be her playing a small role in the shop. She'd been more focused on what the shop could do for her rather than what she could do for the shop.

Michael gave her a small smile. "Anyway. I'm off."

Lani watched him go, a weird feeling in her stomach. She wasn't sure if it was a good feeling or a bad feeling. Maybe it was a mix of both.

Turning her attention away from the closed door, Lani looked over the orders again, prioritized what needed to be done, and got to work.

Time passed quickly, and before she knew it, it was almost ten o'clock. Normally that wouldn't be a problem, but there was no sign of Taylor, and she hadn't heard anything from her.

As she carried the arrangement she'd just finished to the cooler, Lani debated what to do. She didn't have Taylor's cell number, and the number she'd called her from regarding an interview back at the start of the hiring process had been the shop's.

She didn't want to start on another arrangement because she didn't want to leave it half-done if Taylor showed up at the last minute. Instead, she settled for checking the water in the cut flowers at the front of the shop, keeping an eye on the clock as she did so.

Ten o'clock rolled around, and Taylor still wasn't there. Lani paced around the workroom. This wasn't a good thing because even if she could stay, she didn't want to have to handle the front of the store and risk having someone who knew her dad show up.

Finally, Lani decided she had to phone Michael. She hated to do it, partly because she knew she was probably going to have to disappoint him.

She bit her lip as she waited for him to answer his phone.

"Lani?" he asked after it had rung several times. "Is everything okay?"

"I'm not sure," she said. "Taylor hasn't shown up, and I need to leave soon."

There was a long moment of silence before he responded. "Did you try calling her?"

"I don't have her cell number."

"Okay. I'll see if I can get hold of her and find out what's going on."

After he'd hung up, Lani continued pacing, her gaze going to the front door and the sign that should even now be flipped to indicate the shop was open. What was she going to do if Michael asked her to stay?

She still didn't have an answer by the time her phone rang, Michael's number appearing on her screen. "Hello?"

"Hey. I haven't been able to get hold of Taylor yet, but I was wondering if you'd be able to stay for a bit. Maybe open the shop?"

"Okay." The word was out before Lani could give it much thought.

"Thank you so much. I'll try and get this sorted out as soon as I can since I know you have to leave."

When the call ended, Lani made her way to the front door and unlocked it. After a brief hesitation, she flipped the sign to open.

Going to the till, she tried to familiarize herself with the system that Taylor used. She fervently hoped that no one came because she didn't have any money in the till to give anyone change.

"It's a Tuesday," she muttered as she stared at the empty till drawer. "No one needs flowers on a Tuesday."

She could only hope that Tuesday mornings in the Reeds' florist shop were as slow as Tuesday mornings in hers. Anytime she saw someone on the sidewalk through the window, she held her breath, praying that they wouldn't come in.

By the time Michael called her back, Lani was feeling a tension equal to what she experienced when the siblings were present.

"Taylor will be there in about an hour," Michael said with a sigh. "She slept in."

"She slept in?" As soon as she heard the incredulous tone of her question, she wished she could take it back. It wasn't her place to question her boss.

"Yeah." Michael sounded tired himself, but Lani didn't think extra sleep would help him get over that. "Can you stay until she gets there?"

Lani glanced at the time. It would mean opening her shop a bit later, but that likely wouldn't make a difference since, as she'd already noted, Tuesday mornings were a slow time for her.

"Yes. I'll stay."

"Thank you. I'd come to relieve you, but by the time I'd get there, Taylor should hopefully have arrived." Michael sighed. "I'm sorry about this."

"It's not your fault." Even though she didn't know him super well, Lani could tell that Michael felt responsible for Taylor's actions. Not just what was happening right then, but also for whatever was causing the tension between the two of them.

On Michael's end, Lani heard someone yell his name.

"I gotta go. If Taylor doesn't show in an hour, call me back."

Lani assured him she would then said goodbye.

The next hour seemed to drag as she vacillated between concern that Taylor wouldn't show and worry that a customer was going to walk through the front door.

In the end, Taylor showed before any customers did, leaving Lani feeling more relieved than upset at how late her boss was.

"Sorry I'm late," Taylor said as she breezed in. Standing in the workroom doorway, she wrapped the edges of the long loose cardigan she wore across her front. "Thanks for staying."

"You're welcome." Lani didn't say it hadn't been any trouble. She really didn't want Taylor to think it was okay to just sleep in, trusting that Lani could stay later than her usual time. "I finished most of the arrangements."

"Sounds good." Taylor followed her back into the workroom.

"I've got to go, but I'll see you tomorrow."

After grabbing her jacket and purse, Lani said goodbye and left the shop. As she drove home, she couldn't help but wonder what Michael was going to say to Taylor when he saw her next. Lani could only hope that the confrontation would occur when she wasn't around.

CHAPTER EIGHT

Michael stared at the back door of the shop. He didn't need to be there that day since there was no flower order to be picked up. Still, he'd gotten into the habit of coming to let Lani in since Taylor never seemed to be able to make it on time.

That day, however, he wasn't looking forward to seeing his sister. Not that he found himself looking forward to seeing her most days anymore. Anytime the two of them were together, she just gave him the cold shoulder.

Taylor wasn't there yet, though, so he could get himself another cup of coffee before dealing with the confrontation that was headed his way like a runaway train. With a sigh, he pushed open the door and got out. Lani's car wasn't there yet, so he had a few minutes alone in the shop as he prepared his coffee.

Thankfully, after a stressful day the day before, his schedule that day was much lighter. Tree removal brought in more money, but the stress and danger of it made him glad they didn't have to do it too often. Having the distraction of Taylor being a no-show hadn't been a good thing, but at least the guys he'd had there with him had been pros and well able to pick up his slack.

When the door alarm chirped, Michael looked up, relieved to see Lani walk in. While he was glad it was her and not Taylor, he was aware that it meant she was going to witness whatever was to come. The best-case scenario was Taylor accepted she had been in the wrong the day before and apologized for it. He'd happily let it go, but if she was going to cop an attitude about it, it wouldn't go well.

She'd made it clear that her life was no longer any of his concern, but when what she was doing affected the shop, that made it his business.

"Is everything okay?" Lani asked as she approached the table, shrugging off her jacket as she walked. There was concern on her face, and Michael knew exactly what she was referring to.

"I guess we'll see when she arrives," Michael said with a shrug. "I haven't talked to her yet."

Lani frowned, and Michael wondered if it was because she recalled the last time he and Taylor had spoken...argued. He kind of hated the idea that she might hear him speak words in anger.

It wasn't that he was going into the meeting planning to get upset with Taylor. But in some ways, it seemed unavoidable because of the emotions already involved. And yes, he'd been upset the previous day, and some of that anger still lingered.

He'd gone to the men's Bible study the night before and had spent some time talking with Eli after it was over. The Bible study, as always, had been a bit of a struggle since he couldn't easily read the study guide they were using.

He tried to find the time to scan the pages and have his phone read it to him before the study each week. But if he wasn't able to do that, he spent more time listening to the discussion than participating.

Afterward, when it was just him and Eli, Carter, or Kieran, he found it easier to voice his thoughts. Last night, he'd revealed to Eli the troubles he'd been having with Taylor. The other man had listened patiently. And while he didn't have any great advice for Michael, he'd offered to pray with him and had promised to continue to pray for the situation in the coming days.

Michael hadn't been a Christian as long as Eli had, so he sometimes struggled to have the same level of confidence and faith in God. He wanted to be better, which was why he continued to go to the studies even though they weren't a comfortable place for him to be a lot of the time.

As he watched Lani take her jacket into the office then return a minute later, Michael wondered if she went to church. He'd never seen her at his church, but there were a couple other churches that he knew about in New Hope, as well as many in the communities surrounding them.

"Did Taylor say anything to you when she finally showed up?" Michael asked as he carried his mug to the table and sat down.

"Nope." Lani leaned over to grab the binder then settled back on a stool. "Just apologized for being late. I couldn't hang around, so I don't know if she might have said anything more." She gave him an apologetic look. "Sorry about that."

Michael scoffed. "You're not the one who needs to apologize. It's not your responsibility to sort this out. I just wanted to know if she'd said anything that I needed to know before I talk with her this morning."

"Do you think she's going to show up before you have to leave for your day?"

The skeptical expression on Lani's face matched how Michael felt, but he was trying to be optimistic. He wanted to have the conversation over and done with so he could focus on the day ahead. While it wasn't likely to be as dangerous a day as the previous one, he still didn't want to be dealing with distractions.

When Lani opened the binder, she frowned.

"What's wrong?" Michael asked, lowering his mug to the table. He fought the urge to circle around the table to peer over her shoulder at the binder. But he wouldn't be able to make sense of anything written there, so he stayed in his seat.

Her brow furrowed as she flipped a couple of pages forward and then back. "There aren't any orders for today."

"Is that unusual?" Michael hadn't ever really looked closely at the orders in the shop, leaving all of that in Taylor's capable hands.

He'd always assumed the business had plenty of orders since it seemed to be successful. Had she not been truthful in representing the financial achievements of the shop?

"Well...no," Lani said with a quick glance at him. "It's just that in the time I've been here, we usually have at least one order."

"In other shops you've worked in, is that common?"

"Usually, if a store is busy, then it's rare to have a day without at least one order." She bit her lip for a moment. "A smaller, less busy shop can have days without anything but walk-in sales."

"Do you think she closed the shop after you left?" Michael asked.

"Uh...I don't know." Lani lifted her thumb and chewed on it. "I wasn't around this part of town after I left."

"Did she leave you any instructions in place of the orders?"

"No, but usually, there are other things I could do."

"Usually?"

"Yeah. Usually, I would work on freshening up the cut flowers at the front and check the flowers in the cooler. Unfortunately, yesterday while I was waiting for her, I did most of that. I can still check the cooler because I didn't do that yesterday, but..." Her words trail off with a shrug.

"If she doesn't show up, just do what you can find to do, then you can leave. I'll make sure she still pays you for the full time."

"You don't need to do that," Lani protested.

"If you're counting on getting hours here, and you make the effort to show up, she needs to make sure she has work for you. If she knew she didn't have work, Taylor should have let you know, so she didn't waste your time. The least she can do is pay you for showing up."

Lani sighed. "I'm not going to argue with you about it."

"Good."

Michael had to wonder if she felt a bit like she was in the middle of a battle. He hoped that the tension between him and Taylor didn't cause her to quit because it was clear the shop needed her. Plus, even though he knew nothing could ever come of it, his interest in her was piqued. She'd grown from being a bright spot when he saw her to a steady beam, offering assurance and even guidance as he thought of her throughout his day.

As he lifted his mug, needing the caffeine hit even more, Michael watched Lani turn her attention back to the binder and begin to flip through it.

"What are you looking for?" he asked, his curiosity finally getting the better of him.

"Just checking back before I started to see if days without orders are more common than I assumed."

"And?" he prompted when she didn't continue on.

"Well, it's not like it hasn't happened before, but because the shop has quite a few corporate accounts with standing weekly orders, it isn't super common. Maybe I overreacted."

"But Taylor should still have let you know if there wasn't work for you today."

"Maybe she has something she wants me to do and will tell me about it when she gets in."

If she gets in, Michael wanted to say, but he kept that to himself.

After a couple of minutes of silence and no sign of Taylor, Michael said, "Do you happen to know of anyone with a dog to give away?"

"A dog?"

"Yeah. I'm looking at getting a dog."

Her eyes widened. "Really? What kind?"

"I'm not really looking for a specific breed, just something of a medium or larger size. Don't think a dog that could fit in a purse would really work for me."

Lani's face broke into a smile as she giggled. "Yeah. Can't really picture you with a small dog."

"So, do you know anyone?"

The laughter slid from her face. "No, I don't, but I'm sure there are shelters around here with dogs up for adoption. Did you want a puppy?"

Michael considered it for a moment then shook his head. "No. I'm not sure I have the time to train a puppy."

"That's definitely something to take into consideration."

"Do you have a pet?"

"Nope, although my grandma had a dog that I loved. He died a couple of years ago from old age, though."

The sorrow that crossed Lani's face almost had Michael reconsidering his plan. Did he really want to get close to an animal that was almost guaranteed to die before he did? When he said as much, Lani shook her head.

"I know it's hard to think about saying goodbye to a beloved pet, but honestly, the benefits outweigh the loss. Especially if you're getting a dog from a shelter. You're giving it a loving home when it might not have that in a shelter." She gave him an encouraging smile. "If you asked my grandma, she would tell you that she wouldn't trade a moment she had with Donny. He was her shadow."

Michael found Lani's passionate response attractive—though he knew he shouldn't. Although it didn't really matter. Just because he was starting to crush on her a bit, that didn't mean he had to do anything about it. And he wasn't totally convinced that what he was feeling hadn't come about because of the ever-widening distance between him and Taylor.

Part of him wondered if they would have a similar connection outside the shop, but he'd never know. Being out in the real world with him, she'd find out about his...disability. Or as his father liked to call it—depending on his mood—lack of dedication, laziness, or stupidity. He'd never been interested in hearing reasons for why Michael struggled in school the way he had.

He didn't want to see how Lani's interactions with him would change when she found out how he struggled. So their little moments of contact would have to be limited to the shop. Michael told himself that he was at the shop each morning to let Lani in since Taylor was always late. But there was no denying that seeing her each day was a big motivation to him showing up.

As Lani talked more about her grandma and her dog, time clicked by, bringing the time he'd have to leave closer and closer. Were they going to have a repeat of the day before?

"Do you think she's going to show?" Lani asked, clearly having some of the same thoughts he was.

"I don't know. I'm going to have to leave in a few minutes. But if she doesn't show by ten, let me know."

"Okay."

Michael got up and took his mug back to the sink where he washed it before putting it on the small strainer on the counter. Picking up his jacket from where he'd laid it on the worktable, he said, "I'll talk to you later."

Lani smiled at him. "Have a good day. Stay safe."

"Thanks. You too."

Out in the chill of the morning, Michael pulled the edges of his jacket closer together as he strode toward his truck. The further he drove away from the shop and Lani's upbeat personality, the more he thought about Taylor. Those thoughts brought a sick feeling with them. He'd hoped that Lani's presence in the store would help settle Taylor and keep her discontent at bay. Instead, the opposite seemed to be happening.

Michael was mowing the grass at one of his regulars when he felt his phone vibrate in his pocket. Pulling it out, he saw Lani's name on the screen and hesitated a moment before answering. He really didn't want to hear that Taylor hadn't shown up again. But he'd told Lani to call, so he had no choice but to answer it.

Cutting the mower, he said, "Hello?"

"Hi, Michael, it's Lani."

He rubbed the back of his neck as he stared down at the mower. "She didn't show, did she?"

"No, she did," Lani said. "She arrived about fifteen minutes ago. I just wanted to let you know, so you weren't wondering."

"Are you still there?" Michael asked.

"Sorry, no. I just left."

"That's okay. Thanks for letting me know."

"You're welcome." There was a beat of silence, but before Michael could think of anything to fill it, Lani said, "I'll let you get back to work. Have a good rest of your day."

Michael appreciated the words, but he kind of doubted that it would be all that good. After they'd hung up, he turned his attention back to the yard he was working on. Although he didn't usually stop for more than a quick sandwich at lunchtime, he was already planning to take a longer lunch so he could go to the shop to talk to Taylor.

Given that he'd tried his best to avoid confrontation for most of his life, he was uncharacteristically seeking it out for the second time in a month. He was a bit surprised at how determined he was to have this conversation with his sister. Of course, if it all blew up in his face—which, admittedly, would quite possibly happen—he'd think twice about ever confronting someone again.

As a youngster, initiating confrontation would have resulted in a beating, so he'd tried to never let that happen. Michael tended to avoid confrontation as an adult mainly because it brought with it the potential of him losing his temper, and he didn't want that. The last thing he wanted was to become his father—a man with anger issues. While he knew his anger wouldn't manifest itself in a physical way, he was living proof that verbal attacks could be just as devastating.

When he pulled up behind the shop just before noon, he was relieved to see Taylor's car in the lot. Hopefully, they'd have a few minutes to talk without any customers around.

"What are you doing here?" Taylor demanded when he stepped into the office where she was seated behind the desk.

Concern swept through him as he took in her appearance.

Taylor had never been a slender girl, but she'd always taken care of her appearance. She'd always said that just because she wasn't skinny didn't mean she couldn't be fashionable. Paired with carefully done hair and makeup, his sister had always presented a very polished look.

Right then, however, she looked the very opposite of polished—for her, at least. Her hair hung limply around her face—a face that looked bare of her usual makeup. Her skin was pale and blotchy with dark smudges under her eyes.

Tugging the edges of her sweater across her front, she glared at him. "What are you *doing* here, Michael?"

Her repeated question jarred him out of the inventory he was taking of her appearance. "I wanted to talk to you about yesterday."

She rolled her eyes and sighed heavily. "There's nothing to talk about. I showed up."

"Yes, but you showed up *late.* Lani had to stay even though she's told us that she needs to leave by ten."

"Apparently, she doesn't *need* to leave by ten if she was able to stay longer."

"Taylor," Michael admonished. "She may well have sacrificed something in order to stay. That's not her responsibility. That's not what she was hired to do."

"She was hired to do what I tell her to do." Taylor leaned forward to rest her arms on the desk. "She's an employee."

"From what I understand, she agreed to work for three hours a day. So in those three hours, she does what you say. If you need someone to work more hours, then perhaps you should have hired someone who was available for more hours."

"Fine." Taylor shrugged. "Fine. I'll fire her and hire someone who can work the hours I need."

Alarm flared to life within Michael. He didn't want Lani to lose her job. He didn't want to lose the friendship that he felt was growing between them. "Really? That's your solution? Fire someone who is very talented at floral arrangements just because you've suddenly lost your work ethic?"

Anger sparked in Taylor's eyes. "I've worked *hard* for this stupid shop. Excuse *me* if I don't feel like spending every hour of every day in this place."

Michael waited for his own anger to come alive in response to Taylor's. But instead, there was just confusion and weariness. "Then change the hours of the shop. If you don't want to be here for all those hours, then open at noon."

"Like you'd actually want me to do that."

"You're doing a lot of things I don't want you to do," Michael muttered, trying to hide the hurt he felt about that. "I'm just trying to find a solution that doesn't run this business into the ground."

"What about Lani?"

"What about her?"

"If I change the hours, what do I do about her if she can only work until ten?"

"Well, if you trust her, give her keys to the shop so she can still come for her normal hours to make arrangements and any other stuff she can do for you."

"I'll think about it." The anger drained from Taylor's expression, which he'd normally be glad to see. Unfortunately, it seemed like the life had drained from her as well.

"What's going on, Tay?" Michael asked as he sank down into the chair across the desk from her. "Help me understand everything that's going on."

"I just want to live my own life. I'm tired of living it for you. I want to be able to make my own decisions."

It was the same thing she'd said before, but it still didn't make any more sense to him this time around. "So, what are we going to do?"

Her gaze dropped as her brows drew together. "I haven't decided yet."

Michael waited for her to go on, but when she didn't, he said, "Well, just let me know what you're thinking. I'm not going to stand in your way, but I'd rather not be caught off-guard by whatever you decide."

She gave a single nod, her gaze shifting to the monitor on her desk. It was a dismissal if Michael had ever seen one, so he got to his feet. He didn't feel any more settled, but hopefully, she would make some solid decisions about the business rather than haphazard ones that could negatively impact Lani and him.

Lani...

Michael wasn't sure what to think about his reaction when Taylor had said she'd fire Lani. He tried to tell himself it was just because Lani didn't deserve to be fired because of Taylor's early midlife crisis.

But in his heart, he knew that wasn't true. It was the idea of not seeing Lani and having that bright start to his day. Since he couldn't see her outside of the shop, he hated the idea of losing those few moments with her each morning.

CHAPTER NINE

Lani stared at the piece of paper on the worktable before looking up at Taylor. "What's this?"

"It's the codes for the alarm and the back door lock."

"Why?" Lani was unable to keep herself from asking.

Taylor sat slumped on one of the stools, looking rough with her hair up in an actual messy bun, not the artfully messy ones that were popular these days. "I'm changing the hours of the shop."

Lani's brows lifted. "You are?"

"Yep."

"What hours are you going to?"

"Noon to five."

Lani wanted to laugh at the irony of Taylor changing her hours so soon after Lani had changed hers. Of course, she doubted that Taylor cared—or even knew—about that.

Frankly, from what she'd been able to see, she wasn't sure that Taylor cared about much of anything. She still didn't know the siblings all that well, but it seemed like Taylor lacked the commitment that her brother had to the business. Even though he was responsible for a whole other side of the business, he'd never missed a morning delivery. Meanwhile, Taylor was waltzing in whenever she felt like it.

"So, it's still okay for me to come in at seven and leave at ten?" That was pretty much a deal-breaker for her.

"Yeah. That's fine. That's why I'm giving you the codes."

"Okay. I'll just keep to my usual schedule." She paused. "And I'll do the orders in the binder each day?"

Taylor nodded. "And if you finish the orders, you can clean up around the shop."

Lani nodded, a bit perplexed by this latest turn of events. It had been a weird week, with her only seeing Taylor for about five minutes, right at the end of her shift. But it hadn't been a big issue since the other woman had left detailed notes for her about each arrangement in the binder.

She'd actually spent more time with Michael than she had with Taylor since starting to work at the shop. Did he know about this? Was he going to be upset about it?

It shouldn't matter because from what she'd seen, the shop was really Taylor's domain. Just like Taylor had hired her without Michael's consent or knowledge, Lani supposed she could change the hours without him knowing.

"Don't make me regret this," Taylor said, her gaze dropping to the codes for a moment before lifting to meet Lani's again, a trace of challenge in it. "Michael seems to feel that you are more trustworthy than my own roommate, so I hope that's true."

Lani felt a momentary flash of anger that the woman would question her trustworthiness, but she banked it down. Taylor didn't know her beyond the few weeks they'd been working together. She didn't know that Lani would never do anything to jeopardize her position there.

As far as Taylor knew, Lani worked there simply because she needed the paycheck. And while that had been true at the start, the joy of being able to arrange flowers for a few hours without feeling the pressure of needing the job to pay the bills, had taken on even more importance.

"You won't regret it," Lani assured her. "Have you had any issues with my work so far?"

Lani felt confident asking that question. She had learned from the best, so there was no way that Taylor should have any problems with any of her floral work nor her work ethic.

"No," Taylor said. "It's been fine."

Though she might have liked something more than *fine*, Lani wasn't going to push for it. The best thing about this latest change was that it basically removed any chance of someone discovering she was working for the competition.

"So that starts on Tuesday?" Lani asked.

"Yep. New week. New hours."

"Okay. I'll be here." Since it was ten o'clock already, Lani picked up the paper and put it in the pocket of her jeans. "I guess I'll see you...at some point?"

"You'll probably see more of Michael," Taylor said. "But I doubt that will be an issue."

Lani wasn't sure what that was supposed to mean. Instead of asking for clarification, she gathered up her things and said good-bye.

As she drove home, she wondered how this change might impact her business. Would them opening an hour later mean that people might come to her shop? She hoped that it would. Not that she wanted to take all of their business, but maybe just enough of it to help ease the financial strain on her.

Somewhere during the past month or so, she'd ended up invested in the competition. It didn't feel wrong, exactly, but it didn't feel really right either. But what else was new? Her life had never been uncomplicated, so why would that change now?

"I hear that that *other* florist place has changed their hours."

Lani froze for a moment before setting the plate of food on the tray in front of her dad. "Oh yeah?"

"I know you ignored me the last time I told you to open up earlier, but you *need* to do it now." There was no ignoring the forcefulness of his words. "Open at ten. Or nine would be even better."

Lani hummed noncommittally. She wasn't going to do it, but she knew better than to directly oppose her father. He'd never taken that well.

It had been two weeks since the change, and while she hadn't seen a huge jump in sales, it seemed that maybe she'd had a few extra sales. A couple people had mentioned the fact that the other shop had been closed when they'd gone to buy flowers, but it certainly hadn't been enough to bump up her income as much as she would have liked.

"Now if they'd only shut down altogether," her father said as he picked up his bottle of beer. "Then maybe business will improve. As long as you're not doing anything else to screw things up."

She wanted to assure him that she wasn't, but it would be a waste of breath. She'd learned a lot about how to deal with him over the past year and a half. If she'd thought it would make a difference, she would have voiced her opinion more forcefully. But arguing with him was always going to be a lose-lose situation because he had become totally unreasonable, so she didn't bother.

He continued to blather on about how horrible the Reeds were. How they'd ruined her mother's life. How they'd ruined his life. *Blah. Blah. Blah.*

It was a rant she'd heard plenty of times over the months, and in the past, she'd just ignored it. This time, however, she wanted to tell him that they weren't bad people. Well, honestly, she was still a bit on the fence about Taylor. Michael wasn't bad, though. Lani could say that with total confidence.

Except she wasn't going to say it. Blurting that out after not coming to their defense in the past would just result in her father demanding to know how she could possibly know that about them. And then he'd tell her she was betraying her mother's memory.

It wasn't worth the argument. Not right then anyway. No doubt when his little spy let him know that she hadn't changed the hours on the shop, he'd demand to know why, and her answer would spark a heated discussion.

"Do you need anything else before I go?" Lani asked when he paused in his rant.

"Nah. Just change the shop hours."

She left without confirming that plan and made the walk home in the chilly, wet evening. It had been a long day since she'd had to do a flower pickup before going to work at the shop. Even though it was only seven o'clock, and she had still had some bookwork to do, all she wanted to do was crawl into bed.

Her shop didn't have a lot of sales or employees, but there were always things to enter into the system. She didn't want to get behind on any of it, but maybe she could skip that night's work.

When she reached her shop, Lani went straight upstairs to her bedroom, letting her exhaustion make the decision for her.

The next morning, she was already at work when Michael showed up. She wasn't entirely sure why, but he made an appearance every morning she was there, even when he didn't have a flower order delivery.

Maybe it was his way of keeping track of things since Lani didn't see Taylor anymore. Maybe he didn't completely trust her. Whatever his reason, Lani actually enjoyed seeing him. With no friends in town, she found herself appreciating the friendship—if that's what it was—that had somehow developed between them.

It would have made more sense for her to have a friendship with Taylor, but that's not what had ended up happening. And Lani was fine with that.

"Hi there, Wolfie," Lani said, smiling at the dog that came into the shop with Michael. The chocolate lab wagged his tail as she bent over to scratch behind his ears.

"I see how it is," Michael remarked. "Now that there's a dog, I'm chopped liver."

Lani straightened. "Oh, hey, Michael. I didn't see you there."

"Very funny," he said, his eyes crinkling with his laughter.

"How are you two adjusting to life together?"

Michael had had him for a couple of weeks now, and from all appearances, they seemed to be getting along well.

"It's going really, really well. You were right in suggesting I go to the shelter, though I don't understand how anyone could have given him up."

Lani had to agree. The dog was friendly and obedient. Well-behaved enough to come into the shop without worry that he would wreck everything.

"Look what I got him," Lani said, gesturing to a spot against the wall.

Michael glanced over then looked back at her with a big smile on his face. "You got him a bed?"

That smile did funny things to her, but she pushed those feelings aside. "I did. And a water bowl too."

Considering that the most time the dog ever spent in the shop was when they were unloading flowers, those things might have been unnecessary, but she'd bought them anyway. And she refused to apologize for it...not that Michael was asking her to.

"Hey, uh..." Michael shifted from one foot to the other, his hands in his pockets. "Do you enjoy hiking at all?"

Before she could answer that, Lani needed to know why he was asking. "Is that going to be a new part of my job?"

"No." Michael smiled and shook his head. "A group from my church meets at a friend's place outside of town to go hiking some Sundays. I was wondering if you'd be interested in joining us."

Lani felt her stomach knot. She would have loved to take him up on his invitation, but she couldn't risk possibly running into someone who knew her. The town wasn't so small that she knew everyone. But the fact that he was associated with a church where she knew people made it a risk she couldn't take.

"Sadly, I'm not much of a hiker these days, plus I'm usually tied up with family stuff on Sundays."

Michael looked disappointed but also curious. "Are you ever not tied up with family stuff?"

How to answer that question... "Pretty much the only time I'm not is the hours I spend here or when I'm asleep."

His eyes widened briefly. "That's some pretty demanding family stuff."

She nodded. "A lot of it is due to health issues my dad has."

"Are you his primary caregiver?"

Lani fought the urge to fidget under his scrutiny. "Basically. Yeah. We do have some homecare for him, but it takes a lot of my time."

"Well, if you ever have a free Sunday evening, let me know. We don't always hike. Every other week, we have a Bible study. You'd be welcome at that too."

She wasn't sure how she felt about going to a Bible study. Her mom had embraced her faith, giving it a place of importance in her life. For some reason, however, she'd chosen to go to a church in another town rather than any of the ones in New Hope. Though she'd taken Lani with her throughout her growing up years, Lani's father had never attended with them.

Her mom had carried her faith into her work, often telling Lani that as she prepared flower arrangements, she would pray for whoever was receiving them. Being a young child, that hadn't made sense to Lani. Her mom didn't know who was actually getting the flowers, so how could her mom pray for them?

But God knows who they are, my blossom. God always knows.

Though Lani had gone to church while living with her mom's family in Hawaii, she hadn't gone to church regularly since coming back to New Hope Falls. Usually, she just watched the livestream from the church she'd attended in Hawaii, needing the familiarity of it.

"Not sure I'll have time, but I'll keep that in mind."

Michael smiled, and for a moment, Lani considered tossing her reservations to the wind and accepting his invitation. The realization that he wanted to spend time with her flooded Lani with emotions she couldn't quite put a name to. It made her want to spend more time with Michael than just the few minutes they had when he stopped by the shop in the morning.

"Guess I'd better head off." He looked around, his smile growing when he spotted Wolfie on his new bed. "I'm sure you'd love to hang out here, but I think you'd better come with me, Wolfie."

At the sound of his name, the dog lifted his head, then got to his feet and went to Michael.

Lani was sad to see them go, but she had work to do too. "Have a good day."

"You too."

She leaned against the worktable as she watched them leave, then let out a sigh. Michael's presence was a double-edged sword. It was so nice to interact with someone who wasn't her father or a customer, but there was no hope for anything more than what she had with him each day at the shop.

If she had really wanted a friendship, she could have reached out to Sarah or some of her former schoolmates. But she was as much of an introvert as an adult as she'd been as a teen, so she'd never taken that step.

Her friendship with Michael meant a lot to her. But how much of a friendship was it really when she was hiding a significant part about herself?

This wasn't a problem she'd foreseen when she'd made the decision to come work at their shop. Though her father had vilified them, she'd never thought they were actually bad people. She hadn't thought much about them at all. They had been shadowy figures on the perimeter of her life, not fully realized as actual people.

Now, however, the Reeds had been fleshed out, revealing that—even though Taylor was a bit distant—they were just ordinary people. They had moments of happiness. They fought. They worried. They were just like...her.

Her interactions with them brought into focus the lack in her own life, bringing with it a loneliness she didn't want to acknowledge. But she was essentially on her own, and prior to her mom's death, it was never how she'd imagined her life playing out.

Though Michael seemed to want a friendship with her, it was clear he also had other friends. She doubted he had the same friendship hole in his life that she had in hers. He may have been fighting with his sister, but that didn't leave him alone. He still had other people to turn to.

With a sigh, Lani turned her focus to the binder and the work that Taylor had planned for her.

Whatever she might be starting to feel for Michael, there was no way she could allow herself to consider anything beyond the workplace friendship they had. She had no idea what he'd think if he discovered that a competitor was working in his family's shop. He *might* give her a chance to explain, though Lani was pretty sure that Taylor would fire her on the spot.

But after Michael had clearly placed his trust in her, would he see it as a betrayal?

CHAPTER TEN

Michael had just showered and changed and was in the kitchen getting himself something to eat when he heard a car pull up outside the trailer. Frowning, he walked the short distance to the front door. It was rare that people just showed up unannounced, especially late on a Saturday afternoon when he was done work for the week.

Stepping out on the deck that ran the length of the mobile home, Michael paused with Wolfie at his side when he recognized Taylor's car. He'd hardly seen her at all in the last few weeks. He'd been super busy, and the shorter hours she kept at the store meant he didn't see her anymore when he dropped off the flower order.

Seeing her there made him both happy and concerned. He really hoped that she was there to tell him that she was moving back home and was ready to commit her time and energy to the shop once again. Unfortunately, there was a voice in the back of his head calling him a fool for even harboring that hope.

Taylor got out of the car, then opened the back door and leaned in. When she straightened again, she held something in her hands. Something that was covered with a blanket. Moving slowly, she made her way toward him.

"Hey," he said as she got closer.

When she looked up, Michael felt concern unfurl within him. She looked so tired. Just worn out in a way he'd never seen her before.

"I need to talk to you," she said as she walked past him into the house.

Something in her voice told him that this wasn't going to be a conversation he wanted to have. The situation between them had just been simmering over the past few months, but he had a feeling it was coming to a boil. And when it spilled over, it was going to lay waste to his life.

He followed her inside and watched as she set the bulky object she carried on the couch. She stared at it for a long moment before she turned to face him, then gingerly settled down onto the couch next to it.

"I'm leaving."

Michael groped for the nearest armchair and sank down into it, Wolfie pressing against his leg. "What do you mean?"

"I'm not cut out for small town life."

"So you're what...going to move to Seattle?"

"I'm thinking LA."

"LA?" A knot tightened in Michael's gut. "So far away?"

"I just want to live my own life. I can't do that here." She glanced at the thing sitting next to her on the couch. "I had a baby."

Michael stared at Taylor in shock, robbed of words. Taylor could have playful, joking moments, but nothing about her said that she was having one of those moments right then.

"I...I don't understand." He forced the words past tight vocal cords. "How could you have had a baby?"

"I was pregnant, and now I'm not."

Pregnant? Wouldn't he have been able to tell? A pregnant stomach wasn't something that could be hidden. Right?

"How?" It seemed like a stupid question, but it came out anyway. "When?"

"Late last night." Taylor lifted the blanket, revealing a baby car seat. "They discharged me a little while ago because the baby and I were fine."

Michael wasn't sure what to do or say. He watched as Taylor got to her feet, lifted the car seat, and carried it over to where he sat. She put it on the floor in front of him, and Michael stared down at the tiniest baby he'd ever seen. Not that he could remember the last time he'd actually seen a baby.

Wolfie stepped away from Michael, sniffing at the baby, though he didn't get too close.

Taking in the pink cover on the car seat and the pink and white clothes the baby wore, Michael said, "It's a girl."

He couldn't seem to tear his gaze away from the baby. She had wisps of dark hair, and her long, dark lashes fanned out over her pale cheeks. She was just so...tiny. Had she really been strong enough to leave the hospital?

"I named her Vivianne Rose."

That grabbed Michael's attention, and he looked up at Taylor. "You named her after Grandma?"

She nodded and shrugged. "I didn't know what else to name her."

Michael frowned at her words. She seemed a little distant. Was it just the fact that she'd given birth not that long ago?

"I'm sure Grandma would have loved that." He looked back down at the baby, memories of the one good part of his childhood flooding back. During a horrible time in his life, Grandma had been a bright spot, trying in the best way she knew how to let them know they were loved.

"I want you to have her."

It took a minute for Taylor's words to sink in. "What?"

"I don't want a baby. I didn't want a baby when I found out I was pregnant." She paused then said, "I planned to have an abortion, but then I just couldn't go through with it. If you don't want her, I'll give her up for adoption."

"I...I..." Michael scrambled for words. He'd never planned to have kids, and yet now the future of this little one rested in his hands.

He felt like he was losing his sister, but she was offering to leave a bit of herself behind. He couldn't do this, though. What he knew about babies could fit on the head of a pin. Half the head of a pin, in fact. There was no way he could juggle a baby and his job.

Could he let this little girl go to strangers? Could he let her go out into the world, never knowing what kind of life she might end up with?

But if he kept her, would he be able to love her enough to make up for the rejection of her mother?

He had no answers, but it seemed like Taylor was expecting him to give her one right then.

"I don't know how to take care of a baby, Taylor. I have nothing for her."

"It's all here."

"What?" He felt like he was saying that word a lot.

"I came by a few days ago while you were at work and dropped off everything you'll need."

She had been that certain of his decision? Of course, she had. Hadn't he already proved that he'd do anything and everything to protect those he loved? So far, it had just been Taylor that had benefitted from that, but she hadn't been wrong to assume that that love would extend to her daughter. His niece...his daughter?

"It's not that easy," Michael said. "There's legal stuff. You can't just hand her to me and say she's mine."

"I know. I've already been talking to a lawyer who will help us with that. You'll have to have a home study and stuff, but it shouldn't be a big issue."

That was easy for her to say. He had plenty of things stacked against him. He was single. His job was demanding and, at times, risky. On top of all that was the fact that he had a learning disability.

Just one of those things would have been bad enough, but all of them? Was Taylor crazy?

"What about her father?"

"Don't know who he is," Taylor replied with a shrug.

Icy cold fear gripped Michael. "You weren't..." He couldn't even say the word.

She shook her head. "No. Just got too drunk. It was that weekend I met my friends in Vegas."

Michael remembered that trip. Taylor had closed the shop early on Saturday and hadn't come home until late Monday night. As he recalled, she'd barely been functional for work on Tuesday, and they'd had a fight about that. Was that when she'd decided that she was done with her life in the small town of New Hope?

"They'll never let me keep her," Michael said. "How am I supposed to handle my job *and* a baby, Taylor?"

"Hire more guys to work for you. You have more than enough work to run a bigger crew and not have to work so hard."

There was no way he could do this without someone to help him. If Taylor had wanted his help to raise her baby, he would have stepped up in an instant. But this? It was almost a guarantee that he was going to fail and let this precious baby down.

You're a failure, Michael. Why couldn't you have been more like your brother?

His father's voice threatened to drown out everything else. If he listened to that voice, he would say no to Taylor. Let her give her baby up for adoption.

Michael closed his eyes and tried to block out the harsh words, and at that moment, he knew that he would do what he had to in order to protect this little girl. But there was no way he could do that if he didn't know where she was and who she was being raised by.

"Are you just going to leave her with me tonight?" Michael asked.

"Yes. My place isn't suitable for a baby."

"And this place is?"

"It's better than where I am. At least it's quiet."

"Taylor," Michael said. "I know nothing about taking care of a baby."

"Neither do I."

"Yeah, but you've had nine months to adjust to the idea and prepare. You're springing this on me with no notice at all."

Taylor crossed her arms and lifted her chin. "I'm doing what I think is right."

What could he say to that? Emotion clogged his throat, and he looked back down at the baby who, despite her tiny size, was already having a huge impact on his life.

"What do I need to know?" he asked.

When relief crossed Taylor's face, Michael realized that she hadn't been one hundred percent certain he'd acquiesce so easily about keeping the baby that night.

"I'll show you the stuff in the room."

Michael got up and began to follow her to the other end of the mobile home but then stopped and looked back, noticing that Wolfie stayed on the floor next to the car seat. "Do we need to bring her with us?"

"We won't be long, and we'll hear her if she cries."

Deciding to trust Taylor, because he didn't know any better, Michael followed her toward the master bedroom, which had been hers when she'd lived there. He hadn't opened the door to look inside since the day she'd moved out. The room—empty but for the queen size bed she'd left behind—had been too much of a reminder of the hole in his life created by her leaving.

As soon as he stepped into the room, he could see that it definitely held more furniture than the last time he'd looked. He was hard-pressed to name most of the furniture in the room, aside from the chair and dresser. Did a baby really need all this stuff? Apparently, this baby did because he didn't think Taylor would have bought it if she didn't.

Walking around the room, she named each thing and told him what it was used for. Bassinette. Change table. Diaper holder. Wipes warmer. Video monitor.

Michael began to get more and more nervous as she worked her way around the room. There was no way he could do this. But he didn't really have a choice, did he?

He might have said that this wasn't what he'd wanted for his life, but Michael had never really allowed himself to make decisions based solely on what he wanted. It had always been based on what was needed, and this would be no different. If Taylor and this little girl needed him to step up, he'd do that the best that he could and hope he didn't fail either of them.

Once she'd explained everything in the room, she picked up a bag and left the room. Michael stood for a moment, staring at the dresser that already had clothes in it. He was on a roller coaster ride, feeling like he could do this one minute, then questioning how badly he was going to screw things up the next.

He heard a faint cry and spun around, moving toward the door and the crying baby before he even considered what he was doing. In the living room, he found Taylor standing near the carrier, but she didn't pick the baby up. Wolfie had shifted closer, but instead of laying down, his head was lifted, ears perked as he gazed at the baby.

She turned toward him as he approached, her expression shuttered. "Why don't you pick her up while I get a bottle ready?"

Without waiting for him to respond, she moved toward the kitchen with the bag. Michael's heart was pounding as he approached the carrier where the baby no longer looked as calm and peaceful as she had earlier. Her face was scrunched up as she cried, making more noise than something that size should be able to.

"How do I get her out?" Michael asked as he knelt down in front of the carrier.

Without coming over to where he was, Taylor explained how to lower the handle then undo the straps. Once the baby was free from the straps, Michael hesitated. How did he pick the baby up without breaking her?

"Support her head," Taylor said over her shoulder.

"Support her head? That's all you got for me?" Michael asked incredulously.

"That's what they told me at the hospital."

Michael had to wonder what the staff had been thinking, letting Taylor walk out of the hospital with a baby. Had they not seen how inexperienced she was?

"Teenagers manage to do this, Michael," Taylor said as he knelt there, still uncertain about handling the baby. "You'll be fine."

Blowing out a quick breath in hopes that it would take his nerves with it, Michael bent over and slid his hands under the baby. She was still fussing, but she gazed up at him with light blue eyes. Moving slowly, he lifted her, shifting to tuck her into the crook of his arm.

"Bring her here," Taylor said.

Hoping he could get up without falling, Michael straightened carefully. Wolfie scrambled to his feet as well and stuck close as Michael walked to where Taylor stood in the kitchen.

"This is her formula." She pointed at a box that contained a bunch of little bottle things. "It's all pre-made. All you have to do is put a nipple on the bottle. I have a couple tins of powdered formula and different bottles, but I figured this would be easier for you at first."

As she walked him through the process of preparing the baby's milk, Michael once again felt that there was no way he could care for this child. No way he wasn't going to give this baby the worst start in life.

"Here." Taylor held out the bottle. "Go sit down and feed her."

Michael took the bottle and baby back to his favorite rocker recliner. Holding her close to his chest, he touched the nipple to her lips, watching in wonder as she opened her mouth and began to suck. He glanced up to say something to Taylor, but she was walking back toward the master bedroom.

"Do you think I can do this, Vivi?" Michael wished she could tell him what she wanted. What would make her happiest.

He heard Taylor moving around but had no idea what she was doing. If only she'd stay there for at least the first night, just to make sure that he really could do this on his own. But he had a feeling he was about to be thrown into the deep end. Still, he had nothing to lose by asking.

"I need to get home," Taylor said when he asked her to consider staying. "You'll be fine."

Michael wondered how many times she would have to say that before he actually believed her. "But what if something happens to her tonight? Do I just take her to the hospital? I'm not her dad. Will they listen to me?"

"I had my lawyer draw up a document that gives you permission to make decisions for her. It's in the side pocket of the diaper bag."

"She's done," Michael said. "What do I do now?"

"You have to burp her." She handed him a small blanket. "Put that on your shoulder and gently pat her back."

Michael did as she said, shifting the baby gently. When the baby let out a burp, he grinned. "Good girl."

"Let me show you how to do her diaper before I go. Feeding and changing, and you'll be good to go."

As he followed Taylor's directions for changing the baby's diaper, Michael wasn't so sure. This was only a wet diaper. What was a poopy one going to be like?

She showed him where the other sleepers were, then took a couple of minutes to explain how to position the baby in the bassinette that she had moved next to the bed in his room.

"Here's her bathtub, which you can just put in the sink, and these are the bath products for her along with her wash clothes and towels."

Michael was beginning to think he should have been taking notes. He was never going to remember everything.

Before he knew what was happening, Taylor headed for the door. "I need to go. I'll talk to you later about the legalities of making her yours."

"Taylor." Michael started to follow her out the front door but then paused in the doorway. It was a bit cool and damp, and he wasn't sure the baby should be out in that without a...well, he didn't know. A blanket, maybe? "Taylor!"

"I'll talk to you later," she called over her shoulder.

Michael watched with a growing sense of dread as she got in her car and drove away, her taillights disappearing as she turned the corner of the long driveway. What on earth had he agreed to? This had to be a dream... Or maybe a nightmare.

But the weight in his arms belied that.

He stepped back into the house and shut the door, then just stood there. What did he do with a baby? Glancing down, he saw that she had fallen asleep again. Could he put her down? Strangely enough, he wasn't sure he wanted to.

Instead, he picked up his phone, then sat down in his chair. He knew that he needed more information than what Taylor had thrown at him if he was going to feel comfortable caring for Vivianne. Sadly, reading websites wasn't something he could do. But fortunately, there was YouTube.

He pulled up the app on his phone, spoke his request into the search bar, then clicked on the top video. Hoping Vivianne would realize that this was for her benefit as well as his and stay asleep for a bit, Michael lifted the phone and began to watch the first video.

CHAPTER ELEVEN

Lani finished the bagel with cream cheese she'd made for her breakfast, then, after a brief debate, made herself a cup of tea. Hot beverages weren't really her thing, but the dreary morning seemed to call for it. With mug in hand, she headed for her favorite chair and curled up in it, grateful for a slower-paced morning for a change.

The large bay window next to her chair looked out at the houses across the street and the mountains in the distance...when it wasn't a cloudy day. Still, there was something cozy about being inside when it was chilly and gray outside.

Her plans for the day included nothing more than preparing food for the week using the groceries she'd picked up the night before. Cooking had never been something she'd been very passionate about, but thankfully, her father had very simple tastes. Not only did he not mind eating the same thing each week, he pretty much insisted on it.

It made grocery shopping and cooking much more straightforward. Meatloaf. Shepherd's pie. Pot roast. Pork chops. Baked chicken. Basically, anything that could be eaten with either baked or mashed potatoes. Her own food tastes were a lot more varied than her dad's, but to make things easier, she generally ate whatever she fixed for him.

The only time she got something to her own tastes was when she made the trip to Seattle or Everette for her weekly grocery shop and time away from New Hope. The previous night, she'd settled on some sushi, which she'd enjoyed immensely.

While she would have liked to have had a whole day to do absolutely nothing for a change, it had been a long time since she'd had that. However, she could have a leisurely start to the day. As long as she started cooking by noon, she'd have enough time to get everything done. Cooking the same thing week after week for the past year had helped her figure out the timing and order of things to maximize her time.

When her phone rang, Lani sighed and debated ignoring it. No one ever called her except for her dad, and that was usually to issue one sort of demand or another.

It wasn't in her to actually ignore a call, however, so she got up and went to get her phone from where she'd left it on the counter in the kitchen. She frowned when she saw Michael's name on the screen. It was unusual for him to phone her at all, let alone on a Sunday morning.

"Michael?"

"I need your help," he blurted out.

"Um...sure," Lani said. "With what?"

"I'll tell you when you get here."

"Okaaaay. Where is *here* exactly?"

"Oh, my place." He rattled off the address. "Do you know where that is?"

"I have an idea. I'll be there in about half an hour." She hesitated. "Do I need to bring anything?"

"Just yourself." He let out a tired sounding sigh. "I think."

"Well, if that changes, give me a call," she told him. "See you soon."

As she went to her bedroom to get changed, Lani had to wonder why she was so willing to drop everything and go to Michael, especially since she actually had stuff she needed to do that day. Maybe it was a curiosity about his life. Maybe it was because she had a little extra time. Or maybe, just maybe, it was because she wanted to see him again. Outside of work.

She pulled on a pair of jeans and a long-sleeve T-shirt. It wasn't a super stylish outfit, but he'd already seen her in it at work, so it wasn't like she needed to maintain a standard. She brushed her hair back into a ponytail and took a minute to sweep on some mascara before calling it good.

As she drove out of town, Lani focused on finding the address for Michael's rural home. Having lived in New Hope for most of her life, she knew the area fairly well, so she didn't get lost, but it took her a little longer to find his place since it was further on the road than she'd thought it would be. When she finally spotted the numbers on an elevated rustic sign, along with the words *Reed Landscaping*, she breathed a sigh of relief.

The drive in to his home was long, winding through a forest of towering trees. When Lani finally reached the end of the driveway, she was met by a large clearing. A well-kept mobile home sat to one side while a large garage sat across from the house with several pieces of equipment parked in front of it. She pulled her car to a stop next to Michael's truck and got out.

A covered wooden deck ran the length of the mobile home, and colorful flowers filled boxes attached to the railing of the deck. It looked homey and welcoming, and Lani couldn't help but smile as she walked up the steps to the front door.

The door swung open before she could even knock on it.

"Hi...Michael?" The exhaustion on the man's face gave her pause. "Are you sick?"

She'd heard that men could sometimes be babies when they were sick, but Michael had never struck her as that sort of guy. Before he had a chance to answer, she heard a plaintive cry from behind him.

"You have a baby?" she asked, feeling a bit disappointed that he obviously had a family that she hadn't known about.

"I do now," he mumbled before gesturing for her to follow him.

Though she might have looked around at his home, now that she knew there was a baby present, she focused on that. A bassinette sat in the living room with Wolfie sitting next to it, his head tilted up as if keeping watch over its contents.

"Is this your baby?" she asked since his response had been odd. "Or are you babysitting?"

"She's mine. I think." He scrubbed a hand over his face. "Maybe? I don't know for sure yet."

Lani frowned at his words. He didn't know if the baby was his? "Are you waiting on a paternity test?"

He jerked at her words, his eyes going wide. "What? No. She's not my biological daughter. She's Taylor's."

This time it was Lani's eyes widening. "Taylor had a baby? She was pregnant?"

"Okay. Now I feel better." Michael gave a shake of his head. "I was beating myself up for not noticing she was pregnant, but maybe she just did a really good job of hiding it if you didn't see it either."

"So when did Taylor have the baby?"

"Late Friday night."

Lani glanced around then, looking for the woman. "Are you babysitting while she sleeps?"

"Nope. Taylor doesn't want her, so she's giving her to me."

"What?" Lani wasn't as surprised as she should have been by that statement, but when it came to Taylor, nothing really shocked her. "Can she do that?"

Michael shrugged. "I don't know. She said that she's been speaking to a lawyer about it all. I'll need to do some stuff for me to be able to adopt her."

"Oh. Wow. Adopt? That's a big step."

"I know. Yesterday I thought maybe I could do it, but after last night, I'm not so sure."

Lani walked over to look into the bassinette, smiling as she spotted the now-sleeping baby. "What happened last night?"

118 · KIMBERLY RAE JORDAN

"It's what didn't happen," he said as he stood beside her. "Sleep. She kept waking up, and then when she *did* sleep, I couldn't."

"Why's that?"

"I don't know what I'm doing, so worry was part of it. But the other part was being afraid that she would wake up, and I wouldn't hear her."

"Okay." Lani turned to face him. "Show me where stuff is, then you can go take a nap."

"Really?" The relief on Michael's face would have made her say yes, even if that hadn't been what she meant.

He showed her to the bedroom where there was a change table, a rocker, and clean clothes for the baby. Back in the kitchen, he pointed out where the formula was and told her when the baby had last eaten.

"Are you sure you're okay with this?" Michael asked.

"I'm fine with it," Lani assured him because the hope in his gaze wasn't something she could resist. "I've done some babysitting. Plus, when my cousin had her babies, I helped her out a lot. We'll be fine."

"In that case, I'm so grateful that in my sleep-deprived state, I called you."

"Off you go," Lani said, making shooing motions with her hands. "Get some rest, then we'll talk more."

"Thank you. Thank you so much." After a brief hesitation and a glance at the baby in the bassinette, Michael headed to the other end of the mobile home.

"Hi, Wolfie." Lani rubbed the dog's ears. "Looks like you're standing guard."

The dog gave a little chuff like he understood what she was saying. It was only after Michael had been gone for a little while that Lani realized she'd never asked the baby's name. Thankfully, given the baby was barely a couple days old, she wasn't responding to her name just yet.

Now that she knew what was going on, Lani relaxed and took the time to look around. Spotting a pile of dishes in the sink, she went over and started to clean up. By the time the baby began to stir, the nipples were in the sterilizer, and the dishes were in the dishwasher.

Looking more closely at the formula on the counter, it appeared that Taylor had bought Michael the ready-made stuff for the first few days. Before she left that day, Lani planned to help him get organized with the bottles and such so that maybe he felt a little more in control.

What had Taylor been thinking of leaving her baby with Michael like this? It wasn't that Lani was judging her for not feeling she could parent after what Lani could only assume was an unplanned pregnancy. No, she could understand that. What she *was* judging Taylor for was not giving Michael time to prepare for a baby.

Clearly, he was floundering, and that wouldn't be good for him or the baby. By springing a baby on him, Taylor had added stress to an already stressful situation.

When the baby began to fuss, Lani quickly picked her up before she could start full-on crying. She could tell that she was wet, so before anything, she took her into the master bedroom and changed her diaper. Back in the kitchen, she prepped a bottle for the baby then settled down in the comfiest looking chair in the living room.

"Here we go, little blossom," Lani whispered.

As the baby began to drink the bottle, she gazed up at Lani, and at that moment, Lani felt something shift within her. After her mom had passed away, her desire for a family had faded. In her dreams of the future, her mom had always been present when Lani had gotten married and had children. Without her mom there to celebrate those milestones with her, they'd lost their appeal.

Now, however, holding this little girl with blue eyes so like her uncle's, Lani began to think that maybe she could face having a family without her mom. Lifting the baby closer to her face, Lani brushed a kiss across her downy hair.

This wasn't how she'd planned to spend her day, but it was infinitely more enjoyable than cooking all day. She didn't know how Michael was going to juggle everything, but she'd help him out as much as she could.

Once the baby was finished with the bottle, Lani propped her up, gently rubbing and patting her back. After a couple of solid burps, she laid the baby on her thighs, her tiny feet pressed against Lani's stomach. Bending over her, she talked to her about random things, laughing when it became clear that another diaper change was in her future.

She got up and went to take care of that, wondering as she changed her if she'd had a bath yet. Maybe that was something she could help Michael with before she left.

Wolfie had been her shadow, following her wherever she went with the baby, lying on the floor at her feet whenever she sat down. It was clear that he already felt some sort of attachment to the little girl. Lani found it kind of endearing and made her like the dog even more.

Once the little girl had fallen asleep again, Lani carefully laid her down in the bassinette. She didn't know how long Michael might sleep, so while she waited for one or the other of them to wake up, she decided to do a few more things around the house.

Wondering if Michael had eaten anything since the baby had arrived in his life, Lani opened his fridge and took stock of the contents. She frowned when she saw how empty it was, then checked the freezer. That held an assortment of microwave dinners. The cupboards had more in them, but it was all canned goods.

She went back to the freezer and dug further, happy when she found a package of ground beef. After discovering a can of mushroom soup and a pack of instant potatoes in the cupboard, she decided to try and make some meatballs.

It was something she'd made for her dad before, so once she'd managed to get the ground beef defrosted, she quickly mixed up and formed the meatballs. After she'd browned them in a frying pan, she put them in a glass dish she'd found and poured the mushroom soup over them. It wasn't the fanciest food, but hopefully, he'd like it.

Michael still wasn't up by the time everything was done, so Lani just put it all in the oven to keep it warm. She was in the middle of cleaning up the mess she'd made when the baby woke up again, so after washing and drying her hands, she went to pick her up.

As she rocked the baby with a bottle once again, Lani felt a sense of contentment that she usually only experienced when she was arranging flowers. It felt like in the space of a few hours, her world had finally been righted. Her mother's death had knocked it off its axis, and she hadn't known if she would ever regain her balance.

Meeting Michael and arranging flowers at his shop had helped, but caring for this baby had been what she'd needed in order to see that everything hadn't been lost with her mom's death. Lani could find joy once more in the things that she'd shared or hoped to share with her.

She'd just never thought it would be a baby that would help her see that. Especially a baby that wasn't hers.

It was a couple of hours later before Michael finally reappeared, still looking a bit stressed, but at least he appeared more rested.

"What is that smell?" he asked as he approached the bassinette and peered inside.

"That depends. Does it smell good or bad?"

Straightening, he said, "It smells amazing."

Lani got up from where she'd been sitting. "Oh, then hopefully that means it's the food."

"Food?" Michael looked toward the kitchen. "Food sounds wonderful."

"Let me get you some," Lani said then paused. "What's the baby's name?"

"Did I forget to tell you?" Michael smacked his forehead. "Her name is Vivianne Rose."

"That's a beautiful name."

"It was my grandma's."

"Oh, that's sweet. Were you close to your grandma?"

"Yes," Michael said with a nod. "She was very important to me."

He didn't say anything more as he stood looking down at the sleeping baby, so Lani went to the kitchen and took the food out of the oven. She carried it over to the table where she'd set a plate for Michael.

"I didn't expect you to cook," Michael said when he joined her. "I just felt badly in need of sleep."

"Well, I'm sure you're hungry too, so go ahead and dish yourself up."

After a moment's hesitation, Michael sat down. "Are you not going to eat?"

"I'm fine," Lani assured him. She had decided not to eat any of the food she'd made for him since it appeared he needed it more than she did.

He quickly filled his plate then bowed his head. She stayed quiet as he prayed then asked him what he wanted to drink. He'd barely started eating when the baby began to make noises. Michael looked from his plate to the bassinette.

"You eat," Lani said. "I'll get her."

When she returned to the table with the baby and a bottle, she sat down across from him.

"Is she okay?" Michael asked, his brow furrowed. "I watched some videos last night on how to take care of a newborn, but I still wasn't sure."

"She's just perfect," Lani assured him. "She's eating well. Her color is good. She's having wet and dirty diapers. That's what you need to watch for."

Relief flooded Michael's face. "I'm so glad. I've never been around babies before, so I really wasn't sure what I was doing."

"You're doing great."

"I just don't want anything to happen to her because I don't know how to do this baby stuff."

"Well, you've got the basics down. Feeding, changing, and sleeping. Have you given her a bath yet?"

Michael gave a vigorous shake of his head. "I haven't attempted that yet."

"If you want, I can help you with that for the first time."

"Would you really do that?" Michael asked.

"Sure," Lani said with a shrug. "If I have the experience, it would be wrong of me not to help you."

"I really do appreciate all of this." Michael stared at his half-empty plate. "I didn't know who else to call. Aside from Taylor, you're the female I'm closest too. I didn't think my guy friends who don't have kids yet would have been much help." He looked up at her. "I suppose it was wrong of me to assume just because you're a woman that you'd know how to deal with a baby."

Lani laughed. "I think it's a natural assumption, but I do know that lots of men are knowledgeable about caring for babies too. Just like you'll be soon. It'll just take some time to build your confidence."

"Tell me to chop down a thirty-foot tree, and I'll get that thing down safely without injuring anything or anyone." Michael gave a huff of laughter. "But hand me a baby the size of a football, and I'm a mess."

"Do you chop that tree down all by yourself?"

"No. I have a crew that usually works with me."

"Well, you have people who will help you with your baby too. You don't have to do it alone."

Michael sighed. "I'm just not sure how to do this. I have a job that I can't just abandon to take care of her."

"There are people who babysit who could help you."

"But how do I know who I can trust with her?"

"Ask for recommendations. Surely your friends have family or friends with kids that need babysitter."

Michael nodded slowly. "Maybe I could ask Pastor Evans if he knows anyone in the church who could help."

"There you go," Lani said with a smile.

She wished that she could be the one to help him on a full-time basis, but there was just no way she could do that with everything else on her plate. She'd certainly help him when she could, like she was doing that day, but she couldn't commit to anything more.

"I just want to do the best for her." Michael blew out a long breath. "The problem is, I'm not sure if that's her staying with me or giving her up for adoption."

Lani looked down at the baby. "I think you're the only person who can know for sure what's best for her and you."

"I know. It just feels like the biggest decision of my life, and I've had to make some pretty big decisions."

"It is a big decision," Lani agreed. "And I know you'll make the right choice."

"I appreciate the vote of confidence," Michael said, a corner of his mouth lifting in a half-smile. "I think I'll have to pray about it and maybe ask Pastor Evans for advice."

"Has he had experience with adoption?"

"I don't know, but I've discovered that he's a wise man who's also very supportive." Michael lifted a forkful of mashed potatoes and meatball but didn't eat it. "He was the first person I connected with in town. I was driving around the town one day—we hadn't moved here yet—and he was outside mowing the grass at the church. I stopped and offered to help him, and that interaction started me on a completely new path in life."

Lani found that she was curious about his life both before and after he'd come to New Hope. Somewhere along the line, she'd definitely started viewing him as more of a friend and less as the owner of a competing business.

Her father would definitely not approve of that development. She had no idea what he'd do if he discovered what was going on, and she was in no rush to find out.

CHAPTER TWELVE

Michael paid careful attention to everything Lani was doing. He held Vivianne while Lani set things up, talking him through it while she did. She had filled the small white tub with water, making him feel it so he could gauge the temperature for himself. After it had enough water in it, she set up some sort of sling thing that would support the baby.

"Make sure you have everything you need before you put her in," Lani said, pointing at the small pile of things beside the tub.

Washcloth. Towel. Baby wash.

Lani gestured to the towel she'd laid out. "Now, we take off her clothes and her diaper."

Michael laid Vivianne down on the towel and carefully took off her sleeper, then undid her diaper. Lani walked him through the process of giving the baby a bath. Well, it wasn't a real bath. At least not as he defined a bath. It was more like a sponge bath since the sling thing kept the baby from being fully immersed in the water.

"Be careful not to get her cord wet," Lani said, as she pointed to her belly button.

"The video I watched said it would fall off?"

"Yep. I'm not sure when, though. But once it's off, you can cover her with more water."

"How often should I do this?"

"You don't need to give her a bath every day. She's not going to get that dirty at this age. You could actually just lay her on a towel and use a wet cloth to clean her off for the next couple of weeks. I just wanted to show you how to use the tub in case you needed to."

Michael liked the idea of just wiping Vivianne down until he felt a little more secure with her. Plus, the baby hadn't seemed all that enamored with the bathing experience. Lani had assured him that she was fine, and as soon as Vivianne was dressed again, she stopped fussing, so it appeared Lani was correct.

The more he learned, the more his confidence grew. Maybe he *could* do this.

"I've noticed that you have ready-made formula," Lani said, pointing to the bottles on the counter. "But what you have here won't last very long."

"Yeah. I'll need to use the powder stuff Taylor brought."

"Do you need me to show you how to prepare it?"

Michael jumped at the offer like a drowning man being offered a life preserver. "Would you?"

Slowly she walked him through what he'd need to do to prepare bottles and clean them afterward. The process was definitely more complicated than using the ready-made stuff. Maybe he needed to make a trip to the store to pick up more. Could he take the baby with him? Well, of course, he'd have to, wouldn't he?

"What are you going to do about work?" Lani asked once the bottle demonstration was done.

Michael cradled Vivianne, watching as her eyes began to close once again. "I'm going to have to take a couple of days off, for sure. I'm hoping I can get something figured out in that time."

"Is Taylor going to be in this week?"

He shrugged. "I really don't know."

Since he knew Lani relied on the job at the shop, he didn't tell her about Taylor's plan to leave New Hope altogether. He still held out a small bit of hope that she might change her mind.

"I'll let you know before Tuesday what's going on."

Lani gave a nod, then reached out to brush her fingers over the top of Vivianne's head. "I need to get going. Do you think you'll be okay?"

"Thanks to you, I think I will be as long as I can get some more sleep."

"Are you a sound sleeper?" she asked.

"Not really, no." He'd been trained early on in his life to sleep lightly. It had saved him from an unexpected beating from his drunken father more than once as a kid.

"Then trust that you'll hear Vivianne if she needs you," she said. "You need sleep. She'll be up several times through the night, so you need to make sure you go to sleep when she does. That way, you at least get some sleep. Honestly, even if it's not nighttime, you might do well to sleep when she does, just because a fractured night will catch up with you if you don't get sleep when you can."

"I can't tell you how much I appreciate everything you've done today," Michael said, wishing he could give her a hug.

She'd definitely gone over and above what their fledgling friendship might warrant. Michael wasn't altogether sure what he would have done if she hadn't answered his frantic call that morning. Though he could have called Eli and Anna or Carter, at that moment, he'd needed someone a little closer to his situation with Taylor than they were.

Lani gave him a smile that lit up her beautiful eyes. "I'm glad I could help you out. If you have a question or need something, feel free to give me a call. I might not be able to come, but I can always talk on the phone."

Michael grabbed a blanket from the bassinette and covered Vivianne with it so he could follow Lani out onto the deck.

Before she headed down the stairs, she turned to him. "Just remember that you can do this."

"Thank you." He appreciated her faith in him. It wasn't something he'd experienced a lot in his life.

"Bye, baby Vivianne," she said as she leaned close to press a kiss to the baby's head.

With her nearness, Michael got a whiff of her perfume or shampoo. He wasn't sure which it was, but unsurprisingly, it was a floral scent that lingered even after she stepped away and headed down the steps to her car.

As she drove away, he felt a moment's panic that he was once again alone with this tiny human being. Everything Lani had taught him about caring for the baby fled from his thoughts.

There was no way he could do this.

Vivianne squirmed in his arms, bringing him out of his panic.

He gazed down at the baby, seeing little bits of Taylor in her features. It didn't matter if he thought he couldn't do it. He just had to pull it together and do it.

"She's beautiful, Michael." Pastor Evans looked down at Vivianne as he held her, a smile on his face.

Keeping in mind everything Lani had told him, Michael had survived his second night with the baby. He'd slept when she had, trusting that he would wake up when she did, and he had. While he'd been happy about not sleeping through her wakings, he could have done with fewer of them. Unfortunately, every video he'd watched had told him that newborns woke frequently.

After hearing people talk about sleeping like a baby, Michael could only assume that they were up every two or three hours to pee and eat something. It couldn't possibly mean that they were sleeping soundly for eight straight hours.

After checking in with Ryker to let him know he couldn't work that day, Michael had called Pastor Evans to ask if he could meet with him. Thankfully, he'd told Michael to come to the church whenever it was convenient for him.

"Do you mind if I keep holding her while we chat?" the older man asked.

"Not at all." In fact, Michael was happy to share the baby-holding duties for a little while. Who would have thought that holding such a tiny thing would cause his biceps to cramp?

"Why don't you tell me how you came to have this beautiful little one," Pastor Evans said as they sat down on the couch in the man's office.

He didn't know if Pastor Evans thought he'd fathered Vivianne even though he wasn't married or what. But even if he did think that, the man wasn't looking at him with any judgment, which Michael appreciated.

Taking a deep breath, he began to tell the story of Vivianne's life so far. Thankfully, the baby slept through it, and the pastor didn't interrupt him either.

"So, are you going to keep her?" Pastor Evans asked when Michael was done.

"I don't know." Even as he said the words, he knew them for the lie they were. He'd had Vivianne forty-eight hours, and already he couldn't imagine his life without her. "I can't adequately care for her alone."

"What kind of help or support do you think you'll need to succeed at this?"

"I think the first—and probably biggest—need I have is someone to watch her during the day. I don't have the luxury of staying home with her." He hesitated. "I was hoping you might know of someone in the church who could watch her for me."

A thoughtful look settled over Pastor Evan's face. "I think there are a couple of women who might be able to help. I'd have to speak with them first to see if they'd be interested."

Michael felt relief rush through him even though he knew it wasn't a done deal. Even just having the possibility of a solution felt significant. "I'd really appreciate that."

"How is Taylor doing?"

"I'm not sure," Michael confessed. "I've kind of been in survival mode and haven't called her."

Of course, she hadn't called him either to see how he was coping. Was it really that easy for her to walk away from a child she'd just given birth to? He didn't know how it was to carry a child for nine months, but even after having her for just two days, he struggled with the idea of letting Vivianne go.

"That's understandable." Once again, the man didn't appear to be judging him for not having called his sister.

"I'll try and do that a little later today. I need to figure out what she's going to do about the shop."

"Are you thinking of shutting it down?"

Michael shrugged. "I won't have much choice. You know I struggle with the administrative side of things, so I'll already have to deal with that for my own business when she leaves. I'm not sure I can handle the shop too."

"I'll certainly be praying for you as you deal with all these changes. I am sure this is a very difficult time for you."

Pastor Evans was the only person aside from Taylor who knew about his past and the things he continued to struggle with.

"I appreciate that so much."

Though he'd never really believed in the power of prayer before coming to New Hope, he'd seen enough proof of it in the years since he'd become a Christian that he didn't doubt that prayer would help things. He'd definitely been praying lots since Vivianne's arrival in his life. Each time he sat with her in his arms, he prayed for her and for wisdom about the situation.

"I'm proud of you, Michael," Pastor Evans said. "You could have just told Taylor you couldn't do it right off the bat, but even though this will be a significant change in your life, you're considering it."

Michael blinked at the unfamiliar sting in his eyes. Did Pastor Evans know how much he'd needed to hear those words? He was trying so hard to do the right thing, so to have the man acknowledge that, meant the world to him.

Vivianne began to fuss, so Michael quickly got one of the ready-made bottles he'd packed and prepared it for her. When Pastor Evans held out his hand, Michael smiled and gave him the bottle. Though he'd never heard the man speak about children, it was pretty clear that this wasn't the first baby he'd fed.

As Vivianne ate, they talked more about how Michael might be able to handle his business as a single dad, and what hurdles he might have to jump over in order to adopt Vivianne.

When Michael decided it was time to leave a little while later, Pastor Evans prayed for them, one hand resting on Vivianne's head while the other was on Michael's shoulder. He appreciated the prayer as well as the assurance that the pastor would continue to pray for them.

By the time he left the church, he felt another level of confidence, similar to what he'd felt after Lani's visit. It seemed as if a support system was forming around him, and Michael couldn't have been more grateful.

Pulling out of the church's parking lot, he headed to Everett for the order he'd managed to place for more diapers, formula, and some food for himself at a store there, since the one in New Hope didn't have grocery pick up. He hoped he'd gotten everything right. It had taken him ages the night before to work his way through setting up an online account and then placing the order so he wouldn't have to go into the store to shop. He didn't feel too confident doing that with Vivianne just yet.

Back at the house, he was in a bit of a quandary of where it was best to leave Vivianne alone while he unloaded the groceries. Finally, he took her into the house and left her in her car seat on the table while he went back out for the groceries. Wolfie greeted them enthusiastically then waited patiently beside the table until Michael was finished.

When Vivianne began to fuss, he took her out of the car seat. He quickly realized a diaper change was next on the schedule. Hands down, it was the thing he enjoyed the least so far with her. It even topped the chopped up sleep he was getting now.

It took him awhile to get it done, and he could only hope for his *and* Vivianne's sake that he would get better at it. She definitely wasn't any more of a fan of the process than he was.

As soon as it was over and he picked her up, she settled right down. Warmth spread through Michael as he realized that she found comfort in his arms.

"Do you think we can do this, Vivi?" he asked as he made his way out of the bedroom. "Are you going to be patient with me while I get the hang of things?"

As he set about getting another bottle ready for Vivianne, Michael considered phoning Lani to let her know how things were going. He knew it wasn't the phone call he *should* be making, but it was definitely the one he wanted to make.

He'd just put Vivianne down in her bassinette after feeding and burping her when his phone rang. A glance at his screen told him that the decision had been taken out of his hands.

"Hi Taylor," he said as he answered.

"I just wanted to check in about tomorrow at the shop."

"Are you planning to go in?"

"I guess so. I placed an order today for a flower pickup tomorrow."

"Are you sure you're up for it?" Michael asked, unable to keep himself from worrying about her. It was what he'd done for years, so it wasn't something he could just not do even though he was still upset with her for how she was going about things.

"I'll be fine."

"Do you still need Lani to come in?"

"Yes. For now, she can keep coming in as usual."

Michael was relieved to hear that. He wasn't ready to give up seeing her on a nearly daily basis, especially since she hadn't shown any inclination to see him outside the shop. Well, aside from when she'd showed up in response to his panicked call for help. He still wasn't sure why he'd chosen to call her instead of Eli and Anna or Carter.

"Also, I've talked to my lawyer, and he'd like to meet with us to get things rolling for the adoption."

She didn't ask how the baby was or how he was doing with the new changes in his life, just jumped in to scheduling a time for them to meet. When he agreed to the time she'd suggested, she ended the call.

It was only as he sat there holding his phone that he realized that he had a problem. There was no way he could take the baby with him to pick up the flowers the next morning.

One of the videos he'd watched had been about car seats, and since the van didn't have a second row of seats, he couldn't take it. His vehicle wasn't an option either as the truck bed wasn't covered. But more importantly, he wasn't sure how Vivi would do for the hour and a half round trip drive.

His options were to go and hope the order would fit in the truck, ask Taylor if she'd consider doing the pick-up, or ask Lani if she could. He hated the idea of that last one, however. It didn't seem right to ask her to get up so early to deal with the order when that wasn't part of what she'd been hired to do.

Lifting his phone, he recorded a voice message for Taylor. *I'm not going to be able to pick up the order with the baby. She needs to be in a second row in her car seat and the van doesn't have that. Plus, I don't want to keep her in the car seat for that long just yet.*

After he sent it, he got up and went to the kitchen to get himself a drink and something to eat. It took almost half an hour for Taylor to get back to him, but thankfully, she agreed to take care of getting the flower order.

Around five, during a fussy period that Michael didn't know how to deal with, there was a knock on the door. It jolted him because he was so used to hearing a car's engine before someone approached the door. But he'd been so focused on Vivianne and trying to calm her that he'd missed it.

Pulling open the door, he spotted his right-hand man. Michael had forgotten that when he'd called him earlier to let him know he wouldn't be available to work that day, he'd asked Ryker to stop by at the end of the day.

"Why do you have a baby?" Ryker Bennet asked, his brows drawn low as he gazed at the fussy baby.

"It's a long story." Michael sighed. "C'mon in."

Ryker stepped in and greeted Wolfie before closing the door. "This is a bit of a shock, bro."

"Tell me about it. And I'm really struggling with it." He was discouraged at how things had gone downhill later in the afternoon. Vivianne refused to settle, and he couldn't figure out what the problem was.

Ryker stared at him and Vivianne for a moment before sighing. He went to the sink in the kitchen and washed his hands, then returned to where Michael stood with Vivianne. "Let me."

"You want to hold her?" Michael asked, taking in his friend and employee's rough exterior. He was a bit taller than Michael, with tanned skin and broad shoulders.

"Sure. Let me give you a break."

That offer was too appealing to pass up. Plus, he'd be there to watch the man, so if he wasn't comfortable with how Ryker was dealing with her, he could take her back.

"Here we go," Ryker said as he walked to the couch, snagging a blanket from the bassinette as he went.

With careful movements, he laid Vivianne on the couch, then arranged the blanket next to her. Michael moved closer to watch as Ryker picked her up and laid her on the blanket. With deft movements, the man wrapped and tucked the blanket around Vivianne until she kind of looked like a baby burrito.

"Why did you wrap her up like that?" Michael asked as Ryker picked the baby up and held her with swaying movements.

"It's called swaddling, and babies like it because it makes them feel like they're still in the womb."

Michael wouldn't have bought it except for the fact that Vivianne *had* settled down. And even more surprising was how at ease Ryker seemed as he swayed with her tucked into the crook of his arm, close to his chest.

Taking in the soft expression on Ryker's face as he gazed down at Vivianne, Michael couldn't help but ask, "Do *you* have kids?"

He'd never heard Ryker talk about a family, so he'd just assumed he didn't. But he was far too comfortable with Vivianne for this to be his first time dealing with a baby. At Michael's question, however, his expression shuttered.

"No, I don't, but I do have some experience with babies."

Michael wanted to push, to ask more questions, but he got the feeling the man wouldn't be forthcoming with the details. He couldn't risk upsetting the man, not when he needed his help through the challenging days, weeks, and possibly months ahead.

"So why don't you tell me how you came to have this little one."

"She's Taylor's," Michael said as he sank down into his chair.

Ryker's eyes widened. "Say what?"

As he told the story yet again, Michael tried not to let it overwhelm him. With every person he told, with every person whose help he needed, the weaker he felt. Even though he'd needed help many times in the past, he'd had to push on without it. His grandma had tried to help them, but she'd been limited in what she could do.

So to be having to turn to so many different people for help now made him feel like he wasn't strong enough to do what needed to be done. That was a difficult pill to swallow. It made him want to back away and try to do it all by himself, but it was too late now, and frankly, Vivianne deserved better than that.

CHAPTER THIRTEEN

When Lani pulled into the lot behind the shop, she spotted the van there, but no other vehicle. The previous night, Michael had called to let her know that Taylor was doing the flower run in the morning and that she planned to open the shop for the afternoon. She also wanted Lani to be there as usual.

Lani had been happy that it was still business as usual with the shop, though she'd suspected that Michael's life wasn't. He'd as much as confirmed that as he spoke about the changes he was making as he made arrangements for a babysitter for Vivianne.

She'd been happy to hear that he was doing okay with the baby. Even though she'd told him that he could do it, she'd been a bit worried about him. Dealing with a newborn baby was stressful for a couple, or even a single mom, who'd been planning for it for nine months. Lani could only imagine how much more stressful it was for a man who hadn't had a clue that a baby was in his immediate future.

After she let herself into the shop, Lani went straight to the cooler to check that Taylor had already been there with the flower order. Thankfully, it looked like she had been, so Lani was able to get right to work.

She'd been working for a couple of hours when the alarm chimed to let her know the back door had opened. Her heart sped up in anticipation of who might be walking through the door. Turning, she smiled when she spotted Michael come in with a diaper bag over one shoulder, the car seat in his hand and Wolfie at his heels.

"Hey there," she said as he approached the worktable.

With a smile, he put the car seat up on the table, then lifted the blanket that was covering it.

"How's she doing?" Lani asked. "How are *you* doing?"

He looked tired but not excessively so. "I'm doing okay, and I think she's doing okay too. Although she was fussy last night."

"Well, that's not unusual," she assured him as she bent to look at the sleeping baby then gave Wolfie some love as well. She would have loved to give Michael a hug, but that wasn't who they were. "What brings you by so early?"

"When she woke up earlier, I figured I'd continue my habit of stopping by. Of course, she didn't stay awake."

"Car rides can be great for putting babies to sleep."

"I'll keep that in mind," Michael said as he walked over to the Keurig. "I need caffeine."

Lani chuckled as she watched him. "Nice to see some things haven't changed."

Michael started the machine then turned around to lean back against the counter, crossing his arms. He wore a long-sleeve light blue T-shirt and dark blue jeans with worn spots on them. "I have a feeling that's something that can't change if Vivianne and I are to survive this first year."

"Surviving is important." Lani dragged her attention back to her work and tilted her head as she moved the arrangement around to look at it from all angles. "So is thriving, so hopefully you get to that point this year too."

"Hopefully." Michael carried his mug to the table and sat down across from her. "Ryker stopped by last night, and he gave me some tips on how to care for her."

Lani glanced up at him. "Ryker?"

"He's my right-hand man," Michael said. "Shocked me to discover that he knew all about caring for babies."

"Why's that?"

"As far as I know, he doesn't have any kids. But he walked in last night when Vivi was fussing, wrapped her up like a burrito, and boom! She settled down."

"Ah, swaddling. I should have mentioned that."

"I'm still perfecting my technique, but it seems to be working so far."

"I would never be able to fall asleep if I was wrapped up tight like that," Lani said with a laugh.

"I hear you, but as long as it works for Vivi, I'm going to do it." He took another sip of his coffee then said, "Did Taylor get the flowers dropped off?"

"Yep. I didn't see her, but when I got here, there were fresh flowers in the cooler."

"Good. I was kind of worried that she might forget or sleep in."

"So far, I've had everything I need for what she wanted me to make."

Michael leaned forward to brace his elbows on the table as he continued to sip his coffee. "That looks really nice. You definitely have a talent for flower arranging."

"I've had a lot of years of practice," Lani said as she added a final few pieces of greenery. "And I've loved flowers since I was a kid. I even draw them."

"Really?" Michael said, surprise evident in his voice. "You're an artist?"

"I wouldn't call myself an artist." Lani turned the flower arrangement around so she could check it from all angles before calling it done. "All I can draw are flowers."

"I'd love to see something you've drawn."

Lani gave Michael a quick glance then pulled her phone out. After opening her pictures, she found the ones she'd taken to post for sale online.

Sliding the phone across the table, she said, "There you go."

Michael picked the phone up and looked at the picture. "That's very pretty. You utilize watercolors for them too?"

"Yes. As you can see, I don't use a very precise technique."

"I think that works well for this type of drawing."

Lani couldn't help but smile. For some reason, Michael's appreciation of what she did meant a lot. Certainly more than it should. The past year and a half had been devoid of moments like these, so his comments of affirmation were like pouring water on parched ground. She soaked it up and wished for more, though she knew she shouldn't.

Rather than dwell on it, Lani picked up the floral arrangement and carried it into the cooler. Because she'd forgotten to check what she needed for the next arrangement, she had to go back to the work area and check the binder.

Michael was still seated at the worktable, coffee mug held close to his face. It was at that moment that she realized something about the man. Where most people would pull out their phones when they didn't have anything else to do, he never did. In fact, she could count on one hand the number of times she'd actually seen him with his phone in his hand.

"I'm supposed to meet with Taylor and a lawyer at eight on Wednesday," Michael said out of the blue.

Lani looked up at him from where she was trimming the ends of the flower stems. "Is this about the adoption?"

"I would imagine so. She didn't say specifically."

Lowering the stem cutter, she gave him her full attention. "Make sure you read everything thoroughly before signing anything."

Michael frowned. "Do you think I should have a lawyer of my own?"

"I don't suppose it would hurt." Lani hummed uncertainly. "In this case, though, I doubt Taylor would try and pull one over on you. You could probably get away without a lawyer as long as you read through it on your own."

His frown deepened as he stared down into his mug. Lani waited for him to say something, but when he didn't, she turned back to trimming stems.

She wondered what he was thinking about his future with Vivianne. It seemed like he already loved the little girl, so she could only guess that he was going to keep her. But there was always the possibility that he loved her enough to let her go if he didn't feel like he could give her the life he felt she deserved.

Lani didn't envy him the decision.

"I can't read."

The words took a moment to sink in. Putting her work aside again, she looked at him and tried to figure out what Michael was saying. The three words didn't make any sense to her.

"I don't understand."

Michael lowered his mug to the table but didn't look at her. "I struggle with reading. I always have."

"Do you have something like dyslexia?"

Michael shrugged. "I don't know. I struggled through school, but I was never tested for anything. They just kept passing me along until I finally quit school when I was in ninth grade."

"I never would have guessed."

"I don't like people to know."

Lani felt privileged that he had shared this piece of himself with her. "So you won't be able to read any papers the lawyer might give you?"

He shook his head. "I don't think Taylor would try to make the process difficult, but now I'm wondering if I should get a lawyer of my own."

"I would be happy to read any documents to you if you have the time. To see if you need to hire a lawyer."

Michael's gaze lifted and met hers, his brow furrowed. "You'd do that for me?"

"Yes," Lani said without hesitation. "I'd love to help you through the adoption process if you need it."

His shoulders relaxed as the stress eased from his face. "I hate to ask that of you. You've already done so much for me."

"You're not asking me," Lani told him. "I'm offering. And I wouldn't do that if I didn't want to."

"I'm worried that my inability to read will be something they hold against me when it comes to the adoption." Michael's brows drew close again. "In all honesty, I have several strikes against me. So if they aren't willing to follow Taylor's wishes, I don't know what we'll do."

At that moment, words her mom had always said nearly tripped off her tongue. *We'll just have to pray about it.*

Lani couldn't count the number of times she'd heard her mom say that. And it had been about anything. Whether the concern was a spelling test at school or someone who was sick, her mom believed it was worthy of prayer. Lani had never embraced prayer quite the way her mom had, but right then, she really wanted to assure Michael that she'd pray for him and Vivianne.

"Try not to worry too much, Michael." She really wanted to reach out and smooth the furrows from his forehead with her fingertips. "It won't change anything, and it will negatively affect you."

Michael gave her a rueful smile. "I've spent my life worrying about everything. And this thing with Vivianne? It feels like the biggest thing I've ever had to worry about."

Lani struggled to find the words to offer him assurances she wasn't sure she should even make. There was no guarantee the adoption would proceed the way he and Taylor wanted it to. It almost felt wrong to assume that it would. Her life was proof that things didn't always go the way people assumed or hoped they would.

"If you want, bring the baby here before you go to the meeting so you can focus on everything without interruption. I think I can still get work done while she's here."

"I'd really appreciate that," Michael said. "I didn't even think about that. It's like my brain still hasn't grasped that I have something new to factor into all my decisions."

"Your brain is a little tired right now," Lani said with a smile. "Give it a bit of a break."

"If the past couple of days are anything to go by, my brain is going to be tired for the foreseeable future."

"This too shall pass." And yet another saying of her mom's.

Michael nodded. "That is true. I've yet to be in a dark spot that, even though it seemed inescapable at the time, didn't pass. I know this won't be smooth sailing, but as long as I can keep Vivianne, I'll do my best to weather the storms ahead."

Lani couldn't help but admire Michael's determination. She thought about her dad and wished that he would be more willing to move forward despite the difficult place he found himself in. Instead, all he had done was rant about his current circumstances and vent at anyone who would listen.

She knew she wasn't exactly perfect about keeping an upbeat attitude all the time, especially since her mom's death, but at least she was trying to keep things moving. She'd been doing it mainly in memory of her mom, but maybe it was time to start considering herself too.

Michael got up off his stool and took his mug to the sink. When he came back to where the car seat sat, he said, "I should probably head back home before Vivianne starts to fuss."

"I guess I'll see you tomorrow," she said as he covered the car seat with a light blanket.

"Yep. I should be here around seven-thirty. Hopefully, the meeting will only last an hour."

"I can probably stay until around ten-thirty, if need be."

"Well, I'll let them know up front that this can't be a long meeting. If we need to have a longer one, then they'll have to let me have some time to figure out care for Vivianne."

"Do you have any leads on a babysitter for her?" Lani asked as they walked to the back door.

"Pastor Evans said he had a couple of people who might be willing to watch Vivianne, but he didn't tell me who they were."

"That's good that he's willing to help you find someone."

"Definitely. I really appreciate it."

Lani opened the door and held it for him as he left the shop. After he said goodbye, she watched as he headed for his truck then let the door close.

The quiet in the shop seemed heavier now that Michael was gone, which was a little crazy since they had talked about some heavy stuff. She could only hope that the meeting with the lawyer would provide some answers that would put his mind at ease.

~*~

Michael was up early the next day. Although, was it accurate to say he was up early when he really hadn't slept much?

It had felt like he was back in his teen years when he hardly slept for worry over what the next day might bring. Would his father drink himself into oblivion? Or would he drink just enough to bring out his nastiness? That always meant Michael was going to suffer.

All night long, he'd worried about the possible outcomes of this meeting. He'd spent too much time dreaming up all the possible scenarios. Worst case...he lost any right to have Vivianne in his life. Best case...he got to keep the baby and call her his own.

Finally, he loaded up the truck with the things he thought Lani might need. It was crazy how much stuff a baby required, but he wanted Lani to be able to work even with Vivianne there. He was taking the baby sling he'd found in the room along with a collapsible playpen, so Lani could figure out which one she preferred. The diaper bag held several diapers, a pack of wipes, a couple changes of clothes, a blanket, and several bottles of formula.

Hopefully, that would cover anything she might need. If it didn't, he might never leave Vivianne with anyone again because he didn't have enough space in his truck to take the contents of the baby's room.

Lani greeted him with a broad smile when he walked in just after seven-thirty. She took the car seat while he went back out to the truck to get the rest of the stuff.

"I'd tease you about all that," Lani said when he came in with the rest of the baby's things. "But I know it's better to have too much stuff than not enough."

"I left the kitchen sink at home, but only because we have one here."

Lani laughed as he brought everything to the worktable. "Better to be safe than sorry."

"Too true." Michael walked to the Keurig to fill a travel mug with coffee. As he waited for his mug to fill, he watched Lani peer into the car seat at Vivianne. She wore a light purple blouse that had tiny yellow flowers on it that looked very spring-ish. "Sorry I can't hang around."

"No worries," Lani said. "I just hope all goes well for you."

"You and me both." Michael picked up his travel mug then bent to press a light kiss to Vivianne's soft curls. "I'll see you two in a couple of hours."

"We'll be here." Lani gave him a beaming smile, the warmth of which he took with him as he left the shop.

He sucked back the coffee as he left New Hope for the address Taylor had given him in Everett. Since that was where she lived now, it wasn't a surprise that she'd found someone there. He wasn't sure if there were lawyers in New Hope, but he'd prefer to find one there if it turned out that he needed one.

All the way there, Michael prayed that God would guide the meeting and give him the wisdom to ask the right questions. He knew that Pastor Evans was praying for him, and for a moment, he regretted not telling Eli, Carter, and Beau about what was happening. He knew that they would have prayed for him as well.

Why he hadn't told them, Michael wasn't entirely sure. It was odd that he'd turned to Lani and Ryker for help before Eli and the others. Part of him was afraid they'd try and convince him that Vivianne would be better off with a stable couple who wanted to adopt a baby.

But would they really do that? So far, no one else had, even Pastor Evans, who knew everything there was to know about him.

Regardless of how this meeting went, it was time to tell them what was happening in his life. They were his friends, and he needed to trust that they'd support him in whatever decision he made

Already he appreciated so much the support he'd had from Lani, Pastor Evans, and Ryker. For once in his life, it felt good not to be going through the difficult times on his own. After he'd opened up with Lani about his illiteracy and she'd acted like it wasn't a big deal, Michael questioned why he'd hidden that fact from his friends.

He'd been pretty sure that they wouldn't judge him for it. But if he dwelled too long on what he saw as a huge weakness in himself, it made him feel lesser than the other men. The things they took for granted, he struggled with.

Early on, he'd told Pastor Evans because he'd needed someone to confide in about everything, and the older man had presented a safe place for him to do that. He'd shared it with Ryker because he felt he owed it to the man since he'd have to rely on him at times.

When the words had tumbled out of his mouth in front of Lani, his heart had felt like it was going to pound out of his chest. It had felt the riskiest to tell her, but she'd barely blinked before offering to help him. Was it possible she viewed him as less of a man for not being able to read? Maybe? But he'd certainly not gotten that feeling.

Now, all he could hope was that if there were people who needed to know about it, that they wouldn't consider it a black mark against him. He didn't want anything to negatively impact Vivianne, but he didn't think his inability to read would do that.

What he really wanted from the meeting with the lawyer that day was a clear idea of where he stood and what he needed to do to get through the process—all without having any sort of disagreement with Taylor.

CHAPTER FOURTEEN

A receptionist showed Michael into a small room dominated by a large table and several chairs. A tall, middle-aged man stood from the chair at one end of the table and held out his hand.

"I'm Jim Gordon," he said with a friendly smile.

"Michael Reed. It's nice to meet you." He glanced around the room. "Is Taylor not here yet?"

"Not yet, but we can start without her," the man said. "If you have to get back at a certain time."

"My babysitter can only stay until ten-thirty, so I'll have to leave by ten or so."

"That should be plenty of time." The man gestured to one of the empty chairs. "Please have a seat."

Michael settled into one of the chairs, grateful to see what appeared to be a carafe of coffee in the middle of the table. At least he hoped it was coffee and not just hot water.

"Coffee?" Jim asked.

"Yes. Please."

The lawyer poured coffee into two cups. "I imagine you're not getting a ton of sleep these days."

"Not much, no," Michael admitted. "But I received some good advice to sleep when the baby sleeps. Once I realized that I wouldn't sleep through her crying, I managed to get more rest."

"My wife and I were told the same thing," the man said with a nod. "So, can I assume that you have some support around you in dealing with this?"

"Yes. I've had a few people who have stepped up to help me out."

"I'm glad to hear that. I told Taylor that she needed to let you know of her intentions as soon as she made up her mind, but it seems she disregarded that advice."

"Well, unless she didn't decide for sure until after the baby was born. Then yes, I'd say she did."

Jim sighed. "I'll be honest with you. All of this could have been less stressful and better transitioned if Taylor had been more up-front about what was going on in her life."

He couldn't argue with that, and Michael was sort of glad that the lawyer seemed understanding of how he might be feeling. "I definitely would have appreciated a head's up, that's for sure."

"It would have made the adjustment easier for you and would have put us ahead of the eight ball, so to speak, when it comes to the legal side of things."

He didn't like the sound of that. "What do you mean?"

"If we could have done all the necessary paperwork and the home study before the baby was born, it would have been less for you to have to deal with now that the baby is here." Jim tapped the file folder in front of him. "Relative adoptions aren't as common as stranger—for lack of a better word—adoptions, but they can require most of the same steps."

"So even though I'm related to the baby, I'll have to go through the home study and everything?" That wasn't what Michael wanted to hear.

"There is no guarantee one way or the other, but the court may require it given you don't have a family of your own. They'll want to know that you're capable of caring for a baby without immediate support."

"What happens if I fail the home study?" Michael asked.

Jim didn't respond right away, rubbing a hand down his chin. "The thing is, this is a process. Everyone in the process wants you to succeed because we want to make sure that the child is going to a good home. Unless there is something glaring that really can't be corrected, you'll be given the opportunity to fix things that may be a concern."

"Like what?"

Jim picked up his pen and repeatedly clicked the end of it as he leaned back in his chair. "You wouldn't have much of a chance if you have a conviction for felony child abuse or neglect, or for domestic violence. Drug abuse can be an issue. However, Taylor has assured me that none of that is an issue for you."

"She's right," Michael said.

"You do have some things in your favor with you owning your own home and having a successful business."

"I don't own a mansion or anything like that," Michael said, wanting to make sure Taylor hadn't painted it that way."

Jim chuckled. "I'm aware, but everything Taylor has said about where you live tells me that it's a safe home in good repair with plenty of room for a baby."

"Oh, well, yes, that's true." Michael still couldn't allow himself to get his hopes up too much.

Before they could continue talking, there was a light knock on the door before it swung open to reveal the receptionist and Taylor. She walked into the room and circled around to the other side of the table.

"Good morning," Jim said as he got to his feet and held out his hand.

"Morning." She shook his hand then sat down across from Michael.

He was glad to see that she didn't look as bad as she had in the weeks leading up to Vivianne's birth. Her hair and makeup were done, and she was no longer wearing the baggy clothes she'd favored for the last few months. He figured that was because she no longer had to hide her pregnancy.

"I was just explaining things to Michael," Jim said as he settled back in his seat.

Michael wanted to demand to know why she hadn't made this easier for both of them, but he kept his mouth shut. Years of experience with his younger sister had taught him that demanding anything of her was the quickest way to get her to clam up...after she lashed out.

As the conversation turned to the particulars of what lay ahead, Michael felt his head begin to pound. So far, he hadn't been required to read anything, but he knew that would change at some point.

"Michael, you need to get a lawyer for yourself in this process."

Given how comfortable he'd become with the man in the short time he'd known him, Michael wished that he could have kept him and forced Taylor to find another lawyer. But again, he knew better than to suggest that.

"Do you have a recommendation for me?" Michael asked. "I don't know any lawyers."

"I do have a couple that I'd recommend." Jim flipped through the file in front of him and pulled out a piece of paper. He slid it toward Michael. "Either of those would be good choices. I've worked with them both."

Michael didn't bother to look at the paper, just took it and folded it. "So, the lawyer I hire will walk me through what lies ahead?"

Jim nodded. "Though the document I drew up for Taylor giving you permission to make decisions for the baby works for now, we need you to be granted temporary guardianship of the baby, so you can make all decisions related to her care."

"That sounds important."

"It is," Jim agreed. "So we're going to take care of that first. You'll also need to find a pediatrician for the baby because I think she probably needs to have a check-up fairly soon."

By the time he left the lawyer's office, Michael was feeling overwhelmed. His head throbbed as he guided the truck back to New

Hope. He wasn't harboring high hopes for how this process was going to unfold. All his mind could focus on were his weaknesses.

No family—aside from the person who had landed him in this situation and planned to abandon him to it.

Inability to read.

No prior experience with babies...or even children, aside from having been one a long time ago.

And those were just the ones he could squeeze out of his aching brain.

Back at the shop, he sat in the truck for a couple of minutes since it was just after nine-thirty. He didn't want to make Lani stay any longer than necessary, but he just wanted a few minutes with nothing demanding his attention in order to decompress.

After a few minutes, he felt calm enough to move forward with his day. Pushing open the door, he climbed out and headed into the shop. As soon as he spotted Lani with Vivianne strapped to her front, something settled within Michael.

His first priority would always be Vivianne, and that meant he would do whatever was required to make sure things worked out for them to stay together.

"Hey." Lani's face lit up when she spotted him.

"You managed to figure that out, huh?" Michael said, gesturing to the carrier she wore.

"I did. It only took me reading the directions and then watching a video three times. I could have just saved myself some time and watched the video. Much clearer than the written instructions that came with it."

"You'd better send me a link to that video then," Michael said as he cupped his hand briefly over the top of Viviane's head. "Because me and words...we've never been friends."

"I will definitely send you the link." Lani gave him a smile as she bounced and swayed lightly, her hand rubbing Vivianne's back. "How did things go?"

WHEN I'M WITH YOU · 153

Michael sighed as he sat down at the worktable. "Well, my not having a conviction for child abuse or neglect or domestic violence is a point in my favor. As is having my own home and business. Not having a family—or probably more likely, a wife or girlfriend—wasn't a point in my favor. Nor is my lack of experience with children."

Lani frowned at him. "Don't sell yourself short. You're already trying your hardest to move past your lack of experience. You've been more than willing to listen to advice that's been given to you. That can only be a positive thing. Vivianne would be in more danger if you were dismissing what people were telling you."

"Well, that would be a pretty dumb thing to do," Michael said.

"Exactly. But there *are* people out there who refuse to take advice from anyone. Just goes to show you're smart. I think those looking at your situation would consider it a point in your favor that you're accepting help and advice."

Michael sure hoped Lani was right because he had no choice but to rely on others. So if they did decide to count lack of experience against him, he was in even bigger trouble than he already thought.

"Did Taylor show up?" Lani asked as she turned her attention back to the arrangement that was sitting on the worktable.

For a moment, Michael watched how adeptly she did her work, even with a baby strapped to her. Something told him that she wouldn't have balked at juggling her career and a child.

"Yes, she showed up...late."

"Better late than never?"

Michael huffed. "I suppose. Thankfully, her lawyer was a decent guy who was more than willing to walk me through things."

"That's good."

"And he gave me a couple of recommendations for lawyers as I do need one of my own." He grimaced. "Not an expense I really want to have, but if it's necessary, I'll do it."

Lani gave him a sympathetic look. "Yeah, but I know it can be frustrating to have an unexpected outlay of money like that."

"Was she good?"

"Yep. Woke up after you left and stayed awake for awhile then a bit ago, I changed her diaper and gave her a bottle. When I put her in this, she conked back out again."

"Guess she doesn't always need to be swaddled to sleep, huh?"

"My guess is she feels a bit swaddled with the way the sling holds her. Having a warm body close to her probably helps too." Lani ran her hand down Vivianne's sling covered back. "My cousin wore her baby in a sling all the time."

"I never knew such a thing existed," Michael said.

"There's been no need for you to know about them, so that's not too surprising." She grinned. "Did you want to practice putting it on while you're here? You'll feel like you don't have enough hands the first few times you do it."

"Sure, that would be great."

"Let me just finish this last arrangement, then we can work on it together."

Michael got up and headed toward the Keurig machine but then stopped. He wasn't sure that his stomach could handle another cup of coffee when he hadn't had anything to eat yet, but that certainly wasn't going to stop him. "I'm going to head to the bakery to grab something to eat. Can I get you something too?"

"Sure," Lani said as she glanced up at him.

"Anything you do or don't like?"

She shrugged. "I'm not too fussy, although I don't like cooked apple stuff. It's my dad's favorite thing, so growing up, that's all my mom made. Apple pie. Apple crumble. Apple crisp."

"Okay," Michael said with a nod. "No cooked apples."

He let himself out the front door, making sure he locked it before quickly heading down the sidewalk toward the bakery. It was only a couple of blocks away, and Lani would probably be done her work before he got back. *Norma's*, the town's main diner, would have been a good place for a hearty breakfast, but since Lani was working, the bakery was the quicker choice.

After liberating the bakery of a variety of pastries, Michael made his way back. When he walked into the back of the shop, he saw that Lani no longer had flowers on the worktable. Instead, Vivianne lay on a folded blanket on the table in front of Lani, her little hands waving.

"Did she wake up?"

"When I took her out of the sling, she decided to wake up."

Michael set the food on the table then walked around to peer down at the baby. "Hey there, sweetie."

Vivianne blinked up at him. Michael knew better than to expect her to smile or even interact with him, but he found himself looking forward to the day when she would. Provided everything went well with the adoption.

"Which of these did you get for yourself?" Lani asked as she peered into the bag. "I don't want to eat those."

"I'm good with any of them, so take whatever appeals to you." Michael braced his arms on either side of Vivianne, his mind going over what he knew so far of what he'd need in order to make the little girl his for good.

"Was there anything else the lawyer said that was important?" Lani asked. "Or maybe that's none of my business."

He glanced up to find her sitting across from him, a cinnamon bun in her hands. "Given how much you've helped me, I'd say it was definitely your business."

She frowned at his words. "I don't ever want you to feel that in exchange for my help, you have to give me information you'd rather not share."

"I don't feel that way," Michael assured her as he sat down and pulled a doughnut out of the bag. "What I meant was more along the lines of you already knowing so much about what's going on."

"Okay. Sorry. I just don't want you to feel like you owe me anything."

"Well, I can't say I don't feel indebted to you. You've stepped up more than you had to, given that you haven't known me all that long." He paused to take a bite of his doughnut. "I'm not sure why you have, but I'm so thankful that you did. You've become more of a friend and less of an employee."

"Don't you have other friends?" Lani asked. "I mean, I have a fairly small circle of friends myself, so no judgment."

"I do, but most of them are guys, and none of them have kids. Although Ryker definitely surprised me." As they ate their pastries, Michael told her about again about how Ryker had stepped in to help him.

When Vivianne let out a squawk, Lani said, "Guess we'd better try the sling before she starts to really fuss."

She went over to the sink and washed her hands before coming back to where he stood beside Vivianne.

"Okay, so I'm going to show you how to do it on myself first, then you can try. You need to feel comfortable doing it by yourself if you want to use it."

Michael nodded then watched closely as she wrapped straps around herself and then secured them. She lifted Vivianne and held her close to her chest, leaning back slightly as she pulled the wide part up and over the baby. With quick movements, she looped more straps over her shoulders and pulled them criss-cross along her back.

He wasn't entirely sure he was going to be able to do that on his own. Vivianne hadn't fussed for Lani, but Michael had a feeling that wouldn't be the same once he got done trying to fit the sling on properly.

"Your turn," Lani said with a smile.

She walked him through each step, resting a light hand on his back as she helped him brace Vivianne so he could get the straps in place. When the baby started to fuss, Lani said she'd feed her while Michael tried the sling a few more times without the baby in it. By the time Vivianne was fed and burped, Michael felt a little more confident with the sling.

"I'll still send you the link to the video," Lani said as she put Vivianne in the car seat and strapped her in. "Just in case you need to review it."

Michael glanced up at the clock on the wall. "I'm sorry I kept you longer than you were prepared to stay."

Lani waved her hand in the air. "Don't worry about it."

"Well, thank you. *Again.*"

She didn't dismiss his thanks, just smiled at him and said, "You're welcome. Anytime."

After she had helped him carry the baby and all her luggage out to the truck, Lani left the shop. Michael felt a little bereft once she was gone, but he pushed the feeling aside.

For some reason, he'd assumed he'd be able to make it through his life without developing any feelings for a woman. Why would a relationship hold any appeal for him when the most significant relationship he'd seen growing up had been horrible? Clearly, he'd been woefully naïve about relationships. All it had taken to plant a seed of thought in his mind was meeting a woman who, without even trying, drew him to her.

Michael wasn't sure what to do about the feelings that were growing in his heart for Lani. But realistically, he had way too much on his plate to even consider a romantic relationship right then.

Friendship was all he could offer Lani, and in all likelihood, it was all she wanted anyway.

CHAPTER FIFTEEN

It had been a couple of weeks since Michael had met with the lawyer, and Lani was glad that things in the shop had settled down. She still hadn't seen anything of Taylor, and it was only the orders that continued to appear in the binder that let her know the woman was around. From what Michael had said, Taylor was also doing the flower order pickup since there was no way he could do it with the baby.

Michael had found a babysitter, so he was back at work. Unfortunately, Lani wasn't seeing as much of him as she had before Vivianne had arrived on the scene. Every couple of days, however, he'd stop by the shop on the way to the babysitter's.

Lani enjoyed the opportunity to see both him and the baby. Their visits were definitely bright spots in her days, while the darkest part continued to be her daily interaction with her father. He was wearing on her, leaving her spirits extremely low as she walked home from his house each night. The only thing that buoyed her back up again was the prospect of going to work at the shop—the Reeds', not her own—and the possibility of seeing Michael and Vivianne.

Though she knew she needed to, Lani had still made no other move to change the direction of her life. Her big decision had been to apply for a job at the Reeds' shop, then she'd kind of stalled out. She continued to paint her watercolor flowers and was selling a few of them here and there. Unfortunately, not enough to make a substantial difference to the income of her own shop.

But what was she supposed to do going forward? Her aunt and grandma phoned her regularly, encouraging her and reminding her that she'd always have a home with them. Nina continued to encourage her to return to Hawaii where her old job was available to her.

But where she'd once stayed in New Hope out of respect to her mom's memory, now there were a couple more reasons she stayed.

Michael and Vivianne.

Being able to arrange flowers at the Reeds' shop.

But were those reasons really enough to keep her there?

Maybe if she felt like Michael still needed her with Vivianne, but he was clearly taking it all in stride. He may have had doubts about his ability to take care of a baby, but with support, he seemed to be flourishing.

When he appeared around eight that morning with baby Vivianne, Lani felt her heart lighten, and the idea of leaving New Hope wasn't quite so appealing.

"How're you two doing this morning?" she asked as she wiped her hands on a cloth.

"We had a bit of a night," Michael said, and she could see the evidence of it on his face. "But we survived."

Lani moved to look at Vivianne, where she slept in the car seat. It was amazing to see how much she'd changed, even in just two and a half weeks. "You need to let your daddy sleep, Vivi. And you need sleep to grow."

"Maybe she'll listen to you because she certainly doesn't listen to me." Michael yawned loudly as he made his way to the coffee machine. "I need a caffeine IV today. Too bad that's not conducive to what's on the schedule today."

"You need a thermos," Lani said as she watched him. "Not just that travel mug."

"That's probably a good idea. Used to be the travel mug was enough, but that's not the case anymore."

"Do you not have a coffee machine at home?" she asked.

Michael turned and grinned as he screwed the lid on the mug. "Do you think I only drink coffee here?"

"I have wondered."

He chuckled, and for a moment, the tiredness eased from his features. "Believe me, the coffee I drink here is usually not my first cup of the day."

"You're addicted."

Michael shrugged but didn't deny it. "I've never been a great sleeper—even before Vivi showed up. Often caffeine is what gets me through the day. I will say, however, that even though I don't sleep great, before Vivi, once I managed to fall asleep, I usually stayed that way for more than just a couple of hours."

Lani felt for him, dealing with so much on his own. "Well, hopefully, the caffeine keeps you going today."

"I hope so too," he said with a lift of the travel mug. "And now, I must get going. Still gotta drop the princess off."

As Lani watched them leave, she found herself wishing she could offer to go and cook him supper, but it wouldn't work because of her schedule with her dad. Maybe she should expand her weekly cooking to include enough food for Michael. She could give him meals to put in his freezer for the week, so all he'd have to do was pull them out and heat them up.

People made food for new parents, didn't they?

By the time she left the shop for the day, Lani had decided she would go ahead with the plan. The challenge was that she wasn't sure Michael would like the same menu over and over like her dad did. She didn't exactly enjoy it either, so maybe she'd swap out a couple of items each week for both her and Michael's meals.

She was in the back of the shop, working on a watercolor when the bell over the door at the front chimed. Setting aside her brush, Lani went to see who was there.

"Hi, Lani."

Seeing Sarah McNamara in her shop caught her off-guard. It wasn't often the woman stopped by, and when she did, Lani wasn't sure what to make of it. While they'd gone to school together, they had certainly never moved in the same circles.

Sarah had been an outgoing cheerleader while Lani had been more reserved, devoting any free time she had to the study of flowers. After school and weekends had been spent hanging out with her mom at the shop. And since they hadn't attended the same church, they hadn't even connected there.

Still, the woman had only ever been friendly to her.

"Hi, Sarah."

Sarah headed straight for where Lani stood at the counter. "How are you doing?"

"I'm fine," Lani said, though she was sure Sarah was hoping for a less surface answer. The truth was, she *was* doing fine...most of the time. "How about you?"

"Well, life has picked up speed a bit since my exhibit last October. I've had lots of interest in my work, which is nice, but it's also a bit daunting."

"I'm sure that's true," Lani said, though she really had no idea what that would be like.

"Also." She lifted her left hand and wiggled her fingers as a beaming smile curved her lips. "I'm engaged."

"Congratulations!" Lani hoped that her level of enthusiasm was appropriate. She really did mean it, but there was a pang of wistfulness underneath it all.

"Thank you." With her face still glowing with happiness, Sarah said, "I want to order some flowers for an engagement dinner we're having."

"What kind were you thinking of?" Lani walked around the counter. "Whatever I don't have on hand, I can quickly order in."

They discussed different options and colors for several minutes before Lani showed her some pictures of arrangements that would work as Sarah described what she wanted.

"When did you need the arrangements?" Lani asked once she'd taken down all the information about the particular flowers Sarah wanted.

"The dinner is next weekend."

Lani could work with a week and a half. She appreciated that Sarah showed up every once in a while to give her some business and that her orders were similar to those she worked on at the Reeds' shop.

"Hey," Sarah said after everything was finalized. "Would you be interested in joining a group of us who get together to hike and have a Bible study on Sunday nights?"

The invitation was so similar to the one that Michael had extended to her, that it confirmed what she'd thought then—that she was likely to know people at Michael's study. Unfortunately, her response was going to have to be the same for Sarah as it had been for Michael.

"I'm afraid I can't," she said. "I use Sunday nights to prepare food for the week for my dad. It's the only day I really have time to do it."

"Well, if you ever do have a free Sunday evening, give me a call. We'd love to have you join us."

"Thank you for the invitation. I really appreciate it."

"Anytime." Sarah gave her a quick hug, and for a moment, Lani froze.

Since returning to New Hope, she could count on one hand, not including her thumb and a couple of fingers, the number of times she'd been hugged. Her dad might not have hugged her much when she'd been growing up, but her mom had definitely made up for that lack. And her mom's family in Hawaii had also been affectionate and generous with their hugs.

She missed the hugs, and receiving one from Sarah just reinforced the lack of physical affection in her life. Dwelling on that thought, however, would only bring her down further, and she didn't want that.

"Thanks for coming by," Lani said as she walked with Sarah to the door. "See you next week."

Sarah gave her a quick wave and a smile then left the shop. As Lani watched her walk to her car, she wished she could have accepted Sarah's invitation. It would have been nice to do something outside of the shop. But in doing so, she would run the risk of losing what she had with Michael and the shop. Right then, that was more important than reconnecting with Sarah.

She had just closed the shop and was starting to prep her dad's supper when her phone rang. When she saw Michael's name on the screen, she smiled and answered it.

"Michael?"

"Uh, no." The voice on the other end was male, but definitely not Michael's. "My name is Ryker. I work for Michael."

"What's wrong?" Lani asked, sinking down onto a chair at her dining table. "What happened to Michael?"

"He had an accident at work this afternoon."

"Is he okay?" Even as she asked the question, she knew he wasn't. If he was okay, *he* would be the one calling her, not Ryker.

"He has a compound fracture to the lower part of his leg. They managed to get the bleeding stopped, but he will likely have to have surgery to repair it."

Lani's heart sank. "What about Vivianne?"

"That's why I'm calling. Michael asked me to get hold of you to see if you could pick Vivianne up from the babysitter and stay with her tonight."

"Of course." Thinking quickly, she got up and grabbed her dad's supper and put it in the bag to take it to his place, then went to her bedroom to pack a bag. "I just have to do one thing, and then I'll go pick her up. Will that be okay with the babysitter?"

"I'll let her know you'll be a little late."

"Is Michael at the hospital in Everett?" Lani asked, already knowing she'd be going to see him the next day.

"Yes. He's still in the emergency room, but he's a little out of it because of the pain meds they gave him."

"Please keep me up to date on what's going," Lani said.

"I will. He'll be relieved to hear you're able to take care of Vivianne. He was quite worried about that. It was all he kept talking about as he waited for the ambulance. I would have called sooner, but we forgot to grab his phone from his truck. One of the guys had driven it back to his place, so I had to get him to go back and grab the phone for me."

With her overnight bag over her shoulder, Lani grabbed her purse and keys along with the bag of food for her dad then left her place. "Okay. How do I get into his place?"

"He has a code for his door," Ryker said, then gave her the number. "That will get you into the house."

As she climbed into her car and started it up, she said, "Has anyone let Taylor know?"

Ryker sighed. "I phoned her before I called you to see if she'd be willing to watch Vivianne, but she didn't answer her phone. I left a message, but from things Michael has said lately, I doubt she'll call back."

Lani wished that she was surprised by the news, but she wasn't. "Okay. Well, it's not a problem for me to watch Vivianne, especially if the sitter is still willing to watch her during the day."

"I'm sure she will be. At least for the rest of the week. I'm not sure about Saturday."

"I'll ask her when I pick Vivianne up. It's not a big deal if she can't."

"I don't know how long Michael will be in the hospital." Ryker sighed. "It looked like a pretty bad break."

"Tell him not to worry. Vivianne will be taken care of."

"Thanks, Lani. I'll let him know."

"Okay, I just need to drop something off at my dad's, then I'll head over to the babysitter's. I should be there in twenty minutes or so."

After hanging up, Lani pulled her car to a stop in front of her dad's house. She got out, hoping that he wasn't going to argue with her that day. That was the last thing she needed.

"Hi, Dad," she said as she walked into the house.

He grunted in response, which was just fine by her. Moving quickly, she went to the kitchen and put his food on a plate and heated it up in the microwave. When it was done, she carried it with his drink to put on his tray.

Without looking away from the television, he pulled the mobile tray closer and picked up his fork.

"Do you need anything else, Dad?" she asked, eager to be on her way.

"Nope."

"Then I'll see you tomorrow."

He gave no response, so she returned to the kitchen to gather her bag and empty containers. She said goodbye as she walked past the living room but didn't hang around to hear if he responded.

When she reached the babysitter's small house not far from her dad's place, a slender woman answered the door. "Are you Lani?"

"Yes. And you're Sophia?"

"I am. Please come in."

"Sorry I'm a little late to pick up Vivianne."

"Is Michael okay?" Concern shone from the woman's eyes.

Lani wasn't sure what Michael wanted her to know, so she tried to keep it vague. "He had a bit of an accident at work and asked me to pick Vivianne up for him."

"Oh. I hope he's okay."

"I'm sure he'll be fine." Lani noticed a little boy peeking out from behind his mom and smiled at him. "I'm going to be helping him out with dropping off and picking up Vivianne for a few days."

"Okay."

"I was wondering, though, if it would be okay for me to drop her off and pick her up a little later."

"What times were you thinking?"

"I'll probably be by with her around ten-fifteen and then pick her up around this time or just a little later. Will that be okay?"

The woman nodded. "That's fine."

"I guess I'd better get going," Lani said, not wanting to linger in the woman's home.

Thankfully, Sophia had the diaper bag ready to go, so she just had to put the baby in the car seat.

"She ate about an hour ago," Sophia said as she walked Lani to the door.

"Thank you. I'll see you tomorrow."

"Tell Michael that I hope he's okay."

"I will."

After securing Vivianne's car seat in the back of her car, Lani headed for Michael's place. Once she got there, she used the code Ryker had given her to let herself into the home.

As she stepped inside, Wolfie came to greet her. She let him out, then glanced around as she set the car seat on the table. The place was a little messier than the last time she'd been there—no doubt the result of Michael working all day and then taking care of a newborn all night.

"Well, sweetie, you've got me tonight," Lani said as she unbuckled Vivianne and lifted her from the car seat. "But we'll go see your daddy tomorrow."

Cradling Vivianne close, she walked to the baby's room to see if there was a bed for her. If she recalled correctly, there had been one in there, but it hadn't been made. Sure enough, the bed was there, pushed into the corner of the room, but aside from a couple of pillows, it was bare.

She checked the closet in the hallway and found the bedding she needed. Since Vivianne was still okay, she laid her on the change table, knowing she'd be protected by the raised edges and made the bed. Once that was done, she went into Michael's room and quickly grabbed the bassinette that she knew he used for Vivianne at night.

She put it into place next to the bed, then picked Vivianne up and went back out to the kitchen. Since she hadn't eaten yet, she was starving, so she raided Michael's fridge and cupboards. Once again, the fridge and freezer were quite bare, which meant she had to settle for a bowl of soup and some toast.

By the time she was done eating, Vivianne had started to fuss. Lani got a bottle ready then sat down in the recliner to feed her. It felt strange to be there without Michael, but she was so glad that he'd asked for her help with Vivianne.

She had no idea what lay ahead once Michael was out of the hospital, but she was quite certain he wouldn't be able to handle Vivianne on his own. Crutches and a baby didn't seem like a very good mix.

Lani just hoped that this accident wouldn't impact his attempts to adopt Vivianne. He had been granted temporary guardianship of her, but there were still a lot of hurdles for him to overcome.

Would he be able to get over them with a broken leg? And how could she help him?

CHAPTER SIXTEEN

Michael stared out the window of the hospital, but he wasn't looking at the view. It had been a tough few days, and there didn't appear to be an end in sight. He was going home, which he supposed was a good thing, but his injury had complicated so many things.

"Ready to go, man?" Ryker asked as he walked into the room.

Michael glanced over at him. "Ready as I'll ever be."

"Excellent." Ryker stood with his hands on his hips, his eyes narrowing as he looked at Michael. "Stop worrying."

Michael let out a huff. "Easy for you to say."

"You're right. It *is* easy for me to say, but we've got everything sorted out."

"Not everything." Michael was struggling on so many levels, and he didn't know where to focus first.

Lani had taken over Vivianne's care. Ryker was helping with her, too, and with Wolfie, in addition to stepping up to take over the business. The injury would have been tolerable if he'd still had Taylor with him, but she hadn't even deigned to return any of the calls he and Ryker had made to her.

He'd had plenty of time to think during the past several days as he'd had surgery and begun the recovery process. Now he was stuck with a frame around his leg while he waited for the wound to heal enough for a cast to be applied. He was going to be on crutches for the foreseeable future.

And he might not know much about the medical side of things, but one thing he knew with one hundred percent certainty was that handling babies while on crutches wouldn't work. There was no way he could care for Vivianne on his own. Just when he'd felt like he was getting a handle on his new routine, yet another curveball had come his way.

His first thought when he'd heard how bad his injury was, had been how he was going to care for Vivianne.

When Lani had come to the hospital with Vivianne to visit, she'd assured him that she'd be able to help him. She and Ryker had discussed the situation, and together, they came up with a plan.

Lani would keep Vivianne with her at night, then take her to the babysitter in the morning. Michael was a little uneasy about that part of the plan, even though he completely trusted Lani. Though he couldn't care for Vivianne like he wanted to, he wasn't sure he wanted her that far away from him. But what option did he have?

He couldn't afford to pay someone to stay with him indefinitely, and as Pastor Evans had pointed out, having Lani stay with him would not be proper as such an arrangement would surely give rise to inappropriate gossip which Michael wanted no part of. Plus, he hadn't felt it was fair to ask Lani to uproot her life and move out of her home when she could care for Vivianne there.

Ryker had offered to spend nights to help care for Vivianne, but Michael knew that his accident had been in part because he'd been exhausted and thus not as focused as he should have been. He didn't need Ryker to also be exhausted while he was trying to do Michael's job as well as his own.

So that left him with two options. Pay money he didn't really have on a nanny or allow Lani to take Vivianne home with her.

It had been a hard decision to make, made easier only because he knew Lani would take good care of Vivianne. And while he couldn't pay her as much as a nanny might have cost, he *was* going to pay her. She was going to be dealing with interrupted nights, so hopefully, some compensation would help to offset that.

"It's all planned," Ryker said for probably the hundredth time as he gave him a light thump on his shoulder. "We'll get you through this."

He'd told his friends about Vivianne a couple weeks ago, and he'd let Eli know about his accident. The man had offered his help, but Michael hadn't taken him up on that. None of his other friends knew the business or that much about babies, for that matter.

They'd all made that pretty clear when they'd come to visit him and Vivianne, bearing plenty of gifts, but not much advice. Not the way Ryker and Lani had. His friends had other roles in his life, but in this situation, Ryker and Lani were definitely the best choices to help with Vivianne and the business.

"Let's head out," Ryker said once the nurse had let Michael know he was good to go.

The sun was shining as they left the hospital, and while that could be a sign that things were looking up, Michael kind of scoffed at the idea. It wasn't as if things could get much worse.

The drive back to his place passed without conversation, just Ryker's radio playing classical rock. Since it was Monday, Vivianne was with the babysitter, and Ryker would be picking her up later. Lani would be coming to his place after supper sometime.

That was the schedule they'd worked out. Each morning, Lani would take Vivianne with her to work at the shop, then she'd drop her off at Sophia's after her shift so she could take care of the rest of her day. Ryker would pick Vivianne up from the babysitter, when he was done work, and then he'd stay and have supper with Michael until Lani showed up.

Michael felt like he was inconveniencing them, and if it had just been him, he would have found a way to deal with everything on his own. However, with Vivianne in the equation, he didn't have a choice but to accept their help.

"I'll let you get settled while I go grab some supper and the baby," Ryker said after helping get Michael into the house. "Any requests?"

They didn't have many options in New Hope at the moment, aside from the restaurant, the bakery, and a pizza shop. "I'm happy with whatever you choose."

"Takeout burgers from *Norma's*?"

"Sounds good to me."

Once Ryker had left, Michael maneuvered his way over to his recliner and sat down. The therapist had told him to elevate his injured leg to keep the swelling under control, so he didn't feel too guilty about raising the footrest and reclining back. The pain wasn't as bad as it had been during the first couple of days post accident, but it still ached.

He hadn't meant to fall asleep, but given how poorly he'd slept in the hospital, it wasn't too surprising. Ryker's return had him blinking awake.

"Looks who's home, Vivianne," Ryker said as he brought the car seat over to where Michael sat. "Do you want to hold her?"

"Yes," Michael said quickly. There wasn't much he could do for Vivianne right then other than hold her.

Ryker made easy work of undoing her straps, then carefully lifted her out of the seat. When he placed her in his arms, Michael let out a long breath. He'd held her when Lani had brought her to visit in the hospital, but this was different. This was home, where they both belonged.

"Sophia said she might be hungry," Ryker said. "Do you want to eat first or feed her first."

"Let me feed her first," Michael said.

"Sounds good. I'll heat your food up when you're ready for it."

It didn't take too long for her to suck back the bottle and then Michael burped her. It was a pleasure to be able to do that much for her.

As they ate their supper, they talked about the week ahead. Since the accident, Ryker had continued to operate the landscape crew, tackling the jobs they'd already had lined up. As soon as he could, Michael planned to visit the job sites, just to keep in touch. If there was one good thing about his injury, it was that his left leg had been broken, which meant he could still drive his truck.

It was around eight when he heard a vehicle approaching the house. He found himself looking forward to seeing Lani. Though he wanted to chat with her for a bit, he wasn't sure how much longer he was going to last. The few minutes he'd napped earlier had only whetted his body's appetite for more sleep.

Ryker let Lani in and stayed for a few more minutes before saying goodnight and leaving.

"How's the leg feeling?" Lani asked as she sat down on the couch.

Vivianne was currently lying on his lap, her arms waving in the air. "It's letting me know it's there and not happy about its current situation."

Lani gave him a sympathetic frown. "It is better, though, right?"

Michael nodded. "Definitely moving in the right direction, I think."

"That's good." She glanced around the room. "Is there anything you need me to do?"

"Just take care of Vivi. They had me practice walking with crutches and getting in and out of bed before I left the hospital, so I think I'll be okay on my own."

She tilted her head. "Are you okay with the schedule that Ryker and I worked out?"

"I wish I didn't have to rely on you guys like this, but yes, I'm fine with the schedule. But if you need to switch it up, just let me know, and we'll work something out."

"My life is nothing if not predictable most the time, so I think it should be fine."

"Everything at the shop's been okay?"

"As far as I can tell. I have a few orders each day to work on. Some days there are more than others." She hesitated. "Have you heard from Taylor?"

Michael scowled. "Nope, and I've tried to call her a few times since the accident, but no answer."

"I'm sorry, Michael," Lani said, her gaze soft and sympathetic.

"I just wish I understood why. She hasn't always been this way. I never would have thought I'd have to rely on friends over family, not after how close we've always been."

"Is she your only sibling?"

Michael felt his heart clench. "We had an older half-brother, but he was killed in action in Afghanistan when I was eleven years old."

"How old was he?"

"Twenty-one. His mom had passed away when he was eight, then our dad married my mom when he was nine. I was born a year later, and Taylor came along when I was four."

"I'm an only child," Lani said. "Though I'm not sure why. When I asked my mom about having a brother or sister when I was a kid, she would tell me to pray about it. The couple of times I asked about it when I was an adult, she just said the time had never been right. Whatever that meant. I never pushed the topic as it didn't seem to be something she wanted to talk about."

Michael rarely thought much about Davis anymore. He had conflicted feelings about the guy—even now when he'd been gone twenty-plus years. With such an age gap between them, they'd never really been in the same place to have anything in common. Unfortunately, that meant he hadn't really known his older half-brother.

The other unfortunate part of their relationship was that their father had held Davis up as an example and a standard that the man—and Michael—knew he'd never reach. Whether it was schoolwork or sports, Michael struggled in ways Davis never had, leaving him a high school drop out while his brother was a hero, killed in service to their country.

Thankfully, Taylor was more like Davis, though she was the wrong gender for their father to be proud of her accomplishments. Their dad had never shown any sort of interest in anything she did. Michael, on the other hand, had garnered plenty of his dad's attention—always negative—when he failed a class or faltered in some other way—which had happened frequently.

After Davis was killed, his father hadn't even tried to be nice anymore. Not that he'd been a nice man to start with, but he'd been more abrasive and disapproving than mean. After they received the news about Davis, however, he'd turned abusive. It had been a horrible time in Michael's life, and one he didn't much like to think about.

"Right now, I'm thinking maybe being an only child wouldn't be a bad thing," Michael said with a humorless laugh.

"Ah, but then you wouldn't have Vivianne," Lani said. "And I don't think you'd want that."

No, he wouldn't. His gaze dropped to where Vivianne lay on his lap. For all the complications she'd brought to his life in the short time she'd been with him, he wasn't prepared to give her up. She already meant the world to him, which was why it was killing him to think about her spending so much of her time apart from him.

"Are you sure you're okay with me taking her for the nights?" Lani asked, her tone gentle. It was as if she could read his mind—which was a little disconcerting.

Michael looked up, seeing the compassion and concern on Lani's face. "I'm not, but only because I don't want her to be away from me. Of course, she's already been away from me for the past several days." He paused. "I trust you explicitly. If I didn't, this wouldn't be happening."

"I'm happy to be able to help you out."

"I will owe you big-time after this. Honestly, I owe you big-time already for all your help in the shop."

Lani's expression turned serious, and her gaze dropped for a moment. "Helping with the shop and Vivianne has... Well, it's been good for me. I've had to focus on other things in my life for the last couple of years that haven't really brought me much joy. I've felt trapped by circumstances beyond my control."

When she hesitated, emotion clouding her expression, Michael searched for the words to comfort her. Fear of saying the wrong thing kept him quiet because he didn't want her to stop sharing.

"Being able to create the arrangements at your shop lets me, for just a few hours each day, do something I enjoy without any other responsibilities weighing me down. And now, helping you with Vivianne has also given me something to focus on, and I'm very grateful for that. So don't feel like you're taking advantage of me or anything like that because I'm getting something out of all of this too."

Michael was glad to hear that, though he had to admit he was now more curious than ever. Lani was unlike any woman he'd known—though realistically, it wasn't as if he'd taken the time to get to know many women. Those he saw regularly were mostly attached to his male friends, so he kind of knew them more by default. Because of that, he wouldn't exactly consider them friends the way he would Lani. For sure, he wouldn't feel as at ease leaving Vivianne with any of them as he felt about Lani.

"Though I'm relieved to hear that, I still want you to know that I really do appreciate everything."

She smiled at him then, the seriousness slipping away. "Just be sure and let me know if there's anything else you need help with."

"I think you have quite a lot on your plate already, but I'll keep that in mind." He looked again at Vivianne as she let out a small squawk. "I'd offer to help you take her things to your car, but clearly, I'm useless."

"It's fine," Lani said. "Once you agreed for me to take her to my place at night, I packed up what I thought I'd need. The bassinette, some formula, and bottles—though I did leave some for when she's here with you and Ryker—some clothes, and the sling. Oh, and diapers. A couple packages of those."

"I set up an account to do grocery pick-ups instead of having to go out to shop, so if you need stuff, let me know, and I can place an order, and maybe you or Ryker could pick it up."

"I'm sure that would work."

Michael lifted Vivianne up into his arms, cradling her close to his chest. She gazed up at him with her wide eyes, and he found himself looking forward to the moment she'd look at him and smile. He was sure that she would just slay him with that smile, and he couldn't wait.

He heard movement in the kitchen and looked over to see Lani opening the fridge and cupboards. "What are you looking for?"

"To see if you have healthy food to eat," she said without turning around. "To help your leg heal."

"Oh. Well, good luck with that search."

He heard Lani give an audible sigh. "Okay. Here's how that's going to work." She came around to stand in front of him and crossed her arms, looking for all the world like she wasn't going to take any argument from him. "I'll bring you over food each evening when I pick Vivianne up. All you'll have to do is heat it up the next day, or if you want, you could wait to eat your dinner until I show up with the food."

"You don't have to do that," Michael said, though he was incredibly overwhelmed that she was willing to do yet one more thing for him.

"I'm already making a meal each night, so I'll just bring you the leftovers."

"When you put it that way..." Michael said with a grin.

"I'm not a pro cook by any stretch of the imagination, but I haven't killed anyone yet."

"That's definitely a good thing to know, though there's a first time for everything."

"Ha." She gave him a light whack on his shoulder. "Just for that, I won't bring you any dessert."

Michael sighed. "Given how inactive I'm going to be for the next little while, that's probably not a bad decision."

"So maybe we'll go with dessert every few days instead of every day."

"I like that idea."

Lani settled back on the couch. "Are you able to handle everything else you need to do for yourself?"

"I think so," Michael said. "They wouldn't let me leave until they knew I could take care of myself. Not looking forward to sleeping with this thing on, though."

"Do you have follow-up appointments?"

"Yep. Physio, and the doctor also wants to check on my pin sites to make sure I'm cleaning them properly."

"How exactly did it happen?" Lani asked, then added, "If you don't mind talking about it."

"I don't mind. But to be honest, I don't have a clear memory of it. One minute I was over halfway up the tree we were prepping for removal, the next minute I was hanging upside down, my leg tangled in the ropes at an awkward and painful angle." He frowned. "I was tired that day, and I should have let someone else do that climb, but it was dangerous, and I don't like asking others to do that kind of work when I'm able to."

"I guess you have no choice but to trust them now, huh?"

Michael sighed. "Yep. Thankfully, I'll still be able to visit the worksites in a supervisory capacity."

"I really admire you."

Michael's brows rose even as heat suffused his cheeks. Those were words he had rarely heard in his life. "Uh...why's that?"

"In the time I've known you, you've had some nasty curveballs thrown at you, and each time, you've stepped to the plate and dealt with them. I know you've not been happy with some of the things that have transpired, but you've stepped up anyway."

"Don't give me too much credit," Michael said. "You've heard Taylor and me fight."

"I have, but you didn't seem to hold on to the anger that erupted during the fight. At least, not that I saw. I've been around people who get mad, and then hang onto that anger and use it as an excuse to lash out at others, even those who might not be part of the problem. I really appreciate that you didn't do that."

"I never would have gotten angry with you. What's been happening is between Taylor and me. I might vent about it, but I hope I'd never lash out at anyone else."

"Well, you haven't lashed out at me," she assured him. "And you can't know how much I appreciate that."

"You can always tell me if I do something that bothers you," Michael said. "Taylor was really good at telling me when I needed to chill out."

He sighed as he thought of his sister. Her absence in his life felt like a gaping hole. Was he just using Lani to fill that hole? As soon as he thought it, he dismissed the idea. Taylor and Lani couldn't be more different. Lani was stepping up in a way that Taylor never would have for anyone, even her brother. She had a giving spirit that he truly admired.

It was just one of the many things he was coming to admire and appreciate about her. And that was the main reason he'd agreed to her taking Vivianne to her place rather than staying there with him.

It was hard to ignore his growing attraction to her, and having her there would have felt a little bit too much like playing house. Making him consider things that he'd never thought he'd want for himself.

No, it was definitely for the best that he kept what distance he could between them.

CHAPTER SEVENTEEN

Lani finished packing the diaper bag, then picked Vivianne up off the bed and strapped her into her car seat. She fussed a little, but once she found her fist to chew on, she settled down.

Like the baby, Lani was feeling a little out of sorts that morning too. They'd had an up and down night, which wasn't too unexpected. Though Vivianne had started to sleep longer stretches, that schedule had been abandoned the night before.

"Okay, sweetie. Let's go help your daddy out."

She carefully carried the car seat and diaper bag down to her car. It was a chilly morning, so she was glad she'd draped a blanket over the car seat to protect Vivianne from the cold.

Instead of driving to the shop like she usually did, Lani turned her car in the direction of Michael's place. She was getting a later start to her day because she wasn't going to be working in the shop that morning.

Michael had asked her to be present for the home study since she was so involved with Vivianne's care at the moment. He'd said he wanted to show the social worker that he was willing to do whatever it took to get the best care for the baby.

"Good morning," she said a short time later as Michael let her into the trailer.

He wore a pair of black sweatpants that had one leg cut off at the knee to accommodate the leg frame and a long sleeve light blue T-shirt. After a couple of weeks of being on the crutches, he was much more comfortable on them, moving easily around his home.

"Thanks for coming," he said as he made his way to the table where a mug sat. "Did you sleep okay last night?"

Lani set the car seat on the table in front of him and lowered the handle then greeted Wolfie where he sat patiently waiting for some attention. "Vivianne was up a few times. I think she's going through a growth spurt or something because she's been wanting to eat more."

Michael leaned forward and undid her straps before lifting her out. "Are you keeping Lani up, Vivi? That's not good."

Lani removed the car seat from the table, watching as Michael cuddled her close. "She's really a good baby, you know. Seems very easygoing."

"Considering the circumstances of her birth, and the mood Taylor seemed to be in most of the time she was carrying her, she does seem amazingly placid."

"It can change, but I'm hoping, for your sake, that she stays that way. My cousin's baby was colicky, and wow, that was rough for them. Several of us in the family would take turns going over to their place to give them a break."

"What makes a baby colicky?" Michael asked. "Is there anything we can do to stop her from ending up like that?"

Lani shrugged. "From what I understand, there's not one thing that triggers colic. I think it is something in a baby's digestive system, a sensitivity to something in the formula sometimes."

Michael frowned as he gazed down at Vivianne. "So we might have to change formulas?"

"It's possible, but don't worry about it until it happens. We'll cross that bridge when we get to it."

"I'm not sure you're aware of this, but I like to have a plan for every eventuality."

Lani laughed. "Oh, I'm aware, but I'm here to tell you not to worry too much about this particular thing. It's possible that even changing the formula wouldn't work, that the colic will just have to run its course. So worrying about it even before we know she has it will only drive you crazy."

"I think I'm already crazy," Michael murmured.

"Then we're there together." Lani leaned back in her chair and tried to stifle a yawn. "I still maintain you're dealing with all these changes better than most people would have."

"I think it's because I have lots of people praying for me," he said, glancing at her before looking back at Vivianne. "Pastor Evans reminded me the other day that everything that has taken me by surprise wasn't a surprise to God. So I'm trying to keep in mind that if God knew what was coming, He's going to see me through it."

Michael's words reminded Lani so much of her mom that she had to blink back tears. Anytime something unexpected would happen—whether good or bad—her mom would just say *God saw that coming even if we didn't.*

"I wish I could say that assurance has helped me not to worry about everything, though." Michael sighed. "Like I'm especially worried about the visit this morning. I'm worried they're not going to think the decisions I've made were the best ones."

Lani hated seeing the worry on his face and wished there was something she could do to lessen that for him. *Please, God, let this go well. Don't let one more thing go wrong in his life.*

It had been a long time since she'd prayed with such intent. She hadn't really been on speaking terms with God since things in her own life had begun to go wrong. Watching Michael take on the struggles in his life by clinging to his faith was a rebuke to her. She knew that Michael would never have wanted it to be that way, but he was affecting her in a good way without even being aware of it.

"At least I have all my friends and Pastor Evans praying right at the interview time, so I'm going to trust that whatever the outcome is, it's God's will, whether I understand it or not."

Lani slipped her hands under her thighs, gripping the edge of the chair. "Will you really be able to accept it that easily?"

After a moment's hesitation, Michael gave a shake of his head. "If I lost her now…"

He bent his head close to Vivianne's, his eyes closing. His large hand cupped the baby's head, his thumb gently rubbing her head.

As she watched him with Vivianne, Lani felt bereft. She was sure that he was praying over the situation, but though there was a longing in her heart to be part of that moment, she knew why he hadn't included her.

In all the time they'd been together, and in all the conversations they'd had, she'd never given him any indication that she was a Christian. Still, she found that she longed for that connection with him.

As she watched them, Lani wished that she could believe that at one time, her own father had cradled her with such love and gentleness. She was so glad that Vivianne had that in her life, but she wished she could have experienced it for herself.

The past year and a half would have been so much easier if her father had been there to support her in her grief in the same way she would have supported him. Instead, his anger was a wall between them that she was too weary to even try to climb.

The sound of an engine's rumble as a vehicle neared the house had Michael lifting his head and staring at the door. Lani felt nerves begin to flutter within her, hoping that she wouldn't be the reason Michael failed to qualify to adopt Vivianne.

"I'll get the door," Lani said as she stood up. "Unless you think you should."

"No. I've already explained that I have a broken leg, so I think you answering it will be understandable."

When the knock came, Lani took a quick breath and blew it out before opening the door. The woman on the other side offered her a friendly smile.

"Hello. Is this Michael Reed's home?"

"It is," Lani said with a smile of her own. "Please come inside."

The woman looked to be in her late forties or early fifties with light brown hair that she wore pulled back in a bun. Her eyes were a warm brown, and the corners crinkled when she smiled. The navy-blue pantsuit she wore would have been boring if not for her blouse that was covered in splashes of vibrant colors.

"I'm Adele Delano," she said once she'd stepped inside the house.

Lani took the hand she offered and gave it a firm shake. "I'm Lani Alexander."

Michael stood by the table, his weight on his good leg, Vivianne in the crook of his left arm. He held out his hand as Adele approached him.

"I'm Michael Reed."

"Such a pleasure to meet you, Michael. And this must be baby Vivianne."

"Yep," Michael said, looking down at Vivianne. "Hopefully she'll wake up in a bit so you can officially meet her."

"That would be good, but if not, that's not a problem." She glanced around the room. "How about we sit down and let you get off that leg."

Lani stepped up to Michael. "I'll take her so you can use your crutches."

He carefully transferred Vivianne into her arms, then grabbed his elbow crutches and made his way to the recliner. Adele followed him and sat down on the end of the couch closest to his chair. Lani waited for him to settle into the recliner, then leaned over and gave Vivianne back to him.

"What a beautiful dog," Adele said.

Lani glanced around to see that Wolfie now sat next to her.

"He's a rescue dog," Michael said. "I got him a few weeks before Vivianne arrived, and he's become quite attached to her. The day Taylor dropped Vivi off, Wolfie laid down next to her car seat and didn't move."

As if to prove his point, once Adele had scratched his ears, Wolfie made his way back to where Michael sat with Vivianne and after a sniff of the baby's head, he laid down next to Michael's feet.

"That's so sweet," Adele said. "And it's good to see that he's so sensitive to her."

Lani was glad that Wolfie wouldn't be a problem. She could understand a pet might be a concern if he had a more aggressive personality, but from the first day Vivianne had arrived he'd been only affectionate and laid back.

"I understand you have to leave around ten," Adele said, turning her attention to Lani. "When I talked to Michael when we were setting up this appointment, he said that he thought I should speak with you as well as him since you've been helping him out a lot with Vivianne. Do you mind if I ask you a few questions?"

"Not at all." Lani hadn't been sure what to expect of the meeting, so she braced herself for some fairly personal questions. She just hoped that she didn't have to share too much. The last thing she wanted was to have to reveal to Michael who she really was in front of a stranger.

"How do you know Michael?" Adele asked after pulling out a notebook and a pen.

"I applied to work at the florist shop run by his sister."

"Vivianne's birth mother?"

"Yes. She hired me to help out a few hours each morning."

"So you're not full-time?"

Lani hesitated just a moment. "No. I have family commitments that prevent me from working for them full-time. Plus, the position was advertised as only part-time to start with. Which was perfect for me."

"What sort of family commitments?"

And here came the questions she wasn't sure about answering. "My mother passed away a couple of years ago, and my father has required care because of debilitating injuries he received in an accident. I've needed to have time available to help him."

"I'm sorry to hear that." Her expression was sympathetic. "Caring for your father hasn't precluded you from helping with the baby?"

Lani shook her head. "I take her with me when I go to the shop in the morning for three hours, then I drop her off at the babysitter's on my way home. Someone else picks her up and brings her here to Michael and stays with him until I show up around seven or so to pick her up."

"And then you have her for the night?"

"Yes."

"You live with your dad?"

"No. He likes his space, so while I do go over to care for him, I have my own place not far from his, which is where Vivianne stays with me."

Adele looked between her and Michael. "Why wouldn't you just stay here with Michael?"

"Since it was my decision, do you mind if I answer that?" Michael asked.

"Not at all."

"I'm a Christian, and as a single man, I was concerned about the message it might send to people if I had a single woman staying here with me at night."

"So you were concerned about the propriety of the situation?"

"Yes. I wouldn't have agreed to have Lani take Vivianne if I hadn't felt I could trust her completely. And from what I've seen, the arrangement seems to be working well. It's not like I would be able to help her with Vivianne at night anyway. I also figured that since she's still a baby, Vivianne wouldn't actually be aware of where she is."

"Do you feel that this has been working, Lani?" Adele asked.

"Absolutely," she said. "I've helped with babies as sort of a night nanny in the past. My cousin had a very colicky baby, so there were nights when I'd stay with her and care for the baby through the night so my cousin could sleep."

"And you don't feel it's impacted your ability to work and do what you have to do during the day?"

Lani shook her head. "I go to bed a little earlier to make up for any interruptions."

Adele made some notes, then said, "Do you currently have a significant other? One who would have access to Vivianne as well?"

"No. I'm single. My last relationship ended a couple of years ago."

"And how does your father feel about you taking care of a baby as well as him?"

"Since I don't live with my father, and Vivianne is either at the babysitter or with Michael in the afternoon and evening when I'm with him, I haven't felt the need to tell him." Lani paused, trying to formulate her response. "He's struggled emotionally with his injuries...I don't think he'd be all that impressed with what I'm doing. But to be honest, I don't really care. I need to take care of Vivianne. It's given me something positive to focus on, and I really enjoy having her with me."

Adele smiled but didn't comment on what Lani had said specifically. She jotted a few things down in her notebook, and Lani hoped that her father wouldn't throw a wrench in this to mess it up for Michael. She'd give up looking after Vivianne if necessary, but she hoped that she didn't have to.

"So how would you describe your relationship with Michael?"

Lani hesitated, her gaze going to Michael for a moment before shifting her attention back to Adele. "Though I was an employee at the shop, I've always kind of felt Michael was more of a friend than a boss. I mean, technically, I report to Taylor, so maybe that helped to make it feel more like a friendship than an employee/employer type of relationship."

"Is that how you see it too, Michael?" Adele asked as she looked over at Michael.

"It is," Michael said. "Things in the shop were in a bit of a turmoil with Taylor going through what seemed to be a very difficult time. We didn't know she was pregnant at the time, and despite the ups and downs, Lani was a very stable influence. Very calming to have around when everything else felt turbulent."

Adele looked back and forth between them a few times before she said, "Are the two of you not interested in a relationship that might offer more stability to each of you and Vivianne?"

Lani forced herself not to look at Michael. She admired him and, if their circumstances had been different, she might have been more interested in pursuing a relationship if he'd expressed a similar desire.

As the silence grew, Adele smiled. "Well, let's just say that there are worse things to build a relationship on than admiration and friendship."

She asked Lani a couple more questions, then after making a few more notes, she smiled at her. "I think that's all for now. Do you mind giving me your phone number in case I have more questions?"

"Not at all. That's fine." Lani gave Adele her number then got up. "I should probably get Vivianne to the babysitter. Or did you need her here still?"

"I think it's okay for you to take her. I'll be back for a visit another time, so I can see her again then."

Lani went to Michael and carefully lifted Vivianne from his arms. Their gazes met as she bent over, and the moment stretched out for several heartbeats before Michael glanced down at Vivianne.

"Thanks for coming by this morning," he said as she straightened up. "I really appreciate it."

"You're welcome. Anytime."

Adele got up and came over as Lani was putting Vivianne in the car seat. "She seems to be a very good little baby."

"She is," Lani agreed as she finished strapping her in then draped the blanket over the handle. "Not really very fussy at all."

"It was nice to meet you." Adele held out her hand once Lani was ready to go. "Thank you for making time in your day to talk with me."

"I'm glad I was able to be here to help and support Michael." She turned her attention to Michael. "I'll see you later."

He nodded, his gaze serious as he watched her. "Drive safe."

As Lani left the house, she once again found herself talking to God, asking Him to let things go well for Michael with Adele. She couldn't imagine what it would do to Michael if he wasn't able to adopt Vivianne. Lani knew that he would feel like he'd failed her if he wasn't able to continue to be part of her life.

She wished she knew more about the process, and what the chances truly were of this not working out in his favor. Would the fact that he didn't have a wife or a serious relationship really count against him? Adele had seemed to almost hint at that, but Lani really hoped that it wasn't that important.

It felt weird to not be driving to the babysitter's from the shop or going into the shop at all. Michael had said he'd take care of letting Taylor know that she wouldn't be going to work that day, so hopefully, Taylor could take care of any orders that were due.

Once she arrived at the babysitter's, Lani got Vivianne's seat out of the car and looped the diaper bag over her shoulder. As she took in the worn and somewhat overgrown look of the small home, she found herself wondering about the woman and child who lived within its walls.

After she rang the doorbell, it was only a matter of seconds before the door opened. Sophia smiled in welcome and stepped back to let Lani into the house.

"Good morning," Lani said as she set the car seat on the carpet.

Though the interior of the house looked as worn as the exterior, it was clean and tidy. She couldn't imagine that Michael would have wanted to leave Vivianne if that hadn't been the case.

"Good morning."

"Vivianne will probably be ready for a bottle when she wakes up. I fed her around seven, and she's been sleeping off and on since then."

"Okay. I'll be ready for that when she wakes up."

The woman's son crept closer and knelt down beside the car seat. He peered at Vivianne but didn't touch her. "Hi, Vivi."

Lani smiled as she watched him, impressed with his gentleness. "I'll see you tomorrow."

After she left the house, Lani found her steps dragging. Normally, she would've been going to her shop, but that day, she had something to do that she absolutely dreaded. It was time for her dad's monthly doctor's appointment. He seemed to prefer that one of the aides drive him, but none had been available, so it had fallen on Lani.

She had a feeling that the main reason her dad didn't want her to go with him was that the doctor might want to share things with her about his care. He didn't seem to remember that as his primary caregiver and the person who organized care for him, the doctor usually called her if there was anything she really needed to know. Her father had given his permission for that early on, but sometimes it seemed he'd forgotten about it.

It had been several months since she'd last received a call about concerns the doctor had for her father. She was glad that his health had stabilized now that he wasn't fighting quite so hard against the things he needed to have a fairly healthy, functioning body despite the paralysis he suffered from the waist down.

Lani just hoped that the news from her father's appointment and from Michael's time with Adele would all be positive. It was hard not to worry about both situations, though admittedly, she wasn't quite as concerned about her dad since his last few appointments had gone well.

Now, if Michael's appointment went well too, she'd indeed be a happy camper.

CHAPTER EIGHTEEN

Michael closed the door, then leaned his forehead against it, feeling absolutely drained. The throbbing behind his eyes threatened to launch into a full-blown headache, which would just be the icing on the cake.

Wolfie rubbed against his good leg as if sensing Michael's distress. With a sigh, he used his crutches to make his way back to the recliner and lowered himself into it. Wolfie stuck close to him then flopped down next to Michael's feet.

It wasn't that Adele had been mean or aggressive in her questions, but it had been a long, long time since he'd had to delve into the things she had asked him about. And some of it, like his recent relationship upheaval with Taylor, was stuff he hadn't wanted to talk about at all.

But he honestly hadn't known if it was his right to decline to answer, and if he did, how that would look in her report. So he'd answered anything and everything she'd tossed at him, to the best of his ability.

The end result was complete emotional exhaustion, which felt physical even though he hadn't done anything more active than get up and down from his recliner.

He would have killed for a cup of coffee, but he didn't have the energy to get up and make one. And so far, that wasn't something he'd managed to train Wolfie to do for him.

Tipping his head back, Michael closed his eyes and let out a long breath, willing the tension to leave his body.

"Hey, buddy."

"Huh?" Michael opened his eyes to find Ryker standing next to his chair, his hand on Michael's shoulder. "What time is it?"

"Just after five."

"Seriously?" Michael let out a groan as he sat forward, grinding the heels of his hands against his eyes. "I conked right out."

"Rough day?"

"Restless night followed by a semi-rough day."

Ryker dropped down and undid the straps of Vivianne's car seat. "How about you hold her for a bit? Did you eat anything today?"

"Not since toast this morning," Michael said, suddenly aware of the gnawing hunger in his stomach.

"Lani still won't be here for a couple more hours." Ryker handed Vivianne to Michael. "Do you want me to make you something?"

"You don't have to do that, man. You already do so much."

"Don't even think of it like that. If you're hungry, let me make you something." Ryker went into the kitchen while Michael cuddled the baby close. "If you don't give me an idea, I'm going to make you whatever I want. And trust me, I'm not the world's best cook."

Michael gave a huff of laughter. "I think even the world's best cook would have a problem creating a meal with what's in my kitchen at the moment. I need to make another grocery run."

"Want some help with that?" Ryker asked. "Either making the order or picking it up?"

Usually, Michael would have brushed aside the offer of help, but he was too tired at that moment. The most stressful of those two was making the order, so he took him up on that.

"I can make you a ham and cheese sandwich," Ryker said. "That's about the best I can do."

"That sounds wonderful, and it will tide me over until Lani gets here." Michael looked down at Vivianne. "Though sooner or later, she's going to get tired of having to feed me and take care of Vivianne."

Ryker scoffed. "I doubt that. From what I've seen, she's been more than happy to help you out."

"Or she's just too nice to brush me off now that I'm in such a tight spot."

"C'mon now, man. Give Lani the benefit of the doubt. I don't think she's that type of person."

"Maybe not, but eventually, it will end up being too much. Neither Vivianne nor I are her responsibility." He recalled her conversation with Adele that morning. "Plus, she has a lot going on in her own life right now."

He'd felt bad that she'd had to reveal that much about herself to a stranger when she hadn't shared that much even with him. And he couldn't bear to think about that moment following Adele's question about the possibility of a relationship between him and Lani. It wasn't that the idea hadn't crossed his mind, but he felt like she could do so much better than him.

"Just don't dismiss something that could be good because of your own fears. You won't know for sure if you don't even give it a chance."

Michael barely managed to suppress the shudder that wanted to rip through him at the idea of opening himself up in that way. It was bad enough that Taylor had turned on him. He'd thought he could always count on her because she was his sister and they'd been through everything together.

What would protect him from heartache when Lani decided to walk away?

Nothing...

His heart was already aching from how his relationship with Taylor had soured, and then there was the potential heartache looming with the uncertainty of the situation with Vivianne. Why on earth would he take on one more thing that, if things went wrong, would pretty much dismantle his heart in the worst possible way?

He might not be the most intelligent guy around, but even he was smart enough to know that wouldn't be a wise decision.

"Here you go," Ryker said as he set a plate and glass on the small table beside Michael's chair. "So tell me how things went today."

Ryker didn't even bother to suggest he take Vivianne from him. Instead, he just made his way to the couch and dropped down on it. Between bites, Michael told him about most of the interview, choosing to leave out the details of what Lani had shared. It wasn't his place to tell anyone about those things.

"I think it sounds like it went well," Ryker said.

"You do?"

"I do." Ryker frowned. "You don't?"

"I guess it was just so exhausting that I struggled to see that as a positive thing."

"These types of things aren't supposed to be a walk in the park, especially not if someone is doing their job well. After all, the well-being of a child is at stake. It's a good thing the woman was so determined to find out everything she could about you."

"It's too bad they don't make everyone go through something like this before they're allowed to procreate. Maybe it would prevent people who shouldn't have kids in the first place from having them."

Ryker sighed. "Yeah, but you and I know that's never gonna happen."

"So, do *you* have a girlfriend?" Michael asked, suddenly aware that Ryker knew a whole lot more about him than he knew about the man.

Ryker's gaze dropped to Vivianne for a moment before he shifted it to the window above the dining room table. "No. No girlfriend."

"Okay. I was just wondering if I needed to have Lani make a special bouquet to give to someone who might be upset about all the time you're having to spend helping me out."

"No need to make a special bouquet."

"Seriously, though," Michael said. "I'm so thankful for all your help. I couldn't have done this without you. From putting in extra time on the job and helping with Vivianne to writing me a reference letter, you've done so much more than you needed to."

"I'm sure that my letter was the least impressive of the ones people wrote for you. I mean, a pastor, a firefighter, and the police chief? I don't rank anywhere near as high in importance as they do."

Michael frowned. "While I won't deny that having them write letters of reference was very beneficial to me being granted guardianship of Vivianne, you've been able to help me in a more hands-on way, which has meant that I didn't lose everything because of this broken leg."

"I'm glad I've been in a position to help," Ryker said. "There's nothing worse than wanting to help but not being able to. I'm glad that's not the case here."

Though Michael sensed there was a story there, he also knew that Ryker likely wouldn't divulge anything since he had been a closed book from the day he'd appeared in response to the ad Michael had posted for landscaping help. Michael had taken one look at the haunted expression on his face and hired him even though he hadn't had any experience.

Over the past couple of years, the haunted look had eased, but the man hadn't ever opened up. What Ryker had done was absorb everything Michael taught him and quickly become a trusted employee

When Vivianne started to fuss, Ryker got up and went to prepare a bottle.

"I think she might need a diaper change as well," Michael said when Ryker handed him the bottle. "Sorry about that."

Ryker chuckled as he took Vivianne from Michael. "Somehow, I kind of think that's one thing you don't miss doing."

Michael watched as Ryker laid a changing pad on the couch and made quick work of the dirty diaper. He brought the baby back to Michael, then threw away the diaper and washed his hands.

As he fed Vivianne, they discussed what had been going on at work. Michael tried to visit at least one worksite a day, but he wasn't able to be as hands-on as he would have liked. Maneuvering around on the uneven ground with crutches wasn't any sort of fun, and the last thing he needed was another injury brought on by his inability to walk with stability.

Michael was surprised by how alert Vivianne was now when she was awake. As she ate, she looked up at him, her eyes wide as she stared at him. Was she confused by the many people who took care of her? Did she know that he was the one fighting to be able to keep her?

He missed caring for her the way he had before breaking his leg. He'd been able to give her a bath, feed and change her, put her down to sleep at night, and get up with her when she'd cried. Now, he was lucky to be able to feed and hold her. Though he supposed it was better the accident had happened now instead of when she was older and more aware, it was still hard to accept.

From the videos he'd watched and the books he'd listened to, bonding was an important thing in these early weeks of a baby's life. Bonding he was missing out on because he couldn't be there for her like he wanted to be. He just hoped that being cared for by four different people didn't mess her up.

By the time Ryker left shortly after Lani had shown up, Michael was feeling rather morose. He really didn't want to send Vivianne home with Lani that night, but he had no choice.

For the first time in his life, he wished he had a wife. Someone who could take up the slack that had resulted from his injury and, at the very least, keep them together as a family.

"You doing okay?" Lani asked, her brows furrowed as she gave Wolfie a little bit of love. "Did the rest of the time with Adele not go well?"

Michael looked up from Vivianne's sweet face. "I really don't know. It was intense, that's for sure. It was like she turned it up one hundred percent once you'd left."

Lani's eyes widened. "I guess that makes sense since you're the one adopting her, but I'm sure it wasn't easy. No one would enjoy having their life delved into to that degree."

"I'm sorry if you felt you had to talk about things you'd rather not." Michael sighed. "I didn't really think about that until we were in the middle of her interrogation of you."

With a laugh, Lani said, "If you think that was an interrogation, you just wait until teenage Vivianne stays out too late one night. Then you'll understand the true meaning of interrogating some-one."

Michael gave a humorless laugh. "Here's hoping she's still around for me to interrogate."

"If they felt she was truly at risk being with you or being in this situation, I doubt they would have left her in your care."

He heard her words, just like he'd heard Ryker's earlier. But for some reason, Michael just couldn't push aside the worry that some of the things he'd revealed to Adele would ultimately count against him. Though Lani and Ryker knew about his inability to read and some about his growing up years, they didn't know how really horrible those years had been.

He wasn't sure if Adele would consider the potential of him turning into his father as being too great a risk for him to be re-sponsible for a tiny baby. Or that she would be concerned that he'd lacked a good role model for a father.

"Did she say anything about what you might need to work on?" Lani asked. "I mean, would they even mention that while interviewing you?"

"I don't know," Michael said. "She didn't say if there was anything that concerned her."

Lani pulled her legs up, hooking her heels on the edge of the couch, and wrapped her arms around her knees. "Maybe you need to call your pastor? He might be able to encourage you."

Michael knew Lani was right. But honestly, right then, he wasn't sure he could handle someone else trying to tell him he was basically overreacting. Maybe a good night's sleep would help him have a better perspective.

The most ridiculous part of it all was that the one person he wanted to confide in most of all because she'd understand completely why he was struggling the way he was, was Taylor. Only she was part of the reason he was in this situation, and she still hadn't contacted him following his accident. Considering it had been a couple of weeks already, he wasn't holding his breath.

He knew the only reason she was still in the area was because her lawyer had told her it was important that she wait until things had been settled for Michael and Vivianne before she left town. Michael was reasonably sure that Taylor would just give Vivianne up to someone already approved for adoption if it didn't work out for him to adopt her.

The thing was, Michael knew that regardless of the outcome, she was leaving him and the shop. Well, she'd already left *him*, but her leaving the shop was just around the corner. He needed to consider some options and decide where to go with the business once Taylor left.

If only Lani was able to work full-time at the shop. He'd absolutely feel confident letting her take over.

"Let me make you some supper," Lani said. "Sorry, but it's meatloaf again."

"Oh, don't ever apologize for bringing me meatloaf. I could eat that every day of the week."

"You and my dad," she said with a shake of her head. "That's his favorite meal, I think." As she got to her feet, she said, "Do you need a bottle for Vivianne?"

"No. Ryker got me one earlier." He looked down to see Vivianne still awake on his lap. "She's staying awake longer and longer, isn't she?"

"Yep. She is." She lifted a couple of containers from the insulated bag she used for carrying his food each night. "And the good thing about her staying awake more is that she's sleeping slightly longer stretches at night as well. I mean, we're not anywhere near eight full hours, but it's more like three hours in a stretch now instead of two."

"I'm glad to hear that. Hopefully it means you're getting more sleep too."

"It does." She slid a plate into the microwave. "By the time you're back to doing nights, she'll be sleeping close to four hours or more, I bet. I'm going to miss having the little princess hanging out with me in the evenings."

"Well, you know where we live. Feel free to visit whenever."

Lani set the plate on a TV tray and brought it over to him. "Up to trying to eat one-handed, or do you want me to hold her?"

"Let me give it a try, and if it doesn't work, you can take her."

Thankfully, she wasn't old enough to try to grab for his fork or kick the TV tray. With her tucked into his left elbow, he was able to eat with his right hand without having to give her over to Lani just yet.

By the time he was done eating, Vivianne was starting to fuss a bit. Though he hated to surrender her to Lani, he knew Lani had a bit of schedule for her, and she'd probably prefer to be home before feeding her and getting her ready for bed.

He held Vivianne close for a moment, inhaling her baby scent and giving her a kiss before he handed her off to Lani. It didn't take long to get her strapped into the car seat, then Lani came to stand next to him.

When she rested her hand on his shoulder, he looked up at her. She gave him a soft smile, something that looked like affection in her gaze.

"Get some rest."

"Yeah. Thanks again for today."

She squeezed his shoulder, then dropped her hand. "I'll see you tomorrow."

Michael watched Wolfie follow her then sit there staring at the closed door once she and Vivianne had left. The two of them made a real pair. He was glad that he still had Wolfie even after everyone else had left.

He grabbed his crutches and got up, going to the door to let the dog out for a quick run before closing the house up for the night. Even though it wasn't super late, he was ready to go to bed. The next day would be soon enough to update everyone on how things had gone—though clearly, he didn't have an accurate perception of it, if Lani and Ryker were to be believed.

Regardless, he was glad to have this day in his rear-view mirror. Now if he could just manage to keep from losing his mind while waiting to hear the results.

CHAPTER NINETEEN

Over the days following the home study interview, Lani could see that Michael was struggling to stay optimistic. She knew he was scared of losing Vivianne, though he never voiced that. He was coming by the shop like he had in the pre-baby days, but all he did was hold Vivianne. And when she went to his place in the evening, she'd catch him just staring at the baby as he cuddled her.

It made Lanie's heart ache, and each time she saw that look on his face, it made her want to do everything she could to help him keep the baby. But short of offering to marry the man, what more could she do than she'd already done?

When Sunday rolled around, she decided that maybe it was time for a change to the way they'd been doing things. Normally on Sunday, she dropped the baby off with Michael since Ryker had agreed to spend the afternoon with him. That meant she had un-interrupted time to do her cooking for the week ahead.

It was even more important that she do it all at once since she didn't want to show up too late to Michael's in the evenings. Plus, it gave Michael a longer stretch of time with Vivianne than he got during the week.

That day, however, she decided that Michael needed to get out of the house for more than just work. She knew he wasn't out in nature as much as he had been prior to the accident, so maybe it was time to try to rectify that. It had become extremely important to her that his spirits not sink too low.

She understood why he was struggling. He'd been dealt an awful lot of blows recently, but she just wanted him to always remember that he wasn't alone. That if the worst should happen, he had people around him who would be there to support him.

Lani knew that Michael usually went to church in the morning, but she didn't think Ryker did, so she called him around eleven.

"Hi, Lani. Is everything okay?" Ryker asked when he answered her call.

"It's fine, but I was thinking maybe I'd do something different with Vivianne and Michael this afternoon."

"Oh? Like what?"

"I thought I'd get some lunch together and take him and Vivianne out to a park or something."

"That would be great," Ryker said. "Did you need me to come along?"

"I think we'll be okay. Unless you'd like to join us. In which case, you're more than welcome."

Ryker chuckled. "You guys enjoy yourselves. But if things change or you need my help, just give me a call."

"Thanks," Lani said, excited that her plan was coming together.

"Thank *you* for doing this for Michael. I really think he needs to get out of that house and just spend some time with Vivianne and with you, too, if you want me to be honest."

Lani felt heat rise in her cheeks even though Ryker wasn't there. "I think we'll all enjoy it. Even Vivianne, though she won't remember it."

"Take lots of pictures, and I'll see you tomorrow."

After she hung up, she got to work packing a picnic lunch. Since she'd already been considering it the day before when she'd gone grocery shopping, she'd added a bunch of picnic-type items to her basket.

Lani knew the approximate time Michael usually made it home from church, so she made her way over to his place, timing her arrival to a shortly after he would be there. As she turned the final bend in his long driveway, she saw his truck was parked in front of the house, so she knew he was home already.

Though she didn't plan to stay in the house too long, she still took Vivanne's car seat out and carried it with her to the door. She knocked on the door and stood back to wait for him to open it. When he still hadn't appeared a couple of minutes later, she began to worry.

She knew the code to unlock the door, but she didn't want to barge in. Maybe he was in his bedroom or the bathroom. After a couple more minutes, she knocked again, a bit louder this time. She heard Wolfie bark on the other side of the door, so hopefully, that might summon Michael more quickly.

Usually, Ryker was there by the time she showed up on a Sunday afternoon, so it was possible Michael just assumed it was him.

Sure enough, as the door swung open, Michael said, "Why didn't you use the—Oh, hey, Lani. I thought it was Ryker."

As he maneuvered back on his crutches, Lani frowned at him in concern. It didn't look like he'd left the house that day. His chin and cheeks held more than just a hint of a five o'clock shadow, and he wore a pair of long sports shorts and a faded T-shirt.

"You doing okay?" she couldn't keep from asking. "Did you make it to church this morning?"

He gave her a glance as he made his way to his recliner. "No. Not today."

She knew he wasn't in as much pain as he'd been initially, but that didn't mean there weren't days when he experienced more pain than others. If that was the case, her plans might have to take a rain check.

"I made some plans for the afternoon," Lani said. "But if you're not up for them, we can postpone."

"Oh, I'm sure Ryker will be here soon, so you could head off."

Lani stared at Michael, realizing he'd misunderstood. "Nope. You're coming *with* me."

He turned his head to look at her. "What are you talking about?"

"I already called Ryker, and he's not coming." When Michael frowned, she smiled. "And you're coming out with Vivianne and me."

"Hmmm." His expression turned curious. "And where are we going?"

"It's a surprise," Lani informed him. "So, if you need to change or anything, get crackin'."

"Bossy today, aren't you?"

"You bet. Vivianne and I had a talk, and she said that if you balked at all, I needed to get bossy with you."

"Did I fall asleep for a few years, or is Vivianne a talking genius?" Michael asked as he pushed himself up out of the recliner.

"Well, considering she's still in diapers, we're going to have to go with talking genius."

"Good to know." He paused long enough to run his fingers over the sleeping baby's head. "I'll be right back."

Lani was relieved he agreed because it seemed he needed the time out more than she'd even realized.

It didn't take him too long to reappear, wearing khaki cargo shorts and a navy T-shirt. It looked like he'd even taken a few minutes to shave.

"Ready to go?" Lani asked.

"As I'll ever be."

"Then let's go." Lani picked up the car seat and headed for the door.

"Is Wolfie allowed to come, or should I leave him in the house?"

"He can come. Just maybe bring a leash."

After she had the car seat secured, Wolfie jumped up on the seat beside it. He immediately settled down, resting his snout on the edge of the car seat.

"So where are we going?" Michael asked as she turned the car around and headed down the driveway.

"Still not telling you."

They were already partway there since the spot she wanted to go to was further on along the road heading north of the town. There were nice spots to the east of town, but that was the road where her parents had had their accident. Thankfully, she'd had no reason to travel that way since the accident, and that wasn't going to change on that day.

"Do I need a passport?" Michael asked.

Lani laughed. "No. We're not going that far. In fact, we're not going far at all."

She hoped that she wouldn't have to make alternative plans. The sunny, warm day might mean that she wasn't the only one to have this idea, but she hoped there was at least one picnic table for them since Michael needed a proper seat.

There were cars in the small parking lot, but as soon as Lani got out of the car, she spotted a couple of empty tables.

"It's been awhile since I've been here," Michael remarked once he was out and on his crutches. "It's beautiful."

Michael let Wolfie out while Lani got the car seat. "Why don't you choose the table?"

With Wolfie at his side, he made his way to a table in the sunshine, no doubt aware of the fact that sitting in the shade would probably get a bit chilly. She'd packed for Vivianne accordingly.

Once Michael had settled on the seat, she put Vivianne in front of him. The car seat canopy shielded the baby from the sun while a blanket kept her from getting chilled.

"I'll be right back." Leaving Michael with Wolfie and the baby, she returned to the car to grab the picnic basket. It was one her mom had used when the two of them would go on picnics together...picnics her father had had no interest in joining.

When she returned and put the basket on the table, Michael stared at it for a moment before looking at her. "You've made us a picnic?"

"Yep. It's nothing too fancy, so don't be expecting chocolate-covered strawberries or anything like that."

Michael laughed. "I have to say that didn't even cross my mind."

The sound of his laughter made Lani smile as she unpacked the basket. It really wasn't anything all that special. Bread, meat, cheese, grapes, chips, and bottles of water. Oh, and some brownies for dessert.

"This looks amazing," Michael said.

"Go ahead and help yourself," Lani said as she pulled out her phone, snapping a picture of Michael building his sandwich.

He glanced up and arched a brow. "What's that for?"

"Ryker said to take pictures, so I am."

Michael picked up his sandwich and posed, making Lani laugh as she struggled to take a picture without shaking her phone too much. After a couple more shots, she set her phone down and prepared her own sandwich.

"So what prompted this picnic?" Michael asked as they ate.

Lani wondered if she should be honest, not wanting to upset him with her observations. But in the end, she knew that for all that she hadn't been honest with him about some parts of her life, she had to be honest about this.

"I was worried about you."

Michael's brow furrowed, and his gaze dropped to the sandwich he held. "Worried?"

"You haven't been yourself since Adele's visit. I think you've been worried, too."

With a sigh, he nodded. "I just keep imagining the worst, you know." He glanced at the car seat. "I'm torn between wanting to spend every waking moment with her and not wanting to get too attached."

"Let yourself get attached," Lani said, her voice soft.

"Getting attached *hurts.*" Pain laced his words. "Out of my immediate family, Taylor was the only one I allowed myself to get attached to, and well, you've seen how that has turned out for me."

"Do you regret it, though?" Lani asked. "Do you wish you hadn't gotten attached to her?"

Michael's shoulders slumped. "I guess not, but I'm just not sure I'm ready to get hurt again so soon after what's happened with Taylor."

"I know you probably don't want false hope, but I really think that Adele saw what a wonderful man you are."

"She asked a lot of questions about my past, and there are things that aren't great about that."

Lani frowned. "Do you have a criminal record or something?"

"No. Nothing like that. But like I told you, I never graduated from high school." He hesitated. "And my dad was a very abusive man. Both physically and verbally."

She felt her stomach clench and her heart drop at his words. While her father had never been an especially kind man, he had never been physically abusive toward her.

"But that's not a reflection on you," Lani said. "If anything, you removing yourself from that situation shows your character. I never would have guessed you had that sort of background. You certainly have never come across to me as abusive."

Michael gave her a small smile. "I've never looked up to my dad, nor did I ever want to be like him."

"I happen to think you're amazing, and when I see all you've managed to do even after dropping out of high school, I think you're even more amazing. Despite having what people might think as a strike against you, you've managed to run a successful business."

"Not by myself, though," Michael said. "Taylor's helped me with the admin side of things. I couldn't do it without her."

"Oh. I just assumed you had a bookkeeper or accountant working for you."

Michael shook his head. "Taylor has a degree in business administration, so she's been taking care of that side of both businesses. I'll need to figure out another option when she's gone."

Lani wanted to offer her help but held her tongue. She wasn't sure she could get that much more involved in his life and business. More and more, it felt imperative she tell him who she was. But how? And when?

She was kind of surprised that it hadn't all been revealed already. All Michael had to do was mention her name around Sarah, and she'd probably put two and two together. But with so much going on already, was now the time to reveal that she was the competition?

"Anyway, I'm sure you didn't bring me out here to have this depressing conversation."

"Not true," Lani said, pointing a finger at him. "I brought you out here to give you a chance to get out of your head, and if talking is the way to do that, then that's what we need to do."

"I'm not sure what I ever did to have you walk into my life at just the right moment, but I'm so grateful that you did." He smiled at her, and the look in his eyes brought butterflies to life in her stomach. "And not just because of all you've done for me with Vivianne. You've been a calming influence at a point in my life when everything's been cast into upheaval. I've never really had that before, you know? Even with Taylor...well, she's not exactly calming."

Lani felt her cheeks flush at his words, then gave a bit of a shrug. "To be honest, I don't feel that I've really gotten to know her all that well."

"That's not too surprising. Taylor hasn't really connected with many people here in New Hope. She did keep in contact with the friends she made in college, but I thought she was happy here. Clearly, I was wrong."

"Things change. People change. It's possible she *was* happy here, but something changed for her."

Michael nodded as he continued to eat his sandwich. "I just wish that she would have talked to me about everything. Half my struggles lately have come because she didn't tell me what was going on. I hate feeling like I'm behind the eight ball and having to play catch up."

"It's never a fun position to be in," Lani agreed. She'd felt that a time or two in the past few years. "But having to play catch up doesn't automatically mean things won't turn out."

Before Michael could respond to that observation, Vivianne began to fuss. While Michael got her out of the car seat, Lani prepared a bottle. They'd moved away from the prepared formula, so it took a little longer now to get a bottle ready for her.

"That's a cute hat," Michael said as he settled Vivianne into the crook of his arm.

"Isn't it?" Lani asked. "It's a bonnet that I thought would be good for protecting her face from the sun."

"So she'll wear it once a month?"

Lani laughed as she handed him the prepared bottle. "Yeah. Probably not a super useful clothing item, but hey, it's good for today."

As Michael focused on the baby, Lani lifted her phone and took a couple more pictures of him. Maybe she'd get a print made of one of them and find a frame so that he could have a nice memory of this day—the first time Vivianne had come to the river with him.

Turning, she took a couple pictures of the water with the trees and mountains in the background. Though she wasn't much of a photographer and her phone didn't take great quality images, she liked to take pictures of things that she thought she might enjoy a physical reminder of in the future.

She took a couple more of Michael burping Vivianne, capturing the moment he threw back his head and laughed at the burp that came out of the baby. It had been far too loud for such a dainty princess.

"Would you like me to take a picture of the three of you?"

Lani looked up to see a teenage girl standing at the end of their picnic table. Uncertain how to respond, she glanced at Michael just as he said, "Sure. That would be great."

As she stood up, she handed her phone to the girl. She moved around to sit on the bench next to Michael on the side he held Vivianne, being careful not to jostle the frame on his leg.

"Okay. Smile for me," the girl sang out. "Well, I guess the baby's a little young to smile, but you two...cheese!"

Lani couldn't help but smile at the girl's enthusiasm. When the teen was happy with the pictures she'd taken for them, she handed the phone back to Lani. "You are such a cute family."

For a moment, Lani considered correcting her. But honestly, theirs was such a complicated situation that it was easier just to smile and thank her for taking the pictures. After taking a moment to gush over Vivianne, the teen ran back to join her group who were sitting at a nearby table. Lani picked up her phone and returned to her seat opposite Michael.

"Can you send me copies of the pictures?" Michael asked.

Lani looked up. "All of them?"

"Sure. I have a feeling your phone takes better pictures than mine."

It didn't take long for her to text the pictures to him, and he pulled his phone out to look them over. Vivianne was waving her hands, bopping Michael on the chin and making him laugh.

Lani wished that Adele could see them together like this. Maybe things would be moving faster. Or maybe not. What did she know about home studies? She'd tried to search on the internet to find out what to expect time-wise so she could reassure Michael, but it seemed like no two experiences were the same. There were so many variables that impacted the outcome of a home study.

As the afternoon progressed, Lani was happy to see some of the stress and worry slip from Michael's face. Their time away from home was achieving what she'd hoped it would. And not just for Michael.

Even though they'd had some difficult discussions, she felt the happiest she'd been in a long time. Out in nature with someone who was coming to mean an awful lot to her and a cute baby. What more could she ask for? Not much.

Lani kept an eye on the sky, but she was glad to see that even though the sun disappeared behind clouds every once in a while, not one drop of rain fell on them. It truly was a perfect day.

"I wish I could get up and walk with her," Michael said.

"Do you want to go closer to the water?" Lani asked. "If you want, I can carry Vivi so you can walk. There's a nice big rock you could sit on with her."

After the faintest of hesitations, he said, "Sure. Let's do it."

They left their things on the table, and Michael slowly made his way across the uneven ground. He could put a little more weight on his injured leg, but she could see he was still being careful. When they reached the rock, Michael settled himself on it, and Lani handed Vivianne to him.

"I hope Vivianne loves the outdoors," Michael said as he lifted his face to the sun.

"I have a feeling she won't have much choice. You'll be taking her outside all the time, plus living where you do will be a bonus. She can play outdoors without you having to worry about traffic. Maybe you can make her a sandbox or a build a swing set for her." Lani smiled at the idea. "Oh, a tire swing hung from a tree. Or a treehouse! I bet she would love that."

"You're so optimistic." Michael grinned. "I appreciate that."

"I'm not always optimistic," she said. "But out here? It's hard to stay down in the dumps."

"You're right about that. Thank you for making this happen."

She felt warmed from the inside out at his appreciation. It wasn't why she'd done it, but it felt good just the same. "You're welcome. Anytime."

CHAPTER TWENTY

Michael stared at the water, tumbling and flowing freely over the rocks in the riverbed. It wasn't a deep river, and really, river wasn't the most accurate description of it despite its name. It was more like a large stream or a brook. But whatever it was, it brought him peace.

The sounds of nature, interrupted only occasionally by the distant conversations of others in the area, were precisely what he'd needed. He hadn't known quite what to think when Lani had told him what her plan was.

The depressing thoughts and fears that had been weighing on him all week had finally pulled him under that morning. He hadn't even debated going to church, which he knew wasn't good. It had truly been a low moment for him. He'd thought he'd been hiding his depression better than he had, apparently.

But an afternoon out with Vivianne and Lani had been what he needed to lift him out of the pit he'd slid into. Michael hoped that he could carry that feeling through the days and weeks ahead as he waited to hear the outcome of the home study and whether or not he got to keep Vivianne.

When his phone rang, he hesitated a moment before pulling it out.

"Hey, Michael," Eli said when he answered.

"Hey." Michael knew why he was calling, and he appreciated the man's concern for him, but sometimes the concern felt like a weight. He hated that his friends were so worried about him, and they didn't even know everything that was going on.

He wasn't entirely sure why he hadn't revealed everything to them. Why he hadn't taken them up on their offers of help. He knew part of it was that they all seemed to be in such good places in their lives. Things were coming together for them as they fell in love and got married, while it felt like his own life was breaking apart.

It hadn't fractured irreparably just yet, but it felt fragile.

"Are you doing okay?" Eli asked. "We missed you at church this morning."

"I'm doing fine," Michael said, and thankfully, as he sat on the rock next to the river with Vivianne, Lani, and Wolfie next to him, that wasn't a lie. "I just woke up not feeling too good, but I'm okay now."

"Are you going to make it to the Bible study tonight?"

"I'm not sure. You guys aren't hiking on such a beautiful day?"

"It's Bible Study day, so we're trying to be good and not push it off. But we might sit out on the deck instead of staying inside."

"I'll think about it."

"And feel free to bring the baby. You'll have lots of help with her, if you need it."

"I have someone who helps me with her in the evening, so if I come, it will just be me."

"Well, we'd love to have you. We haven't seen much of you since the baby was born."

"The broken leg definitely complicates things too," Michael pointed out. "But I'm managing."

"And you've got enough help?"

"Yep. The babysitter Pastor Evans recommended has worked out really well. Ryker had stepped up on the business side of things, and our employee from the shop has definitely been a Godsend. Among the three of them, things are pretty much covered."

"I hope you know that if you need help, even last minute, you can call any of us, and we'll do what we can."

"I'll be sure and do that."

"I hope so. I feel like we're letting you down in some way."

"You're not at all. If I need help and don't ask for it, that's on me, not you. I've just been kind of leaning on those who were already around me, to help."

"I'm glad they've been there for you, but honestly, we miss you too. Let's do coffee sometime soon."

"Sounds good."

"Okay then. I'll let you get back to your day. Take care."

After Michael ended the call, he slid his phone into his pocket and sighed. He glanced over to see Lani with her head bent over her phone. At that moment, he wondered if she had friends. She hadn't mentioned any in the time he'd known her, but that didn't mean much. There was still so much in their lives they hadn't talked about.

"Do you have many friends here?" he asked.

"Hmm?" Lani looked up from her phone.

"Do you have many friends here?" he repeated.

"Oh. Well, no, I suppose not." Lani frowned. "Growing up, I didn't have many friends outside my family. I was especially close to my mom and her family."

"Not your dad's family?"

She gave a vigorous shake of her head. "I never knew his side of the family. My dad has a brother somewhere, but I don't remember ever meeting him."

Michael would have been shocked by that revelation if not for his personal experience that helped him understand how it might happen that family members didn't have much to do with each other.

He didn't miss family, though he did miss the idea of what his family might have been. And now with Vivianne, he felt bad that she wouldn't have any grandparents to dote on her, but there was no way he was going to let his parents anywhere near her.

Thankfully, Pastor Evans had stepped up, becoming the father Michael never had, and Michael was sure he'd be happy to play the role of grandfather for Vivianne as well. The thing he appreciated most about Pastor Evans was his ability to gently encourage, uplift, and even challenge without making a person feel like he was lecturing them.

Michael thanked God for leading him to the church that day. Meeting Pastor Evans had changed his life in so many ways. All of them good.

"We can leave whenever you're ready," Lani said, clearly not terribly interested in pursuing the friend and family discussion. Not that he blamed her at all.

"I'm really not eager to leave, but I'm ready to go back to the table, I think."

"Good. We haven't had dessert yet, so we need to do that before we head home."

They returned to the picnic table with Lani carrying Vivianne once again. She handed the baby back to him and turned her focus to the picnic basket.

"We've got brownies," she said as she set them on the table in front of him. "Hopefully you'll like them."

Michael smiled and picked up a brownie. "I'm sure I will."

He was so glad that she'd provided food that he could eat with one hand.

By the time they decided to call it a day, it was nearly five o'clock. Michael knew that she usually spent Sundays cooking for the week, so he really appreciated that she'd taken the time to spend her afternoon with him.

"Can I still keep Vivianne for a few hours?" Michael asked as they drove back to his place. "I think I'll go to the Bible Study this evening."

"You don't need to ask me," Lani said with a laugh. "But that's fine."

216 · KIMBERLY RAE JORDAN

"I can drop her by your place once I'm done," he said.

"That's okay. I might be at my dad's, so I'll just swing by to pick her up when I'm done there."

"Are you sure?"

"Definitely. Will you be able to deal with her on your own to get her to the Bible study?"

Well, he hadn't thought about that. "I could probably go over a little bit early. We usually eat around six or so."

Back at the house, Lani repacked the diaper bag, then carried the car seat out to the truck for him.

"I'll see you two later," she said with a smile. "Enjoy your evening."

"You, too. And thank you again for this afternoon." He wanted to give her a hug, which took him a bit by surprise. Hugging anyone but Taylor—and now Vivianne—wasn't something he thought he'd ever want to do. "It was just what I needed."

"I think I needed it too." She wrapped her arms around herself. "Thank you for letting me surprise you."

"Anytime."

"I guess I'll see you later." Lani slid behind the wheel of her car and gave a small wave. "Have fun."

Michael watched her drive away, her car disappearing around the bend of the driveway, then climbed into his truck. Before starting it up, he dictated a quick text to Eli to let him know he was heading their way with the baby on board.

It didn't take him too long to get to Eli's, and he'd barely pulled to a stop in front of the cabin when the door swung open. Both Eli and Anna came out on the porch with their dog, Shadow, at their heels.

"I'm so glad you made it, man," Eli said as he came down the steps. "Where's the baby?"

"In the back seat." Michael maneuvered his legs out of the truck, then grabbed his crutches.

"Is there any special trick to getting the seat out?" Eli asked.

"Pull the latch at the front." He slid his arms through the arm cuffs of the crutches and gripped the handles. "It should release the car seat."

"Got it." Eli backed away from the door, the car seat in his hand.

They made their way up the stairs to where Anna waited, an eager expression on her face.

"It's about time you brought the baby around so I can love on her." Anna rubbed her hands together. "And since I'm here already, I call dibs. The other ladies are going to have to wait in line."

"Let me get her inside first, sweetheart," Eli said.

"Are you worried she might get baby fever?" Michael asked in a low voice as he followed Eli into the cabin.

"To be honest, I'm kind of counting on it."

"Seriously?" That surprised Michael a bit since they hadn't gotten married that long ago. Of course, marriage hadn't been on his horizon, let alone babies, and yet here he was...no marriage, but a baby.

"We're not getting any younger, and I think we're in a good place to have a baby."

Michael couldn't argue with that. Eli and Anna had always given off a very calm and loving vibe. He had no problem picturing them as parents.

When Eli set the car seat down on the coffee table, Anna was right there to lower the handle. "Oh. She's sleeping. I suppose I shouldn't pick her up, huh?"

"She probably won't wake up if you do," Michael said as he lowered himself onto a chair.

"Oh, nice." Anna gently lifted Vivianne up and settled her in the crook of her arm. "She's beautiful, Michael."

Michael watched as Anna and Eli fawned over Vivianne. He enjoyed seeing his friends that way, but it also felt sort of wrong.

Lani should have been there too. He wanted her to be there with him.

She'd already turned him down, though. And though she'd said she didn't have friends, it also didn't seem like she was looking for any. Well, he'd like to think she considered him a friend because that's definitely how he felt about her.

It hurt him to think that she didn't have anyone close to lean on and be there for her. He wanted to be that person for her, but from the start, he had been the one leaning on her.

You're not a man. A man is strong and capable. You are neither of those things. Weak. That's what you are. Weak!

His father's voice echoed in his mind, and tendrils of self-doubt began to search for a place to take root within him. It had been awhile since his father's words and opinion of him had been so loud in his head. Most of the time, he was able to block the memories from that period of his life, but right then—after struggling so much that week—the walls holding those thoughts back were weak and vulnerable.

All the stresses that had been swept away that afternoon with Lani came roaring back, undermining his confidence in his ability to parent Vivianne and do everything he needed to do to provide her with a stable, loving home.

A hand fell on his shoulder, stalling his spiraling thoughts. He looked up at Eli. His friend gave him an understanding look, as if he knew the thoughts circling in his mind.

"How are you doing with being a father?" Eli asked as he sat down on the chair next to him.

Michael thought about brushing aside the comment with a quick response, but Eli had always seemed to see through all of that with him.

"It's been hard because I've felt like I couldn't really fulfill that role very well lately. I mean, I wasn't confident in being able to parent her well before the leg thing happened, and after... Well, I'm just so glad I've had people willing to help me out."

"I think God is teaching you how to lean on people, my friend." Eli shifted on his chair to face him more fully. "I understand how hard it can be to trust people, especially when you've been let down in the past."

Michael nodded. The lesson he'd learned when he was young was that the only person he could really rely on to take care of him, was himself. His grandma had tried to help when she could, but she had been in poor health.

"Why haven't you called on any of us to help you out?" Eli asked. "I mean, you did ask for the reference letters, and we were glad to provide those for you. But we would have been happy to help with the baby. Even make you food or buy you groceries."

Michael dropped his head forward. "I don't know." He rubbed his hands together. "I guess maybe I felt like I couldn't do anything in return for your help. With Ryker and the others, I can pay them for the time they have spent helping me. I had something they wanted and could use."

"You do have something we want," Eli said gently. "Your friendship. You have value in just being you. Not in any money you might have. Not in your business. Just you being you."

Michael swallowed hard. How could Eli see value in him when his own parents hadn't been able to?

His father's voice faded under Eli's words, and Michael took a deep breath, blowing out the emotion that had built in his chest. He was so thankful for the people God had placed on his path, and right then, he was incredibly thankful for Eli.

By the time others began to show up, Michael felt better, and the more he was surrounded by his friends, the more buoyed he felt. He had made the right decision to come to Bible study, and watching the women with Vivianne was kind of funny. The looks of apprehension on the faces of the men who belonged to some of the women was also rather comical.

"Not wanting her to get baby fever yet?" Michael asked Kieran.

The man gazed at his bride of just five months, his love for her clear on his face. "I'm of two minds on that. I've been ready to be a father for awhile now, but I'm also really enjoying it being just the two of us. By the way, my mom doesn't get a vote."

Michael laughed. "I think we all know what her vote would be."

"Exactly." Kieran smiled as Cara, his wife, approached him with the baby.

"Want to hold the baby?" she asked.

"How about you hold the baby, and I'll hold you," he suggested.

"While I do love that idea, that's not on offer right now."

Kieran lifted his arms and waited for Cara to place Vivianne in them. For all that he had seemed to not be sure about holding a baby, the police chief cradled Vivianne like a pro. She was awake by this point, but not fussing at all. Michael was so proud of her—what a trooper.

Even during the Bible study, she only fussed for as long as it took Michael to prepare her bottle. It felt like it had been ages since he'd fellowshipped in that way, and he'd needed it.

Unfortunately, he'd forgotten to bring his guitar. In fact, it had been weeks since he'd last picked it up, and that was something he should rectify soon.

For all the areas of his life that had been a struggle for him, learning to play the guitar had not been one of them. He'd discovered a guitar at his grandma's one weekend, and she'd insisted he should have it. He left it at her place, knowing that if his father saw it, he'd have a few choice words for Michael before smashing it.

Still, even without his guitar, the evening was rejuvenating. And when Michael sat with Vivianne in his arms while his friends stood around them for a time of prayer, tears that his father would have pegged as weakness slipped down his cheeks. They were cleansing tears, and the feeling of his friends' hands on him grounded Michael, reminding him that he was not alone.

And while he wasn't a hugger, his friends apparently were, because he got all kinds of hugs when the prayer was over.

"And now, let's eat some dessert," Eli said with a wave to the dining room table. "Leah has made more than we'll ever be able to eat."

"So the same as always," Michael said with a smile at Leah.

"Someday, I'll show up empty-handed," she threatened.

"And we'll all die from shock," Sarah, her twin sister, said.

The banter between the siblings had always made Michael smile, and that night was no different. Even with his leg still impairing him, he felt hope for the future grow within him. Lani had planted the seed that afternoon, and his time with his friends had watered it.

Before he left Eli's awhile later, he sent a message to Lani, letting her know he was on his way home. He would have liked to have just dropped Vivianne off, but since Lani had said she might not be at home, it worked better to just go on home.

By the time he made it, Lani's car was already there. She got out as he pulled up, and he couldn't help but smile at her familiar form in his headlights.

"Hey, there," he said as he climbed out of the truck.

"How did your evening go?" she asked.

"It was wonderful," he said. "They all loved Vivianne."

"Of course, they did," Lani said as she went to the back door of the truck and opened it. "What's not to love?"

"So true," Michael agreed.

He'd left his porch light on, so he was able to see her. "You should come with me one Sunday evening."

Her hesitation was brief, but it was there. "Maybe."

"I think you'd enjoy it. The people there are just great. So supportive." This time he hesitated. "And I think maybe you could use some of that too."

"You do?" Lani asked.

"I've never heard you talk about friends, and from things you've said about your father, I think maybe you could use some support as someone who is a caregiver in the way you are." He maneuvered himself closer to where she stood with Vivianne's car seat. "You have been a huge support for Vivianne and for me. Even for Taylor at the shop. And also for your dad. Who's there for you?"

Her head lowered. "I do have support, though they're not here."

"But don't you wish you had friends here that you could spend time with? Go for coffee with?"

"I enjoyed our time at the river this afternoon."

"I did too," Michael said. "And I know you did that for me, for which I'm so grateful. I just feel like I'm not able to give back the way you've given to me."

"I don't expect you to give back."

"But maybe I want to support you. You've come to mean so much to me and to Vivianne as well. Even though she can't talk yet, I'm sure she'd say that you're awesome and wonderful, and the best diaper changer and bottle preparer in the whole world."

Lani laughed then sobered with a sigh. "I've loved being able to help you two out. It's been the best thing I've had in my life recently. I know that it probably doesn't make sense, but I enjoy helping people."

She bent down and put the car seat on the ground at her feet. Thankfully, it was covered with a blanket, so Vivianne was protected from the evening chill.

"I don't help people for the thanks, but with my dad, he's so angry and ungrateful, it's...soul-sucking. When I help you and Vivianne, it's different. It satisfies something in me because I know you really need me. And, well, I know you appreciate my help, just like you appreciate Ryker's and Sophia's."

"I do," Michael agreed. "I really, really do. I appreciate each of you. I know that, technically, you're all my employees, but I don't view you guys that way anymore. I haven't for awhile. You've become friends."

Lani beamed up at him. "I'm glad to hear that because I feel the same way."

"Then you have to let me take care of you sometimes too."

She gave a quick nod. "I'll do that."

"Perfect."

"Guess I'd better get her home and us both into bed. Tomorrow is another day."

"And a new week." Hopefully one during which he'd hear the news he'd been waiting for, even though it was probably too soon.

CHAPTER TWENTY-ONE

"Something's different about you."

Lani stared at the small image of her cousin on her phone, trying to figure out how to respond to that. "What do you mean?"

"I don't know. You seem more...settled. At peace with yourself."

It had been a little while since she'd last spoken with Luann, her mom's namesake. She'd just had a baby, bringing her total child count to three, which meant she was fairly busy and unable to chat much recently. Luann had been one of her closest friends during her time in Hawaii, even though they were in different stages in their life. Luann was a couple of years older than Lani and had quickly become the sister Lani had never had.

Deciding that she could use some advice, Lani said, "I think I am."

"Care to share why?"

"It's a long story. Do you have some time?"

"Yep. David took the older two to see his mom, so I just have the baby here, and all she wants to do is nurse." Luann grinned. "I'm a captive audience."

Lani smiled in response. "Well, in that case."

"Spill your guts," Luann instructed.

And so she did, starting back with her decision to apply at *Reeds' Florals* and going right through to her decision to help Michael care for Vivianne after his accident.

"So you're telling me you have a baby with you right now?"

"Not right now, no. I'll go pick her up after I take Dad his supper. I drop her off at the babysitter's six days a week, then Michael's friend, Ryker, picks her up and takes her to Michael so he can spend some time with her before I bring her home for the night."

"Why did you decide to get so involved with these people?" Luann asked. "They're basically the ones who nearly killed your mom's business."

Lani sighed. "That's what I've always thought, but I'm not sure it's true. I mean, I don't think they did it intentionally."

Luann's brows rose. "Really?"

"I haven't said anything to you about it, but as I've reviewed Mom's books from the last few years, I've discovered that instead of leaving money in the business, she'd pulled it out and spent it elsewhere. That meant she had less available cash to use to purchase the supplies she needed to fulfill service the corporate contracts she had."

"Where was the money going?"

"I have no idea. From what I can see, it was transferred into their personal account, but I can't access that to see where it might have gone from there. Dad would absolutely flip his lid if I asked to see his bank account."

"Yeah. No doubt," Luann said with a frown. "Do you have any ideas of where it might have been going?"

"I think at least some of it went to Tutu. I wasn't always able to get enough scholarships to cover the tuition, and she would cover whatever was left, saying that I could pay her back later. Since then, whenever I've tried to give her money, she's just brushed it aside. I know Tutu doesn't have a lot of money to spare, so I think Mom might have been sending her money to cover what I couldn't."

"You could always ask Tutu. She'd probably tell you, especially now."

Lani had considered it, but she had yet to initiate that conversation. It was always hard to talk to her grandma about things that were tied to her mom. Inevitably, the conversation led to tears, and Lani hated it when her grandma cried.

"I'll see how she seems the next time I talk with her," Lani said, making no promises to herself or Luann.

"So about this Michael guy," Luann began. "Tell me more about him."

"Why?" Lani asked, her stomach doing funny things at the thought of talking specifically about Michael.

"It seems like maybe he's important to you. If that's the case, I think I should know about him."

"He's my boss," she said.

"It sounds like he's more than a boss."

Lani couldn't deny that. "He's a really great guy."

"In what way?"

"He's very responsible with a business and a home of his own, plus now taking on the care of his sister's daughter."

"Does he know who you are?"

Lani's shoulders slumped, and she looked down at the table where her phone was propped. "No. I needed the job so bad when I first applied that I didn't tell them. I also had Nina make it seem like I'd just left her business recently, not that I'd been gone a year and a half."

"Are you planning to tell him?" Luann asked as she lifted the baby to her shoulder and began to rub her back.

"I don't know. He's more than just a boss now, but I don't know how to tell him who I am. I mean, he's trusted me with the business and his daughter. Finding out I didn't tell him the truth..."

"Do you think it will matter?"

Lani wanted to say no, but something inside her knew that it would. "I just don't know how to tell him about it now. I really like him and don't want to mess up our friendship."

Luann tilted her head. "You mean you *like* like him?"

"I do."

"Does he feel the same way?"

"I don't know." Lani thought back on their most recent interactions. "There are times he seems to maybe like me too, but then I wonder if it's just him being grateful for all I'm doing, you know? He's been through a lot recently."

"I guess it's possible that it's just gratitude, but there's also the fact that you're a wonderful person, and maybe he sees that."

Lani laughed. "And you're just a little biased."

Luann grinned. "Maybe. But you've had boyfriends before, so obviously, others have seen that too."

"Well, I wasn't wonderful enough for them to want to keep being in a relationship with me." Lani frowned. "Peter wouldn't even consider long distance."

"Peter wasn't good enough for you," Luann said then held up your hand. "And before you say I'm biased again, David agreed with me. And you know that David likes pretty much everybody, but he really wasn't all that impressed with Peter."

"But you never really said anything about him," Lani said.

"No. I mean, I talked to you about him that once, but after that, I didn't think it was my business to keep harping on him. You're an adult. You're responsible for your own life decisions."

"I'm not sure I trust myself to know when a guy is really good for me or not."

"Is Michael a Christian?"

"Yes. I'm pretty sure he is. He's really close to the pastor of one of the larger churches here in New Hope Falls, plus his one friend group is all from that church as well."

"That's definitely a point in his favor." Luann paused. "Have you found a church you feel comfortable in yet?"

Lani sighed and shook her head. "I usually just end up watching our church's stream."

"Does the church Michael attends have a stream?"

"Yes. I've watched it a couple of times."

"Is Michael part of the reason you feel more at peace?" Luann asked.

"Maybe? I think a big part of it is just feeling connected again. Like I have a purpose in life. Running Mom's store and helping Dad out is fine, but my heart hasn't really been in either. Especially my dealings with Dad. Rather than making me feel inspired, I feel drained after being with him. Like the life is being sucked out of me."

"And helping Michael doesn't leave you feeling that way?"

"Not at all." Lani searched for the words to describe how it felt. "It's kind of like a plant. I help it grow by watering it, and in exchange, I get to see a beautiful flower blossom. That's how I feel with Michael. I'm helping him, but I also get to appreciate the joy of seeing him with Vivianne and knowing that I'm playing an integral part in him being able to care for her and adopt her. It all feels so worthwhile."

"Maybe you feel a similar sort of gratitude for him," Luann observed. "Like you appreciate him giving you this opportunity."

Lani considered that for a moment, then dismissed it. "No. I was already sort of feeling something for him before all this happened. When I started to work at the shop, he'd show up several mornings a week to drop off the flowers his sister had ordered. He would always talk with me like he saw me as more than just an employee."

She hadn't told Luann everything about Michael—like the fact that he struggled with reading or about his family history. That was Michael's story to share, not hers.

"He does sound like a really neat guy, but I'd tread cautiously. I don't want you to get hurt again."

"I'll be praying for you about all this," Luann said. "That you'll have wisdom to know what to do." She hesitated, and when she spoke again, her tone was soft, but her words were weighty. "You need to tell him the truth. No relationship—whether it's a friendship or romantic—will survive when it's built on a lie."

Lani's heart clenched at the thought of losing her friendship with Michael. She didn't want that. The big questions were when she should tell him who she really was, and how would he take it when she did? The thought of her honesty ruining everything they'd built made her want to keep that secret forever.

"I'll tell him," she said with conviction. "That'll be the first hurdle. The next will be figuring out how to handle Dad's reaction when he finds out that not only am I working for the enemy, I'm friends with one."

"At this point, I say don't worry about that. Your dad has clearly decided that he's going to live out the remainder of his days angry at the world and everyone in it."

Luann was right. "I guess that's true."

"So don't factor his reaction into whatever you do."

Lani rubbed her hands over her face. "I'll let you know what happens. I think I'll probably wait to say anything until Michael's heard about the results of the home study, and he gets the green light to adopt."

"Just don't take too long," Luann said. "I'll pray about those things too. I'm sure it's been a stressful time for him."

"He hasn't said anything to me about the business, but he's going to have to make a decision soon. I think he said Taylor was planning to leave as soon as he was approved for the adoption. I have no idea what he'll do with the shop, so I'll probably be out of a job."

"Has he asked you to work more?" Luann asked.

"Yep. He offered me more hours, but I said I couldn't. I mean, what am I supposed to do? I've already changed the hours at my shop to accommodate working three hours at his. Dad got mad about me opening later, but I've stayed firm and not changed the hours back."

"If your dad wasn't a consideration, what would you want to do?"

"Like, do you mean if I didn't have to care for him anymore?"

"Well, maybe, but I was thinking more along the lines of you not having to worry about his reaction to things."

"Oh. I don't know. I want Mom's shop to thrive and be a solid business in the community, but I'm just not sure how to do that. I've tried advertising—free because I don't have anything in the budget to work with—and hoped word of mouth would help, but it really hasn't. Before all of this stuff with Michael, I would have said I wanted to close the shop and return to Hawaii."

"And I think that's probably what your mom would have wanted."

Lani sighed. "She really did want me to be around family there. That was why she insisted I go there for school even though it would have been cheaper to stay here."

"I think it's something you really need to consider," Luann said. "I know I'm being selfish, but I miss having you here and would be thrilled beyond all belief if you came back."

"A couple of months ago, I would have absolutely gone back to Hawaii in a heartbeat."

"But now..." Luann prompted.

"Now my heart is involved, and it's saying it wants me to stay here."

"Well, let's just pray that God makes His will clear for you."

Lani hadn't thought much about God and what He might want for her life in recent years. She hadn't been particularly happy when it appeared His plan was for her to leave Hawaii with her degree unfinished to care for an ailing business and an angry dad. She was almost scared to consider what His plans for her in this situation might be.

"But first and foremost, you need to come clean with Michael about who you are."

Lani agreed, even though she felt sick when she thought about it. She'd gotten herself into a situation that could very well rob her of the thing she wanted most right then. If only she'd done what her mom would have done: told the truth from the start and prayed that God would work the situation out.

"I will." She didn't know how, and she didn't know when, but Lani knew it was what she had to do.

They talked a bit more, then Luann had to go, so they said good-bye and ended the call. Lani slumped back in her chair, a maelstrom of feelings swirling within her. She was glad she'd confided in Luann. Her cousin been such an encouragement, but now she was left with the knowledge that she had at least one difficult conversation ahead of her.

She had a feeling that Michael would struggle with the fact that she hadn't been honest with him. Back when she'd made that decision, she'd never thought that she'd come to admire and respect the man who was supposed to have ruined her mom's business. She was just supposed to have gone in to work for three hours and then left to take care of her own shop.

But now...now she had feelings for Michael and had fallen in love with a little girl who, if things didn't go Michael's way, could be taken away from her. How had this happened?

Lani stared out the window next to her, trying to figure out how to untangle the knots in her life. Did she just blurt it out? Did she try to explain why she'd done what she'd done? What would give her the best outcome?

By the time she walked through the back door of the Reeds' shop the next morning, Lani still had no idea how to handle the situation. She turned on the lights, then set the car seat on the wide worktable.

As she glanced around the room, Lani was struck by the feeling that something was off. Right away she noticed that the door to the office stood open and the light was on. Glancing around, she saw that the one to the front of the shop was also open. Usually, both those doors were closed, and the lights were off when she arrived in the morning.

After a peek at Vivianne to confirm she was still asleep, Lani went into the office. It was hard to tell if anything was out of place because the desk was never completely neat and tidy. Papers were spread across the surface of it, but there was nothing on the floor.

Frowning at the idea that she was just imagining things, she went to check the front of the shop. Again, nothing seemed out of place that she could see. Maybe Taylor had been in a rush when she'd left on Saturday and had forgotten to close the doors. Given that nothing else appeared to be out of place, it seemed the most logical explanation for why things were slightly different than usual.

With a shrug, Lani returned to the worktable and flipped open the binder to see what was on the schedule for her that day. She managed to get one arrangement done before Vivianne started to fuss. After she fed and changed her, Lani strapped her into the carrier.

As she continued to work, she swayed and sang, sometimes just talking to Vivianne about the flowers she was using. Now that the baby was staying awake for more extended periods of time, Lani found she enjoyed chatting to her. Not that Vivianne understood a single thing she said, but it made Lani feel a little less alone.

When Lani arrived at Sophia's shortly after ten, the woman greeted her with a shy, but warm, smile. She hadn't been sure what to make of Sophia at first, and it had taken Lani awhile to admit that even though she hadn't been willing to name what she might be feeling for Michael, she'd viewed the woman as competition. And not just for Michael's affections, but for Vivianne's as well.

She knew it was stupid, but after being so disconnected since returning to New Hope Falls, what she'd come to feel from being part of Michael and Vivianne's lives was something she didn't want to lose. A part of her had felt—and still did feel—that she could be easily replaced, and she didn't want that to happen.

But it wasn't Sophia's fault if that should happen. It would just mean that she was more what Michael and Vivianne needed than Lani was. The thought hurt, especially as she stood right in front of Sophia, but she kept a smile on her face.

"She ate about three hours ago, so when she wakes up, she'll probably be hungry," Lani said as she handed her the diaper bag.

"Sounds good." Sophia set the bag down just inside the door beside the car seat. "Bry is thrilled that she's awake more now."

Lani smiled at the little boy who hovered between his mom and the car seat. "I'm sure that makes her a little more fun to be around."

"I think he likes that she's basically a captive audience for him to show her all his books." Sophia smiled down at Bry and ran her fingers through his light brown curls.

That picture made Lani laugh. "It's never too soon to introduce them to books."

"That's what I figure."

"Can I get a book now, Mama?"

"Just a minute, sweetie pie. Vivianne's still asleep, so we have to wait for her to wake up."

"Well, I'd better go," Lani said. "I'll see you tomorrow."

After she left their home, she headed for hers, still wondering how to approach Michael with her story. She puttered around the quiet of the shop, not able to settle on just one thing. After trying to paint for a bit, she abandoned that and tackled the cleaning. When that was done, she tried to concentrate on some bookwork.

Nothing could completely hold her attention, which was frustrating as she usually didn't have that problem.

When the bell rang above the door, Lani eagerly came out from the back where she'd been freshening some flowers. "Hi, Leah."

The woman's brows rose at the greeting. "Hi, Lani. Sarah sent me to order some flowers."

"Lovely," Lani said, grateful for the distraction. "What are you looking for?"

"It's Mom's birthday, and Sarah said we should get her some flowers."

"Oh, that's nice. Did you want to carry out something today? Or place an order?"

"I hate to admit we've kind of left it to the last minute," Leah said with a frown. "So do you have anything I could take right now?"

"I do have roses and a few other flowers ready to go, but if you don't mind waiting a few minutes, I could do an arrangement for you."

"I don't mind waiting," Leah said as she looked around.

"Why don't you come into the back with me?" Lani suggested. "Unless you'd rather wait out here."

Leah hesitated then said, "I'll come back with you."

Lani wished she had a larger selection of flowers on hand, but such was life. After showing her what she had, Leah picked a few blossoms, and Lani got to work arranging them.

"Are you painting these?" Leah asked.

Lani looked up and saw her standing in front of the small easel where she'd been working earlier. "Yeah. I do watercolors of flowers."

"And sell them?"

"Yes. I sell more online than I do in the shop, but painting flowers is something I really enjoy doing."

"They're very lovely." She tilted her head to the side. "Did you know that Sarah had a showing at the gallery in town?"

"Yes. I'd heard that." She been tempted to go but had ended up not attending. "I'm not surprised. She's so super talented."

"She is," Leah agreed as she sat on a stool near the table. "And very busy right now. Between planning a wedding and keeping up with her painting, she's constantly on the go."

"That's good." Lani trimmed the stems of a couple of the flowers to vary the heights. "Are you busy these days too?"

"Yeah. Now that Sarah is tied up with other things, she's not able to help out at the lodge as much. That means Mom and I are busier, although Anna is also a big help."

They chatted a bit more about the lodge as Lani finished up the bouquet. Then, after proclaiming it perfect, Leah paid and left the shop.

As the shop fell into silence once again, Lani let out a sigh. If only she had more customers like that. It would make the time at the shop so much more enjoyable.

Shortly after Leah had gone, her phone rang, and Michael's name popped up on the screen.

"Hi, Michael," she said, pressing a hand to her stomach as butterflies came to life within her.

"Hey, Lani. Did you notice anything weird at the shop this morning?"

CHAPTER TWENTY-TWO

With his phone pressed to his ear, Michael looked across the room to where Taylor stood talking to a police officer.

"Weird?" Lani asked.

"Yeah. Did you notice anything different when you were in?"

"Oh." She hesitated. "Well, yeah, there were a couple of things."

"Like what?"

"The door to the office was open as was the door to the front of the shop, and the light in the office was on."

"Was the alarm armed?"

Lani hesitated again. "Yes, it was, and the rest of the lights were off. The only things that were different were the open doors and the office light, but I thought maybe Taylor had forgotten to close the doors and turn the light off when she was in earlier."

"So there was a fresh flower order in the cooler?"

"There were flowers that hadn't been there on Saturday, but I can't say for sure whether they were brought in yesterday or today."

"Okay. Thanks."

"What's going on, Michael?" Lani asked.

He spotted Kieran walking in. "I've got to go, but I'll call you about it later."

Kieran approached him just as he hung up. "What's going on? Lois said you called in a robbery."

"Yeah. When Taylor came in, she discovered that the safe had been broken into."

"How much did they get?"

Michael sighed. "Taylor apparently hadn't done a deposit in awhile, so it was about a thousand dollars in cash plus the cash register float."

Kieran lifted his brows. "Okay."

Michael lowered himself onto a stool and ran a hand down his face. Kieran asked him more questions about it, taking notes in a small notebook. He had no idea how the theft could have happened. If the alarm had been on when Lani got there that morning, it just didn't make sense.

"Who all has the alarm code?" Kieran asked.

"Taylor. Me. And our employee, Lani."

"How long has she worked for you?"

"A few months now."

"And you trust her?"

"Yes." Of course, he did. If he didn't, there was no way he would have let her help him with Vivianne.

"And only the three of you have the code? No one else?"

"I haven't given the code to anyone else. But to be honest, I don't know for sure who Taylor might have given it to. You'll have to ask her."

"Do you have the code written down anywhere that someone might see it?"

"I have it in my phone, but I haven't labeled it as a code. Plus, no one has access to my phone."

"Do you have any thoughts on who might have done this?" Kieran asked. "An upset ex-employee? An ex-boyfriend or ex-girlfriend?"

"Not sure about the ex-boyfriend thing for Taylor, but there are no ex-girlfriends for me."

Kieran nodded, obviously recalling conversations they'd had about dating and marriage, and Michael's feelings on that for himself. "Okay. I'm going to chat a bit with Taylor."

Michael watched him walk to where Taylor stood, her arms crossed. When she'd called him earlier, it had seemed like the last thing she'd wanted to do. Given that she still hadn't contacted him after his accident, he was sure that was very true.

But since they were both there at the store, he hoped that maybe they could have a conversation about the future of the business. Just thinking about that discussion exhausted him, but he was sure she would hightail it out of the area as soon as things were finalized one way or another with Vivianne and the pending adoption.

He dictated a quick text to Ryker to let him know what was going on. He'd been on his way to visit him at a job site when Taylor had called him. Having never dealt with anything like a theft before, Michael had no idea how long he was going to have to hang around the shop.

Sitting there, Michael wondered if he should go ahead and call Lani back, but he kind of wanted to wait until he knew that no one needed to talk to him again. He wished that she could come to the shop and wait with him, but he knew she had other obligations that made that impossible.

Still, that didn't stop him from wanting her there with him. Was it wrong to want her support in yet another thing? Somehow, whenever she was with him, he felt stronger and more able to deal with the ups and downs of life. Her calming nature settled him in ways that were foreign to him but so very attractive.

He would never have thought he'd be in a place where he'd feel that way about a woman. And yet here he was, feeling emotions that were completely unfamiliar to him. Unfamiliar and, at one time, unwanted. He still didn't know what to do about the feelings. Dating wasn't something he'd ever done or thought much about.

His gaze went to Taylor. If only things were better between them. He wouldn't have hesitated to go to her for advice about what he was feeling for Lani. To talk through everything. Instead, he was trying to maneuver through uncharted waters on his own.

Kieran made his way back to Michael. "We're going to take some fingerprints, but there's not much more we can do here. Too bad you didn't have cameras. That would have been super helpful."

"I really didn't think we'd need such a sophisticated security system. We sell floral arrangements, for goodness sakes."

"Was it unusual to have that kind of money on hand?"

"I think so," Michael said, then shrugged. "But Taylor takes care of all that, so I'm really not certain how frequently she usually makes deposits."

"How about money from your side of the business?"

"We bill the majority of my customers, so we get checks from them, for the most part. Any cash we do get, I give to Taylor to deposit."

"Was any of that part of the money that was stolen?"

"I don't know. That's something Taylor would have to tell you."

Kieran frowned at him, no doubt wondering why Michael didn't know more about the finances of his own business.

"Taylor is the one with the degree in business administration," Michael explained. "So she takes care of all the bookkeeping for both sides of the business."

"Okay. If we have more questions about that, we'll ask her."

Michael sighed. "Sorry, I can't be of more help."

Kieran rested a hand on Michael's shoulder. "Don't worry about that, Michael. We'll do our best to figure this out."

"Can we still open the shop?" They hadn't opened yet for the day, and he wasn't even sure that Taylor wanted to.

"Once we're done dusting for fingerprints, you're free to open."

"Thanks, Kieran. I appreciate your help with this."

"Well, it *is* my job, but I'm glad to help you out. Hopefully, we can determine what happened."

"But there's a chance you won't."

"We'll try our best, but we offer no guarantees, unfortunately."

Michael nodded his understanding, then watched as Kieran spoke to his men before leaving the shop. For the next little while, he watched as a couple of people dusted for fingerprints in the office and the front of the shop. Taylor had retreated into the cooler, doing what Michael didn't know, but he didn't go after her. The conversation they needed to have shouldn't take place in front of an audience.

Instead, he sat on the stool, wondering what else could go wrong. After having several years of calm, he'd been lulled into thinking that's how life would continue on. Honestly, he should have known better.

When the officers finished doing what they needed to, Michael made his way to the front door to let them out. After they were gone, he went to the cooler, gripping the handles of his crutches tightly.

"Can we talk?" he asked.

Taylor glanced over at him for a moment before turning her attention back to the flowers in front of her. "I'll be out in a minute."

He had extremely low expectations for the conversation, which kind of hurt, but he was tired of being disappointed by this new version of Taylor. He made himself a cup of coffee—his...he wasn't even sure how many he'd had at that point—and was sitting at the worktable when she finally came out of the cooler.

"Are you planning to open today?" he asked as she went over to the coffee machine.

"No. I do have one order pick up for this afternoon, but I'll call and let them know that even though the shop is closed, they can come by for it. I'm not up to dealing with customers right now."

Michael nodded, not too surprised by her decision. "Do you have any idea who might have done this?"

She shrugged. "I mean, there's not that many of us that have the alarm code. The fact that the alarm was set kind of limits the possibilities."

He gave her a sharp look. "Are you seriously saying that you think Lani is behind this?"

She took a sip of her coffee as she settled on a stool across from him. "I don't know. There are three of us who know the current code, and neither of us would have stolen our own money."

"It wasn't Lani," Michael said firmly.

It made no sense for her to steal from them. From everything she'd said, Lani loved the work she did at the shop, plus he was paying her even more now that she was helping with Vivianne at night. Not that she'd been happy to take the extra money, but he'd insisted.

Taylor lifted a brow at him. "If you say so."

"I do say so." Michael was done with that part of the conversation. If all Taylor contributed to it was to accuse Lani of theft, he wasn't interested in continuing that discussion. "What are your plans?"

Her gaze dropped to her mug as she lifted it to take another sip. "As soon as you're approved for the baby's adoption, I'm gone."

"And what about the shop?"

"I don't care what you do with it," Taylor said with a shrug. "I'd like ten thousand dollars from the business, and you can have the rest."

"And we have that much in the accounts?" Michael hated that he was ignorant of that side of the business, but he'd never envisioned this particular scenario.

"We have the money we've been setting aside for the greenhouse, so it won't wipe the accounts out. There'll still be plenty in there for you to continue to cover your payroll and expenses."

"I guess I'll have to take your word for it."

Another shrug from Taylor. He was beginning to hate the shrugs. It was like she didn't care one way or another. Which she probably didn't.

"Hire an accountant to take a look at the books. They'll tell you there's enough."

Michael wasn't sure about hiring an accountant just yet, but he wondered if Beau would take a look at everything for him and then give him some advice.

"So I should just shut the shop down?" Michael asked.

"Your call. Maybe, since you trust her so much, you should ask Lani if she wants to run it."

"She's already said she can't work full-time," Michael reminded her. "She needs to be free during the day to care for her father."

"Care for her father?" Taylor asked.

"Yes. He was injured in an accident that left him disabled, so she takes care of him."

"If you're determined to keep it open, then put an ad out or spread the word that you're looking for a full-time florist."

It wasn't that Michael was determined to keep it open, but he hated the thought of having to let Lani go. He could see how much she enjoyed the work and how it gave her a break from dealing with her father. He knew he shouldn't be making business decisions with his heart, but when it came to Lani, it was hard not to.

"Maybe we should just settle on a date, and whether you're gone or not, we shut it down. I assume you've been turning away any major jobs like weddings and such?"

"Yeah. We haven't had many inquiries for them, though, because I've stopped running advertising for the shop."

It seemed like she was confident that he would shut things down, and though he hated to do it, if Lani wasn't able to work full-time, he wouldn't have much choice. He knew next to nothing about running a florist business. That had all been Taylor's doing.

"So, give me a date for shutting things down, and we'll put up a sign to let people know." And then he'd have to break the news to Lani, which wasn't something he wanted to do. But what choice did he have?

"Okay. I'll let you know."

Michael slid his arms into the cuffs of his crutches and got up from the table. "I guess I'd better go."

Taylor didn't say anything. Just kept drinking her coffee. His heart hurt with the distance that existed between them now. He wanted to let her know how much she was hurting him, but if her actions were anything to go by, she wouldn't care.

As Michael drove away from the shop a short time later, part of him was tempted to just go home, but he needed a distraction from everything. So instead, he turned in the opposite direction and drove to where Ryker and a crew were working on the landscaping for a newly built home.

"Everything okay, man?" Ryker asked when Michael joined him.

"We had a theft at the shop."

"Seriously? Someone broke in?"

"Well, technically, it was a theft without a break-in. They either had the alarm code, or they were pretty lucky at guessing what it was."

Ryker frowned. "Well, that would narrow the suspect pool down quite a bit, wouldn't it?"

"Yep," Michael said with a nod. "To me, Taylor, and Lani."

Ryker's eyes went wide, then he frowned. "You don't think it was Lani, though, right?"

"No, but I don't know what the police think. Taylor seems convinced it could be her."

The other man scoffed. "I'm sorry, man, but I don't put too much stock in what your sister thinks these days."

"You're not the only one," Michael admitted with a sigh. "We also decided that she's just going to pick a date to close the shop, so we can put a sign on the door giving people notice of when it's happening. Otherwise, it would have just happened with a day or two's notice."

"That's a shame for Lani."

"It is, but I don't know what else to do. If she could work full-time, I wouldn't hesitate to turn over control of the shop to her and just hire someone to do the accounting for it. But since she's already said she can't, I don't really have a choice."

"Carl!" Ryker called out to one of the guys. "You're gonna need another bag of mulch for that bed." After the man lifted his hand in acknowledgment, Ryker said, "No chance of hiring someone else to work the hours Taylor was working?"

"I don't feel confident in my ability to supervise the shop, to be honest. I wouldn't feel that I had to supervise Lani because she's already proven that she knows what she's doing."

"I feel for you, man," Ryker said. "You've had a lot of stuff dumped on you all at once."

"Tell me about it." Michael rubbed his hand across the back of his neck. "And that's not all of it."

Ryker gave him an incredulous look. "Something more has happened?"

Michael hesitated, wondering if he should tell Ryker. "I think I might have...feelings for Lani."

The man laughed as he slapped Michael on the shoulder. "Is that all? I could have told you that."

"What?"

"The way you act when she's around speaks pretty loudly about how you feel about her."

"Are you serious?" Michael felt a bit queasy at the thought others might see what Ryker did. "Do you think Lani knows?"

"I don't know. Maybe it's just easier for me to see since I get to see the two of you together fairly frequently."

"I'm not sure what to do about it, honestly."

"Why wouldn't you just tell her?"

Michael sighed. "My life is a bit of a mess at the moment, in case you haven't noticed."

"Sure, but she's kind of in the thick of it with you."

"Which is fine for an employee or even a friend, but not necessarily great for a relationship."

"What's the worst that could happen?"

"She says no, and things get awkward?"

"That's always a risk when asking out someone you like." Ryker yelled something to one of the guys then continued, "It's like you've never asked someone out before."

"Well, I haven't."

Michael could sense Ryker's gaze boring into him. "Say what now?"

"I've never dated. Never been interested in dating, to be honest."

"Wow. Okay." Ryker paused. "Why?"

"After the stuff I'd seen in our home growing up and having issues of my own, like not being able to read, I just had no desire to make myself vulnerable to someone."

"Yeah. Vulnerability is kind of a necessity when it comes to a relationship. Eventually, anyway. You don't have to be that way right from the start."

"So yeah...that's why I'm so nervous about even considering asking Lani out. She's been so great, and I really like her, but I don't want to lose her friendship."

"You could offer to take her out for dinner...as a thank you for everything she's doing for you. Then kind of see how things go when it's just the two of you. I'll even babysit."

Michael considered the idea, and while it was a possibility, it also made him really nervous. "I'll see. Maybe I just need to wait until my life calms down a bit."

"That might be a good idea."

"Unfortunately, once I'm off the crutches and the shop has closed, I won't have much interaction with her."

"You'll still have her phone number, and I'm sure she'll be happy for any excuse to see the baby."

"I hope so."

"I can't believe that she's spent all this time with Vivianne without becoming quite attached."

"So then she'll agree to date me so she can be close to Vivianne?"

Ryker chuckled. "I don't really think that's how Lani works."

"As previously noted, I don't have much experience with women. And after having Taylor basically turn into a stranger, I have even less confidence in my ability to understand women."

"Here's your first tip about women," Ryker said. "Trying to understand them as a whole is pretty much impossible. But one on one? If you show yourself to be willing to listen and give them a safe space to share about themselves, you have a good chance of understanding the one woman who's important to you."

Michael eyed the other man. "You seem to speak from experience. Do you date a lot?"

"Not so much anymore, but I did when I was younger."

"Why not now?"

Ryker shrugged. "My priorities shifted awhile back. I'm content with how things are at the moment."

"I guess my priorities are shifting too. Having Vivianne in my life has helped with that."

"Kids will definitely do that."

The pensive tone in Ryker's voice had Michael looking more closely at his friend, but he didn't say anything more.

When a couple of the guys needed more help, he and Ryker made their way over to where they were working. Michael wished that he could get in there and help them. He missed the physical labor aspect of the job. It was something he'd always excelled at, but since the accident, he could literally feel himself losing muscle tone.

Instead, he had to settle for giving directions and guidance while other people did the work. It felt all kinds of wrong.

As he was driving to his place after they were done for the day, Michael realized that he'd forgotten to call Lani back. In the midst of his turmoil about the theft and discussing his feelings for her with Ryker, it had completely slipped his mind. At this point, however, he might as well wait until she showed up later to tell her what had happened.

Michael just hoped that when he did tell her, she wouldn't think that they were blaming her. He didn't know what the explanation was for the theft, but there was no reason to suspect that Lani had anything to do with it.

CHAPTER TWENTY-THREE

Lani waited for Michael to get back to her, but by the time she had to leave for his place to pick up Vivianne, he still hadn't called. She hoped nothing bad had happened at the shop. But if that had been true, why would he have called to ask her if anything had looked off when she arrived for work?

She parked her car beside Ryker's vehicle, then got out. After getting the bag of food from the back seat, Lani hurried up the steps, eager to see Michael and find out what was going on.

"Hey, Lani," Ryker said when he opened the door.

Wolfie was right there with him, his tail wagging madly. She greeted them both then stepped into the house. As usual, Michael was seated in his chair, Vivianne lying on his thighs, her feet against his stomach. By her waving arms, Lani could tell that she was wide awake.

"I'm sorry I didn't call you back," Michael said as soon as he saw her. "I decided I might as well just wait until I saw you to tell you what happened at the shop."

"Have you eaten?" she asked.

"Yeah. We ate what you brought last night."

"Okay. Let me just put the food I brought in the fridge."

"I'm going to head off," Ryker said.

"Thanks again for your help," Michael said as they fist-bumped. "I'll see you tomorrow."

"You betcha." Ryker said goodbye, then disappeared out the front door, leaving the two of them—well, three...four if he counted Wolfie—on their own.

Once she had put the containers of food in the fridge, Lani sat down on the couch. "So what happened?"

"The shop was robbed."

"What?" Lani stared at him in shock. Based on what he'd asked her on the phone, she'd suspected something like that, but it had seemed so unlikely that she'd kind of dismissed the thought. "How?"

Michael sighed. "That's the question of the hour."

"What was taken?"

"Just money from the safe and the float for the till," he said. "But the thing that's so perplexing is that whoever it was, knew the alarm code."

Lani frowned, her stomach knotting. "The cops should be able to figure out who did it pretty easily then, shouldn't they?"

"Yeah, except only three people currently have the code," Michael said. "You, me, and Taylor."

Lani clenched her hands together. "You don't think I did it, do you?"

Michael shook his head. "You've never given me a reason not to trust you."

Though she'd been hoping for an opportunity to tell him who she was, Lani was fairly confident that right then was *not* the time. Lying about who she was might appear to be a motive...especially since she was the competition.

But who could possibly have done it? It just didn't make any sense.

"Did they get a lot?" Lani asked. She wasn't sure how often Taylor made a bank deposit, so it could be anywhere from a hundred dollars to a lot more.

"At least a thousand." Michael sighed. "Taylor will have to come up with a more exact amount."

"When did it happen?"

"We're not really sure, at this point. Obviously, Taylor didn't notice it until she came in today. I would imagine it took place sometime between when she closed on Saturday, and when you arrived this morning."

"So, it was significant that the doors were open?"

"It helped a bit with the timeline, but I think what will help the most is if the person left fingerprints. The only person whose fingerprints should be on the safe should be Taylor."

Lani nodded because she'd never touched the safe or the till at the front. Although she supposed that they could always assume that she used gloves or wiped everything down after opening it. Although she had no clue what the safe code was. Neither of them had ever offered it to her, and she'd never needed it.

And that's precisely what she'd say if anyone came to talk to her about it. It warmed her that Michael didn't seem to suspect that she had a role in the theft, even though she was the only other person besides him and Taylor to have the alarm code.

"Nothing besides money was taken?" Lani asked.

"Nope. Not that there was much else of value in the shop. It's not like they could try and pawn a bunch of flowers or vases."

"I suppose that's true." But it seemed weird that someone would know the code to not just the shop but the safe as well.

Since she knew that it wasn't her, and it obviously wasn't Michael, that only left Taylor. But even as she had the thought, Lani knew she could never voice that. Though his relationship with Taylor had been tested lately, she was quite sure that Michael's loyalty would still lay with his sister.

Lani didn't want to make him feel forced to choose between her or his sister, particularly in this situation, so she kept her mouth shut. If the cops pushed him on Taylor, and if it was possible she was involved, at least it wouldn't be Lani who voiced the idea.

"I hope the cops can get it sorted out."

"Me too, because I don't like knowing that someone has access to the shop."

"Did you change the code?" Lani asked.

"Taylor changed it this afternoon." Michael reached over to pick up his phone. He tapped on the screen, then her phone's text alert sounded. "That's the new code, so you'll be able to get in tomorrow."

Michael talked a bit more about what had gone on that day, mentioning the police chief by his first name, which led Lani to believe he was a personal friend. Kieran Sutherland hadn't been the police chief when she'd left for Hawaii several years earlier, and she didn't recall having heard her mom mention him during any of their conversations.

"I'm sure it was a stressful day for you guys," Lani said.

"Honestly, it feels like it's just been one stressful day after another recently," Michael admitted, his brow furrowing. "I will never complain about a boring life again. Not that I had complained about it before."

Lani wished she could say the same. It was partly why she'd applied for the job at the Reeds' shop. She felt kind of bad as she thought about how the stresses of Michael's life had led to a sense of purpose for her.

If things had just continued on without the developments with Taylor, and if she'd just continued to go to work for the three hours each day without anything else having happened, she probably never would have gotten this close to Michael. And of course, there would be no Vivianne.

"Excitement can be overrated," she said. "Especially excitement of the not-so-great variety."

"I believe that Taylor's issues, my leg, and this robbery would definitely fall into that category," he said, then gently tickled his fingers on Vivianne's tummy. "But this little one is definitely excitement I don't mind."

Lani smiled as he bent over and talked baby talk to Vivianne. Seeing him like this was always such a joy for her.

"Did you plan to have kids someday?" Lani asked.

Michael glanced up at her before focusing on Vivianne again. "No. I can't say that I ever planned to have kids, but I guess God had a different journey for me with this little one." He paused, sighing. "Or at least I hope He has a different journey for me."

Lani knew that he was thinking about the possibility of not being able to keep Vivianne in his life. The very idea made her heart hurt. Part of that was thinking about Michael losing Vivianne, and part of it was thinking of her own life without the little girl.

"I really hope that God didn't bring her into your life like this, only to take her away."

"I hope that too," Michael said, his gaze still on Vivianne. "But sometimes we don't see the bigger picture that God sees. Maybe there is a couple out there who would be better parents for her than I would be."

Lani knew he struggled with the things he saw as lacking in himself, but as she watched him with Vivianne, she knew that no one could love that little girl more than he did. *Please, God, don't take this baby from him.*

It was a prayer that she had said plenty of times over the past several weeks. If God only ever answered one of her prayers, she hoped it was that one.

"When I went to Eli's the other night, the whole group prayed for Vivianne and for me," Michael said. "Those prayers have really buoyed me up, making me feel that if the worst does happen, I may sink for a moment, but I won't drown. I have people who will pray for and support me, and God will keep me afloat."

Lani mulled over his words, thinking of her own experiences over the past couple of years. There were times she'd felt like she was drowning, too weary to try and fight the waves of grief that wanted to pull her down. But she'd never stayed under. Each time, something lifted her above the intensity of the grief, and she remembered the times her family in Hawaii had assured her that they were praying for her.

"I've kind of pulled away from my group of friends during all of this," Michael admitted with a frown. "I'm not even sure why except that they've all had stuff going on in their lives as well. Getting engaged. Getting married. Being busy with their lives, you know. It seemed like my life was sort of falling apart. The situation with Taylor had been building for a while, and I'd been trying to keep it hidden. It felt like a failure on my part, to have invested so much of myself in Taylor and our business, only for her to be able to walk away so easily."

Lani had so many things she wanted to say about that situation, but she bit her tongue. Michael was entitled to how he felt. She didn't know Taylor well enough or have enough understanding about their past to be able to comment knowledgeably. But she would always stick to her belief that Michael was a good man and that Taylor wasn't treating him the way she should have.

"Anyway, I'm glad I decided to go to the Bible study on Sunday night." A smile crossed Michael's face. "It was a good evening." He looked up at her. "I would love for you to come with me some time. They're good people."

She knew that, and maybe, depending on how he took her revelation, she'd accept his invitation sometime. And Sarah's as well. It was a good thing that Michael was closer to Eli and the other guys in the group than he was to Sarah, or he might have already discovered who she was.

"It does sound like they're good friends to you," Lani said, and for the first time since returning to New Hope Falls, she had a strong, undeniable desire to reconnect with people.

In Hawaii, she hadn't had many friends, but she'd had plenty of family who had also been friends. Here, she basically had no family, so if she wanted friends, it would probably be with someone like Sarah.

"And they'd be good friends for you, too," Michael said, repeating a sentiment he'd voiced before.

Lani gave him a smile but didn't commit one way or the other to meeting them. As soon as they discovered who was behind the theft, she was going to reveal to Michael who she was. It was absolutely imperative that she be the one to tell him.

Silence fell then, but she didn't hurry to fill it. Nor did she rush to leave for home, even though she was tired. She wasn't about to rob him of these moments when Vivianne was awake and happy to be with him. If the worst should happen, she wanted to know that she'd done her best to give him more memories with the little girl who'd grabbed hold of his heart.

Plus, she really enjoyed these evenings with him. They were low-key and quiet, but the more time she spent with him—even when they weren't talking—the more her feelings for him grew. She wasn't sure he felt anything remotely similar, and maybe now, with so much going on, he wasn't even thinking about it.

But it was definitely on her mind.

She stifled a yawn, not wanting him to see that she was tired. He'd probably tell her it was time to leave. But even though she'd had a restless night with Vivianne, she didn't want the evening to end.

"I suppose you probably want to leave soon," Michael said after a few minutes.

"No rush," she assured him. "I'll stay until she starts to get fussy so you can feed her before we go."

"Are you sure?"

"I'm positive. Is there anything else I can do for you while I'm here? Laundry or dishes?"

"Nope. Not a thing."

"So is it okay for me to go into the shop in the morning?"

"Yep. Taylor didn't open today because of dealing with the robbery, but tomorrow should be fine."

"Okay. That's good." She relaxed back on the couch, then quickly sat forward again. "Oh, I forgot. I got something for you."

Michael looked at her with lifted brows. "You did?"

"Yep." She got up and went to where she'd left her bag by the door. Opening it, she pulled out the things she'd put in there earlier. "Here you go."

He took the items from her, staring at her for a moment before looking down at what he held. "Oh. Wow."

She'd found a shop that did one-hour photo printing and had uploaded a couple of the pictures from their time at the river. Then she'd made a quick trip to pick up the photos along with some frames.

Michael turned one of the frames over to face Vivianne. "Look at that, baby. Your very first photoshoot. What a little model you are."

Lani grinned as she sat down on the couch again. She was pleased with how the pictures had turned out and even more pleased with how he was reacting to them.

"Thank you so much for these, Lani," Michael said as he turned the pictures back around. "You don't know how special these are to me."

Lani wrapped her arms around herself. "Actually, I think I do."

His gaze held hers, and her heart skipped a beat at the emotion she saw there. But was it for her? Or was it the pictures that had brought it out in him? She hoped that maybe it was a little of both because she found she wanted to have some sort of importance to him...to someone in the life she had now.

Vivianne began to fuss, drawing Michael's attention away from Lani. She got up and went to the kitchen to prepare a bottle then gave it to him to feed her. While he did that, she got a fresh diaper and a clean sleeper ready, knowing that Vivianne would likely conk out on the drive home. Thankfully, most nights, Lani was able to transfer her from the car seat to the bassinette without her waking up.

Lani smiled when she heard Michael begin to sing to Vivianne. It wasn't something he did every time he fed her, but usually, the last feeding before Lani left with her, he would sing as he gave her a bottle. Though she'd originally preferred to leave before Vivianne had her last bottle, she'd changed her mind, wanting to give Michael all the time she could with Vivianne.

And as she listened to him sing to her, Lani didn't regret that decision at all.

While he fed Vivianne, she checked the diaper bag to make sure it was ready for the next day. The more she could do before leaving Michael's, the less she had to do once she got home, which meant she could go to sleep all that much sooner.

Once Vivianne was done feeding and Michael had burped her, Lani changed her diaper and dressed her in a cleaner sleeper then put her in the car seat. Michael used his crutches to come over to where she stood at the table.

"I hope she sleeps well for you tonight."

Lani smiled at him. "You say that every night, and every night she's just fine. She's sleeping around four hours at a stretch now."

"I feel bad that you're getting the worst of it. By the time I get her back for nights, she'll be sleeping through."

That made Lani chuckle. "Hate to break it to you, but unless you think your leg is going to take months to heal, she'll still be sleeping fewer than eight hours at a stretch when you're back to doing nights."

"I'm not sure whether I should feel happy or sad about that."

"I'm sure it's quite alright to feel both. I think mixed emotions is a very real thing for parents."

"I've definitely got those in spades."

"And you probably will for years to come." Lani picked up the diaper bag and the bag she'd brought the food over in. "Let me run these out to the car, then I'll be back for her."

Michael nodded and bent to kiss Vivianne's cheek. Lani made quick work of getting out to the car and back again. Wolfie followed after her like a bodyguard, sniffing around the car like he was checking for a bomb.

When she stepped back into the house, Michael smiled at her. "Thank you again for spending your evening with me. I'm sure you have other things you could have been doing."

It was true she had other things she probably should be doing, but none of them were things she wanted to do as much as spending time with him and Vivianne. "I absolutely don't mind it, and I'll be back tomorrow to do it all again."

He followed her out onto the porch then leaned against one of the wooden posts of the deck. "Have a good night."

"You too. See you tomorrow."

He lingered on the porch as she backed the car away to turn around in the large gravel space in front of the house. And as she drove down the driveway, she saw that he stayed there until the turn in the drive took him from her view.

Lani let out a sigh, trying to push aside the feeling that she didn't deserve his trust or thanks as long as she kept such a large part of herself hidden from him. She hadn't out and out lied to him, but not telling him something so significant was definitely a lie by omission.

She just prayed that the robbery was solved quickly, and once it was, she promised herself that she wouldn't delay telling him everything.

But would that revelation rob her of the desire of her heart to be a part of Michael and Vivianne's lives on a more permanent basis?

Please, God, don't let him be so upset that he banishes me from their lives.

CHAPTER TWENTY-FOUR

Michael sat on the swing on his deck, his guitar propped on his leg, smiling as he watched Wolfie chase squirrels. The dog would dart in one direction until the squirrel was out of reach up a tree before darting in search of another.

It was moments like these when he was thankful that he'd gotten a dog. Now, even when he was the only person at his home, he still wasn't alone.

As he plucked at the guitar strings with the sounds of nature and his dog as harmony, Michael allowed his thoughts to run wild. Normally, he would have been out at a job site with the crew, but he'd needed to make some decisions so had stayed home.

Taylor had texted him that morning, two days after the robbery, to give him a date for closing the shop permanently. When he'd offered her that option, he hadn't been sure what sort of time frame she'd decide on, but he'd kind of hoped it would be at least a month.

Of course, he should have known better than to expect that from Taylor, given her behavior of late. Her text had simply given him a date two weeks in the future. Two weeks!

It wasn't just that the date spelled the end of the shop, it was that it also spelled the exit of Taylor from his life. And at that moment, he couldn't say with any confidence that he'd ever see her again. It wasn't what he'd ever imagined for his relationship with his sister. Still, it didn't seem that she was interested in being a part of his life any longer.

So now he was trying to figure out what to do for Lani. He hated the thought that she needed the income from her job at the shop and was suddenly going to be without it. More than that, though, he'd always gotten the feeling that arranging flowers at the shop gave her an escape from a situation that wasn't all that happy.

He hated that this decision would come at her from two angles, neither of them pleasant. The shop was a lost cause at this point, so all he wanted was to find a way to keep Lani from being too negatively impacted by that development.

And that was what had him sitting on his front porch, seeking calm and wisdom.

He'd already reached out to Beau about meeting with him to look over the shop's books. When he'd asked Taylor for the login to the accounting software, it had taken her so long to get back to him that he'd wondered if she was going to. Finally, she'd given him the information right after the text with the shop's closing day.

By the time Wolfie flopped down tiredly at his feet, done terrorizing the local squirrel population, Michael had come up with a plan. He had no clue if it was going to work, or if it was even possible.

But he wouldn't know if he didn't at least try. He didn't plan to mention anything of what was going on to Lani until he knew if it was going to work or not. He didn't want her to have to worry about anything until it was absolutely necessary.

After all she'd done for him, this was the least he could do for her.

The next afternoon, Michael pulled his truck to the curb on a residential street. The large, towering trees that lined the street spoke to the age of the neighborhood. As always, when faced with the beauty of nature, he felt calmed by it.

That morning, Beau had called to let him know that things were as Taylor had said. The company was in fine shape to give her the ten thousand dollars she'd asked for, even after having a thousand stolen from them.

As Beau had pointed out, however, it was his part of the business that brought in the bulk of the money on a more regular basis. His business had more contracts, which provided a steadier income. The shop's income tended to be lower ticket items with higher dollar events—like weddings—thrown in periodically.

Beau's evaluation of the businesses left Michael feeling confident that he would be able to keep his employees paid and Vivianne in diapers and formula even without the shop's income. Unfortunately, he'd also have to continue to pay the rent on the shop unless the landlord was willing to let them out of their lease.

Figuring that was a problem for another day, Michael got out of his truck and walked up the sidewalk toward the two-story building. A bright sign in the window said the business was open, which answered one of his questions.

He carefully climbed the steps, then pulled open the door, hearing a delicate tinkle of bells as he stepped into the shop. Glancing around, he didn't see anyone right away, but music played softly in the background, and there was a familiar scent of flowers in the air.

"Hi! How can I..."

Michael turned to see Lani standing frozen in the doorway leading to the back of the shop. "Lani?"

"Michael." She clasped her hands to her chest as she stared at him with wide eyes. "What... What are you doing here?"

Confused, Michael wasn't sure how he felt about what was happening right then. Clearly, he'd been led to believe one thing when another thing was actually true. Had other things Lani told him also been untrue?

"What are *you* doing here?"

Her gaze dropped as she hugged her arms around herself. "I work here."

"Wait. You told us you couldn't work longer hours at the shop because you had to care for your dad."

She nodded. "I do have to care for my dad." She waved her hand at the shop. "This is part of that."

Michael didn't understand what was happening, and he was questioning everything Lani had ever told him. Why wouldn't she have mentioned that she actually had another job when they'd asked her if she could work more hours at their shop? It wouldn't have been a big deal. After all, plenty of people worked more than one job, and if she'd had told them, they would have understood.

He tried to push aside his confusion for the moment because he still had something else to deal with at the shop that day. There would be time later to sort through all of this and perhaps have a conversation with Lani to clarify why she hadn't felt comfortable revealing she had a job in another florist shop.

"Is the owner here?" he asked, moving forward with the second part of his reason for coming.

Lani frowned, and her shoulders slumped. "That would be me."

"What?" Michael felt another, larger, shock reverberate through him, and his confusion returned, multiplied by a hundred. "You're the *owner*?" She nodded. "Then why were you in *our* shop?" A sick feeling started to spread through him, bringing with it a wave of anger. "The robbery. Were you trying to sabotage us?"

"No, Michael. Never."

He wanted to believe in the sincerity of her words, but it was hard to do that when faced with the very real fact that she had lied to him. He'd trusted her with so much of his life...and she'd lied.

She'd lied...

Swallowing hard against the anger that wanted to take over, he said, "You don't need to come and get Vivianne tonight."

"Please, Michael. Let me explain."

"You lied to me, Lani. I trusted you with our business and my *daughter*, and all along, you've been lying to me." He didn't look at her. He *couldn't* look at her as he turned for the door, wishing he could move more quickly than his crutches allowed. "Ryker will come by and pick up Vivianne's things, and you don't need to go to the shop anymore."

By the time he reached his truck, his anger burned through him like a wildfire, consuming his confusion and everything he'd ever believed about Lani. Nothing seemed to quench it, and honestly, he wasn't sure he wanted it to end. He normally hated it when his anger was inflamed, but it felt so justified right then.

Lani had had so many opportunities to tell him the truth about herself, but she hadn't. He knew the story behind what had happened to the owner of the rival flower shop—her mother—and he'd even heard that after being shut down for a while, the shop had opened again. Since the shop was Taylor's department, Michael hadn't ever followed up on the situation, and he didn't know if she had either.

Though thinking back, Taylor had mentioned early on after opening their shop that she'd had a few people tell her that the owners of *Luana's Blossoms* hadn't been happy with the competition. It wasn't like he and Taylor had set out to put anyone out of business.

There were enough communities around New Hope that there should have been enough business to support two small shops. Taylor had told him she wasn't going to try and go after any of the corporate places that might hold a regular contract with *Luana's*, and as far as he knew, she hadn't.

That didn't mean they hadn't ended up with those contracts over the years. Taylor wouldn't have turned away any business if they'd approached her. It was possible—likely even—that Lani and her parents had still viewed their shop as poaching their customers.

Had Lani tried to sabotage things on more than one level? Had the robbery been the final attempt to get back at their business?

Even as he thought it, however, the idea didn't sit well with him. Though he wasn't entirely convinced she would go to those lengths, there was no denying that she'd come to work for them without revealing who she was and had gone on to omit that information several times when she could have been honest with them about who she was.

Whatever trust he'd had in her had burned away under his anger at her betrayal.

It actually hurt to think that she hadn't come to realize that she could trust him, and that was probably why he had a hard time accepting what had just transpired. He struggled to trust people. Case in point—how long it had taken him to confide in Eli about what he was going through with Taylor and Vivianne, and that was even after knowing Eli for awhile already.

Michael returned home, wishing for all the world that he could lose himself in work. But all he could do was sit and stew about everything...after sending a voice memo to let Taylor know that she wouldn't have Lani's help at the shop anymore. He was sure she'd wonder about that, but unless she wanted to ask him or Lani what happened—which he was pretty sure she wouldn't—she wasn't going to find out.

"How'd your day go?" Ryker asked as he set Vivianne's car seat down on the table and began to unbuckle her.

"I've had better," Michael said, taking Vivianne when Ryker brought her over to him.

Ryker sat down on the couch across from him, a frown on his face. "What happened?"

Gazing down at Vivianne's sweet face, Michael tried to keep his anger under control. She was not the cause of it, and he didn't want her to be subjected to it. He took a deep breath and let it out before telling Ryker what had happened.

"So you think she got a job at your shop in order to sabotage Taylor?"

"I don't know. I didn't ask." Michael frowned. "It's bad enough that she had plenty of opportunities to tell me the truth, but still kept it from me. I trusted her to care for Vivianne, and yet she didn't trust me enough to tell me the truth."

"Sometimes people are trustworthy even if they haven't revealed everything about themselves," Ryker said, his voice carrying a hint of caution.

"I didn't need to know everything about her except for how it might impact our business. Our shops have a bit of history, which is why she should have been upfront about who she was. She *owns* the competition, Ryker."

"So should I be going home to pack a bag for tonight?"

"No. I can't ask you to do that on top of everything else."

"How're you going to deal with the baby on your own?"

He'd spent time thinking about that earlier and had come up with some options. "If you could go to Lani's and pick up the bassinette and other things, I'd appreciate that."

"And? How is that going to help you tonight?"

"Taylor bought a stroller, and I'll use that to move the baby around." He pointed to the stroller he'd parked beside his recliner earlier after he'd tested his ability to move around with it. "I'm able to put a little more weight on my leg now that I have a walking cast on, so I should be able to use the stroller for support instead of the crutches."

"How about I stay here tonight, and you give it a trial run?" Ryker suggested. "Then, if you do need help, I'm close by. If you feel confident after tonight, then I'll leave you to it."

"Thanks, man."

Ryker gave a nod. "I'll head over to Lani's now, and maybe I'll pick up some dinner from *Norma's,* since I think Lani was supposed to bring dinner tonight, right?"

"Yeah." Michael tried to ignore the pang of pain in his chest. He'd survived without Lani in his life before, and he'd do it again. "I could go for a burger and fries."

"Sounds good," Ryker said as he got to his feet. "Do you need me to do anything before I go? Sophia said she fed Vivianne just before I picked her up, so she won't need to eat."

"I think I'll be okay."

Ryker headed for the door. "See you in a bit."

He felt a bit of panic once he was alone with Vivianne, but he was sure he'd be okay. He had to be okay. There was no calling Lani for help. Not like that first morning after Taylor had dropped Vivianne into his lap.

He'd thought he'd come a long way since then, but when Vivianne began to fuss, he wasn't so sure. Maybe he shouldn't have sent Ryker off quite so soon.

Even as he tried to calm Vivianne, Michael knew that he needed to learn to care for her on his own. He'd relied on Lani and Ryker too much, though he knew he'd really had no choice, especially when he'd first broken his leg.

But it was time that changed.

~*~

When Lani's phone rang, flashing Ryker's name on her screen, she seriously considered not answering it. Her nerves were shot after an angry confrontation with her dad, driving her to escape to the front porch, and the last thing she wanted was to have to talk to Ryker.

Her heart ached at the reminder that she would no longer be caring for Vivianne. She understood why Michael had reacted the way he had. For the last few weeks, she'd worried that he'd learn about who she was from someone else. It had never entered her mind that he might come to her shop and find out that way.

"Hello?"

"Hi, Lani. It's Ryker. How are you doing?"

She let out a quiet breath. "I'm alright. How are you?"

"I'm fine." He paused, then cleared his throat. "I hear I'm supposed to pick up Vivianne's things. I wondered if I could do that now."

"Sure. I'm not home at the moment, but if you go around to the back of the building, there's a door with a code lock on it. I'll send you a text with the code, and you can go in and get her stuff. It's right by the door."

There were a couple seconds of silence before Ryker said, "I can wait and drop by when you're there."

"I'm not sure when I'll be back." She sighed, bending forward to rest her head on her hand. There was a moist chill in the air that made her shiver. But the chill on her skin was nothing compared to the chill that had settled in her heart when Michael had walked out the door of her shop. "I'm at my dad's."

Not that she wanted to be there.

It had been a full-on war with him over the past couple of days. As if it wasn't bad enough that Michael had discovered who she was, someone had seen her leaving the back entrance of the Reed's shop the previous week, and eventually, the word had gotten back to her dad.

Because of course it had.

And when she'd needed a break, she certainly hadn't gotten one because the very next day, Michael had walked through the door of her shop, and her world had imploded.

"Okay. I'll be sure to lock up after I grab the stuff."

"Thanks."

"Take care of yourself."

That sounded too much like a goodbye for Lani, and her eyes burned. Just like she'd gotten closer to Michael over the past several weeks, she'd also come to consider Ryker a friend.

How she had any more tears left, Lani didn't know.

"You take care of yourself too." She wanted to ask about Michael, but instead, she ended the call then gripped her phone tightly as she pressed it to her chest.

Though she wished she could have stayed outside, or better yet, just left altogether, she still had to go back in and finish getting her father's dinner ready. She'd barely arrived when he'd started yelling at her again, picking up where he'd left off the night before, which was why she was out on the front step, resisting the urge to leave and let her father fend for himself.

Forever.

Within the space of a couple of days, her world had changed, and she didn't want to be part of it anymore. She wanted to close the shop, pack up her stuff, and go back to Hawaii to be with the people who loved her. To the unconditional support they offered her.

It was wearying to try to do her best, and it never be enough. She had no one but herself to blame for what happened with Michael, but it still hurt. She could accept his anger, but losing his trust—to have him actually think she would have stolen from him— was like a dagger to her heart.

As she sat on the cement steps in front of her dad's house, she wished that it was dark already. Unfortunately, the longer days meant that even though it was a gray day, there was still plenty of light. Enough for the neighbors to see her sitting there.

When a mom walked by with her two kids on bikes, Lani couldn't keep from imagining a little Vivianne determinedly pedaling a tricycle with Michael trailing after her, a proud smile on his face. She'd wanted to be part of that, but from the way Michael had reacted, she knew she'd ruined any hope of that.

Knowing that the sooner she finished with her dad, the sooner she could retreat to her home, Lani got up. With her hand on the door, she took a deep breath and let it out, bracing herself for what waited for her inside.

"I can't believe how ungrateful you are," her father shouted as soon as he spotted her. "After all the grief your mother suffered because of that other shop, you go and help them out. You took hours away from your mother's shop and gave that time to them."

Lani walked past the living room and went to the kitchen, not bothering to respond to him. He continued to rage at her, so she did her best to block out his voice as she quickly got his dinner together.

She wasn't even sure why she was bothering to make the meal. When he got in a raging mood, he had a tendency to send anything she placed in front of him flying. She'd cleaned up more than one meal and broken dishes off of the carpet.

Once the food was ready, she stared down at it, trying to figure out the best way to prevent him from taking his anger out on the meal she'd prepared. He'd moved on to ranting about all the other things he saw as flaws in her, barely stopping to take a breath.

She picked up the plate and drink, then headed for the living room. He glared at her as she walked in. "It's about time."

Stopping a few feet away from him, she said, "If you dump this on the floor, I'm not cleaning it up, and I'm not making you more."

It wasn't often she stood up to him, but she was at the end of her rope, and frankly, she just couldn't find it in herself to care anymore. She'd prepared the meal for him, and if he threw it on the ground, that was his choice. Her choice would be to leave and not have to listen to his verbal abuse anymore that day.

She set the plate and drink on his tray, then turned and left the room. After checking to make sure there was nothing else that needed attention in the house, she gathered up her things. A glance in the living room showed that her father wasn't eating, but at least he'd stopped ranting and hadn't sent his food flying.

As she made her way home, Lani couldn't help feeling defeated. As if the past year and a half had all been for nothing. And now even the couple of friendships she'd managed to forge were gone.

When she reached home and saw that Vivianne's stuff was gone, tears spilled over. Brushing them aside, she was tempted to call her cousin or aunt. Unfortunately, she had a feeling that if she told them everything, they'd insist that she go back to Hawaii. And she was in just a fragile enough place that she would do it.

Frankly, Lani wasn't at all sure that wouldn't be her final decision, regardless.

CHAPTER TWENTY-FIVE

Michael debated going to Eli's that evening. It wasn't a Bible study night, since they only had those every other Sunday night, but a smaller group of them still met on the off weeks to go on a hike and share a meal. He hadn't always been part of that more intimate group, but in the past year, Eli had drawn him in.

Because of his broken leg and Vivianne's arrival, he hadn't been attending the Bible study or the smaller group as regularly as he once had. And he wasn't entirely sure about going that night either, especially since he couldn't hike. But he felt a strong pull to be around people who had proven themselves to be encouraging in the past because he really felt like he needed that.

In the two weeks since things had gone south with Lani, he'd struggled to find his footing. Every day he battled feelings of being inadequate on several levels. As a boss. As a father. As a friend.

And for some reason, his father's voice—which had faded away to almost nothing in recent years—had once again begun to sound loudly in his head. It reminded him often of how much of a failure he was and how he'd always be that way.

Despite everything going on, he should have been happy. Ecstatic, even. Two days ago, he'd gotten the call he'd been waiting for. Adele had let him know that everything was a go for him to adopt Vivianne. He had been so excited to hear the news, and his first instinct had been to call Lani and let her know. Only he couldn't do that anymore.

But the great news was a double-edged sword. With the approval, there was nothing left to hold Taylor in New Hope Falls.

Adele's call had come on the shop's last day, so he was sure Taylor was glad to finally be free of both him and the shop.

He hadn't bothered to call Taylor with the news, assuming that his lawyer would let her lawyer know, and he'd pass the information on to her. She had made her feelings about their relationship pretty clear over the past few months, and in truth, she felt like a stranger to him now.

At least Vivianne was one step closer to being his. He understood there would be at least one more visit before the adoption would be finalized. But even though he still struggled with things, he was certainly more confident in his ability to be a parent than he had been when Vivianne first arrived.

Not that he didn't think he still had a ways to go. But hopefully, he could learn what he needed as Vivianne required a new level of parenting from him. Maybe by the time she was eighteen, he'd finally feel fully confident in his role as a father. Or maybe not... He couldn't imagine how he was actually going to parent a teenage girl, but he had a few years to figure that out.

In the meantime, he was going to go and spend the evening with his friends. He wished he could go for the hike, but even though he had a walking cast on now, he didn't think it would hold up to something like that. At least not without requiring the group to slow way down.

"Okay, girlie, let's get ourselves together." Long gone were the days when he could just grab his jacket, his keys, and go. Now it was like going on a weeklong vacation even though they would be gone for only a few hours.

He lowered Vivianne into the stroller beside his chair, happy when she didn't fuss too much. As he headed to get the diaper bag, he made a mental list of everything he needed to make sure he had it all. It wasn't like he was going to some sort of playdate where someone might have something if he forgot it. If he didn't remember diapers, they'd be using paper towels.

There had been times over the past couple of weeks when Vivianne had fussed without reason, and Michael had wondered if she'd been missing Lani. He wouldn't have blamed her if she had. He certainly did, and he wasn't sure what to do about it.

The thing was, even though he was now doubtful about her role in what had happened at the shop, he didn't know what to do. He'd come to that initial conclusion simply because he couldn't understand why else she would have come to work in their shop. He still didn't have any idea why she'd want to work for the competition, but he wasn't convinced anymore that it was to commit sabotage.

Michael sighed as he put everything in the diaper bag, then settled Vivianne into her car seat. Every time they left the house, it took him two trips to carry everything out to the truck. But he made it.

The group was back from the hike by the time he got to Eli's. They were met with enthusiasm. Or maybe it was Vivianne who was being greeted with enthusiasm.

"Glad you could make it," Eli said, slinging an arm around Michael's shoulders for a quick hug before he reached in to lift the car seat from the truck. "How's it been going?"

"I'm alive, and so is Vivianne," he said, slipping the strap of the diaper bag over his shoulder. "Let's count that as a win."

"Well, you're also getting a hot meal," Eli said with a grin.

That was a definite plus. He hadn't been eating as well since Lani wasn't coming by each day. Not that that was what he missed most about her. No. That would be her smile. The conversations they shared. The way she stepped up when he needed help. The calm she showed when he panicked.

Was she missing anything at all about him? Probably not. For sure not after the way he'd accused her of stealing from the shop.

"Oh, look who's come to visit," Anna said with a smile when they walked into the cabin. "And it's nice to see you too, Michael."

"Haha," Michael said as he watched the women crowd around the car seat. "Nice to see you as well, Anna."

"Why don't we say a prayer for the food," Eli said. "Then you ladies can all take turns with the baby."

After Eli prayed, they began to dish up their plates from the food sitting on the island. Michael enjoyed listening to the conversations as he ate, though he didn't contribute to them much.

Once they were done eating the meal, they settled in the living room. Though it wasn't a scheduled Bible study, it wasn't a surprise when the discussion turned serious.

Michael debated whether he wanted to share anything, but he knew that he needed to get some things off his chest and perhaps get some advice from these friends. Ryker had definitely made his opinion known, firmly believing that Lani wouldn't have done anything to sabotage things for Michael.

"I've been on a rollercoaster ride these past couple of weeks," Michael said when Eli asked him to share how things had been going with Vivianne. Though he knew it didn't paint him in a great light, he began to tell his friends everything.

"Wait a second," Sarah said when he shared about what had happened with Lani. "Are you talking about Lani Alexander?"

He nodded. "Do you know her?"

"Yes. We were in the same class in high school." Sarah frowned. "There is no way she went to work for you in order to sabotage you."

"I have to agree with Sarah," Leah said. "Lani lives and breathes flowers. She worked in the shop with her mom from the time she was little. They planned to work together once she was finished school."

"But wouldn't that mean she has more reason to sabotage?" Anna asked.

"Not Lani." This time it was Jillian who, from what Michael understood, was also a classmate of Sarah and Leah's, which meant she too knew Lani. "That's not who Lani is."

Michael knew that. He really did. "So why would she have applied to work in our shop?"

The three women exchanged looks, Sarah and Jillian shrugging, leaving Leah to respond.

"If I had to guess," Leah said slowly. "I would say that she just wanted to work with flowers. When I was in her shop the other week, it didn't seem like she had much business. If that's been the case since her mom died, I would imagine she was just trying to find a way to do something she enjoyed and maybe earn a little money as well."

Michael felt sick as he listened. The fact that it was Leah who was telling him this gave even more weight to her words. Leah was reserved, more likely to give a snarky, sarcastic response than a thoughtful one. So if she was talking seriously, it was something to consider.

He thought about what Lani had told him about her father, and he realized that what Leah had said was likely correct. She'd just been looking for a way to do what she loved, and he'd taken that away from her in the worst way possible.

Hopefully, now that their shop was shut down, business would pick up at hers, and she'd once again be able to do what she loved.

Still, though, he owed her an apology.

Just like his dad, he'd allowed his anger to take over and fill his mouth with words he should never have said. Sure, he hadn't lashed out with his fists like his dad had, but what he'd done hadn't been any better. He'd always known what his father was capable of. Whereas Lani had been taken completely off-guard by his angry reaction to seeing her.

He didn't expect her to forgive him, but he wanted her to know that he was sorry and that she'd absolutely deserved better than what he'd done.

"We've all made mistakes," Eli said as he rested his hand on Michael's shoulder. "It's just important that we learn and grow from them."

He knew he'd done more than make a mistake. It felt like he'd made a MISTAKE. A bolded, all caps version of a mistake.

"How do you feel about Lani?" Sarah asked, her brow furrowed. "It seems like maybe you...I don't know...like her?"

"Like her?" Leah said with an incredulous look at her sister. "Are we in high school? Of course, he likes her."

"Why would you say that?" Eli asked.

Leah shrugged. "You could already tell while he was talking about what had happened that he felt really bad. Not just regretful, but really, really bad. And it only got worse for him as we explained who Lani was and what we know about her."

"For someone who doesn't appear interested in relationships, you seem to be particularly insightful about them, Leah," Anna said from where she stood, gently bouncing Vivianne.

"Well, I've had enough relationships going on around me lately to make me a pro."

The others in the room chuckled at her comment, but Michael felt no levity in his heart. He just felt defeated by his own actions. It was a horrible feeling.

He was so used to having other people's actions rob him of what he wanted or needed, making him have to work twice as hard to achieve things. But this time around...he had no one to blame but himself for the fact that Lani was no longer in his life.

"Michael," Jillian said, drawing his attention back to the conversation. "Lani has never struck me as an unforgiving person. She's always been gentle and caring, if a little reserved."

She may have said that to make him feel better, but all it did was make him feel like he'd kicked a puppy...hard. He wanted to make excuses for why he'd acted the way he had—he was tired, in pain, stressed, worried. But none of that mattered. He should have never reacted to the situation the way he did.

The next morning after he dropped Vivianne off at the babysitter's, Michael drove to Lani's shop. He'd thought about bringing the baby with him, but he didn't want the distraction when he was talking with her.

When he pulled to the curb in front of the shop, he could already see that the *Open* sign wasn't turned on. Frowning, he climbed out and made his way to the door. He didn't want to guess when the shop might be open, so he wanted to check the hours and make sure to come back when it was open.

As he approached the door, a sign on the glass snagged his attention.

Luanna's Blossoms is temporarily closed.

Michael stared at the words, then bent to peer through the glass on the door. This seemed to be more than just the shop not being open for the day yet. For some reason, Lani wasn't opening the shop at all.

With a sigh, he returned to his truck, feeling a bit letdown after he'd psyched himself up to talk with her. Without the option of seeing her, Michael decided that he'd call to see if he could arrange a time to talk to her.

Her phone rang several times before going to voicemail. Had she seen it was him and decided not to answer?

"Hi, Lani. It's Michael. I stopped by the shop and saw that it was closed. Would it be possible for us to meet? I really want to talk to you."

Already regretting that he hadn't thought through that message better, he hung up and sat there holding his phone, hoping that she got back to him quickly.

After several minutes passed without his phone ringing or a text appearing, Michael decided he might as well leave. A knock on the truck window made him jump. He turned to see a middle-aged woman standing beside his vehicle.

Lowering the window, he said, "Can I help you?"

"Oh, well, I saw you looking at the floral shop and thought I'd tell you that it's closed."

Michael gestured to the building. "I did see the sign in the window."

"It's a disgrace," the woman said with a fierce frown drawing her dark brows low over her eyes. "She just shut up the shop and left for Hawaii."

"Hawaii?"

"It's where her mother was from."

"Is she coming back?"

The woman shrugged. "Her father is absolutely livid at that girl's ungrateful attitude. She's done a horrible job with the shop. It would probably be best if she didn't come back."

No, Michael didn't believe that would be best at all. Except that was a selfish thought. Maybe, if Hawaii was a place where she was happy, it would be best for her.

"Thank you for letting me know," Michael said, eager to get away from the woman. She seemed to take far too much delight in belittling Lani.

With a nod and a smile, he started up the truck and pulled away from the shop. He didn't know what to think about the woman's revelation. How long had Lani been gone? It felt wrong that she was gone, and he hadn't even known.

If she had decided to leave New Hope for good, Michael would have to accept that he wouldn't have a chance to make things right with her the way he wanted to. And once again, he had no one to blame but himself.

In fact, he was pretty sure that what had happened between them had precipitated her departure. Nothing she'd said in the time leading up to that confrontation had suggested she was thinking of leaving New Hope.

If only he hadn't waited so long to come and talk to her. Maybe he could have caught her before she left.

Resigned to not hearing from Lani, Michael headed for the site where he knew Ryker and the crew were working that day. He still wasn't able to help much, but just being on a job site made him feel connected, and after not being able to talk to Lani, he needed that.

CHAPTER TWENTY-SIX

Lani stared out over the water crashing against the rocks on the shore. Although there was a hint of a breeze, she was grateful for the protection of the roof that covered the large porch as the midday sun beat down on the house. In deference to the heat, she wore a light tank top and a pair of shorts. Quite different from what she would have been wearing had she been back in New Hope.

Every day since she'd arrived back in Waianae—the place she'd called home while going to the University of Hawaiʻi - West Oʻahu campus—she'd been blanketed in heat. At first, it had been almost oppressive. She'd apparently lost her tolerance for it after living in the milder climate of Washington State for almost two years.

She'd definitely made a tactical retreat from New Hope after everything that had happened with Michael and her father. Her desire to work in the shop and to care for her father had plummeted. She was sure that her sudden departure said horrible things about her, but the vitriol her father had directed at her in the days following his discovery that she was working at Michael's shop had only gotten worse.

In the end, for her own sanity, she'd had to leave. After making arrangements for additional care for him—care that had been available from the start but that she'd refused to advantage of since she'd felt compelled to provide his meals for him—she'd closed up the shop and left.

It hadn't been a wise financial decision. The unexpected cost of a plane ticket, plus now there was no money coming in from the shop.

Thankfully, she'd banked most of the extra money Michael had been paying her for caring for Vivianne. She'd tried not to take the money, but he'd pointed out that if she wasn't helping him, he'd still have had to pay a night nurse, so he was happy to give that money to her instead.

She thought of the voice mail she'd woken up to that morning. A voice mail she still hadn't responded to. What was there to say?

The pain she'd felt at his accusatory words still lingered even after two weeks. Everything she'd thought about their friendship had shattered in that moment, taking with it the faint hope that maybe he was starting to feel the same way about her as she felt about him.

"Can you take her?"

Lani looked up to see Luann coming out of the door that led to her mom and dad's small apartment. Lifting her arms, Lani took the baby Luann offered her and cradled her close. Holding the baby was bittersweet. She reminded Lani a lot of Vivianne as they were not that far apart in age.

"You giving your mama a rough time?" Lani asked as she looked down at the little girl.

Luann went back into the apartment then reappeared with two tall glasses of her mom's lemonade. Setting them on the small table next to the Adirondack chair Lani sat in, Luann then sank down onto the chair on the other side of the table with a sigh.

"David at his mom's again?" Lani asked.

"Yep. The kids were going to the park with their cousins."

"Nice break for you."

"Definitely." Luann picked up her glass and took a sip. "How are you feeling today?"

When she'd appeared on their doorstep without any notice, her grandma had taken one look at her and wrapped her up in a tight embrace. The bedroom she'd used when she'd lived there before was just as she'd left it, and that had been exactly what she'd needed.

The large multi-family house her grandma owned was worth over a million dollars now, given its size and location on the shore, but it had been their family home for several decades, long before it had become an expensive property. It was just her grandma and aunt and uncle who lived there full-time, with other family members stopping in periodically and making use of the extra bedrooms in the main part of the house.

"I got a voice mail from Michael." She lifted her glass to take a sip, savoring the tart sweetness of the drink, then pressed the glass to her cheek, appreciative of the cold condensation on her skin.

"What did he say?"

"That he wanted to talk to me."

"Hmmm. That's all?"

"Yep. Apparently, he went by the shop and saw that it was closed."

Luann continued to sip at her drink. "I guess that's a good thing."

"Is it?" Lani asked. "For all I know, he's wanting to ask me more questions about the robbery."

"Or maybe he's wanting to apologize."

Lani scoffed. "I kind of doubt that. He was pretty certain that I was involved."

"People can say a lot of things in the heat of the moment, especially when they don't understand what's going on."

"It's been a couple of weeks, and he's only now coming to talk to me." Lani frowned at her cousin. "Why are you suddenly on his side?"

When she'd first come home, Luann had listened to what had happened and had uttered a few choice words about Michael and his behavior.

"I'm not on his side, per se," Luann mused as she relaxed back in her seat, her gaze out over the water. "It's just that I liked what I saw in you when you talked about him. Well, before all this happened."

"That was all based on what I *thought* Michael was like. Not how he actually is."

Luann didn't reply right away, and Lani didn't feel the need to say anything further. They'd talked at great lengths over the past week about what had happened. It had been cathartic for Lani to let it all out. But once she'd purged it all, she'd felt empty.

The feelings she'd had for Michael had seemed to freeze, no longer a living thing within her heart, and she didn't know how she felt about that. She wanted the warmth of those feelings—the burst of excitement that would spread through her whenever she thought of him.

Now when she had those moments, a sick feeling bloomed in her stomach. The confusion, disbelief, and finally, the anger that had spread across his face when the truth was revealed, was something she saw in her mind far too often.

"Are you planning to stay here?" Luann asked.

It was a question that Lani had been waiting for someone to ask, but until that moment, no one had. She was grateful that they hadn't because she wouldn't have been certain about her answer. The pain she'd felt from both Michael and her father had driven her away from New Hope Falls. The question was: would it be enough to keep her from going back?

"Nina would hire you back in a heartbeat, and you could finish your degree." Luann paused. "And you know your mama would never fault you for coming home."

Lani set her drink down, wiping her hand on her shorts before brushing her fingers across the baby's dark wispy hair. Luann was right. Her mom would never have wanted her to stay in New Hope Falls, especially if it made her unhappy. And truth be told, except for when she'd had Michael and Vivianne in her life, and the time she'd been able to actually do what she loved with flowers, the past two years had been the worst of her life.

Between her mom's death, her father's anger, the failing business, and now what had happened with Michael, she felt drained of all joy and purpose. So while it was true that her mom wouldn't fault her for coming back to Waianae, she'd also want her to return for the right reasons.

"I'm not sure what I'm going to do." Lani stared out at the water. "Even if I decide to stay here, I'll still have to go back to get my things and sort out what to do with the shop."

"You know I'd love for you to come back here," Luann said. "But not if you're not totally confident this is where God wants you. You need to pray about it."

Lani sighed. That was one thing she hadn't been doing much of lately. She struggled to understand how Michael could call himself a Christian and then lash out at her the way he had. When she said as much to Luann, her cousin sighed.

"Michael's human. If he claimed to be God and acted that way, then you might have a point. But Michael made a mistake, and maybe he's realized that and understands he needs to apologize. But..." Luann held up a finger. "Even if he never admits he was wrong and apologizes, you can't base your view of God on that."

Lani knew that since she had attended church for most of her life. It was just that in the time since her mom had died, she hadn't clung as tightly to her faith, and she could see now how that choice had left her weak and vulnerable.

"Maybe you need to phone him back and see what he has to say."

"And if it isn't what I want to hear?"

Luann shrugged. "Then you know. And maybe that will make it easier for you to decide where to go."

They both fell silent after that, and when the baby began to fuss, Luann got up and took her from Lani, disappearing back into her mom's apartment. Lani remained where she was, seeking calm from the turbulent sea.

This spot was where she'd come whenever she'd needed to think. To feel. To study. To talk. It was where she'd come to grieve when the news had come about her mom.

And now she was back again, looking out at the ocean as it stretched to meet the horizon. An endless expanse of blue. It was so different from New Hope Falls, though each place held a beauty that spoke to her.

But where was the place she wanted to call home?

For the next few days, Lani didn't do anything about the voice mail from Michael. Instead, she continued to spend time with her family, soaking up the love and affection she'd been missing over the past couple of years. She hadn't realized how much she'd needed it until she had it in her life once again.

One thing she knew for sure was that if she did decide to make her life in New Hope Falls, she needed to make friends. She also needed to find a spiritual connection with people there. She could no longer be just by herself, dealing with her father's anger and a failing store on her own. A support system was necessary. She'd always have that in her family, but she realized now she'd need something closer if she settled in New Hope.

"I think it's time, *ko'u pua.*"

Lani looked over to where her grandma sat in her chair on the lanai. *My flower.* It was what she'd always called Lani, and it never failed to warm her heart. "Time for what?"

Tutu regarded her with her soft brown eyes, her lined face so familiar. "For you to decide what you're going to do. I don't want you to leave, but living in limbo isn't good for you."

Lani couldn't argue with her on that point. She needed some sort of purpose in her life beyond sitting on the lanai and watching the ocean. Over the past couple of days, there had been an undeniable tug in her heart to return to New Hope Falls. Whether that was to stay or just to tie up loose ends, Lani wasn't entirely sure just yet.

"You're right." Lani drew her legs up and wrapped her arms around them, her heels resting on the edge of the chair. She'd never liked living with uncertainty, and honestly, making major decisions had never been something she enjoyed, especially without her mom's guidance.

"I'm not saying you can't come back here," her grandma said gently. "This will always be your home, Leilani, you know that."

Lani did. She might not have really known her mother's side of the family until she was in her teens, but they'd always lavished her with lots of love even from a distance. Then they'd welcomed her with open arms when her mom had sent her there after she'd graduated from high school.

She'd been horribly homesick those first few months, but her grandma's steady affection had helped to ease the ache. It had made Lani wonder if her mom had suffered homesickness herself when she'd moved from Hawaii to New Hope Falls. And if she had, who had comforted her the way Tutu had comforted Lani?

The break from New Hope Falls had been nice, but it hadn't necessarily given her any clarity for her future. Regardless of what she decided, there was no avoiding going back to New Hope Falls. So while she didn't feel clarity, she felt a bit calmer.

"I'll be praying that God helps you find the path that gives you His peace."

"Thank you, Tutu," Lani said, and she really meant it. If nothing else, she did want peace in her life, whatever that might mean. "I guess I need to book a ticket back to New Hope."

"Good girl." Tutu reached over and patted her arm. "Just give us a couple more days before you go."

That wasn't a hardship at all.

What was a hardship, Lani decided three days later, was saying goodbye to her family again. Luann had said goodbye to her at the house since it was easier than her making the trip to the airport with the kids. So it was her aunt and uncle and Tutu there to send her off.

"It was good to see you again, Leilani," her uncle said, his voice gruff but gentle. Luann's dad was pretty much the opposite of Lani's dad. He was easygoing and affectionate, his big booming laugh something that had always made Lani smile. "Love you."

"I love you too," Lani said as she hugged him.

After she shared lingering hugs with her aunt and Tutu, Lani headed through security to her gate. Though she was leaving in the morning, with the time change and flight length plus a stopover, she wouldn't arrive back in Seattle until later that evening. Then she'd have an hour's drive back to New Hope, after paying what was going to be a large bill at the place where she'd parked her car.

She hadn't slept well the night before, so by the time she pulled her car to a stop behind her building, Lani was exhausted. She carted her things up the stairs and left them at the foot of her bed while she went to wash away the grime of a day of travel.

The trip home had given her time to think about what she needed to do over the next few days. She still wasn't entirely sure when she'd open the shop again—*if* she'd open the shop again. After being closed for almost two weeks, she probably didn't have much of a business left. Not that she had had much of a business to start with.

As she crawled into bed a short time later, she waited for the regret to come at having left Hawaii, but it didn't. Such as it was, the small apartment had become her home over the past couple of years.

When she'd first come back after her mom's death, she'd stayed with her dad. However, when the renter who had been staying in the apartment above the shop left, Lani had gratefully moved in. She'd come to realize that she needed a place of her own where she could escape her father's unrelenting anger. At first, she'd understood his anger and had hoped that it would wane as his grief eased, but if anything, it had gotten worse.

There was no way she would have even considered staying in New Hope if she hadn't been able to have a place of her own.

She still hadn't responded to Michael's voicemail, and as she lay in her bed, knowing that he was nearby once again, Lani couldn't keep her thoughts from going to him and to Vivianne. It was possible that she could avoid him indefinitely. After all, they'd lived in the same town for almost two years and had only met after she'd started to work at Taylor's shop.

But she had a feeling that if she didn't respond to him, he'd eventually come looking for her.

Maybe the first thing she needed to do the next day was to contact Michael and see what he wanted. Just the thought of it made her stomach clench with nerves. How could they move forward from their last interaction?

After yet another restless night, Lani got off to a slow start, taking time to make herself some breakfast then sorting through all the mail that had been shoved through the mail slot of the shop. But as she puttered around doing all manner of piddly jobs, Lani knew she was just avoiding what she had to do.

Finally, after her bags were unpacked, the laundry was done, the apartment dusted and vacuumed, she settled down in her chair with her phone. She drew her legs up and stared out the window, watching as Mrs. Lange came out of her house. Lani shook her head as she saw the woman glare at the shop, obviously looking for any tidbit of gossip that she could pass on to whoever might be within earshot throughout her day.

Even though she knew that it would be easier for Michael if she called him, she just wasn't quite there yet. So instead, she tapped out a message for him.

I just got back to New Hope.

She tried to figure out what else to say, but then finally just pushed send. And waited... She expected him to call her back, so she braced herself for that. Instead, her text alert sounded.

Michael: *Can I come and see you?*

Her breath whooshed out of her lungs at his question. It wasn't totally unexpected, but still, she didn't know how to respond. Part of her wanted to see him again...the Michael of before that horrible day. But instead, would the Michael she'd seen on that day be the one that showed up?

But having made contact with him, she couldn't just leave him hanging. She found herself closing her eyes and praying that God would help her make the right decision.

Finally, she decided that putting it off wouldn't make things any easier. It was time to listen to what he had to say then move forward with her life.

Okay.

Michael: *I'll be there in half an hour.*

Lani was grateful he'd chosen to communicate with her in the way she'd initiated rather than what was most comfortable for him. She prayed that his consideration would carry over into whatever was to come.

CHAPTER TWENTY-SEVEN

Michael had honestly given up any hope of having a chance to talk to Lani again. He'd driven by the shop nearly every day to see if the sign was out of the window. But it had remained there, a glaring reminder of his actions.

When her text had arrived, he'd been so surprised that she'd responded, that it had taken him a minute to get his program to read it to him. It had been straight to the point, giving him no idea what she was thinking about him or their situation. He was flying into this blind, but he could only hope and pray for a good outcome.

Michael maneuvered his way to where Ryker stood with their newest hire, explaining their safety protocols for taking down a tree. This tree was smaller than the one he'd had his accident on, and Ryker hadn't hesitated to use Michael as an example of what could go wrong when a climber was distracted.

"I need to head off for a bit," Michael said when he got Ryker's attention. "Lani agreed to meet with me."

A smile softened the stern features of the man's face as he nodded. "Best of luck."

"Thanks." Michael knew that he needed more than luck. He needed God to guide his words as he spoke to Lani.

He swung by his place to change out of the faded jeans he'd worn to the job site, one leg cut off to accommodate his cast. As quickly as he could, he switched them out for a pair of cargo shorts and a clean T-shirt, then headed for Lani's shop.

The sign was still in the window of the shop, but when he pulled on the handle of the door, it was unlocked. The bells over the door tinkled delicately just like they had the last time, but missing this time was the scent of flowers. She'd obviously not restocked since returning to New Hope.

When Lani appeared in the doorway leading from the back, Michael's reaction was very different than the last time they had met there. The knot he'd been carrying around in his stomach loosened slightly at the sight of her. Not completely, however, because he had no idea how she'd respond to him or what he wanted to say, but seeing her again was *so* good.

There was wariness on her face, and the joy and warmth that had always been present in her gaze were gone. The reserved look she gave him as she stepped up to the counter wasn't something he'd seen on her before. Even from the first day they'd met, she'd been warm and friendly, so it hurt to have her look at him that way.

As he approached the counter, Michael drank in the sight of her, his heart warming. Being this close to her once again made him want to fight hard to have her back in his life in whatever form that would take. But he wouldn't run roughshod over what she wanted. If she wanted nothing more to do with him, though it would be hard, he'd respect her wishes.

"Hi," he said, giving her a cautious smile.

Her brows drew together, and she bit her lip before returning his greeting...without the smile.

"Thank you for agreeing to see me." At her nod, he said, "First of all, I want you to know how sorry I am for how I acted and what I said. It was wrong of me, and I apologize for that. You deserved better."

"Have they found out who robbed the store?"

"Not yet," Michael said, hoping his frustration with the slowness of the investigation didn't show.

"So you don't think I'm that person?" she asked. "Or you do, but you still think you owe me an apology for how you acted?"

"I know you're not that person," Michael said with all the conviction he felt. "I can't explain why I said what I did. I could give you excuses, but the reality is, none of them would justify the way I acted. It was wrong, and I know that."

He'd had no expectations for how she might react, and he was glad he hadn't because she basically didn't react at all. She just regarded him with her beautiful eyes. It pained him that he couldn't read anything from her expression, when before, she'd always been fairly easy to read.

"If you didn't know who I was, why did you come here that day?" Lani asked, not responding to his apology.

"Oh. Well." Michael leaned more of his weight on his crutches. "I came for two reasons. First, I wanted to let the owner know that our shop was shutting down, so they might experience an influx of business. Second, I was hoping that because of the possibility of increased business, they might be willing to hire you."

Lani's brows rose. "You came here to see about a job for me?"

"It seemed like the right thing to do. To try and see if they might hire you to work for them like you had for us." Michael shrugged. "You were a great worker, and you seem to enjoy arranging flowers."

"I do," Lani agreed with a nod. "Don't you want to know why I was working in your shop?"

Michael regarded her for a moment before responding. "Yes, I'd like to know, but I also understand that you don't owe me any explanations."

Lani dropped her gaze to her hands before looking at him again, her brows drawn together.

"I applied mainly because I needed more money for this." She sighed as she waved her hand in the air. "My father had told me repeatedly that your shop had taken away our business, so I kind of figured that by going to work for you, I'd get back a little of what we'd lost. But I only planned to do it honestly. I mean, I wasn't going to tell you who I was, but I was more than willing to work for what you paid me. I wasn't going to take anything from you that I didn't work for."

Her response didn't surprise Michael, and without the shock of discovering who she was, it made perfect sense.

"I know that. I knew it then too, I just... Well, I can't excuse what I said." Feeling hopelessness inside him, Michael's shoulders slumped. "I'm just so sorry for not listening."

"I was going to tell you, but it was hard to find the right time." Lani frowned. "And then when the robbery happened, I was afraid that if I told you who I was, you might suspect me."

"Which is what happened, so you were right to be concerned about that."

Lani shrugged. "Yeah, it did play out like I thought it might, but I still should have said something sooner. Like as soon as we started hanging out outside of work."

"Be that as it may, I should have waited for you to explain instead of going off like I did." Michael felt like they were just going in circles at this point, and since he was still uncertain if she had actually accepted his apology, he wanted to move on from it. "I...uh...I wanted to talk to you about something else."

"Something else?" Lani frowned, wariness reappearing on her face.

"Nothing bad," Michael assured her. "Or at least, I don't think it is."

The frown hadn't disappeared from her face, even at his words, but she didn't say anything. Apparently waiting for him to continue.

"The shop is closed now, which I realize might not seem like a good thing, but I'm hoping it might present a new opportunity for you." Her frown eased into a look of curiosity. "We still have several months on the lease. I'd like to offer you the opportunity to take over the space."

"You want me to take over the lease?"

Michael shook his head. "I will still cover the cost of the lease, so you could get established in the location. Then, if you decide it's profitable, when the lease is up, you could then take it over yourself."

"Why would you do that?" Lani asked, her brow furrowed.

"The shop is going to just sit there empty, most likely. Plus, maybe your father is right. Our shop probably did take business away from yours. We certainly didn't set out to do that. In fact, we agreed that Taylor wouldn't do any local advertising or go after any corporate contracts. However, I'm sure the location alone contributed to our success, which is why I'm offering it to you now rather than have it sit empty."

"I don't know what to say."

"You don't need to give me an answer right now," Michael assured her. "Just consider it, okay? Know that it's an option for you."

"Okay. Thank you." She started to speak, then hesitated before saying, "Uh...how is Vivianne?"

"She's doing good. I got the call last week that my home study was approved."

Finally, the smile he'd missed lit up her face. "That's wonderful. I'm so happy for you both."

"You played a role in that, so thank you. Without hesitation, you stepped in when I needed your help." Michael gave a regretful shake of his head. "And I repaid you badly."

Lani didn't argue that point, which told Michael everything he needed to know about where he stood with her. He just hoped that she'd take him up on the offer of the building. There was no reason she shouldn't take advantage of it, especially if she planned to keep her shop open.

"Anyway," he said, "I'll leave you to your day. Thank you for giving me a chance to talk to you. Let me know what you decide about the space."

"I will."

With a nod, he turned and made his way out of the shop. The knot in his stomach had unwound now that he'd had a chance to talk to her. Still, the knowledge of how wrongly he'd treated her weighed heavily on his shoulders, and he doubted it would ever fully go away.

Knowing that going home would only give him time to stew in his thoughts, Michael went back to the job site even though Ryker would have questions about how his meeting with Lani had gone. He'd told himself not to get his hopes up. But apparently, even the small amount of hope he'd been harboring had been too much because he felt crushed by the loss of her friendship and the potential for more.

But he accepted responsibility for his actions and would learn to live with the consequences.

~*~

Lani moved from behind the counter and went to the door, planning to just lock it. However, she couldn't keep from watching Michael as he used his crutches to make his way to his truck, noticing then that he had a cast on his leg in place of the frame. She'd thought she was prepared to see him again, but clearly, she'd been wrong.

The contrition on his face had been a blow to the walls she'd tried to place around her heart, not wanting to be vulnerable to him again. But even if his apology had been appreciated, it hadn't escaped her notice that he'd come without Vivianne. And even after she'd asked how the baby was doing, he hadn't given her much information, nor had he offered to bring Vivianne to see her.

He may have been sorry for what he'd said to her and even thought he was doing a good thing when he offered her a rent-free space. But it didn't take away from the fact that he didn't seem willing to trust her with Vivianne anymore. What she needed to figure out was how that fit in with her consideration of whether or not she'd take him up on his offer.

She'd come back to New Hope, uncertain if she was even going to stay, let alone re-open the business. Now she had something else she needed to add to the mix.

If he'd made this offer before everything had gone south, she wouldn't have hesitated to take him up on it. But now...now she wasn't sure she wanted to be in debt to him the way taking the shop rent-free would make her feel. It didn't matter that he probably wouldn't view it that way. She would.

Maybe her shop would have an increase in sales even without needing to take over the other location just because the closest competitor was gone.

But as much as she'd like to turn him down based on how she felt about their current situation, Lani knew she needed to put aside her feelings and look at the offer from a business standpoint. One thing she knew for sure already, she couldn't accept free rent, but maybe if they could reach an agreement on that, she could consider it.

The next day, Lani debated going to see her dad. She knew without a doubt that it wasn't going to be a pleasant scene, but she also knew she couldn't put it off indefinitely. The meeting with Michael had been okay...better than she'd expected really. She didn't hold out the same hope for the meeting with her dad.

She still hadn't made up her mind when the doorbell rang in her apartment. It actually took Lani a moment to recognize what it was because she heard it so rarely. No one ever came around to the back door to ring the bell.

Knowing her luck, it was Mrs. Lange, who had seen the lights on in the apartment and was coming to check if it really was Lani. That thought was almost enough for her to ignore the bell when it sounded a second time.

With a sigh, she tossed aside the towel she'd been using to wipe down the counter and went down the stairs to answer the door as the bell rang a third time. Whoever was there was determined.

She unlocked the door then jerked it open, her gaze widening as she spotted one of the McNamara twins on the small porch. Usually, if one of the twins turned up to visit her, she'd assume it was Sarah. But like anyone who had spent any significant time with the two—which she had as a classmate—Lani could tell the difference.

"Leah?"

The woman held up her hand. "Don't give me grief over this."

"Give you grief over *what* exactly?" Lani stepped back. "Did you want to come in?"

"Might as well. I've made it this far."

Lani couldn't help but smile at Leah's snarkiness. She hadn't changed a whole lot in that regard since high school, though she seemed to use her words more now. In high school, it had been a lot more about the looks she'd give people rather than the words.

"C'mon upstairs." Lani turned to lead the way back up to her apartment.

"This is nice," Leah said as she looked around.

"It's nothing fancy, but it's mine."

Leah nodded. "Having your own space must be nice."

"Don't you like living at the lodge with your family?"

The other woman shrugged. "I don't mind it, but sometimes I think it would be nice to have a bit more privacy."

"Have you considered moving out?"

"I have a piece of land that's a part of our family land that I could build on if I want a place of my own."

"That's nice," Lani said as she motioned to the living room. "Do you plan to build soon?"

"I'm not sure. I think about it off and on. But for now, with Eli out of the house and Sarah moving out when she marries Beau, I'll probably stay there with Mom."

"Can I get you something to drink or eat?"

"Water would be nice. Thanks."

Lani filled two glasses with water then carried them to the living room where Leah had settled on the couch. She set the glasses on the coffee table, then grabbed a container sitting on the counter.

"Want a cookie?" she asked. "My grandma sent them back with me. They're her special chocolate chip cookie recipe."

"Well, I won't turn down anyone's grandma's cookies." Leah took one then settled back on the couch. After taking a healthy bite, she said, "Hmmm. I might need you to ask your grandma for her recipe."

"We'd both need luck with that since Tutu has said we won't get a copy of the recipe until she's gone."

Leah chuckled. "I know all about top-secret recipes. Mom has a few."

"And she really hasn't given them to you yet?"

"Nope. I think it's her way of making sure we still need her around the lodge. Like there would ever come a point when we wouldn't."

Lani felt the sting of tears at the thought of her own mom and the plans they'd had together. "So, uh, what can I do for you? Did you need another arrangement? I don't have flowers on hand yet, but if you need something, I can probably order enough to do a bouquet for you."

Leah frowned for a moment. "When are you opening up again?"

Lani sighed and shifted her gaze away from Leah's. "I'm not sure if I am."

"What? Why wouldn't you open again? Especially now that the Reeds' shop is closed."

Though she'd never been especially close to Leah—or any of the other girls in their class, really—she found herself sharing the truth with her. "I'm really struggling here without my mom. For the past year and a half, I've tried to do my best, but it's just not enough." She sighed as she rubbed her hands on her thighs. "I don't know if I want to do it anymore."

"So what would you do?" Leah asked.

"Go back to Hawaii to be with my family. I have a standing job offer from the florist I was working for there when my mom died."

"What about your dad?"

Lani shrugged. "He doesn't want me here. I haven't been able to do anything right, according to him. When he found out that I was working at...at another florist shop, he was livid. The things he said to me." She shuddered at the memory. "And then a couple of days later... Well, let's just say that that was the worst week I've had since my mom's death."

"You went back to Hawaii?"

Though Leah's question held no challenge, Lani felt defensive. "I needed to regroup and figure out what I was going to do."

"Why are you back if you're not going to open the shop?"

"I can't just leave things hanging here. I need to make arrangements for my dad and the shop if I'm not going to stay."

"So you haven't made up your mind yet?"

Lani sighed. "No. I guess I haven't." She hesitated then said, "You don't need to hear all of this. So, did you need flowers?"

"No, although my mom really loved the arrangement you did for her."

"Then, why are you here?" Lani grimaced. "Sorry, I don't mean to be rude. It's just you and I...well, it's not like we're friends."

"I think we're quite alike in our need for friendship," Leah said. "In that we really don't need a lot of friends. Do you have family you're close to?"

"Yeah. I mean, I was always super close to my mom, and now I have my cousin. She's my best friend."

"That's how Sarah is to me."

Lani nodded. "But I still don't understand why you're here."

"Yeah. I'm not entirely sure why I'm here either. Sarah is the one who's better at this kind of stuff. I mean, since she and Beau got engaged, she's become the queen of relationship advice."

"You're here to give me relationship advice?" Lani asked. "I don't have a relationship."

"But maybe you could have one."

"What are you talking about?"

"Not what...who," Leah said with a sigh. "I'm starting to feel like we're back in high school."

"So you're here on behalf of someone who likes me?"

The other woman looked pained. "Yeah. I guess you could say that. Although he's not the one who asked me to come."

"Let me guess. His best friend asked Sarah to ask you to talk to me." Lani was trying to ignore the flutter in her stomach as she considered exactly who Leah might be there on behalf of.

Leah chuckled, a fairly uncommon sound from her. "That would make it more high school-ish, but no, I'm here because...well, I'm not entirely sure why. Maybe because I'm trying to do something good for a change."

"For a change?" Lani asked. "You might not be the friendly, outgoing person that Sarah is, but you're not running around doing bad things."

Leah frowned. "At least not that you know of." Her expression cleared. "But I'm not here to talk about me."

"Then who *are* you here to talk about?" Lani asked, even though she had a pretty good idea.

"I'm here to talk to you about Michael Reed."

CHAPTER TWENTY-EIGHT

Even though she'd been expecting the name, Lani swallowed hard against the emotion that swept through her when she heard it. "Michael Reed?"

"You know him, right?" Leah asked with an arched brow. "I believe you worked for him."

Frowning, Lani said, "How do you know that?"

"He told us." Leah paused, obviously to allow that to sink in. "Michael was remarkably forthcoming about everything that happened between the two of you."

"Everything?" She had a hard time believing that since some of their interaction didn't paint him in a very good light.

"Yes. He told us about what happened when he showed up here unexpectedly, and also what he accused you of."

Lani's eyes went wide. "Really? Why would he do that?"

"Because he was desperate for advice on how to fix what he'd done wrong. At the time, he was unaware that you'd left New Hope."

Lani didn't know what to say to that. Letting out a sigh, she pulled her legs up and wrapped her arms around them.

"He knows he made a mistake," Leah said.

"Yeah. He already apologized."

"He did?" Leah asked. "You mean I've come over here for nothing?" She frowned. "Wait. That came out wrong. This is why Sarah is better at this than I am."

Lani had to laugh, even though she was feeling a bit emotional. "It's okay, Leah. I know what you meant."

"Listen, I'm glad I got a chance to chat with you, regardless." Leah sat forward, pinning Lani with a look. "I think you'll continue to struggle here if you don't allow yourself to have support. You didn't need to struggle on your own after your mom died. We're here for you if you'll let us be."

"We?"

"You want a list? Okay." Leah straightened and lifted her hand, poking up a finger. "Me." Another finger. "Sarah." Another finger. "Jillian." She continued to lift fingers as she added names. "Eli. His wife, Anna. Sarah's Beau. Jillian's Carter. Cara and Kieran. Mom." She had all ten fingers lifted at that point. "And there are others too. You just have to be willing to let people be there for you."

"And you do that?" Lani asked skeptically.

It was no surprise when Leah grinned. "Of course not. I mean, Mom and Sarah are my support. And Eli and Anna, too. The others." She shrugged. "I might not let them close, but I know that if I needed any of them, they'd absolutely be there for me. Just like I'd be there for them."

Lani knew that Leah was only voicing what she had already admitted to herself. If she decided to stay in New Hope, she needed to be willing to put herself out there to build a support group for herself. But did she want that group to include Michael's friends—especially since she wasn't sure about what was going on with Michael just yet?

"If I decide to stay," Lani said. "I'll keep that in mind."

"If you decide to stay, you probably won't have much choice. We let you down once already by not making sure that you were doing okay after your mom died. We won't let it happen again." She grinned again. "Consider yourself warned."

"I'll be sure to take that into consideration when I make my decision."

"Seriously though." Leah leaned forward, sliding her hands under her thighs as her long dark braid swung forward. "Consider giving Michael another chance."

"But he didn't ask for one."

Leah's brows drew together. "He didn't?"

"He apologized and said he had a business proposition, but there was nothing personal."

Leah shook her head as she threw her hands in the air and slumped back on the couch. "Okay. Well. Maybe keep in mind what I said in case things change. Especially the part about us being there for you. That stands regardless of what might happen with Michael."

Lani nodded. "I appreciate you coming by today."

"Just don't tell anyone else about our conversation. I can't have them thinking I'm going soft or anything."

"Your secret is safe with me," Lani assured her.

"Perfect." Leah popped up from the couch then leaned over to take another cookie from the container. "And when things work out between you and Michael because of our conversation, I expect you to share your grandmother's recipe when you get it."

"Deal." Lani laughed. "Except, I hope it doesn't come into my hands for a long, long time."

"I agree."

She got to her feet and walked Leah down to the door. "It was good to see you."

"It's not often someone says that to me," Leah said as she headed down the cracked sidewalk to the front. "Bye, Lani." She spun back around and continued to walk backward. "And if you have nothing else to do on Sunday evenings, you're welcome to join us for a hike and a meal. Sometimes a Bible study."

After Lani acknowledged her words with a nod, Leah turned back around and continued to her car. As she drove away, Lani closed the door and went upstairs, her thoughts and emotions in a quandary, but at least she didn't feel quite so alone anymore. She felt *seen*, which wasn't something she'd felt much in the time she'd lived in New Hope, especially since her mom had died.

But she wasn't sure how to feel about what Michael had shared with Leah and others. It was a surprise to hear that he'd revealed so much to the group of people he considered friends. But what had he said that made Leah think that he had any sort of feelings for her? Nothing about his visit the day before had spoken to that.

Still, it said something about Michael that someone like Leah was coming to bat for him. It also spoke to Michael's character that he was willing to paint himself in a negative light to his friends.

Lani didn't think she'd ever get up the nerve to go to any gathering of Michael's friends, even if some of the people had sort of been her friends first.

Difficult as it was, she wanted to keep thinking about Michael because she didn't want to think about the other situation demanding her attention. Her father.

What would Michael think about her dad? She knew what her father thought about Michael. That had been drilled into her over and over.

It was time she stood up for herself. The shop was *hers.* It had been left to her in her mom's will along with a portion of her life insurance. The rest of the insurance had gone to her dad, but he had no legal right to the shop.

Regardless of that, her dad thought he had a right to lecture her on what to do with it. And she'd let him. But if she was going to stay in New Hope and keep the shop open, she would need to somehow let him know that she wasn't open to his input unless she specifically asked for it. Which, given how things had gone since her mom had died, she never would.

But she still had to face him, and putting it off wouldn't make things any better.

It was time to face him, and then, depending on his reaction, she'd make decisions about the shop. She knew there was no way she could live in the same city as her father and not be somewhat involved with him. But at the same time, she just couldn't deal with any more of his volatile outbursts.

She could let her thoughts go back to Michael later. Right now, she needed to go see her dad. Whether she wanted to or not.

"Where have you *been*?" he demanded as soon as she walked in. He added a few choice words that made her stomach knot. "What would your mother think of you running away like a child?"

Lani pulled her shoulders back. "She would understand, and she would have trusted the decisions I was making."

"Even your decision to collude with the enemy?"

"The Reeds are *not* our enemy, and by working for them, I was able to bring more money into my shop."

"*Your* shop, huh?"

"Mom left it to me. She trusted me enough to leave it to me in her will."

"Except she didn't plan for you to take it over this soon," he ground out. "It should have been years from now."

"And why *wasn't* it years from now, Dad?" Lani asked. "For as long as I can remember, you've never let Mom drive at night. She never *wanted* to drive at night. So why was she driving at that time of night on that road?"

He glared at her with so much anger that Lani had to fight her instincts to not step back from him. But he didn't say a word.

"If—and it's a big *if*—I decide to stay here in New Hope and re-open the shop, I will make all the decisions relative to it, with no input from you. I have the experience of working in a florist shop, plus I now have the schooling to handle the business side of it as well. I know what I'm doing."

"If you say so," he muttered.

"I *do* say so, and Mom also had confidence in me."

She waited for him to respond, but he just pressed his lips together and turned his gaze back to the television. Figuring that was the end of their discussion, Lani considered it a success since, for once, she'd had the last word. She didn't want to abandon him by leaving New Hope, but she couldn't have things revert to how they had been before her escape to Hawaii.

"I'll be back tomorrow with supper for you." She turned and headed out of the living room and then the house.

As she walked back to her place, her steps felt lighter than they had in a long time. The ache in her heart caused by her dad's harsh words from before she'd left eased a little.

The ache wasn't gone completely, however, because even with Michael's apology, they weren't back to where they'd been before everything had blown up.

And she really wanted to be back there. Unfortunately, despite what Leah seemed to think, she wasn't convinced that Michael wanted the same thing.

She knew people might question her desire to pursue a relationship with Michael after what had happened, especially in light of her father's anger issues. But even though she had experienced a flash of Michael's anger, she didn't view him in the same way.

It had only happened the one time under extreme circumstances, and what spoke to her more than anything was Michael's apology. He wasn't forcing her to say she accepted his apology. He wasn't pressuring her to forgive him.

But what she didn't know was whether he was being that way because he didn't care if they ever got back to how things had been. Or was it because he really felt he didn't deserve her forgiveness and another chance?

She didn't really have much hope with either of those scenarios. It seemed almost impossible right then because they could only get back to where they'd once been if they *both* wanted that, and from what she'd seen so far, only one of them did.

~*~

As Michael pulled to a stop behind the shop, he was drawn back to the times he'd come early in the morning to find Lani waiting for him. Her car was there already, just like it had been on a lot of those mornings.

He had actually been surprised when she'd called to say she wanted to meet him to talk about the shop. Surprised, but very pleased. He hadn't allowed himself to get his hopes up after that less-than-wonderful interaction they'd had the previous week.

After he climbed out of the truck, he opened the back door and lifted out the stroller he used to move Vivianne around and offer him some stability when he couldn't use his crutches. Once he had the stroller open, he leaned in to get Vivianne's car seat and the diaper bag then attached the seat to the stroller.

By the time he rounded the front of the truck, Lani was out of her car and waiting by the back door. Her eyes widened when she saw the stroller.

"Good morning," he said as he approached the door.

"Good morning." Her response was a little reserved, and there wasn't much of a smile to go with it.

When she didn't make a move to open the door, he said, "Would you mind unlocking the door?"

Her brow furrowed. "I don't know the code."

"It's the new one I gave you after the robbery."

That made her brows rise, but she didn't say anything. She just turned to punch in the code for the door, then held it open for him. He punched in the code for the alarm, which had also not changed from the one chosen after the robbery, but he didn't want it going off before she had a chance to get to it.

He pushed the stroller over to the worktable and sat down on one of the stools, realizing that perhaps he should have brought his crutches in. Lani followed him, and though he'd expected her to approach Vivianne, she stood off to the side, her gaze going to the stroller.

"She's staying awake longer and longer," Michael said.

Lani looked at him and nodded, crossing her arms over her chest. "That's to be expected as she gets older. Is she...?" Her voice trailed away, and her brow furrowed for a moment before she said, "I hope that means she's sleeping longer at night."

"It does. We're hitting five hour stretches now. Sometimes six, if I'm lucky. It's amazing." When Vivianne began to fuss, he thought that might bring her over to look at the baby, but still, she kept her distance. "Would you like to hold her? I think she's missed you."

"Really?" A small smile tipped up the corners of Lani's mouth. "I would love to hold her."

She moved closer then, bending over the car seat and unbuckling Vivianne. As she lifted the baby into her arms, the smile he'd missed appeared. Though she might not be smiling for him—and he accepted the reasons for that—he was happy that she smiled for Vivianne.

"She looks like she's grown so much." Lani bounced her gently, running her finger along Vivianne's face. "Her cheeks have really filled out."

"The doctor said she's gained over two pounds since she was born."

"That's wonderful. So wonderful."

Michael's heart swelled as he watched Lani murmur gentle words to Vivianne. It seemed like she had missed the baby as well. Emotion threatened to choke him, so he had to look away.

"Thank you for bringing her today," Lani murmured. "When you didn't bring her with you before, I thought you didn't want me around her anymore."

Shoulders slumping, Michael blew out a breath. Was it possible for him to mess things up even more with Lani? Apparently, it was. It only reinforced his feelings that he just wasn't good enough for her.

"That wasn't my intention at all," he said. "I was on the job site when you texted, so I didn't have her with me. Plus, I was just focused on getting to you to apologize, and I guess I now owe you another apology."

"It's okay. I should have realized that."

"Don't ever think I don't want you around Vivianne. You played a huge role in those first few weeks of her life. I couldn't have managed without you, and instead of showing you how grateful I was..." He sighed and shook his head. "My shock and temper got the better of me, and it took me to a place I've tried so hard to avoid. I ended up there and took you with me, and I'll forever regret that."

"It's over and done with," Lani said. "Let's just move forward."

He stared at her for a moment before nodding. Moving forward sounded like a great idea, but he had a feeling that for him, at least, it would be easier said than done.

"So, let's talk shop," she said as she swayed with Vivianne in her arms.

"Okay. Let's talk shop."

"First of all," Lani said as she sat down on a stool. "I'm not comfortable taking this space rent-free."

"But that only makes sense until you get your feet under you. Plus, unless the landlord finds someone else to take over the space, I'll still be paying rent."

"Maybe we can find some middle ground." Lani shifted Vivianne to her shoulder. "How about we do a rent-free first month, then a percentage of sales after that?"

Michael wanted to insist that she just take the shop rent-free like he wanted, but he could see that taking responsibility was important to her. "Let's start with the first month and see how it goes after that."

Lani regarded him for a moment, looking like she could tell he was only giving in reluctantly. "Hmmm. You might not know this about me yet, but I can be stubborn when I want something. So don't think you'll keep pushing back when I start to pay rent."

He couldn't help but smile at her words. He hadn't really seen a stubborn side of her in the time they'd known each other. A determined side, yes. She'd worked hard for their shop even when she could have slacked off and just collected a paycheck. He was pretty sure that she was the reason that Taylor hadn't completely lost her mind in the months leading up to Vivianne's delivery.

"We shall see."

Lani sighed, but the smile on her face let him know she wasn't that aggravated with him. "So how will it work to open up here?"

"I saw you had a business sign on your shop, so we'll need to get that transferred over. We could hire someone to fit it where ours currently is. Other than that, it will just be stocking the shop, right? And maybe you need to hire someone to help you out?"

"I'm not sure if I need to hire someone just yet." Lani bit her lip. "I don't want the expense until I see if I really need the help."

"I hope that you'll need to hire someone soon then. With your talent and the visibility here, I'm sure you'll be busy."

Lani nodded. "It was always Mom's dream to move to a bigger, better location. We thought once I was done school and came back here, we'd be able to take the business to a new level. Mom hadn't wanted to hire anyone else. She was waiting for me." She paused, sadness filling her face. "If only I hadn't taken so long."

"What do you mean?" Michael asked, feeling in some ways like he was seeing Lani for the first time. He was getting to know a side of her that she hadn't been able to share with him before because of the secret she'd been keeping.

"I went to Hawaii to get my business degree, and I was supposed to come back once I graduated." She hesitated, her brow furrowing as she rubbed a hand up and down Vivianne's back. "It took me longer than it should have since I didn't have the money to attend college full-time. I was a semester away from graduating when I got the call about my mom's passing."

"I'm sorry for your loss," Michael offered softly. He didn't know what it was like to have a mom who he would miss if something happened to her.

His mom had pretty much been a non-entity, a shadow drifting through their lives. His father had cowed her as much as he had Michael.

He'd often wondered how long it had taken her to realize that she came in a distant second to his father's deceased wife, just like Michael had been a poor substitute for his deceased older brother.

Taylor might not have come in second to anyone, but that didn't mean she'd been spared their father's anger. All it had meant was that she wasn't constantly being told how much of a failure she was when compared to someone else.

"I really miss her a lot, and I wish we'd been able to spend more time together in the years before she died."

"How has your father dealt with her death?"

"Angrily." Lani frowned. "But honestly, he's always been a bit of an angry man. This has just made him even angrier."

"I know about living with an angry father. It's not an easy thing, which is why I've tried to never let my anger get the better of me." He grimaced. "But clearly, I'm not always successful, and for that, I'm sorry."

"You've already apologized," Lani said. "We all get angry and say things we regret. You need to let go of what happened."

"It just feels like my anger ruined everything."

"But did it?" Lani asked. "You're here. I'm here. You've apologized. I've apologized. And we're talking again. It feels a bit different since we both know things about the other that we didn't before. But isn't that a good thing? I think it will bring an honesty to our friendship that we didn't have before."

Friendship...

Michael was well aware that that was what they'd had, and while he was happy to be back there, he had hoped for something more. Now, though, he didn't feel like there was much chance of that.

Maybe he'd been delusional—even before everything went awry—to think there might have been a possibility for something more with Lani. It didn't seem that she'd had the same feelings that had been growing within him. From her reaction earlier, she was more enamored with Vivianne then she was with him.

So he'd accept her friendship and just be thankful to have such a wonderful person in his life.

CHAPTER TWENTY-NINE

After the meeting with Michael at the shop, things kind of kicked into high gear. With Michael's help, Lani found a company that wouldn't charge an arm and a leg to swap out the signs and could do it as soon as possible.

As she stood on the sidewalk in front of the shop looking up at the sign proclaiming the space as *Luanna's Blossoms,* Lani felt a rush of emotions. This had always been the goal, so to finally be in a much more visible location felt like a reason to celebrate. But at the same time, it felt like an empty accomplishment since she had achieved it without her mom there to celebrate with her.

Plus, she wouldn't be where she was without Michael. He was the reason she'd been able to move her mom's shop to the main drag of New Hope Falls, not anything she'd done.

"Congratulations!" Lani turned to see Sarah approaching her with a beaming smile on her face, her fiancé, Beau, in tow.

"Thank you."

"How soon do I have to let you know that you'll be doing the flowers for our wedding?"

"Depends on when the wedding is," Lani said.

The couple exchanged looks, then Sarah said, "I'll have to get back to you on that."

"Well, as long as you give me a couple of weeks' notice, I should be able to accommodate you. I'm not too busy at the moment."

"That will probably change," Beau said. "If Michael is to be believed."

Lani lifted her brows at that comment.

"Oh, yes." Sarah smiled. "Michael has been telling us how talented you are with flowers. Not that we didn't already know that."

Heat crept into her cheeks. "He's been a wonderful help getting this all set up."

"That sounds like Michael," Beau said. "Always willing to lend a hand."

Lani nodded because Michael had definitely been that way with her, especially recently.

"Are you having a grand opening?" Sarah asked.

"I'm not sure."

"Did you just say yes?" Sarah turned to Beau. "Did you hear her say yes? I'm positive I heard her say yes."

Beau chuckled, gazing at Sarah with affection. When he looked back at Lani, he said, "I would just say yes."

"I wouldn't even know what a grand opening would look like." She glanced up at the sign. "I had planned to just open and pray for business."

"That's not a bad plan," Sarah agreed. "But if you'll let us help you, we can come up with an even better one."

"Us?"

"Us. Me, Leah, Jillian, Anna, Mom, and Cara. We'll help you plan it and carry it out."

"And I'm sure Michael and us guys will help you as well," Beau added.

"Thank you," Lani said, pressing her hands together. "I'd really like that."

"Come over Sunday afternoon, and we'll talk about it," Sara instructed. "And then you can go on a hike with us and eat some food."

Lani wasn't sure the option to say no was even on the table, so she just nodded.

"Perfect! I'll text you the time, okay?"

"Okay."

"Wonderful." Sarah stepped forward and gave her a hug. "See you on Sunday."

Lani watched as the couple headed toward a fancy SUV, Beau opening the car door for Sarah before going around to the driver's side. Though Beau didn't seem as effusive as Sarah, they seemed to strike a healthy balance between the two of them.

Lani had a feeling that a whirlwind was headed her way, and strangely enough, she was okay with that.

Back in the shop, Lani got busy making up a flower order for when the store opened, paring back her initial wish list to the bare minimum of what she'd need. She had to stay mindful of her budget as she basically started from the ground up once again.

When the alarm chirped, alerting her that the back door had opened, Lani looked up, smiling when she saw Michael walk in with Vivianne. The man had made sure to bring the baby any time he showed up other than the usual hours when Vivianne would have been at the babysitter's.

Lani wished that she could still watch Vivianne, but right then, her focus had to be on the business. It also seemed that Michael was managing to handle the baby just fine on his own.

She really missed being able to see Michael and Vivianne every day. Before everything had fallen apart, going to Michael's to pick up the baby had been the highlight of each day.

Talking with him had been something she'd also looked forward to, so now, any time he appeared in the shop, her spirits couldn't help but lift.

"How're you doing?" Michael asked as he wheeled the stroller over to the worktable and sat down. "Ready to open on Tuesday?"

"I am." She leaned over the stroller and, seeing that Vivianne was asleep, didn't unbuckle her. "Sarah and Beau stopped by, and apparently, I'm going to have a grand opening."

Michael chuckled. "That should be interesting."

"You were volunteered to help," she informed him as she sat down across from him.

"I didn't need to be volunteered. I would have been there regardless."

"Apparently, we're having a brainstorming session on Sunday afternoon," she told him. "Followed by a hike and a meal."

"Finally," Michael said with a wide smile. "I've asked you to come often enough."

Lani sighed. "I couldn't say yes, not when I hadn't let you know who I really was. Sarah and Leah knew me. Knew who my mom was."

"I understand. But no secrets now, right?"

"No secrets," Lani agreed, though she was struggling not to let her feelings for him show.

"Are you wrapping up soon?" Michael asked.

She nodded. "This has been an easier opening that I would ever have imagined because I'm walking into an already established shop. Otherwise, it would have taken a lot more time and money to get it all set up."

"Do you have to go to your dad's?"

"Not tonight." Thankfully...

Things with him had been rough going. Since he was still taking his anger out on her, she could only handle dealing with him in limited amounts. Though she had gone back to cooking for him, she only went over to his place every other day. She took him two days' meals at a time, knowing that he could heat meals up for himself if he put his mind to it. So far, it appeared he did because the meals were always eaten.

"Want to go out for dinner?"

Lani froze for a moment, casting him a quick glance. "Out for dinner?"

"I was thinking *Norma's.*"

"Sure." Who was she to turn down the chance to spend more time with him? "Sure. That would be great."

"Excellent. How much longer are you going to be here?"

"Not too long. I just have to place an order for pickup next week."

She finished the order, then gathered up her things. Michael offered to drive, even though it wasn't that far. When they got there, Lani carried the car seat so that Michael could use his crutches.

The restaurant was fairly busy, but thankfully they didn't have to wait too long for a table. The hostess—who wasn't Norma that evening—seated them, then it was only a couple of minutes before a server appeared.

"Can I get you something to drink?" she asked with a friendly smile.

Lani decided to treat herself and order a pop. While this wasn't a date, she was eating a meal with one of her favorite people, her shop was getting ready to re-open, and she'd found a balance of sorts in her dealings with her dad. For the first time in almost two years, her life felt like it was tipping more towards the light, pulling her out of the darkness she'd been submerged in since her mom's passing.

"So, do you have some ideas for your opening?" Michael asked after they'd ordered their dinner.

"No, I have no clue what a grand opening would entail."

"Yeah. Me either. I would assume they're going to suggest food for sure."

"Well, as long as I don't have to make it. I can cook okay, but most of it is fairly basic. Kind of like what I cook for my dad."

"And for me," Michael added with an affectionate smile. "Which was always super good, by the way."

A responding smile tugged at her lips at the compliment. "Maybe. But it's not good enough for a grand opening, I wouldn't think."

"Pretty sure that Leah will be in charge of the food."

Lani could see that, and after the visit she'd had with Leah, she wouldn't be surprised if she wanted to help. "Leah is a fan of yours."

Michael's brows rose at her comment. "What?"

"She came to see me after I got back and told me that you really were a decent guy."

"Huh." Michael's expression turned thoughtful. "Well, she's also a fan of yours because when I told them what happened, what I'd accused you of, she—along with others—were quick to say that you never would have done that. Of course, by that point, I'd already figured that out for myself."

"I can't believe that Leah stuck up for both of us like that. Sarah, I could understand, but Leah's always been more reserved."

"Yeah. I've always had that impression of her, so I was surprised when she spoke up."

Lani had never been really close with any of the girls in her class. Like she'd told Leah, her mom had been her best friend, and they'd always done everything together. Without her and with her cousin so far away, Lani knew it was time she figured out how to make close friends outside of her family.

Michael sat back as the server returned with their food, then said a prayer of thanks for the meal. They ate in silence for a few minutes before Michael said, "So you're going to go to Eli's on Sunday?"

Lani nodded. "I can hardly let them do all the work for the grand opening of my shop."

"With all of you working together, I'm sure it'll come together really well."

"How has your work been?" Lani asked, not wanting their conversation to be all about her stuff.

"Frustrating," he admitted. "But that's only because I know it's going to be awhile before I can get back to doing a lot of the work I was doing before my accident."

"I guess you'll still have to do some physiotherapy once your cast is off."

Michael nodded. "The cast should come off in a few weeks, but I've been told repeatedly that it will take awhile to build up the muscle strength I've lost."

"It's good you've had employees to help you."

"It is. Ryker has definitely stepped up. And not just with the business. He's been amazing helping with Vivianne too."

"How long have you guys been friends?"

Michael's brow furrowed. "He's been working for me for a few years, but I don't know a lot about him, to be honest."

"You don't know him very well?" Lani asked. "I just assumed you guys were good friends from the way he was helping you."

"I do consider him a good friend, but he very rarely talks about himself."

"A man with secrets?"

"Maybe?" Michael said with a shrug. "However, I'd still trust him with my life. I mean, I trust him with Vivianne."

"You trusted me, too," Lani pointed out. "Even though I had secrets."

He seemed to consider his words. "Well, I didn't realize you had secrets, but there was just something in my gut that said I could trust you." He grimaced. "Unfortunately, I quit listening to my gut for a few minutes."

Lani wished she hadn't brought that back up. "But it's all worked out, right?"

"Has it?" Michael's gaze dropped as he turned his fork over and over in his hand.

Before Lani could respond, Vivianne began to fuss, so she turned her attention to the baby, hoping they could return to the conversation. She undid the straps of the car seat and lifted her out while Michael prepared a bottle.

When it was ready, rather than taking Vivianne, Michael handed Lani the bottle. She focused on the baby for a couple of minutes then looked up at Michael. His gaze was already on her with an intensity she'd never really seen from him before.

"Why do you think it hasn't all worked out?" Lani asked, her words making her sound braver than she felt. She wasn't entirely sure she was ready to hear his answer.

"I had hoped that things were moving in a certain direction." His hands dropped below the edge of the table, and from the way his arms moved, Lani could tell he was rubbing his hands on his thighs. "I've always felt like I had several strikes against me. I can hardly read. I never graduated from high school. I come from a bad home."

Lani wanted to assure him that those things weren't strikes against him, except that she knew that to some people, they were. But more than that, a person's own perception of themselves was hard to dismiss. If Michael saw those things as strikes, her dismissing them wasn't being sensitive to how he felt.

Besides, she hoped that not having made a big deal about it when he'd first revealed those things to her would have already shown him that *she* didn't see them as strikes against him.

"I've always been willing to work hard, though, and I did, especially because I wanted to give Taylor every opportunity. But this past little while, it felt like she'd turned on me, and that hurt a lot. Your presence in my life helped to take some of that sting away, especially when you were helping so much with the shop and then with Vivianne. I think that's partly why I reacted so badly when I realized who you were. It felt like another betrayal, you know?"

Lani nodded, but she didn't say anything because she wasn't sure *what* to say.

"Everything that happened made me realize that perhaps I'd been assuming things about our friendship that weren't there." Michael paused, his gaze lifting to meet hers. "I do want to get back to the friendship we had before I screwed everything up. I understand that it might take you awhile to trust me again, but I want you to know that I trust you. All the things that I appreciated about you before are still there even now."

"I already trust you, Michael. Even when you lost your temper with me, I never feared for my safety." She gave a humorless huff of laughter. "I know how to deal with anger, believe me. I understood why you were angry that I'd hidden who I was from you. What upset me more was that you thought I would steal from you."

"I don't like the idea that you're used to dealing with anger, and I never want it to be *my* anger that you have to deal with." Michael let out a long sigh. "I know what it's like to live with someone whose anger dominates everything. It's not something I want for anyone, let alone you or, heaven forbid, Vivianne."

Lani shifted Vivianne to her shoulder to burp her once she finished her bottle. "I think being aware of an anger issue is half the battle. I mean, if you denied you had an issue and lashed out all the time, then I would think it was a problem."

"I never want to become my father."

The words were said with a firmness that Lani admired. She knew that there was no way she wanted to be like her father either. Thankfully, she didn't really have a tendency to anger, being much more like her mother in temperament. Still, after her experiences with her father, she appreciated Michael's awareness of his own issues.

"I think it's important that just as we see qualities we'd like to emulate in our parents, we also recognize the ones we don't want to see in ourselves."

Michael nodded. "I've been trying to be aware of that since I was a teen, but it's even more important now that I have Vivianne and...other important people in my life."

"Is your dad still alive?"

"As far as I know. I haven't been in contact with him or my mom in years. That might sound bad, but honestly, it was absolutely necessary for me to cut ties with them."

"Is Taylor still in touch with them?"

"At one time, I would have said no, but I really have no idea anymore. I will say this much...if she tells them about Vivianne, and they want to see her, the answer will be a resounding no. That's not gonna happen."

"I would have to say that even before my mom passed away, I was pretty much out of touch with my dad. It always seemed that he had no interest in me. I still have no idea why that was."

"I'm sorry," Michael said with a frown. "That must have been really difficult for you."

"Maybe it would have been if I hadn't had my mom. She more than made up for any lack on my dad's part. My mom and I were always very close. I was blessed to have her in my life for as long as I did."

Michael stared at Vivianne, his brows drawn low. "I guess, for now, I'm going to have to be both mom and dad to Vivianne. And wow...that's not daunting at all."

Lani laughed. "I think you have a little while to figure out how to play both roles. Right now, she just wants someone to love her, feed her, and change her diapers."

"I've pretty much got that covered."

"Yes, you do," Lani agreed. Vivianne was a fortunate little girl to have someone who not only wanted her but wanted to be the best person they could be for her.

"Maybe someday I won't have to be both mom and dad to her." Michael's gaze stayed on Vivianne as he spoke.

Lani felt a pang of longing surge through her. She would have loved to help Michael out with that. Was it normal to imagine such a serious future after only having known someone such a short time? But there was just something about Michael that had drawn her in almost from the start. Even before Vivianne had arrived on the scene.

She couldn't let her desire for that future impact their friendship, though. Whether he saw her as a potential mom for Vivianne or not, she would be there to help him out. She loved the little girl and Michael too much to just withdraw.

Lani refused to think too deeply on her feelings for Michael. Because if he didn't view her in a similar light, it would only hurt more. But the presence of that love in her heart—whether it was returned or not—filled her with a warmth that she cherished.

"Do you think that Taylor will try to be a part of her life?" Lani asked.

Michael shrugged, finally looking back at her again. "I don't know. And I'm not sure what I'll do if she wants to have a role in Vivianne's life. Of course, legally, Vivianne will be mine since I've been approved to adopt her. At this point, that's all I want." He let out a sigh. "I'm not happy Taylor has left. I mean, I would have supported her if she'd wanted to keep Vivianne and still maintain the shop."

"I'll admit that I don't understand how she could just give up her life here like it meant nothing to her. Maybe that's just because I've always favored stability in my life, so to give that up for the unknown...I wouldn't have done it."

"I couldn't have done it either," Michael said with a frown. "It all came out of left field. I had no idea how she was feeling, you know? She wasn't talking to me anymore. Which is why I have no idea if she has any intention of being a part of our lives in the future."

Having never had a sibling, Lani didn't know exactly how Michael felt. But she could see that Taylor's actions had hurt him. She understood a bit better why he'd reacted the way he had to finding out who she was. Why he'd felt a sense of betrayal at her lie.

It seemed more important than ever that she let Michael know that she was there for him, and betrayal of any sort wasn't on her agenda. Ever.

CHAPTER THIRTY

On Sunday afternoon, Michael swung by to pick Lani up to drive her out to Eli's for the grand opening brainstorming session. He didn't think that it would take too long since it was very likely that a lot of brainstorming had happened already. Given that several of the women who were spearheading this whole thing lived together, he doubted that they'd waited until that afternoon to start the discussion.

"Are they actually planning a hike for today?" Lani asked as he drove on the road leading out of town.

"I think so," Michael said, with a glance at the sky. "As long as it's not raining, hikes usually take place every other Sunday."

"And you go on these hikes?"

"Well, not recently," he admitted. "But I thought I'd try today. Maybe."

"I'll hang out with you if you decide not to go."

"Thanks. I appreciate that." Michael suddenly found himself torn between going on the hike like he'd planned or staying behind to hang out with Lani.

It didn't take long to get to Eli's, and judging by the cars already parked there, it was apparent that they weren't the first to arrive. Quite possibly, they were the last. Lani got the car seat and the diaper bag from the back seat, though Eli quickly appeared to take Vivianne from her.

"She's the popular one," Michael remarked as Eli headed into the house ahead of them, having gotten used to the fight over his daughter in recent weeks.

"That's not uncommon when babies are involved." Lani walked with him up the steps. "And what's not to love about Vivianne?"

"True." Michael grinned, then followed her into the cabin.

As he'd suspected, pretty much everyone he expected to be there to plan was present. When Eli set the car seat down on the table, the women quickly clustered around the baby. Michael glanced over at Lani in time to catch a frown on her face as she watched the women fawn over Vivianne.

For a moment, he wasn't sure what to make of it as he rarely saw that expression on her, especially when it came to Vivianne. Observing her, a thought occurred to him as he recalled the utter joy on Lani's face when she'd seen Vivianne for the first time again after getting back from Hawaii.

Was it possible that she felt possessive of Vivianne? It made sense, in a way, since Lani had cared for her so much. She might have even loved her like a daughter, but she had no claim to her as a mother. As Michael watched, Lani pulled her shoulders back, and her expression smoothed out.

The truth of the matter was that when Michael thought of Lani's role in their lives, he had no problem seeing her as Vivianne's mother. However, he and Vivianne were a package deal, and Michael still wasn't convinced he was right for Lani.

When Vivianne began to fuss, Lani brought the diaper bag over to him. "Is it time for her to eat?"

"Probably." Michael motioned to the car seat. "Can you bring her over?"

Lani nodded, then made her way to where the women were still hovering over Vivianne.

"Should I take her out?" Sarah asked.

"Just bring her over to me, please," Michael said before Lani had a chance to respond.

Lani picked up the car seat and came over to Michael, setting it on the coffee table in front of him. "I'll get the bottle ready, if you'd like."

"That would be great. Thanks."

She sat down beside him and quickly got the makings for the bottle out of the diaper bag. Michael undid the straps on the car seat and lifted Vivianne out.

"Hey, girly," he said, smiling as he bounced Vivianne gently.

Though she'd begun to give him small smiles, she wasn't having any of it at that moment. The girl wanted her food, and she wanted it right then.

When she screwed up her face and gave a pitiful whimper, Michael couldn't deny her anything, even if he'd wanted to.

"Here you go," Lani said, holding out the bottle.

Michael turned more in her direction and said, "Why don't you feed her? I think she's missed that."

Lani's eyes grew wide before a smile lit up her face. "I've missed that, too."

It took only a moment to get Vivianne settled in Lani's arms with the bottle. And as he watched the two of them together, Michael felt a familiar sense of rightness. He wanted to keep Lani in his life, and if Vivianne was the only reason she stayed, he could accept that.

"I guess it's safe to say the two of you have moved forward."

At the sound of Eli's voice, Michael shifted his attention from Lani to his friend. "What?"

"You and Lani," Eli said. "It's good to see you two together."

"Oh." Michael shot a look at Lani, totally at a loss as to how to respond to that without having to go into detail about how things currently stood between them.

Thankfully, Anna, Leah, and Sarah had moved over to sit near Lani, and from the sounds of their conversation, plans for the grand opening were well underway.

Michael turned to face Eli more fully. "We're not *together* together. Just friends."

"Huh." Eli's brows rose. "Guess I misread things."

Michael wondered what exactly he'd misread. Them arriving together? Lani helping him with Vivianne? Didn't friends do stuff like that?

"So is everything ready for the store to open?" Eli asked, apparently satisfied with Michael's explanation of things.

"Yep. There wasn't much to do aside from swapping out the signs and ordering in some flowers. I'm glad that Lani will be able to re-open without too much delay."

"Are you doing this for her to make up for what happened?" Eli asked, his voice low.

Michael frowned, uncertain of how to answer that. "Well, partly, maybe...? But I'm happy that she's able to take over the space. It was a dream of her mom's to eventually move to a more visible location, and since I was going to have to pay the rent on the space for the rest of the lease, it just seemed to make sense to offer it to her."

Eli nodded. "I suppose it does, and I'm sure she's glad for the opportunity to grow her business the way she and her mom had planned."

"I hope that's what happens because she deserves that after all she's been through with her mom dying, and her dad...well, her dad being the way he is."

"From what Sarah and Leah have said, it seems that there's nowhere to go but up from where the business has been."

Their conversation came to a halt when Beau arrived, and Sarah got up to greet him with enthusiasm. He'd had to drive his brother and sister to the airport after lunch as they were flying to London. Michael had never had the urge to travel, and he'd never left the state, let alone the country.

"So, how are the plans coming along?" Beau asked as he settled on the loveseat next to Sarah.

"Well, we've got the food under control," Sarah volunteered. "And we're going to do up some flyers with a couple grand opening bouquet specials to hand out to people who come by.

"Are you expecting a big turnout?" Eli asked. "Or is there enough space inside for the food and the people who might show up?"

"I don't think we'll have a stampede of people," Anna said. "But you never know when Leah's food is involved."

"Haha," Leah said as she got up and headed for the kitchen. "At least they'll be stampeding *toward* my food. If it was Sarah's, they'd be stampeding away from it."

Michael wasn't surprised that Sarah only laughed at her sister's jab at her cooking abilities. Sometimes it hurt to see the McNamara siblings interacting so affectionately as it made him miss Taylor. As far as he knew, she'd already left the state for LA.

"So food and flyers?" Eli asked.

"Food, flyers, and flowers. Three f's," Sarah said, grinning at the alliteration. "Lani said she'd order some carnations to give away to the first twenty or thirty people."

"I don't think we need anything too elaborate," Lani said. "I'm hoping to just get a little visibility to jump-start business."

"Oh, I think this event will help do that," Sarah said with a nod. "And we should get a sandwich board for the sidewalk so that even from a distance, people can see the shop is open."

Michael could see that Lani wasn't looking for the same level of grand opening that Sarah seemed to want. He didn't try to rein things in as he didn't feel it was his place, but he hoped that Sarah didn't get too carried away with her ideas. Hopefully Leah and Anna would be voices of reason.

"I'll be there," Eli said. "If you need my help."

Michael hoped that he could be there as well. Ryker had already said he'd be okay with supervising the crews that day. Michael had been able to take over supervision of some of the job sites recently. Mainly the ones that were easily accessible for him since he still had his cast on.

"I can't thank you all enough for helping with this," Lani said as she shifted Vivianne to her shoulder and began to pat her on the back, swaying slowly from side to side.

"Thank you for *letting* us help you," Sarah replied, her smile wide. "I know you're not used to that."

"No. I'm really not," Lani admitted, much to Michael's surprise.

"Of course, it kind of pays to be on the good side of the florist when you're planning a wedding," Leah said drolly.

Everyone laughed as Sarah reached out to smack her sister, but Leah managed to evade her. "You know that's not why I'm helping her."

"But it is a bonus," Eli said, getting in on the action.

"Only because I get to give a friend our business and get a talented florist working on our wedding flowers. I think that's a win-win situation. Right, Lani?"

"Right," she agreed. "I'm looking forward to helping you with that."

Cara and Kieran arrived a short time later, interrupting the discussion on the upcoming wedding. After greeting the others, Kieran came to sit near Michael and Eli.

"Hey, man," Kieran said, holding out his hand. "How's it going?"

"Good," Michael said as he shook his hand.

"I had planned to stop by and talk to you yesterday about the theft," Kieran said. "But I got hung up at the station."

"Has something more come up?" Michael had almost given up on ever finding out who had committed the robbery at the flower shop.

Kieran pulled out his phone and checked something on it before looking back at him. "Do you know someone by the name of Brittany Anderson?"

Michael frowned, trying to think if he'd heard the name before. "I don't think so."

"Isn't that the name of Taylor's roommate?" Lani asked as she leaned closer to him.

Michael looked at her, trying to recall the short, intense conversation he'd had with Taylor about her roommate working at the shop. "Britt?"

Lani shrugged. "Short for Brittany, maybe?"

"Do you know her last name?" Kieran asked.

Michael shook his head. "Taylor only called her Britt."

"How about an address?"

"Nope. Taylor never told me where she moved to. Sorry."

"No worries. One of the guys I had reviewing cameras from around the area that weekend was running license plates, and that name popped up. Most of the other vehicle owners live in this area, while Brittany Anderson had an address from Everett."

"Well, Taylor was living in Everett, so it's possible. I can give you Taylor's lawyer's information," Michael said. "He might be able to help you out. I don't even have a cell number for Taylor anymore. The last time I called her, the recording said her number was no longer active."

Kieran frowned. "I'm sorry to hear that."

Michael sighed. "It is what it is." He felt a light touch on his back and glanced over to see Lani looking at him with concern. "I wish things were different, but this is what she wants."

"Well, I'll take that information for the lawyer and see if we can't get this figured out."

"I suppose it makes some kind of sense if it's her roommate," Michael said. "She would have had access to Taylor's phone and laptop, and I wouldn't be surprised if she kept the codes on one or perhaps both."

"We'll get to the bottom of it," Kieran said with a nod. "One way or another."

"I appreciate the work you're doing on it." Michael paused then said, "I kind of figured it was a lost cause."

"I've kept a couple of the guys working on it when they've had time."

"Wish I could give you a more definite answer on whether Britt is actually Brittany."

"Don't worry about it," Kieran assured him. "You've at least given us a direction to follow."

Conversation moved on, and when Andy, another friend of the group who worked at the bookstore in town, showed up, talk switched to heading out for a hike.

"I can stay here with you," Lani said.

"I think I'd like to try hiking a bit. I probably won't be able to keep up with the group, but I'd like to get out there."

"Did you bring the carrier?"

"Yep. It's in the diaper bag, but you'll have to use it. I'm not sure it would be too smart for me to try to maneuver my crutches with Vivianne on my front."

"I don't mind carrying her." Lani dug the baby carrier out of the diaper bag, then began to wrap it around her and Vivianne.

"That looks like you need a degree to use it," Sarah said.

"I had to watch a video a bunch of times to figure it out because reading the directions made my brain cramp," Lani said with a laugh. "It was a godsend, though, when I had Vivianne in the shop with me. I could have her close and still work."

Sarah rubbed her hand on Vivianne's back. "I'll have to keep that in mind."

When they left the cabin a short time later, Michael waited for the others to move ahead. He knew there was no way he'd keep up with them, but thankfully, the well-used path was hard-packed dirt, which made it a little easier to maneuver on with his crutches.

"You don't have to walk with me," Michael told Lani when she fell into step beside him.

She gave him an incredulous look. "I know, but I'd like to walk with you, if you don't mind."

Warmth swirled inside Michael at the knowledge that she wanted to stick with him. It wasn't like he was the only person she knew in the group, so the fact that she wanted to walk with him made him feel better. "I'd love the company."

The path started out wide enough for them to walk side by side, even with him on crutches. It didn't take long for the others to move well ahead of them and disappear from sight, but Michael found that he didn't mind that it was just him, Lani, and Vivianne.

"Have they been doing these hikes for awhile?" Lani asked as they slowly made their way up the path.

"I'm not sure how long, but they've been doing them ever since I've been part of the Bible study."

"I never knew this trail existed," Lani said as she ducked to avoid a small overhanging branch. "But then, I guess it's on private property, so you'd have to be a guest at the lodge or a friend of the family to hike on it."

"You didn't come here as a teen?" Michael asked, curious about how Lani had interacted with the others when they were younger.

"No. I wasn't really part of their group. Sarah and Jillian were cheerleaders, and I definitely wasn't one of them. Leah...well, she didn't really have a friend group, but if she did hang out with others in the school, it was the musical kids. And I wasn't one of those either."

"So did you hike anywhere else around New Hope then?"

"Not very often," Lani said. "But sometimes Mom and I would drive to other trails in the area. There are plenty that are on public land, so we had lots of options."

"Maybe we can explore some of those trails once I'm fully operational on two legs again."

She gave him a smile. "I'd like that."

As they continued to walk, Lani shared more about things she and her mom had done together. The gentle rustle of the leaves around them was a perfect accompaniment to Lani's words, and Michael couldn't think of a better way to spend an afternoon. And it didn't matter that he was moving at the pace of a turtle and that his arms were beginning to ache.

He didn't know if there would ever be anything more between the two of them, which was why he cherished moments like these. Every time he let himself consider trying for something more, Michael couldn't figure out how to move the friendship deeper.

What would happen if he tried to move things beyond friendship, and she wasn't interested? Wouldn't that make things too awkward for them to hang out together? Michael wasn't sure that it was worth it to risk their friendship when they'd only just gotten back to this point.

He really wished he had more experience with relationship stuff because his own belief that Lani could do better than him would always color his view of how she interacted with him. Instead, he resolved to be the best friend he could be to her since it seemed like she didn't have a lot of those.

And even though he had more friends than he'd ever had before in his life, she was by far the one he held closest to his heart.

CHAPTER THIRTY-ONE

Hiking with a baby strapped to her front made things a little more challenging than Lani had anticipated. Apparently, it was way easier to stand at the worktable and put together flower arrangements while wearing Vivianne than hiking up an incline, even if she was doing it at a rather leisurely pace. She was definitely out of shape.

Still, even though her calves burned and her back ached a bit with the extra weight of Vivianne throwing off her center of balance, Lani wouldn't have wanted to be anywhere else. Being outdoors for more than just walking to and from her dad's was a real blessing. Those walks were never relaxing, nor did they allow her to appreciate her surroundings the way she could as she hiked beside Michael.

But more than any of that, the best part was that she wasn't alone.

"Do you mind if we stop for a few minutes?" Michael asked after they'd been hiking for about fifteen minutes. "I think I underestimated how well I'd be able to do this."

"I don't mind at all," Lani assured him. "I think I also underestimated my ability to hike while wearing a baby."

A rare smile lit up Michael's face, taking his features from average to captivating. "Guess we're quite the pair, huh?"

Lani smiled in return, unable to help herself. She just wished that he really did see them as a pair, well-matched in life, not just in the lack of ability to hike well. "It seems so."

"Let's see if we can find a spot with a log or something so you can sit down," Michael suggested.

They walked a bit further before spotting a large rock off to the side that they could rest on. Vivianne had fallen asleep, but she stirred a bit as Lani settled against the rock. It wasn't very wide, so their arms brushed when Michael leaned back on it, resting the crutches beside him.

He shook out his arms then said, "I really hate how breaking my leg has managed to screw up my physical abilities. These hikes used to be a walk in the park for me."

Lani glanced over at him, not too surprised to see him scowling down at his cast. "You're dealing with it pretty good, all things considered. I mean, you've had a lot thrown at you recently, and you've handled it all well."

The smile from a few minutes ago was gone, leaving a tortured expression in its place. "Not everything."

She reached out and slid her hand along his, pressing her fingertips into his palm. "We're not talking about that anymore, Michael. You've apologized, and I've forgiven you. You need to move on."

He stared down at their hands, his fingers curling briefly against hers. "I don't understand how you were able to forgive me so easily."

Lani searched for the words to help Michael understand. "If I did something that hurt you, but I apologized and seemed to be sincere in that apology, would you refuse to forgive me?"

He glanced at her then, his brow furrowed. "No. I would forgive you."

"Then why do you have such a hard time believing that I have truly forgiven you and want to put it in the past?"

"I just hate what I did."

"So try not to do it again." She squeezed his hand, feeling the roughness of his palm against her fingertips. "You're a good man, Michael. So much of what you do shows me that. I'm not going to hold one moment of weakness against you, especially when I can see how much it's eating you up."

Lani knew she should probably let go of his hand, but he had curled his fingers over hers, so she didn't break the contact. Michael lifted his head and stared out in front of him. Though he seemed a million miles away, his thumb brushed lightly over her fingers, so she knew he was still aware of her.

"My biggest fear for most of my life was that I would become like him."

She didn't need Michael to clarify who *him* was since he'd already said as much in previous discussions. Would this one end any differently? There were only so many ways she could assure him that she didn't think he was that kind of man. So instead, she just sat and waited to see if he would add more.

"For the most part, I rarely lose my temper or react in anger. However, it hasn't escaped my notice that recently, the times I have, it has been with two people I care a lot about." He glanced at her. "Those being you and Taylor. That doesn't sit well with me."

"Did Taylor ever lose her temper with you?"

Michael huffed. "Boy, did she ever."

"So you'd get into fights with her a lot?"

"Not really. I kind of chose my battles with her. I'd argue with her if it was something I felt strongly about. But if it was her trying to get a rise out of me, I'd just keep my mouth shut."

"And if I were to lose my temper with you?" Lani asked.

"I'd probably deserve it, since, as of yet, I've never seen that happen. I can only assume that if it did, you had a good reason for it."

"I'd like to think so. I learned a lot from watching how my mom dealt with my dad. She didn't feel that every time he lost his temper, she needed to respond in kind. That's not to say that she never argued with him. She most certainly did. But, like you, she would pick and choose when to fight back. The rest of the time, she'd just let him rant."

"Is that what you do with him?"

Lani shrugged. "I haven't, to be honest. After the accident, I figured his anger was justified, and perhaps a way to vent his grief. But it's not changing any, so I've begun to push back a bit. Things like letting him know that I'm not going to just take whatever he's dishes out."

"How has that worked so far?"

"Well, he still rants and raves when I go over there, but he hasn't dumped any of his meals on the floor after I told him I wouldn't be cleaning them up or making more if he did."

Michael gave her a shocked look. "He would dump his food on the floor?"

"Yep. If he was angry enough with me, he would."

"What does he get angry with you about?"

"It's mainly been that I'm not listening to anything he says about the shop. But Mom left the shop to me, so I can make the decisions I feel are best for it."

Michael fell silent for a few moments. "So if I were to lose my temper, you wouldn't just take it?"

"Well, I won't argue, just for the sake of arguing. But if I feel strongly enough about whatever the argument is over, I'll say something."

She wouldn't have been able to do that prior to that day in her shop because she wouldn't have been sure their friendship could withstand that. And at the time, their friendship was more important than pushing back when he got angry with her. Of course, she still felt that, in some ways, he'd been entitled to his anger over what she'd kept from him.

But inasmuch as what had happened had sort of broken their friendship for a time, it seemed that what they were rebuilding was stronger. More able to withstand differences of opinions and arguments.

Michael seemed to feel the same way because relief crossed his face at her words. "I want that. What I don't want is for you to be scared of me when I get angry. I won't ever hurt you, that much I can promise. But yeah, sometimes I'll lose my temper. When that happens, don't let me walk all over you. Tell me to be quiet or to walk away. Voice your opinion. Hold me accountable for what I get upset over."

"If I promise to do that, will you let go of the guilt you're carrying over what happened in my shop?"

Michael shifted to face her, keeping a hold of her hand. "I will. I think I needed to know that you can and will stand up for yourself. I feel like I just ran roughshod over everything when I got mad, and I didn't like that."

Though she hadn't been aware that they were on uneven footing, this conversation showed that Michael had felt that way, even if he hadn't said those exact words. But now that they'd talked a bit more about what had happened and Michael's issues, Lani could feel that things between them had settled into a better, more stable, place.

Unfortunately, she still wasn't sure if this was just them in a better place as friends or if this could lay the foundation for something more. He continued to hold her hand, so a spark of hope flared to life within her.

"I suppose we should keep hiking," Michael said when silence fell between them.

Lani looked up at the trail where the others had disappeared. "Or we could sit here and wait for the others to come back."

Michael chuckled. "Yes, we could do that."

"I'm just kidding. We can continue on if you'd like."

"I am more than happy to just sit here with you," Michael said. "I'm sure it won't be long until they're back. The hikes aren't really about endurance."

"So they just hike for a little exercise?"

"I think Eli started it as a way to get his sisters and Anna into nature, and it just kind of grew from there."

"Does Leah hike regularly?" Lani asked. "Because she was never a huge fan of exercise or the outdoors in high school."

"No. She only shows up sporadically. Usually, she waits for us back at Eli's with food."

"I would imagine that you all don't mind that."

Michael grinned. "I can't say that we do."

"One of these days, Leah's going to run into a guy who falls in love with her food and then with her."

"It's gonna take a special guy to put up with Leah's snark."

Lani let out a laugh. "Yep. And a persistent one too because she won't make it easy for him."

"I can't wait to see it when that happens."

"I hope to have a front-row seat," Lani said. "After all, she came to talk to me about you, which I think was basically her way of applying to become one of my best friends."

"I hope you plan to tell her that, but make sure I'm there when you do."

"Is that a dare?" Lani asked.

Michael lifted his brows. "Uh. Yes?"

She started to laugh, tightening her grip on his hand. "If this backfires, I'm going to tell Leah it was all your idea."

Vivianne began to fuss, no doubt woken by their laughter. Lani rubbed a hand up and down her back and pressed a kiss to the cloth hat covering her head. "It's okay, baby."

"Should we head back down to Eli's?" Michael said when Vivianne didn't settle right away.

"Let me see if moving around might help her." Lani reluctantly let go of Michael's hand and got to her feet. She moved to stand on the trail in front of Michael, swaying back and forth as she rubbed the baby's back.

"She's a lucky girl," Michael said, affection in his gaze as he watched them.

"She is," Lani agreed. "Not every baby who is abandoned by their mom has a family who is willing to take them in and love them like you have."

"Or a woman who's willing to step up and care for them when she didn't have to," Michael added, his voice soft.

It was hard for Lani not to want the affection in Michael's gaze to include her. The more she was around this man, the more she wanted from him. Friendship was good, but it was just the foundation of what she longed to have with him.

Lani had never been the one to make the first move when it came to a relationship, so she wasn't sure how to let him know she was interested in taking things to the next level. What she felt for him seemed to grow each time they were together. Each time he showed a little bit more of himself to her.

"You're a natural with her," Michael said as Vivianne calmed with Lani's movements. "Do you plan to have kids?"

"I had kind of stopped thinking of having kids when my mom died," she said after a moment. "I mean, I had always assumed she'd be here to be a grandparent to them, you know? When I realized I wouldn't have that with her, that dream kind of faded."

Michael nodded like he understood how she felt. "That's one thing I feel bad about for Vivianne. She'll have no grandparents, although I think Pastor Evans might be willing to fill that role for her."

Lani hesitated then said, "That could change if you marry a woman whose parents are still in her life."

"Honestly, getting married and having kids was never part of my plan." Michael regarded her for a moment then gave a shrug. "I've come to realize, however, that circumstances can make you reconsider things. Vivianne coming into my life so unexpectedly has shown me that while I might plan things one way, God can sometimes steer things in a different direction."

Lani wondered if that meant he'd changed his mind about marriage the way he had about kids. "Yeah, and sometimes people come into our lives who make us rethink things as well."

Michael nodded. "That's been true of a lot of people who are in my life now. Pastor Evans helped me consider the role God could play in my life even though I wasn't sure that God was actually real when we first met. Eli and the others offered me friendship that I had never even hoped to have."

And what about me? Lani wanted to ask. Had her presence in his life made him reconsider anything? Fear of the answer, however, kept her from voicing the question.

She tipped her head back, looking up at the trees towering above them, their leaves rustling in the breeze. How she wished that God would send her a clear sign to show her which way to go. She'd never been one to take risks, mainly because life hadn't really ever presented her with them, so the risk of possibly losing Michael's friendship loomed large.

At that moment, the hole left in her life by her mom's death felt huge. This was the sort of thing that she would have talked to her about, and Lani just knew that her mom would have had good advice for her.

Tears pricked at her eyes as she closed them, wishing more than anything to hear the sound of her mom's voice. Even just the whisper of it, telling her if she should take the risk or not. Assuring her that she wouldn't be alone, even if pressing for a deeper relationship negatively affected the friendship she shared with Michael.

But no advice came to her, and she knew she would be alone once again if Michael told her he didn't feel the same way. After spending almost two years basically on her own, Lani knew she didn't want to go back to that.

"You okay?" Michael asked, his voice gentle.

She blinked a couple of times, then lowered her gaze to meet his and gave him a smile. "Yeah. Just thinking about my mom."

"I'm sure you must miss her a lot."

"Especially now with opening the shop. She would be so happy." Lani kissed the top of Vivianne's head. "And I know she would have loved Vivianne."

"I wish I could have met her." Michael's brow furrowed. "I'm not sure if Taylor ever talked to her."

"If she did, Mom never mentioned it."

"Would she have mentioned it if they did meet?"

Lani shrugged. "I suppose it would have depended on how the meeting went. I've discovered that Mom really only chose to tell me the positive things happening in her life. If something didn't make her feel happy, she didn't mention it to me."

"Does that bother you?" Michael asked.

"That my mom only told me the good things?" Michael nodded. "A little. I mean, I understand the urge to protect someone you love from the negative things in life. On the other hand, I wish she'd shared that stuff with me because I'm not sure she had anyone else in New Hope to talk to about it."

"She must have loved you very much."

Lani felt emotion begin to rise and let out a quick breath. "Yes. She loved me enough for two parents, which is why I never really felt the lack of love from my dad. The downside to that was that when she died, I felt the absence of that love acutely. Especially since I've here and not in Hawaii with the rest of my family."

"I hope that maybe, with more people in your life who care about you, you won't feel that lack so much."

She smiled. "I don't most of the time, but there are moments when I miss her horribly."

The care and concern from those around her now helped, but at times, it wasn't enough. Especially when she wanted more from Michael. She tried to be grateful for what they did have. Was it selfish to want more?

At the sound of muffled conversation, Lani turned to look up the trail. "Is that how long they usually hike?"

"Nah. I think they probably cut it short for our sake."

Within a couple of minutes, the group had rejoined them.

"Are you guys okay?" Anna asked, concern on her face.

Michael laughed. "We're fine. I just discovered that my arms aren't quite up to using crutches on a trail like this."

"And I didn't realize that hiking with a baby on my front would be more difficult than walking normally."

"As long as you're both okay," Anna said.

"You didn't need to cut your hike short on our account," Michael said.

"That's okay." Eli gestured at the sky. "I think we might be getting rained on soon anyway."

Lani looked up, actually paying attention to the darkening sky this time. Instinctively, she cupped the back of Vivianne's head.

"You guys go first," Michael said. "And I'll bring up the rear."

After the others had preceded them down the trail, Lani once again fell in step beside Michael. All in all, the afternoon had been perfect, and given the opportunity, she'd definitely do it again. Now that she had no reason to avoid Sarah and Leah, Lani hoped that she'd be able to spend more time with the group.

But most especially, with Michael.

CHAPTER THIRTY-TWO

On Tuesday morning, Michael peered through the doorway to the front of the shop, pleased with how many people were there. He hadn't been there right when Lani had opened, but after dropping Vivianne off and checking in with Ryker, he'd made his way to the shop.

When Lani turned and spotted him, her face lit up. Emotion flooded Michael at the sight of her. It was something he'd never felt for anyone before, and he was feeling it more and more intensely every time he was with Lani.

"How's it going?" Michael asked as he walked to where she stood at the counter.

"Wonderfully," she said with a big smile. "I've already gotten some orders, and someone—not Sarah—said she was going to call me about doing flowers for her wedding."

"That's great." Michael wanted to give her a big hug, but he held back and settled for returning her smile. "I'm so happy for you."

Lani reached out and lightly gripped his forearm. "I couldn't have done this without you."

"I'm just glad that it's going well. I really want this to succeed for you."

"That makes two of us." She tugged lightly on his arm. "You need to try some of the food Leah brought."

Michael allowed her to lead him to a small table that was set up with a large coffee urn and some platters with goodies on them. There was also some cut up fruit and veggies.

Lani handed him a small paper plate. "I would recommend trying those tiny cinnamon buns. They are *amazing.*"

Michael took one along with some fruit and a couple of other little things Lani recommended. Leah had definitely come through.

"Here you go," Lani said.

He looked over to see her holding out a cup of coffee. Taking it from her, he said, "Thank you."

"I can't believe you would betray your father like this."

Michael jerked, then swung around, hot liquid spilling out and burning his hand. He ignored the pain as he faced the speaker. Right away, he recognized her as the woman he'd spoken to outside Lani's shop after she had left for Hawaii.

Silence fell in the shop, and Michael's heart sank at the look of dismay on Lani's face.

"That you would hook up with the competition like this is disgraceful." The woman's face was distorted with anger. "Your mother must be rolling in her grave."

"Do not speak to Lani like that," Michael growled. "You are not welcome in this shop if that's how you're going to act."

The woman crossed her arms as her gaze swept over him. "I suppose you think you've won because you've taken over the competition."

"Taken over the competition?" Michael was incredulous. "Did you not read the sign outside?" He gestured with his half-empty cup to the front of the shop. "That's not my name on it. The sign is for Lani's mother's business. You don't know what you're talking about."

The woman's head lifted, her chin jutting out as she let out a bark of laughter. "You don't know what *you're* talking about."

Michael felt Lani's hand grip his forearm again, and he looked down at her.

"Just ignore her. Please." Lani looked like she was trying not to cry.

He set his cup and plate down, then gathered her into his arms. "Okay. I'm sorry."

"She's going to ruin your life, just like she ruined her father's," the woman screeched. "Just like she ruined mine."

Lani turned her head to face the woman. "How on earth have I ruined your life?"

"If it hadn't been for *her* being pregnant with *you*, Tom never would have married her. He would have married *me*."

Michael waited for Lani to respond to the woman, but instead, she just stood stiffly in his arms.

"Judy, I think you need to go."

Michael watched as Nadine, Eli's mom, took hold of the woman's arm and forcibly walked her out the front door.

"Hey." Michael turned Lani to face him. "Are you okay?"

When she looked up at him, he was surprised to see that her expression was clear. "That explains so much."

"What do you mean?"

"I always wondered why my parents got married because it didn't seem to be for love."

Nadine came back to where they stood, concern on her face. "Are you okay, sweetheart?"

"I am. Thank you."

Michael let his arms slide away from Lani as she spoke to Nadine. Anger burned inside him toward the woman who had tried to hurt Lani with her words. He could only hope that the woman kept her distance from Lani and the store.

When Lani turned back to face him, she must have read his thoughts because she took one of his hands in hers. "Don't be mad about this. She actually did me a favor by answering a question for me that my mom never would."

"She shouldn't have spoken to you like that." Michael didn't want to let go of his anger just yet. "Especially here."

"I know. C'mon." Turning, she led him into the back of the shop. Once there, she faced him again. "Thank you."

"For what?"

"For standing up for me." She smiled up at him. "I really appreciate that."

Under the warmth of her smile, Michael's anger melted away. "For you, always."

At his words, her expression softened, her beautiful eyes gazing at him with emotions he was afraid to name. "You don't know how much that means to me."

Nerves knotted Michael's stomach. Maybe his dad was right when he'd called him weak and cowardly because fear had a tight hold on his tongue. After losing Taylor, he wasn't sure he could handle losing Lani, which was likely to happen if he let her know how he felt about her, and it turned out that she didn't feel the same way.

But what if she did? What if he was reading her actions and expressions correctly?

"You don't know how much you mean to me," he said, trepidation keeping his voice low.

"Really?" Lani's lips parted as she gazed up at him. "You...care about me?"

Michael knew he was at the point of no return. Either he manned up and admitted how he felt about her, or he backed away. He'd been praying about this, and it seemed like maybe this opening was God's way of answering that prayer.

"I do," he said. "So very much."

A smile lifted her lips again, and her hand gripped his more tightly, like she didn't want him to walk away. "I care a lot about you too."

Relief rushed through Michael, and all he wanted was to pull her into his arms and hold her. Unfortunately, he knew it wasn't the time or place to get into any sort of discussion about their feelings.

"How about we talk about this later over dinner?" Michael asked. "And to celebrate your grand opening."

"I'd like that." The expression on Lani's face made Michael think that he'd been worried for nothing. "Consider it a date?"

"Definitely." He squeezed her hand gently.

She stood there for a moment, smiling up at him, then said, "I should probably get back out there."

Michael nodded. "I'm going to hang around for a bit. I told Ryker I was taking some time off today."

"I'm glad you came by." She gave his hand a squeeze then let go with apparent reluctance. Giving him a small smile, she headed through the door to the front area.

Michael watched her go, his heart pounding in his chest. Was this really happening? He sure hoped he wasn't misreading things. With his lack of relationship experience, he would have preferred to have flashing neon signs to tell him how she really felt. Of course, he'd have a hard time reading those signs, so he wouldn't be any better off.

"It's about time."

Michael turned to see Sarah regarding him with a wide smile. "What do you mean?"

"What do I mean?" Sarah scoffed with amusement. "The two of you have been dancing around each other for the last little while. We've all been waiting for one of you to finally take the first step."

"We haven't talked about it yet."

Sarah let out a huff as she crossed her arms in exasperation. "Just ask her out on a date already. She'll say yes. I can almost guarantee that."

"I did ask her out," Michael told her. "We're having dinner tonight."

"Oh! That's great." Sarah practically glowed with happiness. "Where are you going?"

"Uh... We didn't get that far. Probably just to my place, since I'll have Vivianne."

"I'd say you should get a babysitter, but something tells me that the two of you would be just fine talking with the little one around. Lani adores her."

Michael knew that was true. He just hoped she adored him too. "I think I'll get food from *Norma's.*"

"I approve of that," Sarah said with a nod. "And I can't wait to hear how it goes."

"Well, hopefully it goes well, or it's going to be kind of awkward."

Sarah reached out and patted his arm. "I think it will go just fine, but we'll still be praying for the two of you."

"Thank you."

With that settled, Michael followed Sarah back into the main area. Nadine was speaking with Lani and another woman, but it appeared that Leah had left. And thankfully, there was no sign of the woman who'd verbally attacked Lani.

For the next little while, he watched as customers wandered in and out of the shop. Most seemed to just be curious, but a few bought some of the ready-made bouquets Lani had on hand. A couple even placed orders for the bouquets she was advertising as being on special for the grand opening.

To Michael, it seemed like it was a success, and he couldn't be happier for her. After everything she'd been through, he was glad that things finally were going her way, and he was thankful he'd been able to play a small role in that.

He wanted to give her the world, but he'd never be able to offer her wealth, the way Beau could offer it to Sarah. But if she would consider a life with him, it would be a comfortable and stable one.

She knew his limitations, so she understood what she was getting into with him.

Michael hung around for a little while, speaking to a few people who he recognized from church. They had all been curious as to why the shop had changed hands, and though he'd been reluctant to talk about it at first, he finally decided to just be upfront about Taylor leaving town after having Vivianne and then leaving her with him. Though he'd anticipated some judgment, there had been none—only words of sympathy and support.

Mid-afternoon, he told Lani he had to leave, then asked her to come to his place when she was finished for the day. With a broad smile, she assured him she'd be there, and he left with nerves of anticipation fluttering in his stomach.

He drove to the job site where Ryker was supervising the planting of some trees on a new client's property.

"How did it go?" Ryker asked when he saw him, rubbing his forehead on the sleeve of the T-shirt he wore.

"Really well." Michael couldn't keep the smile off his face. "We're having dinner tonight."

Ryker's brows lifted. "Like as in a date?"

Michael paused for a moment, then nodded. "We're going to talk about...us."

"Well, it's about time," Ryker said as he clapped Michael on the back. "I'm happy for you, bro."

"Thanks."

"Want me to babysit Vivi?"

"You know, I think Lani would like her to be there. I'm just going to pick up some food from *Norma's.*"

"That sounds like a perfect date for the two of you," Ryker said. "But if you change your mind, let me know."

He stayed for a bit, talking to Ryker about the job, then headed over to another site where a smaller crew was doing weekly lawn maintenance for a long-time client. It would be another couple of weeks before he would finally be free of the cast, and he couldn't wait to do more than just stand around and supervise.

It seemed that all the things that had upset his world were finally balancing out again. Only nothing was the same, and with the exception of Taylor no longer being in his life, he was okay with that.

By the time Lani arrived at his house, Michael had managed to grab the order he'd phoned into *Norma's* and pick Vivianne up from the babysitter's. Unfortunately, Vivianne was a bit cranky, so he hadn't had any time to set the table.

"Okay. Do you want me to take care of the baby or the food?" Lani asked as she greeted Wolfie with scratches behind his ears.

"How about you take Vivianne," Michael suggested, knowing how much Lani enjoyed taking care of her.

Lani quickly washed her hands, then took the baby so that Michael could get up from his recliner and begin to unpack the food. He'd based his order for their meal on food he'd heard Lani mention she enjoyed before, so he hoped she liked one of the two meals he'd gotten.

"I have two dinners. Fried chicken or roast beef. Both have mashed potatoes and gravy, and I got two sides. Corn and green beans."

"Oh, that sounds yummy." Lani brought Vivianne to the table along with the bottle she'd prepared. "Do you have a preference?"

"Nope. I'm good with either."

"Well, as long as you don't care either way, I'll take the chicken and the green beans."

"Sounds good. And thank you for choosing the green beans."

Lani sat down in the chair opposite the chair he usually sat it and gave Vivianne her bottle. "I actually don't mind them, but I also remember you saying that you didn't care much for them when I was bringing you food."

"I'd forgotten that," Michael said as he set her food in front of her. "Sorry. I should have dished this up on plates."

Lani reached out to touch his hand. "Don't worry about it. I'm fine with this."

"Maybe I should have taken Ryker up on his offer to babysit so we could have gone somewhere nicer."

"Michael, I don't need fancy restaurants or gourmet food," she said, her expression earnest. "Being here with you and Vivianne is just perfect."

Michael felt a weight lift off his shoulders. She'd never shown herself to be someone who needed expensive things, but to have her confirm that was a relief. He made enough money to be able to treat her every once in a while. But if she'd expected that to be the whole of their dating experience, they'd have been off to a rocky start.

Still... "I do hope you'll be okay with us going out on our own occasionally."

Her smile grew at his words. "I'd be more than okay with that."

Michael was glad to hear that because, while it was easy to have Vivianne with them now, as she got older, it would likely be more difficult. He looked forward to the three of them being able to hang out together, but he also was eager to have some time with just Lani. They'd already shared a lot of their time with others, so they were overdue for some one-on-one time.

He said a quick prayer for the food, then they began to eat, taking turns holding Vivianne once she was done with her bottle. At first, their conversation circled around the shop, his business, and their friends, but soon it began to shift to more personal things.

"So, uh..." Michael began when there was a lull in the conversation, but then words failed him as he took in the expectant look on Lani's face. What exactly was he supposed to say?

She seemed to understand his hesitation because she leaned forward and took his hand. "I think we're both a bit uncertain about how to move forward."

Michael nodded. "But I'm not uncertain about the fact that I want to, or about how I feel for you."

Lani's eyes lit up as she smiled. "I'm not uncertain about how I feel about you either, but I was scared to risk our friendship in case you didn't feel the same way. I've kind of felt like I needed a friend more than a boyfriend."

"And you don't feel that way now?" Michael asked, trying to ignore the butterflies that were beating frantically in his stomach.

"I'm kind of hoping that I get both." She gave a shrug, and her fingers tightened briefly on his hand. "I know I have others who I'd consider friends now, but you were the first friend I felt I had here after so many months of trying to survive on my own. I consider you..." Her gaze dropped, and she cleared her throat. "Well, I consider you one of my best friends here."

Love flooded Michael's heart until it felt like it would burst. "Though I've considered Eli and Ryker my best friends, they only know parts of me. Aside from Taylor and Pastor Evans, you're the only one who knows all about my life. Everything that happened with my dad. My inability to read well. My struggles with Taylor. You know all of it...the good, the bad, and the ugly...and yet you've still stuck around."

"I'm not scared of the bad or the ugly in a person's life because I've had that in my life too."

"You're so strong," Michael said. "It's one of the things I love about you."

As soon as the words left his mouth, Lani's eyes widened as her mouth dropped open. Michael felt a flare of panic, but it quickly receded. A part of him wanted to take the words back or try to explain them away, but he ignored that urge. Maybe it was too soon to be saying stuff like that, but honestly, it was how he felt.

"I'm sorry if my saying that makes you feel uncomfortable—"

"It doesn't." The words came out in a rush. "Not at all. I was just...surprised."

Michael chuckled. "Well, that makes two of us. I hadn't planned to say anything about that yet, but I guess it just kind of popped out because it's what's in my head and my heart whenever I think about you." He gave her a small smile. "Which is pretty often."

"Well, there are lots of things that I love about you too, Michael." She leaned closer and gripped his hand in hers. "Not the least of which is your devotion to those you care about. Also, your perseverance when faced with setbacks. I really love that about you because I know that you'll be willing to stick with me, even if things get rough."

"I will," Michael said, wishing he could hug her. Unfortunately, their positions, plus him holding Vivianne, made it impossible. "I never planned to be in a relationship, but that all changed when you came along. I may have started coming to the shop each day because I wanted to make sure you could get in. But soon, I was there every morning because seeing you made my day so much better."

"That long ago? I thought I was the only one feeling things back then."

Michael nodded. "You came into my life at a chaotic point, but instead of adding to the chaos, you brought calm and joy. Even before Vivianne, you were already becoming important to me. Kind of like coffee."

"Ooooh," Lani said, her eyes going wide. "I'm as important as coffee to you? That's really important!"

He couldn't help but laugh at her words. "And that's another thing I love about you. The way you can make me smile and laugh. I haven't had a lot of that in my life." The levity faded away as Michael considered the beautiful woman in front of him. "Seriously though, Lani, I love you. I really do."

Her eyes closed for a moment, and when she opened them again, they were damp with unshed tears. "I love you too."

Vivianne apparently wanted in on the declarations because she let out a squawk. They laughed, then Lani said, "No worries, little one. We love you too."

"Yes, we certainly do," Michael agreed.

He might not have thought love was for him, but whenever he was with these two, he couldn't imagine *not* having love in his life. It scared him a bit, how much he loved Lani and Vivianne. What would happen to him if he lost either of them?

Though that worried him a lot, Michael knew that he had to trust that God would be there for him should that ever happen. Still, he would pray every day that nothing would happen to them. After having to walk away from his parents, losing his grandma, and having Taylor leave, Michael didn't want to lose anyone else.

Lani squeezed his hand. "Well, I think we can consider our first date a great success."

"I'm not sure we can really call this our first date," Michael said. "I mean, we've spent a lot of time doing things together that could be considered date-like before this."

She tilted her head as if considering his words. "I suppose we did have some early morning coffee dates, even though I didn't drink coffee."

"We also had countless dinners together after I broke my leg, and let's not forget our picnic lunch by the river."

"I guess we were kind of dating without actually calling it that, huh?"

"It certainly gave me plenty of time to fall in love with you," Michael admitted. "So I wouldn't have it any other way."

"Me either." Letting go of his hand, Lani scooted her chair closer to his then leaned her head against his shoulder as she reached out to rub a finger along Vivianne's cheek. "Despite the painful journey I've had to take to get here, I'm so glad it led me to you and Vivianne."

Michael turned his head and pressed a kiss to her forehead, relishing in her closeness. He would never take for granted her presence in his life after spending so long believing that he didn't want a love like that. "I'm glad too."

Lani slumped back in her aisle seat and let out a long sigh. She wasn't a morning person at the best of times, so even though she was excited to be heading to Hawaii to see her family, she was still tired.

"I'm guessing you're gonna want some coffee this morning?"

She turned her head to smile at Michael. He was in the window seat while Vivianne was strapped into her car seat in the middle. "You're guessing right."

They had been able to pre-board so were settled in their seats waiting for the rest of the passengers to file on and find their seats. She had never traveled with a child before, so she hoped that Vivianne proved to be as good in an airplane as she was in the car. Unfortunately, Lani had heard plenty of horror stories of flying with a baby, so she was braced for the worst.

Thankfully, it was a direct flight, so they wouldn't have to deal with layovers and an even longer day. Of course, their day had started well before sunrise since their flight had a six-thirty AM departure time. Eli had generously offered to drive them to the airport, so she hoped he'd be able to get some more sleep once he got back home.

Vivianne was wide awake, her eyes big as she watched people moving past them. Lani decided to pick her up until it was time for take-off. Hopefully, keeping her awake now would mean she'd fall asleep once they were in the air.

At the end of November, when Michael had suggested they go to Hawaii for Christmas and New Year's, she hadn't been sure about leaving the shop. In the six months since she'd re-opened, business had been steady. Steady enough that she'd had to hire help.

She'd ended up hiring someone part-time who helped prepare the flower orders. At Michael's suggestion, she'd also hired Emma, the woman Taylor had used on a casual basis to watch the shop when she'd needed to be out doing wedding set-up or deliveries. The final person she'd hired was a young man to make deliveries to the corporate customers with standing weekly orders. She'd never imagined she'd actually need staff for her shop.

Still, she hadn't been sure about leaving someone else in charge of the shop for the ten days they'd be gone. It was only the confidence she had in her part-time flower arranger and her willingness to work full-time hours for the time they were gone, along with Ryker's promise to check in on the shop, that had her finally agreeing to go.

She was excited to see her family, but even more than that, she was looking forward to introducing Michael to them.

"Are you ready for your first airplane ride?" Lani asked, resting her hand lightly on Vivianne's stomach.

Michael took her hand in his. "I'm so nervous I feel like I'm going to throw up, so I guess so."

"You'll be fine," Lani assured him. "I'm more worried about Vivi deciding that now would be a great time to have her first prolonged crying fit."

"What if I have a prolonged crying fit?"

Lani laughed then said, "Well, I'll see if they'll put a cup of strong coffee in one of Vivi's bottles for you."

Michael grinned. "Hopefully, that won't be necessary."

She let go of his hand, then cupped his chin and used her fingernails to scratch the five o'clock shadow that was nearly always present on his face. "I think you'll be fine, but I'll hold your hand for the trip, if it will make you feel better."

"I appreciate your sacrifice for my benefit." He captured her hand against his cheek, then turned to press a kiss to her palm. "Definitely makes me feel loved."

Though they had been joking around, Lani's smile softened at his words. He had been so good at making her feel loved over the months since that day they'd had dinner at his home, and she hoped that she'd been able to do the same for him.

She rested her head against the back of her seat, keeping her gaze on Michael. "I do love you, so that's good."

Michael mirrored her position and gave her a soft smile. "Love you too, baby."

When he moved closer, she closed the remaining distance and pressed her lips to his for a quick kiss. The love she'd felt six months ago was nothing compared to what she felt for him now. Though their lives had already been intertwined through the shop and Vivianne, in recent months they'd gotten even closer because she'd started to attend church with him as well as the Bible study at Eli's.

As she'd grown closer to God, she and Michael had grown closer as well. Encouraging one another spiritually had added depth to their relationship that she wouldn't have understood if she hadn't experienced it for herself. She was so grateful for that. But at the same time, she was sad that her mom had never enjoyed that sort of relationship with her dad.

When the plane jerked into motion, Michael's hand tightened on hers briefly. "Guess there's no turning back."

"Nope. They don't offer parachutes." Lani returned Vivianne to her car seat and strapped her in.

Michael gave a huff of laughter. "As if I'd jump out of the plane into the air instead of staying inside it."

"Here." Lani pulled the diaper bag out from the seat in front of her. She quickly prepped a bottle then shoved the bag back into place before someone told her to. "How about you give this to Vivianne when we start to taxi? I read that the sucking motion will help with her ears and the altitude change."

She handed him the bottle then pulled out the pack of gum she'd put in her pocket earlier. "Chewing gum will also help with your ears."

Michael took a piece and popped it in his mouth as the plane continued to taxi away from the airport. Lani hoped that sucking the bottle worked, but she also had a pacifier to try if it didn't. And she also hoped that keeping Michael focused on the baby would help with his own nerves.

She couldn't remember her first plane ride, but she'd never been afraid of flying, so she wasn't really sure how to reassure Michael. Lani hoped that his nerves had more to do with having never flown before and not because he really was scared of flying. Having an uneventful first flight would likely go a long way to alleviating his nerves for future ones.

"Go ahead and give it to her," Lani said as the plane paused at the end of the runway.

Michael gave Vivianne the bottle, holding it for her, even though at almost nine months, she usually held it herself. As she watched the two of them together, Lani couldn't help but wonder how Taylor was doing and if she ever thought about the daughter she'd walked away from. Michael hadn't heard anything from Taylor, and Lani knew that it weighed on him.

"Oh boy," Michael said as the plane lifted off.

Lani laid her hand on his arm. She could honestly say that take-offs and landings weren't her favorite parts of a flight, but she wasn't about to tell Michael that.

Vivianne's dainty brows drew together, and she paused in her sucking. Lani leaned over her and smiled. "Hi, Vivi, baby."

The baby's eyes widened at the sound of her voice, then she smiled around the silicone nipple of the bottle, a dribble of milk in the corner of her mouth. Lani kept talking to her as the plane climbed in the sky, watching Michael out of the corner of her eye. His attention was on Vivianne until the plane eventually leveled off.

The longer they were in the air, the more he relaxed, and after Vivianne finished her bottle, she took her pacifier and fell asleep. Lani breathed a sigh of relief. So far, so good.

Once they had been in the air awhile, the attendants came around offering them coffee, which both she and Michael took. Lani shifted in her seat to face Michael.

"Doing okay?"

"I am, actually. Bit of a weird feeling, that take-off. It kind of reminds me of a rollercoaster ride Taylor talked me into going on once." Lani had a hard time imagining Michael on a roller coaster, and when she said as much, he grinned. "Well, it was definitely just a one-time thing, so don't be thinking you'll get me on another one."

"As long as you'll get on airplanes with me, I won't force the rollercoaster issue."

He glanced out the window then turned back to her. "I think I can safely promise to get on any airplane you want me to."

Lani beamed at him, her love for him swelling within her. "I love you."

"I love you too." She never doubted that he did because it always showed in his expression and in his actions.

They lapsed into silence for a little bit, and Lani was considering a bit of a nap when Michael spoke again.

"Did you go by your dad's last night?"

Lani blew out a breath. "Yes, but he wouldn't talk to me, so I didn't stick around long."

"I'm sorry, sweetheart," Michael said as he reached over to take her hand.

"I'm okay with it," she told him. "I know that I'm doing my best for him, and if he can't accept things about my life, then that's his problem."

Things had gotten worse with the older man in the weeks following the grand opening. But that had been nothing compared to what had happened when Lani finally told him that she was dating Michael. She'd tried to continue to take him food, but going into his home even every other day had been super stressful for her as the verbal abuse intensified.

In the end, she'd decided to take all his meals over to him along with his groceries for the week each Monday. She spoke more frequently with the aides who were there to help him each day, keeping track of how he was doing that way. A couple of them had mentioned that he'd had a female visitor a few times a week, so Lani assumed that Judy Lange was stopping by. Frankly, she was perfectly fine with that.

She prayed daily that he would choose to let go of his anger and embrace peace and joy. But she knew that some people held tightly to their unhappiness, and if that was his choice, she couldn't do anything about it.

The only downside to keeping her distance from him was that there were questions she was likely never going to get answers to. But if that was the payoff, so be it.

"I wish your dad could see how wonderful you are," Michael said.

"Just as I wish your parents could see that about you, too."

Lani knew that wishing changed nothing, but prayer could. In the months since she had returned to New Hope and had begun to attend church once again, she had embraced her faith in God in a way she never really had before. And it was in that faith that she had entrusted the future to God, trying her best not to worry about things beyond her control.

She and Michael now attended the Sunday gatherings at Eli's, along with a growing number of others. At the beginning of December, they'd all celebrated Sarah and Beau's wedding. It had been a beautiful day of love centered around a touching ceremony. While Beau's siblings had been in attendance, his parents had not been there, nor had Sarah's dad.

Her heart ached for them, knowing how hard it was to move forward with life and all its momentous occasions without the love and support of parents. Though she hadn't, as of yet, faced a wedding without her parents, she figured it would only be a matter of time.

That was one of the reasons Lani wanted her grandma to meet Michael now, so that when the day came for them to get engaged, she would know and approve of the man Lani wanted to marry.

In a few short hours, she'd be making that introduction, and she couldn't wait. Lani couldn't imagine a better way to celebrate Christmas and the New Year than to be with the people she loved the most.

~*~

Michael watched Lani hold onto Vivianne's hands as she waded in the very edge of the ocean where it lapped at the sand. The little girl squealed with delight as gentle waves pushed against her legs.

It was hard to believe that just a year ago, none of this was even on his horizon. He'd certainly not been thinking about what it would be like to fall in love with a woman and adopt a baby. But here he was, and despite the rough road he had traveled to get to that point, he wouldn't have wanted to be anywhere else.

The light blue-green waters of the ocean sparkled in the fading sunlight, the perfect background to his two loves. He wasn't sure he'd ever seen anything so beautiful.

There was a bustle of activity behind them as Lani's family finished up the preparation for the luau they had planned for their New Year's Eve celebration. They'd traveled a little ways from where they'd been staying with Lani's grandma and aunt and uncle to another family member's home since the beach along her grandma's property was too rocky for easy access.

Lani scooped Vivianne up and buried her face against the baby's tummy, resulting in a torrent of laughter from her. Michael grinned at the sound. There truly was nothing as wonderful as the sound of his daughter's laughter.

Turning, Lani headed his way, a beaming smile on her face. It was something he'd seen an awful lot during the time they'd been there, and he was glad they'd made the decision to come and spend the holidays with her family. He had to say it was probably the best Christmas he'd ever had, and Tutu had gone out of her way to let him know that he had a place in their family.

As Lani reached him, Michael opened his arms, and she walked into his embrace without hesitation. He gave Vivianne a quick kiss on her cheek, which brought on another round of giggles. The kiss he gave Lani was a bit longer, and then they turned to join her family.

Bamboo torches were lit in the grassy area above the beach, and the flames flickered in the waning sunlight. They were on the west side of the island, which meant they could watch the sun sink into the ocean. The gorgeous streaks of color on the horizon were unlike anything he'd ever seen before.

It wasn't that he'd never watched the sun set into the ocean before. New Hope Falls wasn't that far from the coast. However, being with Lani and Vivianne in Hawaii, surrounded by Lani's loved ones, made this moment particularly beautiful.

Parents were trying to corral children of all ages to get them to the long tables that had been set up. Once everyone had settled into their seats, Lani's grandma said the blessing for the food, then they began to eat.

Though he was usually a pretty basic eater, he happily tried a variety of new foods that night with Lani patiently explaining what each dish was.

They passed the hours until midnight eating, talking, laughing, and even singing. As younger children fell asleep, they were laid down on blankets that had been spread for just that purpose. No one left, that Michael could tell anyway, and there was lots of excited chatter about what was still to come.

With around twenty minutes left until midnight, Lani's grandma approached him and squeezed his arm. When she gave him a nod and a wink, nerves flared to life.

"Let me take her, *ko'u pua,*" the older woman said to Lani, holding out her hands.

Lani didn't hesitate to hand Vivianne over. She'd been sleeping but had woken up a short time before. Her schedule was all out of whack, but Michael figured there would be plenty of time to fix it once they were back in New Hope.

"Walk with me?" Michael asked once Lani was free of the baby.

"Always." She took his hand then let him lead her back toward the beach where a couple of bamboo torches had been lit.

As they stepped between the torches, Michael stopped walking. Lani turned toward him, a questioning look on her face. Her eyes went wide as Michael slowly lowered himself to one knee.

She pressed her free hand to her chest. "Oh, Michael."

"Before you walked into my life, I had no idea how much love a heart could hold," Michael told her, emotion almost choking him.

He swallowed hard to loosen his vocal cords because he had more to say. "But then I met you and learned that there is absolutely no limit. Or at least I hope there isn't because every day I love you more, and I don't want that to ever stop. You've not just brought me love, but you've brought me so much happiness.

"Even though you've accepted every part of me, I still want to be a better man for you and for Vivianne. When I'm with you, I feel like I can take on the world, and I want to do that with you by my side."

He paused to take a deep breath and pull out the ring box he'd placed in his pocket earlier. Because he'd been practicing, he managed to open the box one-handed, then held it up to her. "Lani, will you marry me?"

Dropping to her knees in front of him, she flung her arms around him. "Yes. Always yes." She gave him a quick kiss then pulled back to look at him, her hands resting on his shoulders. "I love you, Michael, and there's nothing I would love more than to spend the rest of my life with you."

Michael pulled her close and buried his face in her neck, emotion getting the better of him. "Thank you, sweetheart. I love you so much."

He prayed that he would be worthy of her love in the years to come. With God's help, he knew he'd be able to take care of her, Vivianne, and any other children God might give them.

The clapping and whistles from Lani's family were suddenly drowned out by the sound of fireworks. Michael got to his feet, drawing Lani up with him. In the illumination from the exploding fireworks overhead, he slid the ring on her finger, then kissed her with all the love and passion he felt in his heart for her.

When the kiss ended, Michael smiled down at Lani, then took her hand once again. They made their way back up to the blanket, where Tutu sat with Vivianne. When Michael sat down on the blanket, leaning back on his hands, Lani settled beside him, tipping her head back against his chest as they continued to watch the rest of the fireworks.

Though Hawaii wasn't their real life, Michael knew it would always be a part of their future together, and nothing could make him happier. He missed Taylor so much, but God had given him a family to replace the one who'd tossed him aside, and he'd be forever grateful.

When the fireworks reached a crescendo and then finally faded away, Lani sat up and turned to face him. She reached out and took his hands in hers.

"You're amazing," she said. "Do you know that? I really can't wait for us to be a family. How long do you want to be engaged?"

Michael chuckled. "I'd marry you tomorrow if I could."

Lani's brows rose. "Really?"

"Well sure," he said. "I've already committed to marrying you. Sooner rather than later definitely works for me."

"Think we can plan another trip back here for a wedding in about three months?"

Michael smiled. "I think we can. In fact, I'll make sure of it."

"You don't mind getting married here instead of New Hope?"

"No. This is where your family is, this is where the wedding should be. We can always have something in New Hope afterward for our friends there."

"You don't know how happy you've made me." Lani leaned forward, bracing her hands on his knees, and pressed a kiss to his lips. "I love you so much."

"I love you too, and you've made me happier than I'd ever thought I'd be in my life."

Michael hoped that the next three months would fly by because he was more than ready to start the next chapter of their lives together.

As he sat there with Lani being congratulated by her family, he was reminded of the verse Pastor Evans had shared with him when he'd gone to him with Vivianne, uncertain of what to do with the abrupt change in direction that his life had taken.

A man's heart plans his way, but the Lord directs his steps.

Since he'd figured his life would continue on the path it had been on for the last several years, that prospect had been a bit daunting. He hadn't wanted his plans to change.

But during the ups and downs of the past year, Michael had learned an important lesson. God's plan for his life would always be better than anything he planned for himself.

Michael just hoped that after bringing Lani into his life, God's plan included many, many years together for the two of them.

ABOUT THE AUTHOR

Kimberly Rae Jordan is a USA Today bestselling author of Christian romances. Many years ago, her love of reading Christian romance morphed into a desire to write stories of love, faith, and family, and thus began a journey that would lead her to places Kimberly never imagined she'd go.

In addition to being a writer, she is also a wife and mother, which means Kimberly spends her days straddling the line between real life in a house on the prairies of Canada and the imaginary world her characters live in. Though caring for her husband and four kids and working on her stories takes up a large portion of her day, Kimberly also enjoys reading and looking at craft ideas that she will likely never attempt to make.

As she continues to pen heartwarming stories of love, faith, and family, Kimberly hopes that readers of all ages will enjoy the journeys her characters take in each book. She has no plan to stop writing the stories God places on her heart and looks forward to where her journey will take her in the years to come.

Printed in Great Britain
by Amazon